Never Too Late

by
Susan L. Tuttle

Bling!
Romance
An imprint of Iron Stream Media

Bling! is an imprint of LPC Books
a division of Iron Stream Media
100 Missionary Ridge, Birmingham, AL 35242
ShopLPC.com

Cover design by Elaina Lee

Iron Stream Media serves its authors as they express their views, which may not express the views of the publisher.

This is a work of fiction. Names, characters, and incidents are all products of the author's imagination or are used for fictional purposes. Any mentioned brand names, places, and trademarks remain the property of their respective owners, bear no association with the author or the publisher, and are used for fictional purposes only.

Library of Congress Control Number: 2021942976

All scripture quotations, unless otherwise indicated, are taken from the Holy Bible, New International Version®, NIV®. Copyright ©1973, 1978, 1984, 2011 by Biblica, Inc.™ Used by permission of Zondervan. All rights reserved worldwide. www.zondervan.com. "NIV" and "New International Version" are trademarks registered in the United States Patent and Trademark Office by Biblica, Inc.™

ISBN-13: 978-1-64526-350-0
E-book ISBN: 978-1-64526-351-7

PRAISE FOR *NEVER TOO LATE*

Never Too Late? Quite possibly the best contemporary romance I've ever read. Susan Tuttle's latest novel has it all—the warm backdrop of family, humor that will make you chortle, multi-dimensional and relatable characters, heart-tripping romance, multi-layered plot, and a beauty from ashes theme that will leave you wiping away a happy tear at the end. Did I leave anything out? *Never Too Late* deserves a spot at the top of the charts.

~**Denise Weimer**
Author of *Fall Flip, Spring Splash,*
A Holiday Heart, and *A Harvest Heart*

The romance in *Never Too Late* quickly reminded me why Susan L Tuttle has become one of my favorite authors. The friends-to-more trope will have readers swooning with delight as Evan and Rachael navigate the waters. But just as the romance will have readers sighing with all the feels, the faith element will touch the heart and remind us of One greater than all our fears. *Never Too Late* has it all.

~**Toni Shiloh**
Author of *An Unlikely Proposal*

Never Too Late is an intricately woven, tender second-chance romance that will leave readers savoring it long after they turn the final, satisfying page.

~ **Jessica R. Patch**
Publishers Weekly bestselling author

Never Too Late is so much more than a "friends falling in love" romance. Author Susan Tuttle writes a well thought out, multilayered story, deftly showing how love influences our lives in different ways. One overarching theme is how love welcomes in the best parts of life, but Tuttle also doesn't avoid the risks that come with loving others.

~**Beth K. Vogt**
Christy Award-winning author

Acknowledgments

My first thanks always goes to Jesus Christ. I could never start or finish a book on my own strength, and that has never been more evident to me than with this story right here. There were moments I didn't think it would all come together, and yet here it is in your hands. Jesus Christ. Ever faithful. My provider. And the love of my life. I thank you for once again reminding me that in you I can do all things.

To Jessica R. Patch, Joanna Politano, and Kelli Tipton. Three friends from three different places in my life, and I couldn't love you all more. Jessica and Joanna, you help me see story world in a different way, push me to be a better writer, and pray for me constantly. Kelli, you have believed in me before I even knew how to believe in myself, and you encourage me in this writing world even though reading isn't your thing. When it comes to my books, you've made it your thing because that's what best friends do. Thank you each for the blessings you are in my life.

To my Bible Bootcamp ladies. Thank you, thank you, thank you for your excitement for my books, and your constant prayer for me. When God placed us all at the same table, he knew what he was doing, and I am thankful for each one of you.

To my agent, Linda S. Glaz, thanks for once again championing my story. Your honesty and steadfastness to your authors is priceless. Thank you for all your nonstop hard work to help us find success while also constantly reminding us to keep our eyes on Christ.

To my editors, Jessica Nelson and Linda Yezak. Ladies, you never allow me to be a lazy writer, and I am so, so thankful for that. You've nailed the "sandwich method" and encourage me while also calling out things I can improve on. You listen to aspects that are important to me, allow me to write in my own voice, yet bring high expectations that push me to succeed. It has been both a privilege and joy to have you as a part of this writing journey. Thank you.

To My Love and my kiddos. Thanks for loving me and supporting me even when I spend hours secluded in the office or, even better, staring off into space. Writing is a strange and unique job, but we've never been ones to do things the normal way. ☺ I cannot imagine another family I'd ever want to call mine. God blessed me greatly when he gave you all to me. Love you MORE.

DEDICATION

To my mama who taught me the beauty of art through both her paint brushes and her petals. You are my favorite artist, gardener, and mom.

Chapter One

If Rachael Stark wasn't being held at gunpoint, she just might laugh.

"Abundance PD," the officer repeated. "Hands where I can see them!"

Inching her hands out and up, she slowly turned. Nothing was visible beyond the bright light cementing her in place, but she knew that voice. She was also confident the man it belonged to held the said gun on her, which was why she complied with his order rather than rush him for a hug.

"Hey, Evan, it's me." She added a smile to try and defuse the situation. "That light's kind of bright. Mind shifting it?"

"Rachael?" Evan Wayne's confusion escaped from behind the blinding halo surrounding his position. He didn't, however, douse it. "What are you doing here?"

Outside, a bolt of lightning sliced through the night and rain pounded against the windows. This late-summer storm had knocked out power, forcing her to navigate through her brother's vacation cottage on the shore of Lake Michigan by the tiny penlight on her keychain. Obviously, the sight had caught Evan's attention from his house next door. He was currently on injury leave from the police department, but that didn't prevent him from watching over Jonah and Penny's vacation home when they weren't here.

She squinted against the haziness. "Visiting my brother's lake house, which— to be fair—I didn't know was a crime."

The light shifted as Evan came closer. She still couldn't see his face, but his voice remained void of amusement. "It's not. But it tends to look like one when you show up unexpectedly. Last time we talked, *three hours ago*, you were nearly home."

His confusion was understandable. Chicago wasn't anywhere near where she now stood in Holland, Michigan—the small town where he lived that was situated beside Abundance, Michigan, the even smaller town where he worked. Plus, he had no way of knowing that in another lifetime she, the ultimate planner, had been spontaneous. That portion of her had been dead and buried for so long now, she'd surprised herself by resurrecting it tonight—an epic failure, it now seemed.

She shivered as cold drops of water slipped from her soaked hair and trailed over her skin. "Yes, but then I decided on a detour."

"Detours don't involve backtracking a hundred and fifty miles."

"Depends on the kind of detour you're talking about."

Hers was more of the metaphorical type, because when she'd neared her final exit in Chicago, it hit her. After fourteen years in her home, all that would greet her tonight was silence. She knew dropping her only child, Gavin, at college would be difficult, but she didn't know she'd feel so … aimless and alone. Even her dog, Clooney, was staying the night at Jonah and Penny's house. Thus, her impulsive decision to turn around.

Evan pointed his flashlight at the floor, enveloping them in a hazy circle. "How about the kind that has you skulking around in the middle of the night, looking like a criminal to anyone watching."

"I didn't figure anyone would be watching as most people are asleep by now."

"Not me."

"Right. My bad for forgetting Batman lives next door." She quirked her lips into a smirk. Hopefully, by deploying it along with his nickname, she could shift them from sarcasm to camaraderie.

Her tactic met partial success, and she was rewarded with a fleeting smile as he brought himself nearly toe to toe with her. "I could have shot you."

"But you didn't."

"Batman's notoriously cool under pressure." He shoved his gun into his waistband, then swapped the flashlight from his injured right side to his left so he could travel the beam over her. He was right-handed, but thanks to the bullet that had torn his shoulder apart six weeks ago, that arm didn't have much range of motion, other than in his wrist and elbow. She wanted to ask where his sling was, but now didn't seem the time.

As the light touched the floor, he asked, "What's going on, Rach? You look like a drowned rat."

"Don't you know how to charm a woman. A drowned rat? Really?"

His lips wiggled in another attempt to break free from the thin line he'd jammed them into. "Where's your car?"

"Up the road a little ways."

"Define little."

She turned her face sideways and quietly mumbled, "Two miles."

But she didn't call him Batman only because his parents named him Bruce (Evan) Wayne. The man's hearing rivaled that of those winged creatures.

"Two!" Flashlight returning to his right hand, he gripped his neck. "You broke down two miles from here on a deserted forest road, at night, in the middle of a thunderstorm, *and you didn't call me?*"

"Okay, take it down a notch." She understood his freak-out. He didn't have all the facts. "I would have much preferred calling you over my midnight stroll, but my phone was dead"—she thrust her hand up before he could offer further opinions on that tidbit— "because Gavin swiped my charger from my car. He forgot to pack his."

Evan's jaw tensed, and he paced away, then back to her. "I'm going to shove chargers into every crevice of that rust bucket—"

"Sally."

"Rust bucket"—he ignored her like he always did when she tried to get him to use Sally's name— "so that doesn't happen again. Better yet, you should finally trade that heap in for something from this century."

"I can't do that to her." She had a soft spot for her 1992 forest-green Jeep Wagoneer with wood paneling. It had been her Gigi's, and she'd given it to Rachael a month after Gavin was born. Said she needed something safe to drive her great-grandson around town in. "We have too much history."

"It's a car. It doesn't have feelings."

"Well, I do. And I'm rather attached to her."

"Even after she left you stranded on the side of the road in a storm?" His head tipped.

"She didn't leave me stranded. I ran out of gas." She realized her mistake the second the words left her mouth. Even in this dim light, she could see him stiffen.

"Your gas gauge." He looked up at the ceiling. "I never got that fixed for you."

Her hand went to his good arm. "Because you were shot. You had more important things to think about." She waited for him to meet her eyes. "And I am an adult, Evan. Perfectly capable of bringing her in myself. Better yet, I should have filled up at the last station, but my head's been elsewhere." Getting Gavin packed. Figuring out what came next. And worrying about Evan too, but she wasn't about to give him any more ammunition for his misplaced guilt.

Neither was he about to let it go. "I knew you had a lot on your plate. I should have reminded you. Made sure it was done so this wouldn't have happened." Deep lines forced his eyebrows down while others bracketed his mouth. Even his voice dropped a notch. It wasn't the first time she'd seen him lost in distant shadows. This man held himself responsible for all the weight in his world, and she wished she knew why. But she wasn't prepared to get into her own mood, so she couldn't very well ask about his.

"You know"—she wiggled his arm, her lips tweaking up— "you do brooding male really well. You may not be a fan of your name, but you're giving it some serious justice right now."

Took a second, but finally the words seemed to penetrate his melancholy, and his full smile came out to play. She shouldn't have coaxed it because the sight sent another round of shivers through her. Ones that warmed rather than cooled her. Strange.

His remaining tension gave way to concern. "You're cold."

"I'm fine." She let go of his arm and stepped away.

"You're soaked through."

"You're not exactly dry yourself."

Water splotches created a mosaic on his T-shirt, and his nearly black hair lay tousled in a wet mess above his high forehead. Small droplets trickled through charcoal whiskers that coated his cheeks and square jaw. That scruff nearly covered the dimple in the bottom center of his chin. The tiny spot seemed perfectly fit for her fingertip, not that she'd ever allowed herself to test the theory. Might weird out their friendship.

"Drier than you." He pointed to his mainly dry jeans, then to her soaked everything.

Thunder shook the walls as the storm rolling off the lake intensified. Dry clothes did sound pretty amazing right about now.

She took another step. "I'm sure Penny has some things here I can wear."

"Go change. I'll fire up your generator." He held out the flashlight. "Take this. I know where Jonah keeps others."

With a nod, she accepted it and escaped upstairs to Jonah and Penny's room. She rummaged through Penny's closet to find a pair of leggings and a sweatshirt, then exchanged her wet things for comfier ones. Already she felt ten times better.

Next she navigated to their bathroom, set the light on the counter, and found a towel to dry her hair. In the dim haze, she stared at her darkened reflection in the mirror.

Her sole focus since losing her husband Chris and their daughter Brianna nine years ago had been raising Gavin. Those years hadn't been easy on either of them, but they'd made it. She'd been so busy celebrating his safe arrival to adulthood that it took time for reality to catch up. She'd worked herself right out of her favorite job.

While Gavin spent his last few nights at home, she curled up in bed with an industrial-size container of cheese puffs. By the final night, reality seeped into her cheddar-coated depression. She needed a new job. One that would fill both her empty hours and her bank account, because idleness was no friend of her or her hips, and Gavin's college wasn't going to pay for itself. Chris had left her a hefty life insurance policy, enough to allow her to raise Gavin as a single, stay-at-home mom with some excess to cover his school. But they hadn't planned on the medical bills from Gavin's battle with cancer. Her accounts were nearly tapped out, and there was a real possibility she'd need to sell her home to replenish them.

So she'd set her cheese balls aside, intent to figure out her work situation. Except she couldn't seem to shake the encroaching sadness. For the past eighteen roller coaster years of her life—teenage pregnancy, loss of Chris and Brianna, Gavin's cancer—she'd managed to elude it. Oh, she'd grieved at all the appropriate moments, but then she'd moved on. Held her life together because there was no other option. Her fortitude became a trademark of her personality. Admitting she'd lost that strength made her feel like a fraud. What she needed was a quick breather so she could clear her mind and regain her emotional muscle.

Hence, her impetuous U-turn toward Holland tonight. As she drove, the detour made more and more sense. Time at the lake commiserating with her best friend was exactly what the doctor ordered. After all, Evan had plenty to commiserate about. Stories about the suffocating, yet well-meaning, women in his family laced his last phone call. The man needed his own breather, and she could provide one by stepping in to care for him. She always functioned best while helping others. Her mind would clear and her emotions steady. She'd discover her next step. And Evan would gain some space from his family.

Yep. Her visit was the perfect idea for them both.

Minus her unintentionally surprising him.

With a chuckle, Rachael draped the bath towel over a hook, then crossed through the master bedroom. Passing by Jonah's side of the closet, she grabbed one of his hoodies. Her feet landed on the last stair as the living room flooded with light. Looking across the open space, she found Evan flipping on the kitchen lights as well.

"Coffee?" he asked without sparing her a glance. It never ceased to unnerve her how in tune he was to her presence. It shouldn't be a surprise, though. Beyond being a patrol officer in the Abundance Police Department, he also served on the area's tri-county Special Enforcement Team, a version of SWAT, which had only sharpened his natural bent toward an alert personality.

"Yes, but let me make it." She hurried into the kitchen. "My taste buds can't handle your sludge tonight." Passing Evan, she tossed him Jonah's sweatshirt.

He snagged it from the air with his left hand. "Thanks."

"No problem." She opened the cupboard and grabbed the coffee grounds. "Ooh, look, there's Tate's Cookies in here. I know you're a homemade-cookie snob, so I'll eat yours for you." She turned to punctuate her tease with a smirk. Her lips froze in place, and she swallowed hard.

Evan had managed to strip out of his wet T-shirt, and two sights slammed into her. The yellowed bruising that seeped from under the bandage on his wound and, as she averted her gaze, his abs. Those toned muscles were a familiar sight, thanks to long summer days on the beach. She'd had no clue they existed until the first day they swam together. Hands down, they were his best-kept secret—and a feature she lived to tease him over. Things like, they were his ticket to the cover of a police calendar. Women would take his six-pack over one of Diet Coke any day. Laundry could be done on that washboard.

Yet in this moment, her thoughts strayed light years from funny.

"Trying to come up with another one-liner?" His tone was dryer than him, and his eyes met hers with a challenging spark.

"Nope. Too tired." She jerked around and reached for the coffee maker. "How many cups are you having?"

There was a slight hesitation before he responded. "One's fine."

Scooping grounds into the basket, she heard him struggling behind her. His frustrated mumbles pricked her heart. Evan's independence played such an inherent part of his character. With him two feet away, wrestling with something as simple as putting on a sweatshirt, her own internal struggle fired up. She was who he vented his frustrations to over his mom and sisters babying him. Did she turn around and help him, or let him finagle things himself? He wasn't wearing his sling, and she worried he'd hurt himself. But she didn't want to embarrass him.

She also wasn't entirely sure she wanted to be that close to his bare chest.

"Um, Rach?" His muffled voice reached out.

She turned around. The hood had inverted and become stuck, capturing him in a cotton prison.

"On it." She hurried over and yanked the hood out of the collar. "Better?"

With his left hand, he freed his face. "Yeah. Can you pull it down in back?"

Gripping the edges of the sweatshirt, she tugged. Her fingers skimmed over his skin and heat flushed her cheeks. She'd put sunscreen on this man's back and never felt a tinge of weirdness about it, for goodness sake. She had to be more exhausted and lonely than she realized, because friends simply didn't get flustered about stuff like this. And of all her favorite things about Evan Wayne, one stood out: he was unequivocally her best friend.

Evan had plenty of practice under his belt in maintaining control of his actions during situations that provoked him. None of them required more restraint than that blush on Rachael's face when her fingers touched him.

Probably because for the past year he'd done his best to keep his focus off her lips and the rising desire to kiss her. In not one of those moments, though, had she looked at him like she did right now. But it had been an emotional day for her and a heart-racing night for him. Neither of them were in the right place for him to act, and the last thing he wanted was to risk their friendship with one ill-timed kiss. If he finally did kiss her, he planned on it being a beginning, and right now he feared it could wind up an ending.

She licked her lips. He clenched his right fist, still hidden in the sweatshirt, as she reached for that empty sleeve. "Um, do you need me to help you get your arm into this part?"

"No." He cleared his throat. Got his hormones under control. Easy to do when she looked as if with one wrong move on his part, she'd bolt. "I'm not going to sleep in this, so I'll need to change at home anyway. This keeps it easy."

"Unless you get snagged by that hood again. I should have grabbed you a crewneck."

"It'll be fine." He winced as he readjusted himself so his forearm rested on the counter, taking the pressure off his shoulder joint. He wasn't supposed to be out of his sling this long, but—unable to sleep—he'd been readying for a shower when he caught sight of Rachael's light wandering through the shadows. He couldn't sit by and watch someone break into his friend's house when he could prevent it.

His pulse still beat erratically from pulling his gun on her. That was a mental picture he'd gladly erase. Right along with the slideshow of what could have happened on her run here. An avoidable situation if he'd done something about her broken gas gauge. Underneath that baggy sweatshirt, she was lean muscle, but that didn't mean she was strong enough to fight off someone intending to do her harm. If something had happened on his watch … it would have been Mandie all over again, only this time he wasn't sure his heart would have ever recovered.

Rachael regarded him. "You're wincing. Did you pull something when you raced over here?" Lines dug into her forehead as she cast a sideways glance as if following a thought. "You had your gun in your left hand, flashlight in your right, but you're not supposed to use that arm at all."

Her concern did something to him. "I didn't lift my shoulder. I only manipulated my elbow and wrist. That's why I had my gun in my left hand." Thunder shook the walls, the rumble competing with the pelting rain against the roof. "Too hard to take a shot if you can't lift your arm."

"Comforting thought," she groused.

"See, I don't only do brooding male well, I specialize in warm fuzzies too."

That earned him an eyeroll. The coffee pot behind her beeped, and she rose to grab mugs. "Anyway, back to my point. You're hurting, which tells me you used that arm too much."

"I may be a little sore, but it'll pass." He flexed his fingers. "I forget sometimes that I'm not fully up to speed. But I'll get there."

Mugs in hand, she turned. "Not if you ignore doctor's orders."

"I wouldn't dream of it."

"Isn't sounding convincing an important part of your job?"

"Yeah."

"Then you might want to brush up on that skill."

That right there, her scrunched-up nose and teasing eyes, was quite possibly one of his favorite things to look at. "I've missed you, Rach."

"Like an annoying little sister, I'm sure."

He'd had plenty thoughts about Rachael Stark. Not one of them sisterly.

"Only when you taunt me with coffee." He nodded at the pot behind her.

"Oh, right." Quickly turning, she poured the warm brew and bypassed adding cream to his without asking. She'd made him enough cups to know how he liked it. Nabbing the cookie box under her arm, she rejoined him at the counter.

She'd been right about his preference for homemade cookies, but when faced with the choice of no cookie or store-bought, well … He reached for one. After swallowing a buttery, chocolatey bite, he twisted on his stool to face her. "So what brings you here in the middle of the night?"

She shrugged. "Nothing too surprising. I just couldn't face my quiet house."

"So you came to this quiet one instead?"

Another shrug. "It's quiet, but not empty."

Over the past few weeks, he'd checked in with her often to see how she was handling Gavin's impending departure. Her words and voice provided him with opposite answers. He'd wondered which would win out. Everyone always commented how strong Rachael was—and that certainly proved true—but her strength also prevented her from showing her weaknesses. She might have resurrected his childhood nickname of Batman, but she was the one playing Superwoman with her emotions. He'd made it his mission to sneak past her disguised strength to the real woman below. That she'd shown up practically on his doorstep gave him hope in his progress.

"You know I'm here if you want to talk."

"I do." She sipped her coffee. "But not tonight. I've exceeded my emotional quota for the day."

"Tough dropping Gavin off?"

She held up her hand, thumb and forefinger nearly touching. "Just a tad."

He couldn't handle her forlorn expression. Reaching out, he knocked her fingers farther apart. "You know what *wasn't* just a tad?"

"What?"

"The number of photos you took while dropping him off." She'd texted him the impressive count while there. "Two hundred and thirty-one? Fifty-seven alone of his dorm room? Not sure how, exactly, you managed to take that many of a ten-by-ten space."

Her dimples returned. "It's a gift."

"One I cannot wait to be the recipient of. Thankfully, in person rather than you texting them to me. All two hundred and thirty-one," he reemphasized.

She stood. "You sound as excited as Gavin while I was taking them."

"More than, I'm sure."

"Not yet, but you can muster that enthusiasm while I run and grab a phone charger. Lucky for you, Penny keeps one in the guest room."

He was waiting for her when she sailed into the kitchen. Jumping up, he clicked his heels together. "Enough excitement for you?"

She tolerated him with a smirk. "You still need to teach me how to do that, along with skateboarding."

She'd been begging to learn since his offhand comment about some teens they'd walked past earlier this summer. But he hadn't been on one since he was a teenager. Too many memories. At least now he had a legit excuse for not teaching her. "I doubt I'll be on a skateboard anytime soon." He resettled on his stool. "How long are you here for anyway?"

"That depends on how long you need me." She plugged in her phone, then set it aside. It would take a few minutes to turn on. "I heard your cry for help, and with my suddenly empty schedule, I figured I'd answer it."

"How noble of you, except I don't remember sending up the Bat Signal."

"Because you're Batman. You don't send it up, you answer it."

"But you said you're answering it." He snapped his fingers. "So, wait. That makes you my sidekick. Like Robin?"

"I am nobody's sidekick."

"You're right. You're more like a leading lady."

She held his look, and for the briefest of moments, the atmosphere charged between them. But she'd boxed him so firmly into the friend zone, he'd need a battering ram to get out.

As if to remind him of his place, she punched him in his good shoulder. "That's right, and don't you forget it."

He couldn't. That was the problem. Because offering her the role felt like an all-or-nothing risk—too costly to take yet becoming all too impossible to ignore.

Chapter Two

Last night's storm passed, leaving clear skies filled with early morning sunshine that beckoned Rachael awake. Typically a morning person, today she had half a mind to pull the comforter over her head and ignore the dawning day. But ignoring life didn't mean responsibilities disappeared. Her car remained two miles away with an empty tank, and her brother deserved a phone call. He and Penny expected her to pick up Clooney later this morning at their home in Chicago. Being a no-show would raise their concern, so calling wasn't something she could shirk. But her brother was bound to have questions about her late-night detour, and the thought made her itchy. If she was going to haul out suitable answers for him, she needed food first. Much like her car, her brain and body did not work on fumes.

Tossing the fluffy duvet off, Rachael stretched, then sat up. Unlike Penny's personally colorful nature, her guest room was decorated in neutral tones with cozy fabrics that invited you to snuggle in and rest awhile. A fiddle-leaf fig plant with a wicker basket covering its pot took up one corner, while an upholstered glider and tiny bookshelf filled the opposite side of the room. Centered on the wall opposite the bed hung a macramé creation, courtesy of Penny's newest hobby. She might focus on antiques at her Chicago shop, but she could easily sell these too.

Stomach growling, Rachael dragged her hands through her knotted hair, then shuffled to the bathroom to at least brush her teeth. She grimaced at the sight in the mirror. Thank the sweet Lord that nobody was here. No brave soul would try and coax words out of her or be forced to pretend she didn't resemble something the cat dragged in.

She trudged down the staircase, the scent of coffee reaching her as she hit the last step. Evan sat at the kitchen counter, sipping from his mug. This morning he wore his sling, which secured his right arm snugly against a wedge stabilized with straps around his neck and waist. He glanced up before her wrinkled self could retreat.

"Not one word, bucko," she warned.

Laughter danced in his eyes, and he pointed toward a plate of toast and slices of cheese. Without a word, he returned to reading something on his phone.

Bless him. He understood her need for silence and food in the morning. Since they'd eaten through the only thing in the cupboards last night—cookies— he obviously had brought over much-needed sustenance. Hello, cheese! He knew her so well. Plus, they'd been friends long enough that he'd seen her messy self before. Still, she ran a hand through her hair as she scooted to the toast. After nabbing two pieces and a hefty amount of cheddar to tide her over until breakfast, she quickly poured coffee, then beat a hasty retreat upstairs.

She bypassed the guestroom to grab another outfit from Penny's closet. Quickly downing the toast, she headed for her bathroom. Within ten minutes she'd showered and braided her wet hair. Evan waited downstairs, but she really should call her brother.

She stared at her phone, sucked in a breath, and pressed Jonah's number.

He answered on the first ring. "How're you doing?"

"Good. But I'm not in Chicago. I stayed at your cottage last night."

"You're in Holland?" Curiosity and concern revved up in his voice.

"Yep. And so you know, your watchdog is still as sharp as ever. He nearly shot me last night." She cringed as she tossed out the words. Not nice to throw Evan under the bus, but it would divert Jonah's attention for a few minutes.

"What?!"

Okay. So maybe she could have found a less dramatic redirect. "Calm down. I'm only kidding."

"Not a funny joke, Rach." He blew out a hard sigh.

"Evan did think I was breaking in, though. Since I sort of did."

"Why didn't you knock on his door for a key?"

"I figured he was sleeping. He is recovering from a gunshot wound, you know."

"Yeah, I know," Jonah softly replied.

They'd all been worried about Evan. Her stomach still tensed with the memory of the phone call that he'd been shot. An all too familiar reminder of how quickly life could change.

"Actually, that's why I headed this way." At least partly the reason, but Jonah didn't need every specific detail. "Evan's getting along fairly well, but he could still use some help in areas, and I offered my services."

"Kind of you." He sounded like he wanted to say more but didn't. God bless him.

She strolled to the window overlooking Lake Michigan. "I plan to come home tomorrow and grab a few things."

"Clooney being one of them?"

"Of course. But if you need me to, I can come that way today and get her."

"Are you kidding? Abrielle loves having her here. I'm going to have to prepare her for Clooney leaving." She suspected he'd have to ready himself as well. He'd purchased Clooney for her and Gavin during Gavin's battle with cancer, but he spoiled her like she was his.

"Maybe it's time for me to buy you a dog."

"How about we make it past the toddler stage with Ellie first?"

"Oh, dear brother, you haven't even entered the toddler stage. She's only turning one. You could potty-train her and a puppy at the same time." In fact, the more she thought about it …

"Your silence is scaring me. It's like you're plotting my demise."

"Or returning the favor you so graciously did for me." And in all honesty, Clooney had been a huge favor. She'd been a constant companion during some really tough times.

"No return needed." He paused, then, "So everything's okay?"

No. But it would be, and that's all anyone needed to know.

"It's all good. Promise. I'm just taking advantage of having a clear schedule and offering it to Evan. It's rare for me to have nothing on my plate."

"Have you thought of painting again?" He'd been nudging her toward her return for some time now. Even found her studio space. And she'd tried, she really had.

But every time she picked up a brush, memories pressed in. Chris seeing her talent and encouraging its growth. Brianna toddling nearby, dipping her tiny fingers into paint and sliding them over crisp, white paper Rachael laid out for her. Gavin joining them after school, munching on Cheetos, then chasing Brie with his sticky, orange fingers. She'd loved those moments. If only she'd allowed them to be enough to satisfy her, perhaps things would have been different. But slowly her love of painting eclipsed her love of family, which was why she hadn't been with Chris and Brianna when they died.

They were all supposed to attend Gavin's Christmas concert, but she'd stayed home to finish a project. Told Chris she needed quiet and sent him on his way with the video camera. Had Gavin not gone home with friends, she'd have lost him too. Either way, she'd been permanently granted her silence to paint. What she wouldn't give to have them all underfoot again. She hadn't treasured the beautiful chaos and noise. Now the atmosphere was too quiet—even when she turned her music full volume.

After completing only a few nonstellar paintings, her canvases remained blank. It was a situation with no obvious remedy. So had she thought of painting again? "Not really." Though finding her way back to it could produce the answer to her money problems.

Right now she didn't have it in her to search. "Not to cut this short, but Evan's downstairs, and after last night I think I owe him some bacon." They could head into town, and she'd buy him a plateful.

"By all means, go eat then. I'm not about to keep you from your breakfast. A hangry you isn't fair for Evan."

"Hey!"

With another deep laugh, he said his goodbye and hung up. Overall, the conversation went well. Hand on the door knob, Rachael squared her shoulders. A few weeks with her friend. Then she'd figure things out whether she was ready to or not.

But next, breakfast.

In the kitchen, Evan still sat at the island. "Safe to greet you now?" His eyes remained on his phone.

"Marginally." She beelined for another slice of toast. "What are you doing in my kitchen anyway? Not that I'm complaining, just curious."

"I knew the fridge was empty, which meant your stomach would be too, which would result in a hangry you on my doorstep. I chose to head off that problem and bring food over."

"Thanks, Batman." This time she slathered blueberry jam on her bread before adding a slice of sharp cheddar.

"Not bucko?"

"You saved me from empty cupboards. That makes you my morning hero, so definitely Batman."

He chuckled, then grimaced. "I brought bacon and eggs too. You don't have to eat that nasty combination."

"This isn't nasty. It's delicious." She took another bite to emphasize the fact. "But because I know your taste buds aren't quite as refined as mine, I'll cook up those bacon and eggs." Seemed they were eating in, not out.

He stood. "I'll help."

"Oh no, you don't." She jabbed a finger his way. "Sit. I've got this." Grabbing the ingredients from the fridge, she peeked at him. "Need a refill on that coffee?"

"I'm good. This was already my third."

"Third?" She set out two skillets. "How long have you been up?"

"Long enough." He watched her work. "I really can help, Rach."

"You really can sit there too." She started the bacon as he glowered at her. Cracking the eggs, she added them to a bowl to whisk. His glower continued. The man did not like being inactive. "How's your shoulder this morning?"

"A little sore, but I'm sure after PT I'll wish it felt this good." Then, as if he could no longer contain himself, he joined her at the stove to flip the bacon. Between his bulky sling, the angle of the pan, and having to use his nondominant hand, his movements were awkward. The bacon popped. "Ouch!" He jerked away, knocking her arm as she scooped the scrambled eggs, and some spilled to the floor.

Rachael reached for a paper towel. "I'll clean them up."

His lips thinned into a straight line, and he beat her to them. "I've got it."

She skirted his mood. Had to be hard on him, wanting to act normal when his body refused to let him. "All right, then I'll finish the bacon."

Evan didn't respond, but he didn't stop her either. Another minute and they sat side by side at the island much like last night. Rachael took her jellied toast and topped it with scrambled eggs, then a slice of bacon and, of course, cheese. "Thanks for bringing over food."

He shook his head. "Your taste buds aren't refined, they're in line with a toddler's."

"Aww, you truly do give the sweetest compliments." She tossed him a syrupy smile before taking a huge chomp out of her concoction. After swallowing, she began creating another perfect bite. "It's all the same food as what's on your plate. It shouldn't matter how you eat it."

"We've been over this before." He carefully scooped a forkful of eggs. Not a morsel of food on his plate touched. "This isn't like your paints. Each item needs to remain separate."

"What a boring world. Think of all the amazing colors we wouldn't have if someone hadn't swirled those primary tones together. Your food is the same."

She reached over with her fork, intending to mix his plateful together and finally win this old argument.

He deflected her hand and shoved her chair away all in one move, then kept his leg braced against it so she couldn't scoot closer again. "So, besides coming to my rescue, what else instigated your late-night detour?"

A devilish idea sprang to mind. "Let me fix you a perfect bite, and then I'll tell you."

"I don't think I want to know that badly." He stabbed at his eggs. "Besides, you'll tell me eventually. You're a talker. You can't help yourself."

"Better a talker than a chicken." Though she hid her most vulnerable places from him, maybe she was a little of both.

He side-eyed her. "Smack talker."

She laughed. "But is it working?"

With a sigh, he shifted in his seat. "Fine. Fix me one bite."

"*And* you eat it."

He feigned disgust. "You drive a hard bargain."

"Take it or leave it, bucko."

"I thought I was Batman."

"Your status with me remains fluid."

The confident grin sliding across his face sparked a warmth through her middle she'd rather ignore. "I'll keep that in mind." He swept his hand over his plate. "Fix away."

Oh, she'd fix away all right. Starting with these rogue thoughts she couldn't seem to corral. She'd erroneously thought a good night's sleep was the only thing required to cage them. She'd been wrong. What she needed was a list of reasons to combat his enticing behaviors. Every time he did something that elicited a gooey response from her, she'd whack it down with something from her list.

She began assembling his sandwich as she contemplated.

First. He was just a friend.

Second. Moving from friendship to something more equaled awkward. How did one kiss their best friend?

Third. If she kissed her friend and it didn't work, their friendship was a goner.

Fourth. She wasn't looking for love anyway.

Fifth, and most important. Even if she was, his job was way too dangerous. She'd already had enough loss in life.

She stopped there, set down the knife, and triumphantly handed him his toast concoction. "All set."

Already her list was working. Points One through Four formed an impressive show of force between her recalcitrant emotions and Evan's charm. She didn't foresee any way for him to topple them, but on the off chance he did, Point Five stood at the ready, impenetrable.

"That was awful." Evan reached for the last sip of his coffee, hoping it would remove the mixed-up taste she'd gleefully delivered him. "How do you eat such craziness?"

"I take a bite, chew, then swallow."

He narrowed one eye at her. "Funny." Then took his plate to the sink, rinsed it, and stowed it in the dishwasher. "You owe me an answer, by the way."

"Look at the time. You mentioned last night that you start PT this morning. Need a ride?" She brought her items to the sink. Dressed in another pair of Penny's leggings and a tunic, with her long brown hair in a braid and no makeup on her fresh face, she didn't look near old enough to be the mother of a college student. Of course, she'd had Gavin right after turning sixteen, but she'd also lived a whole lot of life since then. She'd come through with a strength everyone commented on, and he had to admit he found attractive. Yet, it was her struggles he hoped she'd share with him. Those moments where she grew quiet, forced a smile that didn't reach her eyes, lightly fisted her hand to rub her thumb against her nails.

He scooted over to make room for her to rinse her dish. "I do. And I really appreciate your help." Though he fully planned on returning the favor. Which was why he wasn't letting her skirt her end of their bargain. "It'll provide plenty of time for you to give me your promised answer."

"I never actually specified *when* I'd provide my response."

"It was implied to be immediately following my fulfillment of the deal."

"Or did you merely infer that?"

"Your stall tactics won't work with me. You're filling me in while we drive." Grabbing her shoulder, he steered her to the foyer. "Let's get moving. I don't want to be late."

"Fine." She bypassed her still wet tennis shoes and slipped into a pair of flip-flops he recognized as summer leftovers. "We'll have to stop by my Jeep on the way so I can grab my purse. Think we can get some gas after your appointment?"

"Yes and no." He held the door for her.

She stepped through, then stopped short at the sight of her Jeep. "Sally!" She whipped around and faced him.

"I told you I'd been up awhile."

"But how'd you do this all by yourself?"

"Well, first I waded through several layers of barrels to reach my gas can, and then I marched through the pine tree forest past the swirly tops of the sandy dunes until—"

"Okay, Buddy the Elf, I get it." Her face lit at the reference to their favorite Christmas movie. "And my car key?"

"I took it with me last night when I left."

"But I thought you couldn't drive. Hence why I'm your chauffer?"

He crossed to his own Jeep, a Wrangler, bright red, and twenty years newer than hers. "It was two miles down a country road. I figured I could make an exception." He held open his driver's door for her. "Now come on, I don't want to be late for my first appointment. Who knows what kind of extra torture they'll prescribe me if I am."

"I'm more comfortable driving Sally."

"And I'm more comfortable riding in my Jeep. Since I'm the patient, I win."

"Definitely trying my patience." A playful tone outlined her grumble, and she settled into his vehicle. Her familiar scent of apples carried on the breeze as he shut her door. He rounded to climb into the passenger seat.

They started down the road, splashing through puddles from last night's rain. She squinted against the bright sunshine. He reached into the console between the seats and handed her his sunglasses. "I believe our agreement was you'd fill the silence of this ride."

"Right." She slipped the shades on. "Like I said, I initially headed this way because I couldn't face a quiet house." She cast him a glance. "I blinked, and Gavin grew up on me. I'm still not sure how it happened."

Oh, he completely understood life changing in a blink of an eye. His first experience had been the sudden loss of Mandie. His last experience had been six weeks ago with what should have been the routine stop of a maroon minivan.

Rachael kept talking. "I'm staying, though, so I can help you."

He didn't necessarily require any aid, but people seemed intent on providing it. And he had to admit, accepting assistance from Rach was much easier than from his mom and sisters. Not only did it provide an excuse to be around her, but he sensed in her a deep need to focus on someone else. Caretaking ran thick in her blood, and for the first time since she was sixteen, she didn't have anyone to take care of. He'd happily sacrifice himself to aid in the transition.

Those were both answers he already knew though, which meant there was more. "What else, Rach?"

She hesitated, glancing over her shoulder to change lanes. Finally, "I've got to find a job."

That surprised him. As far as he knew, she'd been living off of Chris's life insurance. They probably hadn't planned on Gavin's medical bills. "You didn't mention anything about job hunting this summer." Normally she talked through things with him. They were constantly bouncing ideas off one another.

"I only just decided."

He looked her way. "I'd heard rumors of your once spontaneous nature, and now I'm starting to believe them."

Her cheek pulled up in a smile. "This isn't spontaneity, it's me adjusting to what needs to be done next and doing it. Right now, that's getting Gavin through school. Money's tight, and he wants to be a doctor." Her fingers drummed the steering wheel. "After everything he's been through, he'll make an amazing one, too."

"Plus, you want him to have his dreams." Last year, when he was applying to colleges, Evan had caught Rachael in a rare emotional moment. When he'd asked why she didn't restrict Gavin to local schools, her answer only made him admire her more.

We lost Chris and Brianna when he was in elementary school. In junior high, he battled cancer. High school was all about catching up. If I can help him have the best college experience, then that's what I'm going to do because he's more than earned it.

Rachael loved with a rare abandon and fullness. But she also guarded that love, refusing to extend it any farther than her current sphere. She remained kind and caring to all but reserved the depths of her heart to few. Knowing her past, that was understandable. Didn't stop him from wanting farther inside her tiny circle.

"I do. And, as you know, he didn't receive much in the way of scholarships."

"But he did manage to graduate with his class. That says way more about his abilities than a GPA."

"If only you were in charge of doling out college funds."

He'd give her all of them and then some.

She shrugged. "Even with the financial aid he received, his yearly school and living cost still runs just north of fifteen thousand."

"Yearly?" This was the first time she'd shared that info with him, and he had to have heard her wrong.

"Yep." She cast him a glance. "It can take thirteen years to become a pediatric oncologist."

He did the math. "How can anyone afford that?"

"Welcome to my dilemma." She merged onto the highway. Luckily, her friend and Penny's brother-in-law, Micah—already a doctor himself—had offered some hard-earned wisdom and assistance. "Micah's been pointing Gavin to more scholarship and grant applications. He also had some connections who helped Gav get a part-time job at Sparrow Hospital, so that income will go toward some of his undergrad. And once he's a resident, he'll get paid."

"But in the meantime ..."

"In the meantime, I need to come up with a lot of money." She navigated around a slow car. "I know he'll have some debt, but I'm hoping to mitigate how much."

"What about painting again?" Seemed an obvious choice for her. She'd been very well known in the art world—something he'd googled after Jonah let that info slip. Since then, he'd visited her work studio in Chicago. Seeing her paintings in person impressed him even more.

Her fingers twitched against the steering wheel, and she glanced his way. "Seeing as how I only have a GED, nothing other than Mom to put on my resume, and no money to change either of those facts, that suggestion makes sense on paper." Her attention returned to the road. "But I'm experiencing some ... major painter's block, so painting isn't a current option."

"Like writer's block, only for painters?"

"Exactly."

The car bounced over ruts in the road. "Then hopefully this unplanned visit will spark something."

"Hopefully." She didn't sound convinced. "If I can't find a way to make money, I may need to sell my house." She darted her eyes his way for a moment, then back to the road. "And I'm not ready to sell. Chris and I fixed it up, and there's still marks from where Gavin swung his tiny hammer alongside us. It's the only home Brianna ever knew. And Gavin beat cancer there." She swallowed, and her voice softened. "It may be too quiet for me right now, but I'm not ready for that chapter to close as well."

He set aside his hope of writing an entirely new book with her and focused on being her friend. Reaching over, he grasped her hand resting on her leg and gave it a squeeze. "You won't have to sell, Rachael."

She sniffed and pulled away. "You can't know that."

"I can. We'll get you past your painter's block or figure something else out. I promise."

She sighed, her thumb rubbing circles against her other nails. They passed a sign for their upcoming exit. "Like I said, my resume is sorely lacking, and as far as painting … I'm not sure there's a way around the block."

Her deliberation over words perked his senses. Something lurked under her surface, and it was a deeper truth than the one she offered. He'd fish it out sooner or later.

"Then I guess we'll both be helping each other while you're here."

She offered him a quizzical look.

"I'm going to find you a way to make money," he supplied. "I am a police officer, after all. Finding things is kind of my specialty."

"Still, that's a rather tall order."

"I'm a man of many talents. One of which I'm offering you. So how about you take me up on it?"

Her hesitation felt unending, but eventually she answered. "Okay." She navigated the exit. "But first we have your appointment at the torture chamber."

"Wow, your preparatory skills are A-plus."

"I like to keep it real. That way your experience always comes in above your expectations."

If that were true, then he was setting his expectations even higher when it came to a future with Rachael Stark.

Chapter Three

Rachael had made the right decision. During the past hour, while she was in Chicago to pack, that realization had become crystal clear. Yes, she loved this home, but the memories inside were too much to handle on her own while maintaining her trademark strength. If she was going to get on top of these unplanned emotions, she'd need to do it from a distance. So yes, she'd made the right decision to spend the next few weeks in Michigan, taking care of Evan.

"I packed all of Clooney's toys." Evan appeared in her doorway. PT yesterday wound up being only an initial evaluation so his therapist could determine a plan. With nothing on his calendar today, he'd made the three-hour trip with her to Chicago to grab clothes and collect her goldendoodle child. The furball hadn't left her ankles since they'd picked her up at Jonah and Penny's. Evan leaned against the doorjamb, a hedgehog squeaky toy in his hand. "I think we need to have a talk, though, on how many toys this dog has."

"Direct that conversation to Jonah. He's the one who keeps her supplied." Jonah spoiled her like any other member of his family. Clooney barked as Evan squeaked the toy. "You do realize if you start playing with her, we'll never get out of here to meet Jonah and Penny."

"She's not letting you out of her sight unless we distract her." He nodded to her sitting at Rachael's feet.

"True." She knelt and grabbed Clooney's fluffy face. "You're coming with me this time, I promise. But first we're going to go see some sea life."

Evan's brows arched in amusement. "You know she doesn't understand you, right?"

"Sure she does." Rachael ruffled the top of Clooney's head. "Don't you, girl?" Clooney barked. "See?"

He simply shook his head and strolled into the room. "This all you're taking?" He nodded to the two stuffed overnight bags on her bed.

"Don't sound so surprised."

"Can I look it?" He parted his mouth and widened his eyes.

She stood and swatted at him. "No, you cannot."

He dodged her attack and picked up one of the duffels, then followed her into the hall and down the stairs. "When are we supposed to meet Jonah and Penny?"

"One. That gives us time to grab lunch and stop by my studio for a few art supplies."

Evan had encouraged her to bring some things with her to try and push past her painting block. It was easier to agree than explain her refusal.

They walked through her living room. The last family picture of her, Chris, Gavin, and Brianna hung on the wall over her couch. Perched together on their front porch swing, pumpkins and mums decorating the space, she'd been tickling Brie while Chris and Gavin talked football. Jonah captured the moment after their huge Thanksgiving meal. She'd had no way of knowing that only a few weeks later, her life would forever be altered. But that was how life worked. Change hardly ever came with a warning, and it was her job to keep up.

Evan followed her gaze. "Great picture."

"It was a great moment." Simple and true, but she knew those days would not return. It wasn't that she longed for them anymore. No, what she yearned for was stability. Security. She couldn't predict the future, but she could minimize its emotional impact by controlling how far she allowed her emotions to roam. "We had a lot of them."

"I bet." He scanned other pictures in the room. The remainder were of Gavin and Brianna. A few years ago she'd packed away the photos of her and Chris along with her wedding ring, thinking it would ward off the questions on how long she planned to grieve—as if grief had a timetable. Instead all she did was invite a whole bunch of attempted blind dates. She no more wanted the dates than she did the questions. Evan pointed at another. "That's one of my favorites."

She turned. Smiled. "Brianna loved painting with me." Chris caught them early one morning, sunlight streaming into the dining room as they'd stood side by side at their easels. Brie's stance mirrored her own.

"She was a mini version of you, wasn't she?"

"One hundred percent."

They stood in silence for a long moment, then Evan continued through the room to drop her bag at the front door. The plan was to leave everything here while they ran to Shed's Aquarium, then return for her bags and Clooney. "I turned off the water to your washing machine and your upstairs toilets."

She dropped her other bag. "I'm only going to be gone a few weeks."

"I know, but you really should have done that when you left to drop off Gavin. If a leak happens when you're not home, it can cause a lot of damage." He grabbed his keys from the entrance table. "You should always be prepared. You'd hate to come home to a flood and wonder what if."

The man would prepare for a tropical storm in the middle of a desert. Opening the door, she stepped onto her porch. "Sometimes you're more Boy Scout than Batman."

His grin said he took that as a compliment.

He joined her outside, then waited as she patted Clooney goodbye and locked up. They hustled to his Jeep, and she drove them to her studio. Jonah had originally rented the space, but a few years ago he purchased the building and used the extra square footage to house Penny's antique shop as well. Hopping out, Evan waited for her by his door. "Need much from here?"

"Not really. You can wait in the car if you'd like."

"I'll come in, if that's okay."

She hesitated. One of the pieces inside would require an explanation she wasn't prepared to give. The painting belonged to a personal series she worked on around this time each year, and only Gavin knew about it. The heartfelt watercolor was the one and only thing her fingers could create. All other attempts at painting made her remember what she lost. But this series helped her regain a few of those precious stolen moments. Most of the pieces were tucked away, but the beginnings of this year's stood in the open.

"If you don't want me to—" Evan prompted.

"No. It's fine." She could distract him easier by acquiescing. If she stonewalled him, he'd only grow curious. "Come on in." Unlocking the door, she pushed it open and flicked on the lights. She directed Evan toward her paints and away from her project. "Mind packing everything on top there into the tote on the floor?"

"Sure thing." He set to work.

That provided the perfect opportunity to visit her painting. Her heart swelled at the face taking shape on the canvas. She reached out and traced the lines she'd sketched. This year they'd lost some of their soft curves. Moisture blurred her vision for a moment before she blinked it away. Her emotions lived too close to the surface lately. She needed to muscle them into submission, but they seemed to be growing stronger than her resolve.

"Rach?" Evan called. "Do you need any of these on the lower shelf?"

"Nope." She quickly covered the portrait with a thin, quilted blanket and secured it with a twill rope. "Just those." Before she could second-guess herself, she tucked the bundle under her arm to bring with her.

Duffel of paints in his good hand, Evan joined her on the other side of the space and pointed at her quilt-covered package. "What's that?"

"Just a canvas." She scanned the room. "Let me grab my brushes, and then I think that's everything."

Evan strolled the perimeter of the room while she worked. His voice reached hers from the opposite corner, where several pieces lay propped against the wall. "I didn't know you painted people too."

Her gaze swung that way. Drat. She'd left out last year's painting, having used it as a jumping-off point before beginning this year's. She scurried over to tuck it away. "Sometimes."

He followed her. "Why're you putting it away?"

"I can be shy about certain pieces."

"You shouldn't be about that one. It's amazing. Almost like a photograph." Looking around, he studied her floral landscapes and close-ups of individual flowers. Nearly all of them she'd painted a decade ago. "Your flowers are beautiful"—he turned to the painting in her hand— "but that's one of the best portraits I've ever seen. Instead of hiding it, you should paint more."

She tried for an amused laugh but it sounded hollow. "You're an art critic now, huh?"

"Just saying what I see."

She tucked the canvas away before he could look any closer. Already he'd done that squinty thing like he thought he recognized the subject and was trying to place her. "Then you need to broaden your art horizons."

Shaking his head, he strolled away from her and stopped by a painting of a massive dahlia, one of her favorite flowers. This had been her first attempt at something so detailed. She'd used saturated merlot tones with highlights of claret along the dips and curves of its individually cupped leaves. Chris challenged her to create it—and she had, with Gavin at school and Brianna napping nearby. Her agent, Lanette, took her on because of the promise she saw there. And Jonah hung it when he purchased her the space.

Evan peered over his shoulder at her. "I can see why they called you the next Georgia O'Keefe."

"You actually know who she was?"

"Sure. A famous painter known for her enlarged flowers." He turned. "I may have looked her up after googling you and seeing the comparison. Personally, I think yours are better."

She was a little stuck on the fact he'd googled her and a whole lot stuck on the fact he liked her old paintings. "You may be a little biased."

His smile fired off nerves inside like those crazy trick candles. She kept trying to snuff out the sparks, but they kept firing right back up. "Maybe."

She darted for her things. "We should get moving if we want to have time for lunch before meeting Jonah and Penny."

"Wouldn't want that. A hangry you is scarier than the sharks."

True. But right now she wasn't thinking about food. All she wanted was something to douse these sparks popping between them. Moving to Holland for a few weeks was supposed to be her escape, not an ambush for her heart.

"I don't think she's going to sit much longer." Penny bounced a wiggling Abrielle as they followed the crowd out from Abbot Oceanarium situated inside Shedd's Aquarium.

They reached the top of the cement steps, then scooted to the side as Jonah left to retrieve Abrielle's stroller. Evan watched the massive screens used for the aquatic show's video presentations roll upwards. They covered the floor-to-ceiling glass wall overlooking Lake Michigan and the Chicago skyline. An enormous aquarium with dolphins, sea otters, and beluga whales stretched between that wall and these steps, which doubled as a seating area. An indoor forest bordered the sides of the space. Not something he expected to find when he'd approached the Shedd's entrance this afternoon. Climbing the marble steps and walking past the towering, thick pillars that made him feel about two feet tall reminded him of structures he'd seen in DC. He knew this one housed fish, not government, but he hadn't imagined it would do so quite this impressively.

Jonah showed up with the stroller, and Penny tried to buckle Ellie in, but their little girl went stiff as a board.

"You want to take her to the Polar Play Area so she can run around for a little bit?" Rachael suggested. From what Jonah had proudly shared, Ellie took her first steps last week.

"Yes." Penny puffed the word as she scooped Ellie up. "The dolphins put on a great show, but I think she'll enjoy it better when she's a little older. Right now, all she wants to do is walk."

As they started toward the elevators, Rachael sympathized. "I remember that stage well."

Evan followed their little group, his mind working to picture Rachael as mom to toddlers. The first time she'd been a mother, she'd had to tackle the role of parent on her own. He'd still like to find that guy—Kurt—and knock him upside the head. If he'd thought himself man enough to sleep with her, he should have been man enough to support her and Gavin. And sure, Kurt had only been a teen himself, but in the eighteen years since then—enough years for him to grow up—he hadn't once contacted her. She brushed it off like it didn't matter, but that abandonment still touched parts of her. Yeah. He'd definitely like to hit something resembling Kurt's face.

"You okay?" Rachael stopped beside the beluga tank. A few feet away Jonah and Penny held a giggling Abrielle so she could see the white whale swimming beside the glass. Water cascaded down the man-made rock to their right, and he leaned closer to better hear her over the splashing noise.

"Fine. Why?"

"Your eyebrows slant any more, they might slide off your face."

The woman sure knew how to pull him from frustrated to amused with a few well-placed words. Across the walkway, the sea lions barked. "Sorry, but I don't like those guys."

"I didn't realize you felt so strongly about sea lions."

"They're a bunch of showboats. I prefer more humble sea life."

She stared at him, a slow grin lifting her lips and lighting her bright blue eyes. "You're weird."

"You hang out with me. What's that say about you?"

"That I need better discernment when it comes to my friends." She spun and continued up the walk toward the elevators where Jonah and Penny waited for them.

Rachael snuck up beside Penny to take Abrielle from her. The two ladies chatted about mom stuff, while Evan joined Jonah. "I replaced your furnace filter when I did mine. Before we know it, we'll need to turn our heat on."

"Can't believe summer's practically over." Jonah leaned against the wall. "Send me the receipt, and I'll get you a check."

"It was twenty bucks. I think I can handle it since you paid Rach's and my way in here today."

"How're things going with my sister, anyway?" Jonah had a way of assessing someone with an accuracy that was, quite frankly, scary. He could use him during interrogations. Didn't like that ability turned on himself like it was now, though.

"You'd need to ask her."

"I will. Right now I'm asking you."

All summer Evan had swerved and dodged Jonah's attempts to probe his intentions, though he had no doubt his friend was fully aware what they were. Rachael showing up in Holland last week only made her brother more curious. Well, get in line, buddy, because Evan's own curiosity was stoked, and Racheal wasn't answering any of the questions she'd provoked in him.

"Things with Rach are fine. She needed a bit of a break, and it just so happened I needed an extra hand." He wiggled his fingers strapped to his chest. "Literally. So it's worked out perfectly."

"She does love helping others." Jonah watched his sister blowing raspberries against Abrielle's cheeks.

Very true, sometimes to a fault. When Rach focused on someone else, she didn't have to deal with her own emotions. He had a feeling that's what she was doing with him. Adjusting to an empty nest was no easy task—especially for someone with a caretaking nature. Made sense she'd focus on Evan, and he'd happily let her. What he wouldn't allow was her skirting her own feelings. Not indefinitely at least. Especially when his gut said there was more going on with her than empty-nest syndrome. "I'm sure that played into things."

Jonah's intense focus swung to him. "Anything else at play here?"

The elevator arrived and the girls stepped on. Might as well be blunt or this conversation wasn't ending. "I like your sister, but there's no developments in that area currently. If there are, you'll be one of the first to know."

"Fair enough." With a nod and a smile, he pushed past him and entered the elevator, moving toward Penny.

Rach appraised Evan with a penetrating look that rivaled Jonah's. Man. Those two must not have gotten away with anything in their household because those looks were no doubt inherited.

He scooted beside her to allow others into the space. They rode down one floor and exited into a carpeted area depicting the depths of the sea. Varying tones of blues covered the walls and ceiling with some overhead sections dipping down like waves. Giggles echoed from a cartoon-like yellow submarine as kids pressed their faces against the glass. As they walked farther down the corridor, the room opened wide. People stood in front of a glass wall, their outlines dark against the brilliant blue water where belugas and dolphins played on the other side.

Penny put Ellie down and she toddled toward the glass, her eyes wide as she pointed at the dolphin swimming by. Moms with strollers and toddlers scurried around the area. How on earth did they keep track of where everyone was? This was worse than trying to police an outdoor rock concert. Loud, lots of movement, and most of the civilians were only knee-high. He navigated to a wall with a vantage point of the space, stuck his shoulders against it, and scanned the room.

"Ellie seems much happier down here, now that she's free." Rach leaned against the wall with him.

"Mm-hmm."

"She's going to give them a run for their money. Brianna and Gavin didn't start walking until nearly fifteen months."

He merely nodded, his eyes on a mom of two who tried unsuccessfully to calm her crying baby girl with a bottle. She dug into the depths of a diaper bag, and her toddler took advantage of the distraction to race the opposite way.

Evan pushed off the wall and intercepted the little boy. "Hey there. Let's go find your mama." He gently scooped him up with his good arm and walked him toward his mom, who popped her head up and darted a look around. Her eyes widened as she realized her son was missing.

"Carter!" She called before Evan could placate her fears.

"He's right here." Evan hustled over and deposited Carter at her feet.

She hugged her son. "Don't you run off like that." Then straightened. "Thank you."

"No problem."

Grasping her boy's hand, the exhausted-looking woman headed for the elevators, no doubt ready to end today's excursion.

Rach sidled up beside him. "Come on, let's grab you a snack."

"Penny and Jonah aren't finished yet."

"They may be here awhile, and you're going to put the security guards out of a job if I leave you down here much longer."

"Maybe they should *do* their job then."

She nodded toward one of them as she tugged Evan toward the steps. "He was halfway to little Carter. You happened to reach him first."

"Oh."

"Oh," she mimicked.

They ascended the stairway, coming out near the food court. Here, the musty smell that permeated the entire building swirled with the odor of fried foods and burgers. They both secured trays and snacks, then met at a table he'd chosen along the edges of the room. Rach shook her head good-naturedly. "Can't shut it off, can you?"

"That's about as likely to happen as you letting me steal one of your mozz sticks."

She chuckled, then yanked the paper bowl closer to her. "You know me so well."

Probably better than she liked to think. Like how, right this moment, her attention caught on the mom to their left handing out snacks to her three littles, and he could read every emotion swirling in Rachael's eyes. Tenderness. Longing. And almost a stunned expression, as if she couldn't quite grasp the speed at which life moved. It wasn't the only time today he'd caught her watching the moms here. Or the only time he'd seen her blink away tears—not that she ever allowed them to fall.

"Rach." He swathed her name in a gentle tone.

She pasted on her smile and switched her emotions with a speed that could teach a seasoned undercover cop a thing or two. "I'm not sharing, so don't try to bargain with me."

The reference clearly applied to her feelings as much as it did her mozzarella sticks.

"Maybe another time then."

"Don't count on it."

"Oh, honey, you know I don't give up that easily."

Her cheeks reddened, and she bit into her snack rather than respond. Typical Rachael. When she didn't want to talk, she'd reroute the conversation, take a bite of food, or find a distraction. She was so good at her sneaky redirects, people often didn't recognize the tactic.

He spotted it every time.

But this time he noted something else. Straightening, he watched her as she avoided his attention and scanned the crowd. As she did, he could virtually see her pack herself up tight. Her back straightened. Her shoulders stiffened. And then she gave a nearly imperceptible nod.

This wasn't about sidetracking tough conversations. Rachael was distancing herself from any emotions too difficult to feel by convincing herself she didn't feel them. But by cutting off emotions, she missed all the good ones too. Such as joy and love.

Like a paradigm shift, the revelation brought understanding that her defense mechanism wouldn't topple in one conversation. He needed to retreat and rethink his approach. So he allowed her diversion tactic to meet success today.

They chatted for nearly forty-five minutes before Jonah, Penny, and Abrielle joined them. Abrielle looked ready to conk out. Good time to call it quits, especially if they wanted to beat rush hour.

In the parking lot, Jonah hugged his sister. "You sure you're doing okay? Penny and I can come stay with you for a while if you want the company."

Rach waved him off. "I'm perfectly fine."

"Your spontaneous detour says otherwise."

"Yeah. It says Evan needed a break from his family. You know how overbearing family can be at times." She framed her comment with an arched brow.

Evan watched as the pro redirected her brother, and Jonah went right along with her.

"Fine," Jonah relented. "You're staying at least until Labor Day?"

"Yep."

"Guess I'll next see you at the annual potluck. Gavin coming in for it?"

"He wouldn't miss it."

With a few more hugs, they all climbed into their cars. Rach started up his Jeep and pointed it toward her house to collect her things and Clooney. Evan studied her, completely amazed by what he had witnessed. For as aware as Jonah was, he had a huge blind spot, and Rachael lived smack-dab in the middle of it. He wasn't any more aware of her emotional struggles than he was her financial ones. To be fair, she was doing an epic job of hiding them, and if he was used to seeing her strength, he might not have the perspective to see anything else.

Evan did, however. And he fully intended to be the one to help her regain her footing—with him right by her side.

Chapter Four

"What about lion tamer?"

At the sound of Evan's crazy suggestion, Rachael peered across the kitchen table to find him peeking over the rim of his laptop. Apparently, he was resorting to a new approach after she'd shot down his last five legit career options.

"Hmm ... tempting, but I think I'm gonna have to pass." She grabbed a Babybel cheese from the plate in front of her and pried open its red waxy coating. They'd spent Wednesday grabbing groceries for both their houses then taking a drive to the Silver Lake Sand Dunes since his therapist had to cancel his second PT appointment due to an emergency. Today they were hard at work trying to find her a job. After helping her string together a simple resume, Evan started perusing job sites with her. She hadn't let him upload her resume to any locations yet, which, no doubt, instigated his lion-tamer comment.

"Maybe a Professional Line Stander then?" he suggested.

"People get paid to stand in lines?"

He scanned his screen. "To hold someone's spot. Yep. Seems they do."

"I do not have the patience for that." Then again. "How much does it pay?"

"This guy says he earns up to a thousand a week."

Hmm. "Mark it."

Evan looked at her. "You know I'm only teasing, Rach. You're way overqualified."

"How do you figure? You padded my resume, and it's still emaciated."

"Doesn't need to say a lot to convey a lot."

"Look at you, rhyming and everything."

He shrugged and quirked his lips. She'd never seen a grown man make adorable so attractive, but Evan Wayne nailed the look. Feeling heat rush to her cheeks, she stood and headed for his laundry room. "Time to swap out loads." She cast a glance over her shoulder. "Hey, look to see if any hotels in Chicago are hiring maids. We could add my time here to my experience section."

"Funny," he called after her.

Ducking into the small room, she inhaled the mixture of Tide and April Fresh Downy. That combo always reminded her of Evan, only on him it was typically tinged with sage and cedar. She took her time swapping the wet towels into the dryer and his sheets into the wash. As she finished, she heard him chatting with someone.

Heading up the hall, she reentered the open living room area. Evan's friend, Dierks Holden, sat at the kitchen island. Lone detective of the Abundance PD Criminal Investigation Division, Dierks used to be a patrol officer with Evan when they both worked in Holland, but they'd been friends since the academy.

He smiled when he saw her. "Hey, Rach. I heard you were in town."

"For a couple of weeks. Evan needed some help."

Dierks' gaze moved between her and Evan. "I'm surprised he's letting you. I know he hasn't been the easiest patient for his mom and sisters."

This snapped Evan's attention to Dierks. "Where'd you hear that?"

"Hattie." He tugged on the edges of his suit jacket. "I ran into her last week."

The Wayne family had four children. The oldest, Justin, whom Rachael had only met over Facetime because he lived in Seattle. Nora was next. She and her family lived in town, and Rachael saw her often over the summer when she'd bring her boys to play at the beach. Then came Hattie and Evan who made up spots number three and four. Rachael didn't know Hattie all that well, but what she did know was how protective Hattie could be toward her little brother.

Rachael also knew how much that dynamic bothered Evan. "It can be hard to accept help from family. Especially when you're the youngest."

"Since I'm the oldest, I'll have to take your word for it." He redirected to Evan. "I don't want to keep you, but I thought I should stop by and give you an update."

Evan cut a sideways glance her way.

"Need me to go?" she asked.

"No." Dierks answered. "Nothing you can't hear."

"Which means there's nothing new." Defeat and a hint of anger edged Evan's voice.

"Nothing new on what?"

He looked at her. "The guy who shot me."

Oh. She'd read every article she could get her hands on but hadn't asked him much about that day. She knew what it was like to repeat conversations she'd rather not have in the first place. Now she looked to Dierks. "Is he right?"

"Unfortunately, yes." Frustration creased his forehead as he refocused on Evan. "The possible lead someone called in after seeing the video from your dashcam didn't pan out. We questioned him, but he's not our guy. Drives a maroon minivan, but it's registered with a plate, and he was on a business trip the day you were shot."

"You confirmed it?"

"Have him on video at the airports and checking into his hotel in Maine an hour before you pulled over the van."

Evan turned toward the wall, his good hand gripping his neck. "This guy is dangerous, and he's still out there because of me. If something else happens—"

"It won't," Dierks answered firmly. "We'll catch him, Evan. He shot one of ours. Every cop out there is looking."

"They shouldn't have to be. I should have stopped him."

"How?" She hadn't meant to verbalize her question, but as it echoed in the room, she was glad she had. She crossed to Evan and stood in his space, looking him directly in the eye rather than letting him hide. "I've no doubt you've watched your dashcam video, probably repeatedly. Did you miss anything when you pulled over that van?"

"Yeah," Evan bit out. "I missed he had a gun."

She fought the urge to shake him. He was intent on blaming himself. "Why?"

He stayed silent. Dierks watched from across the room. She shifted her focus to him, and he nodded his agreement that she continue pressing. "Evan?" she prodded.

"I couldn't see it." This answer arrived in a slightly softer tone. Still he continued, as convinced of his guilt as her niece Anna was that unicorns were real. Neither were true, but she couldn't persuade either to believe that. "Doesn't matter though. No plates meant I had no idea who was behind that wheel. I should have been prepared for anything."

She pressed her palm against his chest. "Maybe. But the fact remains, it's not on you to prepare for every contingency in life, Evan. You're only human."

He looked at her hand and then to her. "Thought I was superhuman."

With that cockeyed grin, he was doing his best to move them to lighter ground. She could understand that desire and respect it. Thing was, he might be attempting a joke, but at his core he was completely serious. He had it in that handsome head of his that he should be superhuman. And she had no idea why.

Across the room, Dierks cleared his throat. She slipped her hand from Evan, her palm warm from the heat of him. He shared a brief smile with her before turning toward Dierks. "Thanks for coming over to give me the news."

"You'd have done the same."

Evan simply nodded.

Dierks headed for the door. "Good to see you, Rach."

"You too."

"Try and make sure he doesn't overdo it."

She grinned. "Nothing like attempting the impossible."

With a laugh, Dierks slipped outside. Evan turned her way. "Don't know about you, but I'm ready for lunch."

"Me too. Let me go grab Clooney, and then I'll whip us up something." The dog hadn't wanted to come inside earlier. She loved the fenced-in area Jonah created for her when he'd purchased his place. Evan had built it with them during their second weekend here. Their first weekend, he'd brought over his homemade guacamole and joined them for a cookout. Only took those two visits to cement his place in their tiny group that had slowly expanded over the years to include his family and friends as well.

She ducked outside to grab Clooney while Evan cleared off the table they'd been working at. He might have become a part of their circle, but the two of them had formed an even tighter bond with each other. She couldn't remember having a friendship form more quickly, but from the start Evan's easygoing personality and dry sense of humor clicked with hers. They went from hanging out on weekends to texts daily that morphed to regular phone calls and him visiting Chicago when she wasn't in Holland. She hadn't been looking for a best friend, but he'd found her anyway.

Lately people challenged them on their *"just friends"* status. She supposed she could see why. He was everything a woman would want—if she were looking. Funny, kind, and supportive, the man respected women, loved his mama and Jesus, and protected strangers and loved ones alike. In her book, he really was hero material. Even had the classic good looks, at least the kind she was attracted to. But attraction didn't hold together relationships—she'd learned that at sixteen. And those qualities that did were what led to searing pain when torn away.

Clooney met her at the gate, greeting her with a bark as Rachael opened it. "Come on. Let's go see Evan."

Clooney tore off towards his door. See? Even her dog was smitten with him.

She simply needed to ensure that Clooney was the only girl in her household who'd fall for Evan Wayne's charm.

It took more strength to sit on the couch while Rachael finished up the dinner dishes than it had to complete his stretches this afternoon. "You know, I can at least dry them."

"You can also sit on that couch and ice your shoulder like you're supposed to at night."

Her tone brooked no argument. Not that he'd give her one. Since throwing herself into caring for him, she'd relaxed some. The shift in her attention seemed to loosen the hold of whatever had been plaguing her, at least enough for her creativity to wiggle. These past few days he'd discovered flower doodles on his pads of paper and his book of crossword puzzles. Her head might be experiencing painter's block, but her heart wasn't. Now to get them both on the same page.

"Fine," he groused. "I'll sit here. But I won't like it."

She chuckled and continued with the dishes.

He reached for his puzzle book and flipped it open. Scanned to the first clue. "Four letter word for 'small salamander.'"

"Newt."

His eyes met hers. "How on earth did you know that?"

"Boy mom." She smiled.

"Gavin was into lizards?"

"Salamanders aren't lizards. They're amphibians," she corrected. "But yes, he was into them both."

Evan penciled in the answer. Together, they finished the rest of the puzzle while Rachael tidied his kitchen and folded the laundry she'd washed earlier. Felt a little weird when she headed upstairs to make his bed, but there was no way he'd get that fitted sheet on. He hated being sidelined from life, but it was his own doing. Sometimes it seemed no matter how hard he tried, failure found him.

Glancing at the clock, he turned on the TV, then scrolled through the guide. AMC had a Schwarzenegger movie playing, and he quickly scanned past it.

"Hold up." Rachael's voice reached from the stairs. "I saw that."

"What?" Never give more info than needed. She could be talking about anything.

"What AMC has playing."

But she was talking about Arnold. "There's got to be something else you want to watch. Please. Anything."

"Funny you should say that." She made her way over, stopping between him and the TV. Her lips twitching, she produced from behind her back one of his high school yearbooks. "Because look what I happened across in your spare bedroom."

"What were you doing in there?"

"Changing those sheets too." Said as if everyone routinely changed the clean sheets in their spare bedroom. "Now scoot over so you can tell me all about young Evan." She plopped down beside him. "This definitely beats Arnold."

He wasn't so sure. The date on the cover showed she'd grabbed the year Mandie had passed away. He took the book from her, set it on the table, then notched up the volume to snag her interest. "Nothing beats Arnold."

She hit mute on the TV remote. "Okay. You've only stoked my curiosity, because those words would never come out of your mouth unless you were trying to hide something." Reaching across him, she snatched the yearbook. "Bad haircut? Poor fashion choices? An embarrassing photo?"

Painful memories?

He swallowed. While he knew all the tender spots of Rachael's past, he'd never mentioned Mandie to her. Wasn't an intentional slight. He didn't talk about her with anyone. No one enjoyed admitting how they let someone they cared about down when that person needed them most.

Beside him, Rachael flipped pages. "Let's see. You'd have been a freshman." She navigated to that spot. Her hand stilled as she opened to the two-page tribute to Mandie that preceded his class. Didn't take her but a moment to recognize him in nearly every picture with her. She traced the page, her fingertip stopping on one of him and Mandie skateboarding together. Her eyes, full of questions, lifted to his.

"Mandie Johnson. We grew up together." He left off that she'd been his first best friend. No doubt Rach could see the evidence in the pictures, but the words wouldn't leave his dry mouth.

Her fingers ran over each photo as she studied them. "She had a beautiful smile."

"Yeah. She did." He could still see it sometimes when he closed his eyes.

Rach lifted her eyes to his. "What happened to her?"

Anticipating the question still didn't prepare him to answer her. "She died."

"I can see that, Evan." His answer had been too simple. He realized the moment her eyebrows drew together that she sensed something more. "How?"

He looked at Mandie, lying down with her hair spilled all around her as she smiled up at the camera. He'd taken that picture. They'd both been so happy to make yearbook staff together. She'd hoped to be a journalist and was always telling him stories. If only he'd listened more closely to the hints about her own.

Or to the shouts that night.

"She was murdered…" He paused at Rachael's sharp intake of breath. "… by her stepfather."

The day remained lodged in his mind. Sitting in class, worried that she wasn't at school. Being called to the office and seeing his teary-eyed mother waiting for him. Evan pushed to his feet and tried to outpace the memory.

"Oh, Evan. I'm so sorry." Rachael set down his yearbook and stood too, crossing to stand in front of him. He stopped and she wrapped her arms around him, careful not to hurt his injured arm wedged between them. "That had to be unimaginable at your age."

"At any age," he muffled into her hair.

She nodded, her cheek pressed against his chest. After a moment, she stepped back, but her hands still cupped his arms. "I didn't mean to bring up these memories tonight. I'm sorry."

He shook his head. "You didn't know."

Again, her brows pushed together as she stared up at him. No doubt she wondered why she'd been in the dark when he knew everything about her. But then, as if his omission provided a revealing clue, her eyes widened. "Do you somehow feel responsible?"

He'd never been a liar, and he wasn't starting now. Still, he'd only give her enough to satisfy her curiosity. The deepest part of his guilt was his alone to carry. "Her stepdad was physically abusing her. I saw the marks, and I did nothing."

"Oh, Evan." She reached for him again, but this time he sidestepped her. She allowed him his space. "How old were you? Fourteen? Fifteen?"

"Fourteen." But that was no excuse. He'd been old enough to wonder if something was going on. He'd prodded even. Then allowed Mandie to downplay things. When she'd called that last night ....

Scrubbing a hand through his hair, he tried to quiet the haunting echoes of so many voices. He'd lost count of how many times after her death he'd heard the words *why didn't you do anything?* directed at him. From her grandparents. His older brother. People at school.

It was a question he promised to never have to ask himself again.

Rachael's voice filled with compassion he didn't deserve. "You were a kid. There was nothing you could have done."

"The school assemblies afterwards said otherwise." Her crinkled brow prodded him to elaborate. "The month after Mandie's death, her grandparents started a program that went into schools to teach students how to spot friends who were hiding problems. Their goal was to ensure nothing like what happened to their daughter and grandchildren ever happened again."

"That doesn't mean Mandie's death was your fault. That blame lies squarely at the feet of her stepfather."

Her words sounded good, but they weren't true. He backed away. Roughed his hand across his cheek. "Yes, he pulled the trigger, but if I'd said something, he wouldn't have had the chance."

And no one would convince him otherwise, because no one knew about that last phone call.

They stood in silence for a minute, then Rachael slowly shook her head. "You're wrong. But so much about you makes sense now."

Over the heavy moment, he offered her a teasing grin. "Well, that's not fair, because I feel like there's still things about you that don't."

Her head tipped. "As in?"

"How you can mix your food together. Your crazy obsession with cheese. But most of all"—pointing his thumb over his shoulder at the TV— "how you can love Arnold Schwarzenegger."

She watched him for a split second before allowing him to shut the conversation down. "The man's humor is seriously underrated."

"Or nonexistent."

"Okay. Take it off mute. We're watching this movie so I can point out how you're wrong."

She'd started for the couch, but he grabbed her shoulder and steered her to the kitchen. "I'm going to need popcorn if you're submitting me to this torture." After changing her direction, he plopped down on the cushions and tucked his yearbook into the side table drawer. "Lots of butter, please. And none of that cheddar-flavored powder."

"That's the best part." A pan smacked onto his stove top.

"It's awful."

Kernels pinged against stainless steel as she poured them. "Fine. I'll split the batch." The burner popped on. "But you're really missing out."

"Hardly." He couldn't stand the processed flavor, and he'd already had enough nasty-tasting memories to fill his night. Least he could do was enjoy his popcorn.

Chapter Five

Most people loved naps. They looked forward to them. Planned them into their afternoons. Woke up rested. Evan was not most people.

He reached for the ringing phone responsible for waking him from his spontaneous siesta. Groggy, he cleared his throat as he answered. "Wayne here."

"Did I wake you?" Captain Larry's gruff voice snapped him to attention.

Stifling a groan at the movement, he rubbed his sore shoulder. He'd had his first real PT appointment this morning only to discover his physical therapist, Becky, defined the saying *don't judge a book by its cover.* Under her easy smile and kind eyes lurked a taskmaster worse than the bear of a sergeant who conducted the physical agility test at the police academy. He'd only had to survive Sergeant Miller's torture once. Becky would inflict pain on him three times a week for the foreseeable future.

Lucky him.

"I was resting my eyes." And all the muscles in his right arm. Thankfully, it was Friday, and he didn't need to see Becky for three whole days. He was all about pushing himself hard but wouldn't mind the pain level dropping some.

"Your eyes. Right." Captain Larry's distinctive laugh peppered the words. "Have it in you to come to the station today? There's something I want to speak with you about."

Evan stole a glance at the clock on the microwave. Nearly four. Rach had mentioned bringing something over for dinner, but they could go out instead. "Sure. Give me about a half hour?"

"I'll be here."

They disconnected, and Evan dialed Rach's number. After dropping him at home, she'd left to take Clooney for a walk. She invited him, but he passed. His response generated concern, but she restrained it to a look, then gave him his space. Still, she must have kept her phone close because she picked up before the first ring finished. "How're you feeling?"

"Like Becky lied to me Monday when she said we were going to be friends."

"It's probably a line from her employee handbook."

"They need to rewrite the handbook then." He scanned the room for his ball cap. "Also, now that I've had the full PT experience, I'm downgrading your preparatory skills to a C-minus."

"Hey. I told you it was going to be a torture chamber."

"Yes, but you didn't tell me the degree of torture. Listening to Bieber on repeat level or hearing someone chew. I was woefully unprepared for the pain I've endured."

"I beg your forgiveness." Drier words he had never heard. "So which is it? Bieber or chewing?"

"Neither. It's on par with having to watch your Schwarzenegger movie the other night." He grinned at his image of her facial expression.

"Hey! Don't insult Arnold. Like I pointed out, he had some classic lines."

"Right up there with Shakespeare."

She *pffted* him. "Did you call to bother me, or is there a point to this conversation?"

His University of Michigan hat sat under his side table. Must have knocked it off when he reached for his phone. He nabbed it and pulled it on. "I need a ride to the station. Can you take me?"

"Sure." Keys jangled as if she'd been standing by them. "I'll meet you by Sally."

"Remember, we agreed it's my Jeep while you're in town."

"That was before you insulted Arnold."

He headed outside and found her standing beside Sally. She pocketed her phone and held open the passenger door. "Your chariot awaits."

"What was that? Did you say rust bucket?"

"You have no appreciation for the classics."

He stood beside her but didn't hop in. "How old does something have to be to make it a classic?"

"At least twenty."

He drew a lazy stare from her sandals to the ball of hair she'd piled on top of her head. "I think I appreciate classics just fine then."

She rolled her eyes. "Get in the car."

With a chuckle, he did.

She rounded the hood to climb in the driver's side, then fired up Sally's engine. "What's happening at the station?"

"Not sure. Cap called and asked if I could come in." Most likely to talk about his return date. Becky had probably sent in her initial assessment. "I'm hoping it's about my light duty assignment. I requested to be placed in dispatch."

"Taking calls and sending patrols out?"

"Yep." Not that it was up to him, but their department was small enough, and he had a good relationship with his captain, so he felt he could ask. "If I can't be out there for a few more weeks, at least I can stay in the action."

She glanced his way. "Didn't Becky say it'd be more like several months?"

Right. He'd mentioned that on their drive home this morning. "Yes, but see her preparatory skills *are* actually of the A-plus sort. She set an expectation I can definitely exceed."

Rach's hands flexed on the steering wheel. "You really want to be on patrol again? After getting shot?"

"It's where I belong." Stepping between the innocent and impending harm, helping prevent life-changing moments no one should ever encounter, that was who he was.

Several miles passed under Sally's tires. Rach turned onto Rainier, the main street through Abundance's downtown. Storefronts lined several blocks, each one with a unique façade and entrance. The last of summer's flowers cascaded over pots dotted along the sidewalks, and aqua-painted iron benches created places every few feet for shoppers to rest. Murals covered the brick sides of several stores. Repainting them was an annual tradition that began a decade ago, then morphed into its own contest during Abundance's Fall Flower Fest.

The festival would begin soon, drawing artists from around the Midwest for the competition. They'd paint new murals over the old ones, and then visitors along with the town's residents voted for their favorite. The artist won a cash prize, while the location that hired them won bragging rights. The event kept the artwork around town fresh while also bringing in tourism. A definite win-win.

Rachael pulled into a slanted parking spot in front of the police department and shut her engine off. "Any idea how long this appointment will take?"

"None." Her silence during the drive bothered him, but he wasn't sure what brought it on. "I can text you when I'm finished."

"Sounds good. I think I'll walk over to the farmer's market." It took place every Friday in the large lot to the south. "Belle is selling some of her lotions there."

Belle Shaw, Penny's little sister. While Rachael and Penny lived in Chicago, Belle lived here in Abundance. "Tell her I said hi."

"Will do." With a wave, Rach headed across the street.

Evan watched her for a moment before stepping inside the old brick building. The terrazzo floors gleamed beneath his feet, and he followed them to the wide staircase that rose to the second floor, which housed the department offices. The middle of this floor stretched wide open with cubicles for officers' shared desks. A corridor that ran the entire perimeter held offices for sergeants, Dierks, and their captain. He crossed the bullpen toward Captain Larry's door.

Abundance wasn't a very large town and as such, the police department was on the small side. If it weren't for his relationships with Dierks and Captain Larry, he wouldn't have transferred here out of Holland PD. But Dierks made the move two years back, then Cap followed for a promotion. Within six months he called Evan and asked him to join his team. Evan couldn't say no. He respected the man greatly. Plus, he missed working with both him and Dierks. What he found when he arrived was a tight-knit community of brothers that immediately pulled him into their ranks. Wound up being one of the best decisions he'd ever made.

Dierks stepped out of his office as Evan approached. He leaned against his doorframe. "You're looking a little stiff. How's PT going?"

"Becky puts Sergeant Miller to shame." He rolled his shoulder and winced.

Dierks laughed. "I won't tell either of them you said that." He nodded a greeting to another officer, who passed by. "What brings you here today?"

"Not sure. Cap called so here I am."

"Really." The way the word left his mouth …

"You know something." And it sounded like something Evan needed a heads-up on.

Dierks's hands lifted. "Nothing definitive."

"What?"

Before he could answer, Cap stuck his head out his door. "Good. You're here. My office."

The smirk on his friend's face had every inch of Evan's nerves on alert. He slipped into Cap's office and closed the door. Settling into the brown leather chair opposite the desk, he voiced his most pressing concern. "You make a decision on where I'll be assigned for light duty?"

"I have." Cap took his own seat, then closed a file on his desk. "Becky gave me an update on where you're starting at." Age and wisdom lined the creases of his eyes, along with compassion. "She said she can't guarantee you'll regain full mobility of your arm."

He appreciated her honesty and told her as much this morning. Didn't mean he agreed with her. "I will."

"I know you'll do everything in your power to reach one hundred percent again. I also know it's going to take longer than you hoped."

Maybe by a few weeks, but this would not be permanent.

Cap drummed his fingers on his desk. "You asked for dispatch, and right now I don't have a spot for you there. But when Robin goes on maternity leave, you can fill in for her."

That was in three months. "I'll be back on patrol by then."

"If you've regained full ability to execute an arrest and you can pass the gun range, then yes, you will be." Cap agreed while outlining the nonnegotiables. Ones he didn't sound convinced Evan would hit in that time frame. Made him wonder what exactly Becky had told him. "Meantime, I do have another place I could use you."

That had him sitting forward. "Where?" Maybe he could work intake. Or help question suspects.

"You know the Fall Flower Fest is right around the corner."

Okay. Not at all what he expected. "I do."

"It appears the artist we hired to paint our mural can no longer do it. She was due in town today, but she's had a family emergency and can't come to Michigan."

"That's too bad." Seemed the appropriate answer but didn't explain why he was a part of this conversation.

"It is. Especially this year."

Oh, right. Blake and Harlow Carlton—Hollywood's charming couple with roots to this town—had agreed to put up money for this year's contest. Not only would the artist win cash, but the Carltons added an additional ten thousand dollars to the charity of the winning location's choice. The department had chosen Searchlight, a local nonprofit that helped families of missing children through support groups and counseling. They were connected to the National Center for Missing and Exploited Children.

Cap leaned across his desk. "I'm putting you in charge of our mural this year and all that comes with it. Interviews with local news outlets. The dinner with our charity. Running point with the artist. Attending the gala." His mouth twitched under his mustache like he was enjoying this way too much. Made sense, as Cap preferred remaining behind the scenes. "Basically, you'll run the show and be our face."

Evan straightened. "Come again?"

Cap steepled his fingers. "Festival organizers request each venue has a spokesperson, and this year, you're ours."

"Why me?" It was the last thing Evan wanted to do.

"Two reasons. You have the time." Cap regarded him. "And I've recently been informed that you're friends with a well-known artist."

He'd guess that informant looked an awful lot like Dierks.

"A *once* well-known artist," Evan cautiously responded.

"Who was known for flowers. When I researched Rachael Stark, I discovered her reputation as the next Georgia O'Keefe." Cap pressed into his chair. "Sounds perfect for a Fall Flower Fest art contest."

"Except she's never painted a mural that I know of."

"Do you think she could?"

"Yes." No doubt in his mind—if she could move past whatever was blocking her.

"Then you'll ask her?"

Frustration gave way to budding possibility. After all, knowing Cap, he wasn't really giving him a choice. So he needed to find the silver lining in this.

Painting was the career choice for Rachael—he fully believed that. Not only did he see her talent, but he sensed her love for the craft hidden under her reticence. She produced an excuse against all the businesses he wanted to send her resume to but shot him down when he suggested she contact her old agent. Yet she couldn't stop doodling on every surface around her. And today he caught her drawing a vase of flowers on the whiteboard at his PT's office while she'd waited for him to finish. Whatever emotions kept her from returning full time to the art world, he wanted to help her process and work through them.

"I will."

This contest would be the best thing for her. Move her past this creative block while also presenting a possibility to win a pretty nice cash prize. Plus, it could relaunch her art career and—with this year's elevated coverage thanks to the Carltons—boost her notoriety again.

Then there was the personal side. If he could convince her to do this, she'd extend her stay. And since Cap was adding the contest to Evan's plate, they'd be working together. She'd gain new vision for painting—and hopefully for their relationship.

Looked like he'd found more than one silver lining to this assignment. As long as he could convince Rach to come on board.

This was a near perfect afternoon. Sunshine filled the clear cerulean sky overhead, and a light breeze tickled Rachael's skin. With late summer temps, she wasn't too cold or too hot—which quite perfectly fit her Goldilocks temperament when it came to weather. The scent of popcorn, cotton candy, and fried foods intensified to a delicious level as she neared the farmers market. Her growling stomach begged for a treat to tide her over until dinnertime. That growling turned to a roar the second she saw the menu. The only thing better than a hunk of cheese was a hunk of fried cheese.

She purchased the deliciousness-on-a-stick and strolled the booths. At the far end she spotted Belle with a few of her employees. In her yoga pants and pink tank, Belle looked annoyingly adorable for a woman eleven weeks pregnant.

Rachael's own pregnancies with Gavin and Brianna at this stage had left her a Grinch-shade of green with marshmallow-puff bags under her eyes.

Belle spotted her and ducked out of the booth for a hug. "Rach! Penny said you were in town."

Holding her cheese out to avoid greasing up Belle's shirt, Rachael returned the embrace with one arm. "Yeah. For a few weeks."

Belle motioned to a set of chairs in her booth. "How did it go dropping Gavin off?"

"Fairly well." She picked up one of the tubes of AnnaBelle's lotions. "Is this a new scent?"

"Fresh Laundry. Another of Micah's creations."

"He's really getting into this, isn't he?"

"He and Walter both."

"How's it going? Them working together."

"Good. Professionally and personally. There's really been healing in that relationship."

Hers and Micah's too, evidenced by the glow on her face as she palmed her belly. Baby number two on the way, but baby number one was conspicuously absent. "Where's Anna?"

"With Astrid and the gang." A gaggle of retirement friends who Belle and Anna had lived near before Belle married Micah. "They get playtime, and I don't have to chase her around here. My energy level isn't currently on par with a three-and-a-half-year-old's."

"I remember." Although it had been a long time. Brianna would have been twelve this December. People often reminded her that, at thirty-four, she was young enough to remarry and have more children, as if replacements for what she was missing would fix everything. But Chris and Brianna weren't possessions she'd lost. They were pieces of her heart, and she didn't have enough fragments left to chance giving them away again. "You look like you're feeling well though."

"For the most part. I do have some food aversions, but so far things are going well."

"Glad to hear it." Setting down the tube of lotion, she savored more of her cheesy treat.

Belle answered one of her employee's questions, then refocused on Rachael. "How's Evan doing?"

"Good. He's meeting with his captain right now."

"Is he starting back to work soon?"

"He hopes so."

Belle's blue eyes widened. "Not on patrol, right?"

"No, but he would if he could. His PT thinks it'll be several months."

"What does Evan think?"

"That he'll be out there in weeks."

"How do you feel about that?"

Swallowing the last gooey bite, she tossed the stick. "It doesn't matter how I feel."

Belle's perfect eyebrows arched.

Rachael knew that look. She'd seen it on way too many faces. "We're just friends, Belle."

"Okay."

That tone did not say okay. Why did no one ever believe them? "Anyway," Rachael drew the word out, "I wanted to stop by and say hi. I should head back. He'll be done soon."

Belle hopped up, immediately contrite. "Don't leave. I'm sorry I teased you."

She knew people didn't mean anything by it. But lately the joking prickled her in new ways. It had gotten under her skin and was starting to affect how she saw Evan. In fact, everyone's insistence that they were attracted to each other must be partly to blame for her weird reactions toward him lately. That made complete sense and gave her a measure of relief. She wasn't battling new feelings toward her best friend. She was fighting the power of suggestion from those around her.

"It's okay. Really." She let Belle off the hook with a goodbye hug just as her phone dinged a text from Evan. "That's him, so I'll see you later. Promise." With a wave, she slipped from the booth and headed up the street. Evan sat on the concrete wall outside the precinct, waiting for her. He rose as she approached.

"How'd it go?" she asked.

"Let's grab dinner, and I'll tell you all about it."

"What sounds good to you?"

"Anything. You pick."

There were several restaurants throughout the downtown shopping district. "The Gathering Place?" she suggested. They had amazing farm-to-table cuisine served on small, shareable plates. That way she didn't have to make a decision on one dish alone.

"Sure." Evan shoved his hand into his pocket and followed her the block to the restaurant. He held the door for her. Once they were seated, he glanced at the menu. "I'm guessing you want the blue-cheese fritters."

While she loved cheese, he tolerated only some of it. Blue cheese did not fall into that category.

"I already had an entire mozzarella wedge at the farmer's market."

"Never stopped you before."

"My waistband is stopping me." Maintaining her weight grew harder each year.

Evan peered over his menu. "Switch to stretchy pants then, and enjoy your cheese."

"Says a man who's never had to struggle with his weight." He was all muscle and—if anything—only defined them more each year. Men had all the advantages when it came to aging.

"Says a man who cares more about the size of your smile than your waistband. You don't smile enough."

"I smile all the time."

"True. But it doesn't reach your eyes."

She skirted the feelings welling from his scrutiny. He saw too much of her, and she wasn't really sure if she liked it or not. "And you think if I eat more cheese, it will?"

"In this moment, yep. I'll find other ways in the future."

"Like what?"

He landed a devastating smile on her. One that tumbled through her middle, leaving jumbled nerves in its wake. "Guess you'll have to wait and see."

She swallowed to ease her suddenly dry throat. Since when had their friendly flirting moved to such dangerous ground?

Their waitress arrived right then, bless her, and took their order, which included plenty of cheesy dishes. After she left, Evan reclined in his chair and fiddled with his straw. He was processing something. Better not be those other ways to instigate her smiles.

"Tell me about your meeting," she prodded, just in case her smiles had been his line of thinking. "Did you receive your assignment for light duty?"

He maintained his interest in his drink. "I did. Though it's nothing I ever expected."

"How so?"

With a blink, he focused in on her. "You know about the Fall Flower Fest, right?"

"Kind of hard to miss all the signs around here." She'd heard about it for years but had never actually been able to attend one. Things were too busy at the start of the school year. This year, though, Gavin could handle that busyness all on his own. "Will the precinct's wall be repainted this year?"

"It was scheduled to be."

"What happened?"

"The woman we contacted had a family emergency, so she can't come to town."

Ah. So that's what was bugging him. Evan had a competitive streak a mile wide, and the townspeople took bragging rights from the mural win seriously. The police department had yet to be victorious. "Sorry."

Their waitress delivered the first two small plates, and Rachael picked up one of the fritters. Evan snagged a bacon-wrapped, cream-cheese-stuffed pepper from the other dish. "Thing is, this year not only will the artist win money, but so will the charity of the location's choice."

"Really?"

"Yep. Blake and Harlow Carlton are donating. It's sure to up the awareness of the event too."

"Sounds like a great opportunity for everyone involved."

"Definitely. Ten grand for the artist and another to the venue's chosen charity."

She dunked her fritter into the creamy sauce accompanying it. "I sure could use ten grand," she said absently before popping the perfect bite into her mouth. Munching, she realized Evan's silence, then glanced his way to find him staring at her.

"What?" She wiped at her cheeks. "Do I have cheese on my face?"

"Nope." The way he said it raised all her antennas. He was up to something. "What then?"

"You specialize in painting flowers, right?"

"I did." What he was up to suddenly became clear. She held out her hands. "Oh, no. I've never painted a mural in my life."

"Doesn't mean you can't. You're a painter."

"Artist," she corrected. "Of watercolors and acrylics. And all ones that can hang on a wall." Albeit she'd completed some rather massive pieces, but never anything the size he was talking about.

"So you make things a little bigger."

"That's like hiring someone who plays with model cars to be your mechanic."

He had the good grace to look slightly chagrined. "Okay. Point made. But I believe you can do this, Rach."

"Then you obviously haven't been listening, because I told you painting is currently not an option for me."

"Due to your painter's block." He pointed his glass at her. "See. I was listening. But what if I brainstorm ideas with you?"

This was exactly why she didn't like to allow people to operate under misconceptions. At one point or another, it'd come back and bite her in the rear.

He latched on to her hesitancy. "If you win, you'll get a good chunk of change."

"That's a mighty big *if.*"

"I've seen your work. I feel like it's more a certainty."

Maybe once upon a time. "Sorry, Evan, but I'm going to have to pass."

The creases around his eyes briefly deepened, but one thing about Evan, he was practiced at holding in unexpected reactions. "Not a problem." He reached for another pepper. "I'll find someone else."

Her relief lasted a second before, "Wait." She leaned to the left to allow the waitress to refill her water glass. "Why do *you* have to find someone?"

"Turns out this is my light-duty assignment. Handling our entry and all that entails." He wiggled his sling. "Though my handling is currently limited to one hand."

"Funny."

"I try." His hazel eyes locked on hers. "Think you could toss me some suggestions of people I could contact?"

"Definitely." More small dishes arrived at their table. Some meatballs with dipping sauce and another plate with local pickled veggies. She reached for a carrot. "Who's the charity your department chose?"

He stabbed a meatball with his fork. "One of our groups."

"Thanks, o fount of information, but which one exactly?"

Popping the bite into his mouth, Evan took his time chewing. He chased it with a long drink of water. Seemed like he was stalling. Finally, he provided the answer. "Searchlight. It's a local group that helps families with missing children. They're connected to the National Center for Missing and Exploited Children."

No wonder he hesitated. Of all the charities he could have named. Her child was missing. Maybe not in the same way, but she understood their loss, nonetheless.

Evan leaned across the table. "I wasn't going to tell you because I didn't want you to feel manipulated into saying yes."

As if that was possible with him, a man who had her best interests at heart. He would never force her hand in any situation. Which meant he genuinely wanted her to do this because he thought it would be good for her. And that she truly had a shot at winning.

She wasn't entirely convinced he was right, but maybe she'd made a hasty decision. After all, she'd stayed to help him, and this provided another way to do that. Plus, this charity spoke to her heart. She shared a similar pain with the families they served, but at least hers held answers. Parents of missing children were left with too many questions. Winning this contest could provide the means for Searchlight to continue being there for them.

Could she paint a mural? The emptiness inside said no. But her desire to help said yes.

Evan leaned in. "I promise I'm not trying to unfairly influence you."

"I know, and you're not." She played with a loose string on her napkin. "I really don't think I'm who you need, Evan."

Calm and sure, he focused on her as if she were the only person in the room. "You most definitely are." His response was strong enough to support her doubts.

"Okay. I'll do it." She reached for another fritter. "But I'm going to need a lot more cheese."

Chapter Six

What on earth had she been thinking?

Helping Evan recover? Good.

Agreeing to paint the mural? Not good.

Saturday afternoon Rachael sat in a small room in Abundance's township office building along with fourteen other artists. Many had flown in for today's meeting and to acquaint themselves with the wall they'd paint. After the weekend, they'd return home to prep and plan until the start date.

The township supervisor, Chad Douglas, spent the past half hour going over the history of the Fall Flower Fest and how they'd added the mural contest a decade ago. Then he spent time talking about this year's significance, seeing how the Carltons had donated so generously. Finally, he zoned in on the rules. About then, Rachael realized she had not, in fact, been thinking when she'd given Evan her yes. That little revelation only amplified as Chad clicked through photos of past murals, highlighting the winner of each year.

Evan leaned over from his seat beside her. "You have totally got this."

She side-eyed him. "No pressure or anything, right?" The liveliness and vibrancy of those murals captured her. Made her wish for the feeling not only in her own project, but her life. Not one of her ideas came anywhere close to what Chad displayed in front of her.

"That's not pressure. That's me believing in you. Get used to the feeling."

She could. Easily.

Instead, she refocused on the PowerPoint presentation in front of her. Wrapping up, Chad addressed the crowd. "The location will remove last year's mural and prep your wall for you. They will also supply any equipment you'll need. Please see your Dates to Remember in the packet we handed out. Big ones to note are the painting kickoff in four weeks on September twenty-first. There'll be a small celebration downtown the day before that all artists are to attend. Painting must be finished by October ninth, when the Fall Flower Fest—and voting—officially starts. Also, our gala for the artists and to announce the winner will be held at the end of the festival on October twenty-fourth. If you have any questions, please contact my office."

With that, he dismissed the meeting and everyone stood. Rachael slipped to the rear of the room where a few refreshments waited for them. She grabbed a glass of lemonade and stared down her BFF. "What have you gotten me into?"

"You're not having second thoughts, are you?"

"Second? No. I'm well onto my thousandth."

He popped the remainder of his iced almond cookie into his mouth and munched it as he studied her like she was conducting suspicious activity. Then he swallowed and nodded to the door. "Come on. What you need is some inspiration."

"Thought that was what you were providing with all the brainstorming you promised," she mumbled as he tugged on her arm.

"Precisely."

He had the nerve to sound like there wasn't a question about coming up with an idea for the mural. Yet there were plenty of them. Huge, looming ones hot on her tail.

They exited the township offices and made their way to Sally. Evan held her door for her, then crossed to the passenger side. "Take a left out of the parking lot."

"You're not going to tell me where we're going?"

"I just did."

"No. You gave me a direction, not a destination."

"Just drive, Grumpy."

"Ooh, are we using the Seven Dwarf names now? That makes you Pesky."

"That's not one of the Seven Dwarfs."

"And yet it fits you so well."

He puffed out a groan, then pressed into his seat, arms crossed. "I think we need to hit a drive-through on the way. Someone's a little hangry."

He wasn't far off. The only part of her that worked when she was hungry was her attitude. "I did warn you I'd need cheese."

They hit a Culvers drive-through, and she munched on cheese curds as Evan directed her toward the heart of Abundance. The murals she'd seen in pictures only a half hour ago dotted the landscape as they scooted up Rainier. Rather than stopping, they overshot the shopping district. About two miles past the Civic Center, they took a curve and as the road straightened, tall pines with their thick arms of evergreen needles stood sentry on either side of the asphalt. "I've never been this far outside of town."

"I know." He pointed to his side of the road. "See that yellow reflector up there?"

She squinted. A little ways ahead, the sunshine glinted off a metal post with a shiny yellow top. "Yep."

"Pull over near it."

"Okay." She drew the word out, more from pure curiosity than concern. She trusted Evan implicitly, and now that her belly was full, didn't mind admitting it. Slowing to a stop, she cut the engine. "Now what?"

"You follow me." He grinned like a kid about to lead her on a grand adventure.

Her stomach summersaulted as her brain sent out the rogue thought that life with Evan could be her grandest adventure of all.

No.

Nope.

No way. She already had her lifetime's share of adventure *and* the ensuing heartache when those amazing journeys ended. Now it was about staying strong and doing the next thing. There was a calm assurance that came with certainty. She craved the even-keeled feeling of placing one foot steadily in front of the other and a job well done.

"You coming?" Evan stared at her from the passenger side. He'd climbed out and peered in the doorway, his dimple tempting her.

Point One. Just friends. They were just friends.

She busted out of Sally. "Yep."

He shut his door and strode to the pine trees where she joined him. "Come on," he urged as he ducked through the branches.

She dodged the prickly needles, inhaling the woody scent of their sap, and emerged on the other side of the thick berm of trees into a magical land. As in, she half expected unicorns and fairies to materialize.

Evan grinned her way, his good arm spread wide as if he was a ringmaster showing off his marvelous production. "How's this for inspiration?"

Marvelous, indeed.

Flowers sprawled out in front of her in varying heights. Inside this alcove, more trees stood tall and vines climbed several wooden arches. Multiple colors formed a diverse blanket of vibrant hues. A few trails allowed access into the heart of the beautiful landscape, and she inched toward the closest one. "It's a secret garden." And a large one. It had to be at least an acre tucked away from the world. "How did you find this place?"

"I'm a police officer. I know where all the secret spots are and how to keep them that way."

"So it's like your take on the Bat Cave." She made a show of looking around. "It's kind of flowery." His chuckle followed her toward a wooden bench in the center of the garden. She bent to read its bronze plaque. "For Ruth Cummings.

May the kindness and beauty you shared with others spread, and may our memory of you grow stronger each day like the flowers you loved." Straightening, Rachael peered at the garden once again. "Who was she?"

"My mother," a female voice sounded from behind.

Rachael twisted to see a petite woman with her honey-blonde hair tugged in a high ponytail. She wore a pair of denim overalls over a cream shirt dotted with flowers. The legs of the overalls bunched around her shins where they met the top of green rubber boots with pink soles.

"I'm sorry, I …" Rachael glanced at Evan. "Are we trespassing?"

The woman's face spread with a smile that made her a near twin to Reese Witherspoon. "If you were, he'd have to arrest you himself. Evan's talented, but I don't think he's quite that talented." She stepped up and gave him a gentle hug before offering her hand to Rachael. "Hi. I'm Aundrea Cummings, but you can call me Auna."

Rachael shook her hand, a little speechless that this beautiful woman knew Evan, yet he'd never mentioned her. "I'm Rachael Stark."

Auna's face registered recognition. "You're our mural artist. Thank you so much for agreeing to do this." She peeked at Evan. "Bringing our secret weapon out here to give her a little inspiration?"

All right. She was completely confused.

Evan must have sensed it because he steadied her with a soft touch on her lower back. "Auna works in our communications department when she's not knee-deep in flowers. Her mother, Ruth, was responsible for Abundance's Fall Flower Fest."

"Actually, it was my dad, as a way to remember her." She held her hands wide. "This entire garden wasn't enough, apparently." The words were spoken with a tenderness that conveyed how much she loved her parents.

Rachael took in the expanse of flowers around her. She'd never seen so many varieties in one area. "I didn't know this garden existed."

Auna nodded. "Because it's not on the public map. It's more of a treasure for the townspeople, and not telling outsiders about it is kind of an unspoken rule." She looked between them. "But Evan brought you here, so that says a lot about you."

He shrugged. "You haven't been an outsider for a long time, Rach. Not to me."

His rough voice tickled her nerve endings, pulling out goosebumps. But it was his eyes, brown and green with that golden fleck through them, that she sank into. Their steadiness cocooned her much like the pine trees insulated this space. A light breeze encircled them, pulling her deeper into the trance and toward the curiosity of leaning into him.

A throat cleared.

Rachael straightened. For a second—goodness she hoped it was only a second—she'd forgotten Auna stood here with them. Evan Wayne did indeed possess superhero capabilities. He contained the power to make the rest of the world disappear. How was she, a mere mortal, supposed to keep her heart away from him?

She needed space and a deep breath not filled with the heady scent of him. "If you don't mind, Auna, I'd love to walk some of the paths through the garden."

Lips tipped slightly, Auna glanced between the two, then nodded. "Go right ahead. I'll keep Evan company."

Rachael tensed at the thought. Oh, seriously, she needed to get a hold of herself. "I won't be long," she informed Evan. In full retreat mode with a green monster chasing her, she took off down the closest path.

Behind her, Auna asked Evan something about his recovery. Rachael kept moving until she couldn't hear their voices anymore.

Inspiration of all kinds spread through her mind, much of it pointing toward Evan. She focused on the creativity she could indulge in with her painting rather than her heart. All other thoughts she purposefully turned in other directions. Like the fact she needed to double down on Point One. Just friends. Time to reestablish friendship-only boundaries with Evan. Maybe then she could purge these new feelings that had taken seed and were doing their best to spring up.

Those weren't any kind of flower she needed to pick.

Evan understood cloudy, gray moods. If he were being honest, it was one way he felt he resembled the crazy Batman nickname Rachael had latched onto. He'd shut down its use in his teen years, but she brought the moniker back to life the moment she discovered his full name. Funny thing was, hearing it from her lips didn't grate his nerves like it had from his siblings. His current situation, however, scraped against every single raw ending. More often than not, he could soothe what chafed him. Recent events challenged that ability.

With a clink, he settled his one-pound weight into the metal tree intended to hold it. Until he'd been shot, he hadn't owned such a light amount. Now his hand shook with his attempts to lift one pound to a ninety-degree angle. His loaded gun weighed two.

That alone could sour his attitude. Then Cap gave him this cockamamie assignment for the Fall Flower Fest. He'd tried to look at the bright side—

working with Rachael. But she'd been squirrelly since their garden excursion yesterday. Holed herself up all last night and hadn't popped out for breakfast or to drive him to church. He had the distinct impression she was avoiding him.

Piled onto that, he'd allowed himself to be shot, and the perp remained at large. A dangerous man out there in his community because he hadn't done his job. Couldn't offer much more than what his dashcam recorded. He only remembered that maroon van and the guy's height and build. Not enough to create a useable sketch. Some cop he was. His attitude dipped way past sullen and neck-deep into surly.

He gripped the weight and lifted for his final set of fifteen. Ten in, and sweat dotted his temple, but he at least managed to stave off the groan that wanted to escape. He'd anticipated a tough recovery. He had not, however, prepared himself for the way his body manhandled his mind. No matter how hard he concentrated, he couldn't stop his arm from shaking. There was no gray area here. Either he regained full use of his steady arm, or he wouldn't return to the streets.

And that topped his bad mood. There was no other job. He couldn't fathom never putting on that uniform again. Since fourteen he'd understood his path, and he'd diligently followed it. Why would that be taken from him now?

Aching, he dropped the one-pounder and picked up the forty-pounder for his left side. Those muscles felt weak too. As he hit the final set, someone knocked on his door. Before he could answer, his older sister, Hattie, stepped inside holding Tupperware that emitted amazing smells in one hand, and a bag of what appeared to be chocolate chip cookies in the other. She was only fifteen months older, but she acted like the oldest of all of them. And her overprotective nature toward Evan had shifted into overdrive since his injury.

He stood, wiping his face with the towel draped around his neck. "What're you doing here, Hattie?"

She stiffened. "Good afternoon to you too, dear brother."

"Sorry." Every inch of Hattie functioned like exposed nerves. She was what doctors called a "highly sensitive person." All of her senses operated as if someone had twisted their knobs full throttle. Even if he thought his voice and face were neutral, she could pick up on the tiniest expression. It had taken him years to learn how to soften himself around her. "You surprised me is all." He'd hug her, but he was sweaty and she liked her personal space. "A good surprise though."

With his easy tone, she relaxed. "Good. I don't want to be a bother."

"Never."

She crossed to his kitchen island. "Mom made pot roast for lunch. I told her I'd bring leftovers since you didn't show up."

Typically, Sunday mornings involved attending church together and then heading to Mom and Dad's for lunch. "Sorry. I didn't have a ride, so I watched online."

"Thought that's why Rachael was here. To take over all of that."

"She is, but there was a minor miscommunication that kept her from being here this morning." Easiest answer to provide his sister since he was still trying to deduce the real motivation behind Rach's curious absence.

"You could have called me."

"Guess I don't want to be a bother either."

"Never." Hattie mimicked him as she placed the dish on his granite countertop. "Anyway, Mom sent enough for you both. She figured Rachael would eat with you since you two have been hanging out a lot lately."

Hattie wasn't the only one good at reading tones, and both times she'd mentioned Rachael, hers bordered on unfriendly. "Say what you really came to say, Hattie."

Leaning against the counter, she crossed her arms. "I don't want you hurt. Any more than you already are, at least." Somewhere along the line she'd added guardian of his heart to her list of big-sister duties. "Your physical healing is going to take everything you've got. You can't be emotionally distracted."

"Who says I am?"

Through thousands of conversations, she'd perfected her big-sister look. "You haven't hidden how you feel about her, at least not to your family. But it's obvious she only sees you as a friend." She straightened and reached for the cookies. Pulling one out of the bag, she offered it to him, then waited while he took a bite.

"These are amazing."

That answer pleased her way too much. "I didn't make them."

Oh, no. He'd stepped right into that one. Like a pro, she'd shifted his attention elsewhere so he wouldn't catch her sneak attack. "Don't say it."

"Felicity made them."

Hattie had been trying to set him up with her best friend, Felicity, for the past year. She ramped up her siege after he'd been shot. In her world, Felicity owning a bakery specializing in cookies only added another check mark in their compatibility column. She'd already harped on how their schedules gelled, Felicity's dad had been a police officer, she loved the outdoors, and she kept a tidy house. If he were choosing a wife from a checklist, Felicity would definitely be in the running. But no matter how many times she'd stopped by to look in on him, no matter how amazing her cookies were or how well she understood his hard days, she wasn't the woman who held his heart.

"You'll have to tell her to enter them into Abundance's Christmas bake-off."

"I'm sure I can convince her if you'd come cheer her on."

"Don't you know anyone else to set her up with?"

"No one better suited."

"Isn't the biggest qualification a guy who's actually interested in her?"

"Maybe you'd discover you are if you spent a few hours really getting to know her." Hattie handed him another cookie. He might not want to date Felicity, but he'd eat her cookies all day long. "At least admit she's gorgeous and she can bake."

He was a man. He could admit the obvious. "I can acknowledge both of those facts."

"One date, Evan. Just one."

But he didn't want to toy with anyone's emotions. His heart was hung up on Rachael, and as long as that door remained open, he wouldn't be pursuing anyone else. "Not until I figure things out with Rachael."

"One date with someone else may be exactly what you need. Maybe you'll recognize Rachael is only friend material."

Their connection and flirting said otherwise. And maybe, just maybe, he could have continued to ignore all that, but then she'd shown up on his doorstep. She'd tossed out a whole host of reasons, but the one that clocked him right in the sternum was her loneliness. Could have gone home to be near Jonah and Penny. She chose to be with him. That wasn't something he could simply walk away from.

"Agree to disagree at this point." He snagged one more cookie.

"Fine," Hattie conceded. "I'd love to stay and argue the point, but I'm meeting someone for dinner."

Hattie was a homebody. He could only think of a few people she'd meet for dinner, and any one of them she'd have named. "Who?"

"A friend."

"Does this friend have a name?"

"Everyone has a name, Evan." She grabbed her purse from the table where she'd dropped it, then headed for his door.

He followed. "They do. And I find it interesting that you're not offering me his."

"I never said it was a guy."

"You never said it wasn't."

She opened his door. "And I'm not going to." On the porch, she turned. "And don't you dare *Find My Friends* me, or I'll turn my location sharing off."

He'd had her share her location with him years ago. She lived alone and, as a legal assistant, sometimes worked late at night. Someone needed to keep an eye on her.

"At least tell me it's not a blind date." Highly doubtful since she wouldn't tell him a name. Between their personal and professional lives, they had several overlapping circles. He'd probably recognize whomever she was dining with.

"I wouldn't meet a stranger alone. You taught me better than that." She tipped her head toward the kitchen behind him. "Warm up the potatoes for a minute first before you add your meat." She started down the steps, calling over her shoulder, "And enjoy those cookies."

She was determined, he'd give her that.

Closing the door, he eyed the cookies on his counter. No question, things would be easier if he'd fallen for a woman ready to fall too. Nothing in his life felt easy right now, and that wasn't necessarily bad. He'd long since subscribed to the old adage that the best things in life were worth fighting for. Rach definitely fell into that category. So did his job. And he didn't intend to lose either.

Chapter Seven

White had never been an intimidating color. Bland. Boring. Stark. But not intimidating.

Until now.

Rachael glared at the watercolor paper block in front of her. Winsor & Newton. Eighteen by twenty-four. One hundred forty pounds. Her favorite brand, size, and thickness. Next to the block she'd laid out her brushes and filled her palette with bright colors waiting to saturate the space around all that white. And after one hundred and twenty-three minutes, nothing had happened save staring down this blank paper from different angles.

She'd sat. Paced. Twirled in her chair. Plopped on the couch. Nothing worked. She'd cranked up her playlist—Skillet, Thousand Foot Crutch, Switchfoot—but all that did was shake the walls, not her creativity. It had been the same thing all week long. She spent her days with Evan, taking him to appointments, tidying his house, mowing his lawn, whatever needed doing. Nights she climbed the steps to the third-floor office Jonah had told her to use for her painting. Kind of him, but no painting had happened yet.

Evan tossed out ideas whenever they were together. Some sounded like something she might use. Then when she sat here, her mind went as blank as the paper in front of her. What used to bring such joy now brought frustration. Worse yet, if she couldn't pull herself together, she'd not only let Evan down but a charity she truly wanted to help. They shared the pain of deep loss, but at least her loss had answers. If she could lend support to Searchlight in their quest to find closure for families, then that's what she wanted to do.

With a heavy sigh, she looked over at the easel in the corner. In the nearly two weeks since she brought the canvas here from her studio in Chicago, she'd finished the outline and begun adding the depth and colors that would breathe life into the image. This piece she enjoyed spending time with. She never rushed but rather savored her moments spent here with her paint brush in hand. Known for her watercolors, she'd developed her abilities with acrylics through the years while working on the additions to this series. The art world would classify them as hyperrealism. Paintings so lifelike they resembled photographs. Probably why

Evan was so enamored with last year's piece when he caught a glimpse of it at her studio.

Hyperrealistic art wasn't a genre she'd set out to learn, but once she started, she discovered a natural ability for the style. Not that anyone other than Gavin realized she possessed the hidden talent. Well, and now Evan, she supposed, but he hadn't mentioned anything about it again.

Her phone dinged a text. Evan. Did the man have some kind of sensor warning him she was thinking of him?

She picked up her phone and opened Messenger. How goes it over there?

After breakfast she'd left him to his PT exercises while she'd come to make progress over here. No doubt he'd long ago finished and showered, but he'd allowed her privacy to work. Too bad she had nothing to show for her solitary hours.

She typed out a quick response. About like a lead balloon trying to fly.

Sounds like you could use some fresh air. I volunteer to help you get some.

Aren't I supposed to be helping you?

You are. You're rescuing me from my boredom.

How very heroic of me.

It'd be even more heroic if you brought me a cookie when you come this way.

She chuckled. Two nights ago he'd sat at her counter while she whipped up a batch of chocolate chip cookies. The man could add Cookie Monster to his list of nicknames. She'd sent him home with two dozen. How on earth did he eat so many and still look as good as he did?

I'll see what I can do.

Meet me by the Jeep.

She was already up and walking, typing as she descended the stairs. Where exactly is this fresh air we're going in search of?

Ford Square.

A block off Rainier yet still considered a part of downtown Abundance, Ford Square was a spot for people to congregate. Year-round, the town held activities in the space, mainly on weekends. Today was Saturday. No doubt something was happening there right now.

Slipping into her Birkenstocks—with September nearly here, there were only so many days left to wear them—she called for Clooney. By the time she gave her a quick bathroom break and made sure she had water and a treat, Evan was standing beside his Jeep.

"How's your arm feeling after your exercises?" she asked as she passed him to climb in the driver's seat. He tended to push himself right to the line of what Becky instructed. Sometimes beyond.

"Sore, but I'm used to it." He clicked his seatbelt in place. "How's the rendering coming?"

She needed two actually. The contest required that each artist create a smaller scale of their mural to be placed on display as they worked. The second would act like a construction map of sorts. After researching, then chatting with an old friend who had experience painting murals, Rachael decided the best way to tackle this task was to draw it out and break it into a grid. This would enable her to envision the placement on the wall, and she could work in sections.

All doable if she could think of something to draw. "About as good as it was yesterday. And the day before that. And the day before that."

"You've got time. Something will pop."

If only her creativity was as readily available as his confidence. "It's a massive project, and I have just under a month."

"More than enough time."

He reached out and flicked the volume knob up. The strands of "Piano Man" filled the cab, and he tapped his good hand on the dash in time with the music. Then he started crooning along with Billy Joel. He glanced her way and sang louder, wiggling those brows with an invite to join him.

Seriously. Resisting him was impossible when he proved so darn irresistible.

They sang through two more Billy Joel songs from his playlist before parking near the square. Already her chaotic brain felt calmer. Somehow Evan always managed to quiet her unrest.

"Lots of people." She dodged a group of teens strolling the width of the sidewalk. "What's going on here today?"

"Sidewalk Chalk Saturdays."

"Huh?" Ahead, upbeat music played from the stage. Something canned, not live. Whoever controlled it maintained the volume at a level to fill the background but not eclipse conversation.

"The township leaves buckets of chalk on the stage each Saturday in summer and people can come create whatever they'd like."

She side-eyed him. "This your sneaky way of calling out my creativity?"

"I'll let you know after I see if it works." He led her up front and grabbed a bucket. "Shall we?"

"You go ahead and start. I'm going to walk around a little if that's okay?"

"Sure." He motioned to an empty space of cement. "I'll be over there, starting on our masterpiece."

"You sound pretty confident for a man with one hand."

"Because I have a secret weapon."

She made a show of looking around. "Magical chalk?"

"You."

How did he infuse so much emotion into one word? Confidence. Admiration. Assurance. All those packed-in feelings landed in her heart, unfurling and making themselves at home.

Except she didn't have room for any new feelings when it came to Evan Wayne.

"You'd have more luck with magical chalk." She left on the heels of his deep laughter, heading in the opposite direction to stroll the perimeter. Families and teens milled around Ford Square right along with their creations. Everything from hopscotch grids little kids played on to detailed chalk drawings covered the ground. Her favorite gave off the optical illusion of precariously standing on the lip of a cliff. She actually became a little lightheaded teetering on the fake edge.

As she turned to head toward Evan, she caught sight of Auna Cummings filling a large black urn outside one of the businesses. Once again dressed in denim overalls with smudges of dirt on her skin and her hair in a messy bun, she seemed very much in her element. Flower clippings of all colors and sizes lay around her, and Rachael studied them as she approached. "Those are gorgeous."

Auna smiled as she greeted her. "Thanks. It's Rachael, right?"

"Yep." Rachael looked at all the flowers Auna had brought to play with. Vines of varying green shades, white pansies, tall grass, and hydrangeas flowing from blue to pink. "I didn't know you arrange flowers too."

"A hobby that's slowly morphing into more."

Exactly how her painting started. "I understand."

"Yeah?" Auna motioned to one of the potato vines. "Mind handing me that?"

"Sure." She picked it up, then passed it off. "Painting started as a hobby for me too. My husband is the one who encouraged me to make it something more."

"I didn't know you were married." She stood back and assessed the vine's placement.

"He passed away nine years ago this December."

That grabbed her attention, as it always did with everyone when she shared. "I'm so sorry."

"Thanks."

Before things could grow awkward, Auna pointed to the long strands of grass. "Those next, please." She took them from Rachael and continued talking as she added them to the arrangement. "Did you find your hobby lost some of its joy when it became a job?"

"Not at all." There was something about waking up each day and using the gifts she'd been given. Growing in what she felt created to do. Yes, deadlines and expectations sometimes added a level of challenge to her work, but joy had always been present in those days. Now it was as elusive as water in the Sahara.

"Good." Hands on her hips, Auna dragged her attention from the urn to Rachael. "That's my biggest concern in making a leap to this becoming full time." She nodded to the flowers. "Hydrangeas, please. The pink ones, I think."

Rachael reached for them. "I love hydrangeas. I have a bush at home, but it hardly ever blooms. Seems my talent with flowers didn't extend past painting them."

Auna laughed. "It's not only you. Hydrangeas are tough for most people. Typically it's because they're pruning them when they're not supposed to."

"Oh, I leave it alone until fall, then I cut it back so I don't have those ugly dead stems all winter."

A knowing smile spread on Auna's face. "Those dead sticks are exactly what you shouldn't cut if you want blooms in spring."

"Huh?"

"Hydrangeas bloom on those old, dead limbs." Auna played with one of the pink petals in the cutting she'd added to the urn. "What you think is dead is actually the breeding ground for new growth. It's one of the reasons I love the plant so much. Life springing out of something dry and barren. We hardly think it's possible"—she clipped one of the blooms and handed it to Rachael—"yet we have these little messages left in nature that prove otherwise."

Rachael took what she offered, staring at it for a long second. "So you're saying if I don't cut anything away this fall, that next spring I'll have flowers like this?"

"Yep."

Across the square, Evan caught her attention and waved. Pieces of chalk littered the area around him, along with multiple colors dusting his jeans. He'd drawn something on the ground, but she couldn't make out what it was from here. "I should go rescue him."

Auna followed her gaze to Evan, then laughed again. "He's in his element. A giant kid in a grown man's body."

Something close to adoration rolled across Auna's face, the sight awakening a possessive feeling in Rachael. "He may be a goofball sometimes, but he's definitely all man."

Auna's eyes cut to Rachael, her perfectly sculpted brows slightly arching. "That he is."

Her cheeks heated, provoking too many questions with no favorable instigators as their source. All led to deeper feelings than friendship for Evan as their root. And that simply wasn't going to happen. She consulted her five points. Just friends. Kissing Evan would be awkward. They could lose their friendship. She wasn't even looking. And he worked an incredibly dangerous job.

With a decisive nod and her emotions sliding back where they belonged, she waved goodbye to Auna and went to join her Just Friend.

There was something incredibly attractive about a woman's laugh. Particularly, Rachael Stark's. The full, rich sound had snagged his attention, creating an initial impression that still made him grin. He heard it the first time Memorial Day weekend three years ago. Standing on his deck, preheating his grill for a solitary steak, then a peal of rich laughter hooked him around and had him searching for its source. Intriguing target acquired, he turned off his grill, beelined it indoors, and whipped up his famous guacamole. Looked like a party happening next door with his new neighbors, and he intended to join.

The chips and dips gained him entrance and a group of friends. But what he developed with Rachael far surpassed that. Her sense of humor clicked with his. The way she cared for her family demonstrated her selfless heart. She loved classic rock and crazy eighties movies that made him groan. And she held a deep faith that challenged his. Those were only a few reasons he'd fallen for her. Every day added more to his ever-growing list.

Like how right now, she moved to allow a little four-year-old boy to color in the dinosaur she'd drawn for him. His attempts included mostly scribbles outside the line, but rather than take the chalk from his hand and finish the illustration, she encouraged him to continue coloring. Exactly like she had with the unicorn, hippopotamus, and llama other children now embellished with glee.

Other little kids noticed her contributions and began clamoring for their own animals. Evan snuck up beside her. "You doing okay or do you need me to help you make a break for it?"

Her blue eyes were brighter than he'd seen in weeks. "I'm good. Unless you need me to get you someplace."

He was on empty, but he'd starve his stomach in favor of feeding her heart any day. "Nope. I'll grab another bucket of chalk. I think you're going to need it."

An hour later she'd created a chalk zoo full of zebras with rainbow stripes, a teddy bear dressed like Luke Skywalker, giraffes with purple spots, and monkeys swinging from floral vines. And those were just his favorites.

She completed the ears on an elephant resembling Dumbo, then stood and dusted her hands against her now chalk-covered jeans. "I think that's the last one."

"Good thing, because you're nearly out of chalk." He'd snagged the last two containers twenty minutes ago.

They returned the now empty pails to the stage, and several parents wandered over to express their thanks as their kids continued to fill in the animals Rachael had created for them. He patiently waited until the final person walked away, then motioned toward the west side of the square. "Could I interest you in a late lunch?"

"Or early dinner?" She grinned and followed him. "Where to?"

"The Landing?" It served a little of everything, including a killer grilled cheese he knew she loved and, situated between here and the shopping district, was only a short walk away.

"Let's go."

As they turned south, he peeked down at her. "You're a whole lot more talented than you let on."

"Because I drew a few chalk animals?"

"With incredible detail."

"Psh," she puffed out. "You're easy to impress if that's all it takes."

"No. This confirmed what I already knew."

"Which is?"

"You can create anything with those hands of yours." He thought back to her art studio and the piece she'd tried to hide. "Like that portrait in your studio. I've never seen anything like it." A young girl around ten or eleven; the details and style creating a lifelike quality. "She looked so real."

Rachael stumbled beside him. Swallowed. "That technique's called hyperrealism."

"Good term for it." Such a beautiful day outside, others filled the streets too. They moved around them. "I still think you should paint more pieces like that."

"Maybe someday." They reached the restaurant, and she pulled open the door before he could for her. "First I need to paint this mural someone convinced me to do."

"You mean asked." He approached the hostess stand. "Two, please."

Grabbing menus, the hostess led them to the outside patio. Once they were seated, Rachael dropped her napkin across her lap. "Tomorrow night is the dinner with your charity, right?"

"Yep."

"Where's it held again?"

"At Chief Platte's house. They have a farm on the east side of town."

Her eyes lifted from the menu. "I don't speak compass. Give me landmarks."

"We seriously need to work on your directional abilities." Their server delivered waters with a promise to return in a few minutes for their orders. "Near Nicole's Antiques."

"Ahh. Okay. Now I know where you're talking about." She set down her menu. "They're not going to ask to see any preliminary sketches, are they? Because I have nothing to show them."

"I doubt they'll ask, but if they do, I'll redirect them."

"How?"

"By telling them you're a temperamental artist who doesn't like sharing her work until it's finished."

She laughed. "It's not a lie."

"I know." He smiled. "But you seemed okay with people watching you create your chalk creations today."

"Those don't count. It was for kids. They're easy to please."

Was that why her creativity had flown so effortlessly this afternoon? No pressure. Just fun and a captive audience enamored with whatever she put out there. All week he'd studied her and at times gently prodded and poked, accumulating clues as to what built her painter's block. If he could figure out the pieces involved, maybe he could tear down the barrier. "Is that part of the holdup? Are you worried people aren't going to like whatever you come up with?"

"Putting yourself out there for the public to critique definitely is daunting, and I'm a little out of practice with it." Sunshine warmed their table, and she slid the butter for their bread into a patch of shade. "Art is so subjective, and people are quick to share their opinions—especially when they're negative. Sometimes they don't do it in the most constructive of ways."

"But like you said, it's opinions, not facts." He waited for her eyes to lift to his. "Fact is, you're an amazing artist. And before you go and say that I'm biased, I'd like to remind you I'm not the only one who's said so. If you'd like, I can pull up all the articles I read."

"From nearly a decade ago."

"Talent doesn't disappear simply because you took a break from using it. It might need a little dusting off, but after what I saw today, I'd say you've got this."

"If only your confidence equaled assurance."

Their server arrived and took their orders, and shortly after she delivered their food. Conversation flowed as they ate. Rachael often filled the quiet moments, but she rarely did so with words that held any sort of vulnerability. She deflected difficult questions and offered what she believed were suitable answers intended to satiate his concerns toward her. So while she'd answered his question moments ago—and he believed her words truthful—she'd used her response to throw him off the scent of a deeper reason causing her inability to paint. But both her even tone and the way she'd rubbed her thumbnail hinted at more for him to discover yet.

He'd simply need to continue digging. Creatively. Because when it came to Rachael, the only block *he* was experiencing were the roadblocks she tossed up herself. Good thing he was trained in how to dismantle strategically placed barriers.

Forty-five minutes later, they climbed into his Jeep and pointed it toward home. "What are your thoughts for the rest of the day?"

"Walking Clooney. Staring at a blank canvas. Maybe some popcorn."

"Want some company?"

"I was planning on it." A motorcycle blasted past them. No helmet, short sleeves, no jacket, and way over the speed limit. He'd have pulled the guy over. Rach's look said she shared his conclusion. "You want to be out there, don't you?"

Understatement of all time. "It's where I belong, and I'm a little tired of sitting on the bench."

"Be patient. You'll get out there again."

"If only your confidence equaled assurance." He repeated her earlier words, finishing them with a wry grin.

She shook her head. "You know, you've talked to me a lot about my art career lately. All I've ever really sold were my floral paintings, but you've encouraged me to try different aspects. Including this mural." She glanced his way. "Why?"

He could see where the track she was laying led, and he wasn't about to hop on it. "This is different, Rach. Painting in a different medium is still doing what you were created to do."

"And working in a different department at the station isn't?"

"No. I'm meant to be on the front lines, preventing bad things from happening."

"Because you couldn't with Mandie?" she softly asked.

He fisted his hand on his knee. She wasn't trying to upset him. Rachael wouldn't do that. But tension worked through him all the same. "Too far, Rach."

She slowed and turned into their shared driveway. "Sorry." Pulling to a stop between their houses, she turned off the engine. "It's just ... maybe consider that there are a lot of ways to help people. And if you're forced to have to do so in a way you never expected, it wouldn't be the end of the world." She placed her hand over his fist. "You will always possess the opportunity to make a difference in someone's life. It's up to you if you choose to take it." Then she released her grip and hopped out of the car.

He sat there for a second longer, her words echoing through his mind until they faded away. Because he couldn't reconcile what felt like truth in her words with the truth churning inside him. Being permanently sidelined might not be the literal end of the world, but it certainly felt like the end of his.

Chapter Eight

"It's perfectly fine, dear, if you don't have anything to show us. The minute Henry heard you'd be our artist, I looked you up online." Dolly Platte, tonight's host and wife to Chief Henry Platte, smiled at her. Sixty-something, she stood tall and thin and had short hair that reminded Rachael of a night sky, pitch-black with silver shooting through it. Most women would look frail with that build, but Dolly commanded the area around her with the calm strength of the teacher she once was. "I showed everyone your work, and we are honored that you'd agree to paint the department's mural."

An unconfessed hope that Rachael could pull out the win for them shined from her eyes.

Quelling her nerves, Rachael returned her smile. "Glad I can be here."

However, if she didn't come up with an idea, they might not return the sentiment.

Rachael weaved through the crowded barn, chatting with others along the way. Everyone was sweet, but many didn't possess Dolly's reserved nature. They were all too happy to share their faith in her. She was an amazing artist. The answer to the charity's prayers. This year the department would win. Their expectations chipped away at the false bravado she'd strapped on.

She darted out the wide-open doors of the barn and gulped a breath of air free from the buzzing anticipation. Within minutes of their arrival, Evan had been hauled off by his captain. Something about a known dealer in one of his patrol areas. Whatever it was, Evan's eyes lit like someone hooked him up to a fresh battery. He lived and breathed his job, and these two months on the sidelines were fatiguing him more than that time he'd run a marathon without adequately training. Mental hurdles often required more endurance than physical and always proved more draining. A truth she intimately knew.

A late summer breeze brushed her bare arms as she scanned the area around her. Tonight's party spilled from the catered food inside Dolly and Henry's barn onto the grassy field beside it. A few tall tables with long white cloths dotted the yard, and bouquets of varying flowers in saturated fall tones perched on top. Rachael strolled to one and fiddled with a dahlia, her favorite.

Her inability to paint notwithstanding, she truly did love flowers. Each one delicate and unique, they'd captured her attention from the first swish of her brush across a canvas. They allowed her to play with color, sometimes creating with soft, tender tones and delicate lines. Other times she'd use vibrant, bold shades with huge sweeping swashes of paint. A gentle smile curved her lips, and she closed her eyes, remembering. Chris walking through the door with a new flower for her to paint. Brianna gathering them from a field they'd visited, her nose pressed against the petals as she twirled.

Laughter spilled from the barn, trickling its way to her, and she opened her eyes. Painting without Chris and Brianna wasn't the same, but like every other area she'd moved forward in, it was time to do the same here. Put her head down and do the work. Gavin needed her, as did this charity.

"You like dahlias?"

The question pulled her around. Auna walked her way, looking noticeably different than the last two times they'd seen one another. Her honey-colored hair fell in soft waves to the middle of her back. She wore an adorable flowy dress with huge flowers smattered all over the soft, creamy fabric, and strappy sandals that added a little height to her frame. Her best accessory was the wide smile that seemed a permanent fixture.

"Hey," Rachael greeted. "I didn't know you'd be here today."

"I volunteered to put together the flower arrangements. Can't say no when the chief's wife contacts you." Auna joined her at the table. "Not that I would have anyway. Arrangements are one of my favorite things to do."

"You're definitely talented at them." Rachael fingered the dahlia's stem. "And to answer your question, these are my favorite flower, actually."

"One of mine too." Auna smoothed a wrinkle from the tablecloth. "Do you know their meaning?"

She tipped her head. "Meaning?"

"Oooh." Her eyes lit up. "Someone who doesn't know about floriography." She clasped her hands together. "Get comfy, we could be here all day."

"Flori-what?"

"Oh, no." Evan joined them. "I know that look. Make a break for it, Rachael. I'll hold her off."

She knew he was joking, so why did his offer cause an uncomfortable twinge inside? Casting a look between them both, she leaned into the table instead. "Actually, I'm interested in what she has to say."

"You've done it now." He glanced at his watch, then looked at Auna. "Just so you know, there's only two hours until sunset, so maybe give her the abridged version."

Auna nudged him away. "Go help Felicity in the kitchen and stop bothering us."

"Felicity, as in Hattie's friend?" The one Hattie had tried several times this summer to set Evan up with?

"Yep. She volunteered too. Catered this entire event for free." Auna turned to Evan. "That woman isn't only great in the kitchen, she's a sweetheart."

"Sounds like quite the catch." Between Auna and Felicity, there didn't appear to be a shortage of eligible bachelorettes around Evan, and Rachael should be happy about that for her friend. But like someone playing a trick and pouring lemon juice when she expected lemonade, these sour thoughts weren't what she expected, and they left a bad taste in her mouth.

"She is," Auna agreed. "But enough about her, let's talk flowers." She scooted closer. "Something I love to do, especially with another flower-lover like yourself."

Somehow she didn't feel they were on the same level, but she could pretend. "So what is floriography?"

"I'm so glad you asked." Auna practically glowed with excitement. "Floriography is the language of flowers …"

As she spoke, Evan propped his elbow on the table and cupped his chin. He leaned toward Rachael and whispered. "I'll stay close by. Shine the bat signal when you need me to rescue you."

His nearness and his breath on her neck sent shivers through her in a much too pleasant way. She edged away from him and managed a tiny nod in response. Working hard, she brought her focus to Auna, who was still talking, but not before she caught Evan's low chuckle. She refused to goad him by looking his way.

"… has meaning." Auna picked up two of the pieces from the bouquet. "Rosemary symbolizes remembrance, and daisies refer to childhood innocence." She then pulled out a green-leafed stem along with the dahlia and a carnation. "This is eucalyptus, which means protection. And both the dahlia and pink carnations mean eternal love, but the carnations refer specifically to a mother's eternal love."

Hearing all the meanings completely changed the flower grouping in front of her. Rachael looked it over with new eyes. "So you don't simply arrange the flowers. You put them together to create a specific meaning or message."

"Exactly. Pretty neat, huh?"

It actually was brilliant. Rachael looked around at the people mingling outside, and an idea began to form in her mind. "I knew roses mean love, but how did I miss that all flowers have meanings?"

"Not many people have ever heard about it. The idea was huge in the

Victorian era. Men and women used it to secretly communicate their feelings toward each other. The groupings and the way they accepted the flowers meant something."

Evan straightened, a grimace on his face. "It's hard enough to ask a woman on a date. Glad I didn't live back then with all that added pressure."

Rachael tipped her head and added a tiny smile. "I think it's romantic."

"Right?" Auna added. "They didn't just stop by the convenience store and pick up the closest bouquet. Men had to think about each flower. It added intention and meaning."

"Every flower I've ever given a woman already had those things." He nearly looked offended that they'd think otherwise. "Love isn't lazy."

His words surprised her. Not their bold sentiment from his lips, but what they meant. "You've been in love before?" The thought was new and a little unsettling. Again, it made no sense. She'd given her heart away before, so why would it surprise her that he had? Whoever the woman was, she'd have been the lucky one.

"I have."

Oh, she had about a million and one questions. She just wasn't sure she wanted the answers.

Auna skillfully replaced the flowers in the vase she'd stolen them from. "I'm going to see Felicity. I'm pretty sure she has a boatload of desserts to put out and could use the extra hands."

She headed for the barn, and Rachael turned toward Evan. "How come you never told me you were in love before?"

"You never asked."

"Who was she? Did she break your heart or was it the other way around?"

His palm lifted. "Hold up there, Nosy Nelly."

She batted his hand out of the way. "Not nosy. Curious." Because somehow it mattered if he'd suffered a broken heart. She just might need to find the woman and—

"Neither."

"Wait. What?"

"It was a mutual thing. We both realized we weren't right for each other."

"Do you still know her?"

He nodded.

"Well?" Rachael held her hands out. "Who is it? Have I met her?"

His gaze shifted over her shoulder. Rach turned to follow it, and saw Dolly headed their way.

"Oh, there you are, dear," she called as she approached them. "Felicity's putting out the dessert, and we'd love to have you come join us. Not everyone's had the chance to speak with you yet, and they really want to show their appreciation."

Evan straightened. "By all means, you should go then." The twinkle in his eye marred his solemn expression. He no doubt sensed an opportunity for escape and was snatching it.

Dolly parked herself beside Rachael and threaded their arms together. She patted her hand. "I won't keep you from your man for too long."

Whoa now, what? "Uh, we're just friends."

Another pat. "Sure you are, dear. I look at all my friends that way." Her laughter trickled across her words.

"No, seriously." Rachael telegraphed a look Evan's way, silently pleading he chime in. When he responded with a smirk, she switched to words coated in a menacing syrup. "Tell her we're just friends. Please."

Clearing his throat, he gravely nodded. "Dolly, Rachael and I are just friends."

Dolly looked from Evan to Rachael and back to him. "Ah. I see. Well, then, my mistake." As she spoke the words, she looked like a parent agreeing with their child that Santa Claus was real. She knew the truth and was allowing Rachael hers. Then she disengaged from Rachael's arm. "Goodness me, that's Mary over there, and I've been waiting to speak with her. I'll meet you by the dessert table. I'm sure Evan can walk you over." She toddled off under that lame excuse.

Rachael turned to Evan. "What was that?"

His intense focus rested on her. Eyes a mixture of dark brown and green, she typically likened them to camouflage in color, though not in expression. Evan never hid his emotions, at least not from her. But right now she couldn't read his thoughts.

"What was what?" Feigned innocence dripped from each word.

"Your response to Dolly."

"I told her we were just friends, like you asked."

"Not very convincingly."

"Well, you didn't specify that requirement." He said it so matter-of-factly she nearly let things drop there.

Except she couldn't. She had to be clear. "I didn't think I had to, since it's a truthful statement."

His full attention hadn't lifted from her, and now his forehead scrunched as he sucked in a deciding breath, then stepped closer. Hand skimming the table, it came to rest with his fingertips brushing hers. Then he leaned down until their eyes were level. "I disagree." The gold lines through his irises glittered in the evening sun. "I'm not sure how to label us, but I'd say we've been beyond *just friends* for quite some time now." For a breath, he held her captive without blinking. Or maybe she wasn't breathing. Then he tapped the table, straightened, and extended his hand toward the barn. "Shall we see about dessert?"

Right then she knew. She was in trouble. Because he'd decimated Point One without breaking a sweat. With a few well-placed words and a smoldering stare, he'd completely changed how she saw that *just friends* term, and she'd never go back.

"Sure." She followed him, consoling herself with the fact that being more than just a friend didn't have to mean anything romantic. Points Two through Five still held strong, and there was no way he was toppling those.

"Finished?" Evan motioned to Rachael's plate that moments ago held a slice of chocolate cake.

"Yes." Her arms crossed over her stomach. "That was delicious."

"It was." He piled her plate on top of the cookie crumbs left on his. "Be right back." He walked to the trash cans a few steps outside the barn. When he turned, a familiar woman approached him. Short with blond hair, blue eyes, and only a few wrinkles showing in her middle-aged face, she looked vaguely familiar, but he couldn't place her.

Evan nodded at her. "Hello."

"Hello. Are you Officer Evan?" She squinted up at him.

"I am."

"I hear you're the one who brought Rachael Stark on board."

"I did." He wasn't giving up excess information until he better assessed who this was.

Her face pulled into a warm smile. "Thank you. My husband, Alvaro, and I truly hope the department wins this year, especially since you're donating to Searchlight." She shuffled her weight from foot to foot. "Could you introduce me to her?"

"Maybe you could introduce yourself to me first."

Her cheeks reddened. "Oh, goodness, I'm sorry." She held out her hand. "My name is Hope Perez. I volunteer with Searchlight. My daughter, Liliana, has been missing for fifteen years."

Ah. That's where he knew her from. He'd run into her on one of his first days with Abundance PD. She stopped by the station about once a year to ask if there were any updates on her daughter.

"Yes. I've heard about her case, and I'm so sorry she's still missing." He motioned inside. "Come with me." He led her to the table and introduced her to Rachael.

Standing, Rachael shook Hope's hand. "Nice to meet you."

"You too." Hope settled onto a chair at their table. "I wanted to thank you for stepping in and taking on our mural. For families like myself, it means everything." She opened her purse and pulled out a picture. "This is my daughter, Liliana."

Rach accepted the picture and studied it. Evan peered over her shoulder at a beautiful preteen who bore many of her father's Hispanic features. Tan skin, a wide smile, and hair so black it held a blue sheen. Her eyes, though, were what always captured him. Brilliant blue like her mom's. An unique and unusual combination.

"She's beautiful." Rachael peeked up at Hope.

"Thanks. That's my last picture of her. She's been missing for fifteen years."

To her credit, Rachael absorbed the shock and offered compassion in its place. "I'm so sorry. The loss of a child is life's hardest loss."

As if sensing a kinship, Hope nodded. "You've lost a child?"

"My daughter Brianna passed in a car accident when she was almost three. My husband too." She sucked in a deep breath and refocused on Liliana's picture. "How old is Liliana here?"

"Twelve."

"I guessed eleven or twelve. Her cheeks still have some of their childlike roundness." Her eyes remained on Liliana's face.

"She had the chubbiest baby cheeks," Hope recounted with tenderness. "She'd be twenty-seven now. I often wonder if she'd look more like me as an adult or still be all Alvaro."

Rach's eyes narrowed as they traced Liliana's features. After a moment, she blinked and returned the picture to Hope. "I have a feeling she'd take after you." Then she shifted to Evan. "Does your department have Liliana's case?"

Hope responded before he could. "It's a cold case. No movement. I check in each year, but there haven't been any new leads." She slid Liliana's picture into her purse and locked eyes with Evan. "I'm thankful your department still takes the time to speak with me. I only wish there were more you could do."

Evan leaned forward. "Most cold cases aren't for lack of concern, but lack of manpower." He swallowed the other reasons, like the truth to her lack of leads. Or the fact Liliana could be thought of as a runaway. He hadn't studied her case, so he wasn't prepared to speak into it.

Hope nodded. "I understand. I do. But she's my daughter, so there's not a day that goes by when I'm not thinking of her." Then she stood and turned to Rachael. "I only wanted the chance to thank you. Searchlight is so important. We do our best to keep our children's stories and faces out there, but too often people walk or scroll past them. Being the charity this year will keep our name—and theirs, we hope—in the public's eye. We cannot wait to see what you paint."

Little lines dug into Rach's forehead and around her mouth. "I hope I can do you proud."

"The mere fact that you stepped in so we'd still have a mural already has. Thank you, again." With a little wave, she left.

Rach watched her, then she blinked at Evan. He spoke before she could. "I'm sorry. Tonight wasn't supposed to add so much pressure to you. I should have come alone and told them you were working."

Rather than mollify him, she abruptly stood. "Can we head home?"

With a sigh, he stood. "Sure." He'd intended for this mural to draw them closer together, but tonight he seemed to keep striking out. The first swing and a miss had been his attempt to knock them out of the *just friends* category. After his honest answer, she'd spent the rest of the night introducing him as her *best friend.*

Potato, potahto in his book.

Then he'd failed at shielding her from everyone's expectations. Now she'd gone mute, no doubt regretting her agreement to help him but unsure how to admit it. After making their goodbyes to Chief Henry and Dolly, they walked to his Jeep in complete silence. They climbed in and rode home the same way. Her leather seat squeaked as she shut off the engine and turned to face him.

He braced himself for her letdown.

"I think I know what I'm painting," she announced.

Color him surprised. He straightened, trying to catch up with her thoughts. "You do?"

She nodded, excitement edging into her eyes. "Sorry. That's why I went all quiet. I was processing an idea that sprang up after talking to people tonight." She rubbed her thumbnail against the pads of her fingers. "It's different though."

"Different how?"

"Let me play with it a bit, and once I have it where I want, I promise—if it works—I'll show you."

"All right." They hopped out, and Clooney's barks greeted them from behind Rachael's front door. "Planning on taking Clooney for a walk?"

"A quick one. Then I'm working. That's why I wanted to head out."

Her explanation buoyed his earlier concern. "Mind if I join you?"

"Sure, but I need to change clothes first."

They met on her steps. She'd switched into distressed jeans and a white T-shirt and tugged her hair in one of those knots. She looked good dressed up but even better dressed down.

They descended the steps, her oblivious to him checking her out. Clooney barked and raced into the lake. Still lost in her thoughts, Rachael walked silently beside him. At least now he understood that her quiet centered around trying to fine-tune the idea playing in her mind. They walked about a quarter mile before she stopped to throw a piece of driftwood for Clooney.

"I really felt for Hope tonight. For all those families," she said.

"Me too." He stood ankle deep in the surf with her. "I wish there was something more we could do for them."

She clapped for Clooney, who came racing her way and dropped the stick at her feet. "Interesting you should mention that because isn't part of your job finding missing people?"

"That falls more in line with detectives like Dierks."

"Okay, but you do work missing persons cases sometimes."

Rarely. There were times, however, on the front end of investigations where he conducted interviews or chased down leads. "When they first come in. Not when they're cold."

Turning her neck, she looked at him. "You told Hope cold cases weren't for lack of concern, but manpower."

"I did."

"And you told me you were tired of sitting on the bench."

She was good. Listened to details and filed them away to use them against a suspect later. He was good too. And he picked up where this was headed. "Also correct."

"And you have lots of time on your hands right now." She lobbed another shot.

This one he blocked. "Actually, no. I don't. All my excess time is going toward my recovery."

"Twenty-four seven?" Skepticism lined her voice.

"I said excess time. Remember, I'm also in charge of the department's Fall Flower Fest contributions."

"A few events here and there, but I'm doing the bulk of the work by painting the mural." She tossed Clooney's stick again. "Something you encouraged me to do even though it was out of my wheelhouse. Now I'm returning the favor."

"Convenient."

"Come on. You have the time, access, and know-how to look into Liliana's case. It would get you off that bench and help a family who really needs it." She brushed hair from her face, blinking as it caught on her eyelashes. "Please?"

He didn't want to give Cap any reasons to find a new permanent slot for him. "Rach, I—" His words dried up with the expectant look on her face. Darn, but she could bring him to his knees and twist him in circles with only a look. "It's that important to you?"

She nibbled her lip for a moment, then, "I can't have Brianna back, but Hope, she at least has a chance. I know what it's like to lose a daughter, but I have no idea what it must be like to always wonder where she is." Clooney dropped the stick again, and as if sensing Rachael's distress, she nudged her head under Rachael's hand. Like a soothing habit, Rach dug her fingers into Clooney's fur. "You could maybe answer that question for her."

"Or find no new leads." Because that was entirely possible.

"We won't know until we try."

Her words breathed something into him, because they were true. It was the same hope he had for the two of them. How could he withhold possibilities from someone else?

"Okay. Let me talk to my captain, but I think he'll let me look into it." He already had access to the files, and anyone could ask questions, but he should keep Cap abreast of any digging he'd be doing.

Rachael threw herself at him, hugging him tight. "Thank you, Evan."

Unprepared, he wrapped his good arm around her tightly in attempt to steady them both. Her face tucked into his neck, and her hair brushed his cheek. Between her soft curves pressed against him and her apple-scented shampoo, this was the best thank-you he'd ever received. He brushed his hand along her rib cage, smiling at her quick inhale. Her nose slid up along his neck as if she were breathing him in, and he held perfectly still.

Clooney barked and Rach stiffened, then stepped away. "I should get back."

"I'm going to walk a little farther." He waited out her nod, then watched as she patted her leg for Clooney to follow her. "And Rach?"

She turned. "Yeah?"

"You're welcome."

Chapter Nine

She'd forgotten what it felt like to enjoy painting. When creativity met purpose and passion like a perfect storm and spilled onto her canvas in brilliant colors. Experiencing it again felt like a piece of her had reawakened from a long slumber. A bit hazy, not quite ready to face the world, yet feeling energized.

It was also a little scary. Taking a step, she assessed the start to the scaled rendering of her mural idea. The flowers were the easy part. Choosing faces and contacting families for permission to use them would be more difficult. What she contemplated doing required a vulnerability she wasn't quite ready for because in sharing her painting direction, she'd inevitably share its genesis. But if baring that piece of her produced exposure for children like Liliana, then she'd make herself ready.

Peering across the room to the canvas that acted as a catalyst to her mural, Rachael breathed out her worries and focused on the face of her daughter. Just this morning she'd layered in laugh lines around Brie's smile, hearing her giggles as she did so. Her little girl laughed from her belly with a joy Rachael couldn't seem to recall in her own heart but with a sound she'd never forget. These annual paintings healed her in ways many might not understand, but the people from last night's dinner could.

That connection planted this seed for her mural. Learning about floriography, then hearing Hope's story fertilized it, and the idea flickered to life. Now she strived to flesh it out on paper. She knew she'd use Liliana's likeness, but there was space for more children. Until she figured out who those would be, she'd pore over flower meanings and decide which ones needed to grace this painted garden.

She had three weeks to nail everything down and complete both smaller-scaled versions of the mural. Having a direction, albeit a broad one, at least made things feel doable.

Her phone buzzed in her pocket, and she pulled it out. Smiled. "Hey, Bud."

"Hey, Mom." Gavin's deep voice still surprised her at times. In so many ways, he was turning into a man. "How goes it over there?"

"Good. I'm actually painting as we speak."

"Oh. I can call you later if that works better."

"Nope. You always come first."

Silence crept in for a moment before he answered. "I can't wait to see your entry."

Something felt off, but it was most likely all part of the process of letting go. "I can't wait to show you." Footsteps pounded up the stairs. Had to be Evan. She set down her brush and hustled into the hall, shutting the door to her studio before he could enter. Sure enough, she bumped into him on the landing. She held up her hand, pointed to her phone, and mouthed *Gavin.* "How're things there, Bud? Do you like your job?"

They'd texted some, but so much was lost without the actual tones. "I do. I'm definitely low man on the totem pole, but I'm making friends. Glad I came over early so I was able to settle into things before classes started last week."

He certainly sounded settled. "Me too. It's a whole lot of change."

"Yeah, it is. How are you doing?"

"Me? Great?" Always great. "What time Thursday do you think you'll be home? In case I want to have some cookies ready for you." His Friday classes had been canceled, so they planned an early start to their weekend. Jonah and Penny were set to arrive Thursday too.

Evan's brows lifted at the mention of his favorite treat, and he pointed to himself, nodding. She waved him off as Gavin chuckled in her ear. "I have to work until three, then I'll head home, change, and hit the road. Should be there in time for dinner."

Home. The word rolled off his tongue effortlessly while she was still grasping the fact she wasn't included in that space anymore. The only time she would be was in reference to a nostalgic destination, not a daily occurrence.

She gripped her phone. "I'll be ready for you."

"I'll see you then." With an *I love you*, he disconnected.

She slid her phone into her pocket.

"How's he doing?" Evan asked.

"Good. I can't wait to see him." She started for the stairs, knowing he'd follow her. "It'll be almost three weeks since I dropped him off. That's the longest we've ever been apart."

"You've been away from me longer, and I've never gotten cookies out of it." He clomped behind her. "I feel I should at least get a half dozen of his."

"You'll have to battle him for them, then."

He harrumphed. "Pit me against a kid."

"That kid is practically as big as you now." They turned into her kitchen. "So what do you want for dinner? Besides cookies."

"You're really not going to make me any?"

"No, but I will paint your mural for you."

He leaned against her counter, and regarded her like she was the most entertaining thing he'd seen in a long while. "How long will I be paying for this one?"

"I'm not sure yet." She opened the fridge. "At least until Christmas. I'm pulling for a good gift."

"Last year's wasn't?"

Evan had numerous amazing qualities. Gift giving was not one of them. "A pair of socks inside a coffee mug?"

"Those socks had pictures of cheese on them and that mug was a Starbucks exclusive. Two things you love."

She peeked over the edge of the fridge door, met his eyes, and shook her head before digging for tonight's dinner ingredients. "How's spaghetti sound?"

"Good."

They worked side by side, as best as Evan could one-handed, and every few minutes Rach snuck a glance his way. Conversation flowed at a normal pace between them, and tonight she intended to keep it that way. When her brain hadn't been working on the mural today, it'd been contemplating ways to rid herself of these crazy new feelings bubbling up. She definitely needed to reinforce her points. And no more hugs like yesterday. But she might also need to resort to something more drastic, like encouraging Evan to take Hattie up on the matchmaking she was always pushing. Not Rachael's favorite idea, but Evan dating would force them both to maintain strictly friendship boundaries.

Dinner ready, they fixed their plates. Rather than sitting shoulder to shoulder at the counter, she directed them to the table and took the seat across from him. Evan's forehead wrinkled, but he didn't press her on the change.

"Did you make any progress today?" he asked, digging into his dinner.

"I did." She spun her fork in the center of her noodles. "I have a direction now, but it's going to require a bit more work than I'd anticipated. And possibly your help." Evan would have a much easier time finding contact info when it came time to reach out to the families about using their children's likenesses.

"I'm there." His look and tone promised that. "But you may rescind your request once you see my artistic abilities."

"Right up there with your gift giving?"

"Even better." There came his lopsided smile that left her stomach feeling off-kilter.

"Yes, well—" She paused her fork spinning— "what I'm referring to runs more along the lines of research, so I think we're safe. I'll know more after this weekend. For now, I'm going to flesh out a few flowers, and then I'm setting everything aside while Gavin's here." Lifting her fork to her mouth, she grinned. "I plan on driving him crazy by never leaving his side."

"A little advice from a man who loves his mom dearly but was once a teen?" He grabbed a slice of garlic bread. "Be Tupperware, not Cling Wrap."

"Huh?"

"Give him a little breathing space. You'll up your chances of him coming home again."

"Good point. Crazy way to make it, but still a good point." She grabbed her water. "What about you? Did you have a chance to talk to your captain?"

"Late this afternoon, yeah. Since it's a cold case and I'm still recouping, he's fine with me looking into it. Not in any official capacity, but he does want me to keep him aware if anything comes to light." He hesitated. "So you know, they did classify Liliana as a runaway, which is why they haven't revisited her disappearance."

"Hope doesn't believe that."

"I know. Most parents don't."

"And you? What do you think?"

His mouth swished back and forth. "I'm reserving judgment until I look over her file. But either way, Rach, she's been missing fifteen years. Our chances of finding her are pretty slim."

"All the more reason to bring her case back to light. She'll never be found if people stop looking." And for whatever reason, she felt the need to help. Painting this mural was more than a shot at prize money for Gavin's college bill or a way to relaunch her art career. Those things had become the wonderful side effects of possibly finding a lost child.

"Which is why I agreed to do this. I want your expectations to be realistic, though."

"You've mentioned that."

"But I'm not sure you're listening." His hand shot up to ward off her response. "If I can head off you getting hurt, that's what I'm going to do."

Ah. Now she understood. Evan's main goal in life was to prevent harm—in every form—from reaching people, especially those close to him. Something she understood much better since hearing about Mandie. Her budding frustration fizzled. "I understand, and I promise, my expectations are very realistic. But that doesn't mean I'm not hopeful."

He studied her for a long minute. "Okay." Though based on the creases in his forehead, his internals and his response didn't match.

"Have you told the Perezes that you're looking into Liliana's case?"

He shook his head. "Not yet. I want to acquaint myself with the details first. I'll speak with them later this week."

"That makes sense." Hazy evening sun glowed through the window behind him, bringing out the golden tan still clinging to his skin. He was one of the most attractive men she'd ever met. Especially that big ol' heart of his. "No matter how this works out, Evan, thank you for at least looking into it. I know it seems funny for me to ask. I don't even know Hope."

"You made a connection with her. I get it."

"Understanding it and being willing to help are two separate things."

Sopping up some sauce with his garlic bread, he cocked the right corner of his lips. "At least one of those things should earn me a cookie."

She laughed.

"I bring you cookies." Rachael's announcement preempted the squeak of Evan's screen door. He popped up from his couch, doing his best to hide his pain at the fast motion. PT had been killer this morning. Afterwards, Rachael dropped him at home, then took off to paint again. She'd been focused on the mural, and he'd been trying to find out what he could on Liliana. Labor Day weekend quickly approached, and they'd be able to play then. Her family and his always joined together for a potluck, plus they'd be celebrating Abrielle's first birthday. Best of all, as far as Rach was concerned, Gavin was coming home tomorrow.

He blinked past the grogginess of his pain meds to accept the plate she offered him. The warm scent of oatmeal, butter, and chocolate made his mouth water. "Ah. My charms worked." He grinned up at her as he peeled off the tinfoil. M&Ms and chocolate chips made these monster cookies one of his favorites. "These smell amazing. Thanks, Rach."

"What are best friends for?"

He'd officially grown tired of that term. Ever since the Searchlight dinner when he'd challenged her about their status as *just friends*, *best friends* had made a strong showing in her vocabulary. If she used it one more time in regard to them, he was going to petition to have the phrase struck from the English language.

"More than cookies, I can assure you," he muttered under his breath before biting into one. Sweet heaven, what had she done to this poor cookie? He forced his jaw to continue chewing what tasted like a mushy salt lick and did his best to smile. "Mmm."

Rach's eyes narrowed in on him. "What's wrong?"

"Nothing." He swallowed and reached for his water on the coffee table. "Just a little thirsty."

She picked one up, chomped into it, and her eyes jarred open wide. Shaking her head, she dashed for his trash can and emptied her mouth. "Oh! That is awful!" She grabbed a water bottle from his fridge and took a long swig. "Why didn't you say anything?"

"I thought maybe it was my taste buds, not your cookies."

"Sure you did." She drank more water. "Penny keeps all her pantry items in these clear plastic containers. She labeled them, but I was distracted while baking, and I think I swapped salt for the sugar."

"That'd do it." Cookies in hand, he joined her in the kitchen. "On the plus side, you probably won't make the same mistake when you're baking Gavin's batch."

She took the plate from him and tossed it into his trash. "Change of plans. He's not coming home."

Her words floated out effortlessly, but when she faced him again, he caught the lines bracketing her mouth like little sentries forcing what she really wanted to say to remain inside. "Why not?" he asked.

Her shrug was a valiant attempt at looking like she hadn't a care in the world. "His text mentioned something about being added to the schedule at work, some project that's due, and a football game with the guys."

"His text?" Surely Gavin had called her, not texted the news.

"That's what I said." She leaned against his counter and crossed her arms.

"How are you doing with that?"

"Fine."

He wasn't sure if she was trying to sell that answer to herself or him, but he wasn't buying it. "I know you were looking forward to seeing him, so it's okay if you're not fine."

"He'll come home another time. What's important is he's taking his job and classes seriously, and he's making friends."

Her bottom lip trembled, and she sucked it in, no doubt hoping he hadn't noticed. But he had. He stepped closer to her. "Rach—"

She twisted around and began rummaging through his cupboards. "I came for some parsley. I'm out at my place, and I need it for the chicken and rice."

Per usual, she defaulted to her distract-and-retreat mode rather than face her emotions head on. He'd gone along with that status quo long enough. Rachael believed strength was not allowing any weakness. But true strength faced weakness.

He gently gripped her shoulder, wishing he had use of both arms so he could wrap her in a hug. She tensed beneath his hold. "Need something?" she asked, continuing to rummage through his cupboard. The one she'd organized last week, so she knew exactly where she'd placed the parsley.

"For you to admit you're upset."

"But I'm not." She lifted a tiny spice bottle in victory. "Found it." As she turned, her attention caught on a Ziploc bag filled with chocolate chip cookies. "Looks like someone else had the same idea as me."

He eyed her for a long minute, wanting to press. The way she set her jaw promised there'd be a fight if he did. That wouldn't lead anywhere productive. He'd give her space to settle, but as a reprieve, not a retreat.

Nodding to the bag, he took a step back. "Hattie brought those earlier this week." A repeat attempt at encouraging his taste buds to talk him into a date with Felicity.

"Mind if I have one? My mouth is all kinds of salty."

"Go ahead."

She pulled two out and handed him one. As she bit in, she released a tiny groan. "These are heavenly. Think Hattie will share her recipe with me?"

"She didn't make them."

"Who did?" Rachael popped the rest of hers in her mouth, then reached for another.

"Felicity."

Second cookie halfway to her mouth, Rach stopped. "Oh?"

He much preferred the slight tinge of jealousy she'd had in her eyes the other day around Auna to the curiosity there now. This reminded him too much of the look on Hattie's face every time she brought up Felicity. "Don't go there."

"Where?" She swiveled a glance around. "I didn't realize I was moving."

"You are. Right into matchmaker mode. I get enough of it from Hattie."

"You're an eligible bachelor. Of course your sister wants to set you up." She took another bite. "And for a cookie monster like yourself, I'd say she's on target if she's trying to set you up with Felicity."

"I agree these are delicious." No harm in that. "But I don't need any help being set up."

The curiosity in her eyes flared brighter. "No?"

"No. A guy doesn't need his big sister to find him a date."

"But what about his best friend?"

That was it. The petition started tonight.

"No."

As if the air between them swallowed his answer, she continued with her crazy notion. "Actually, it's a great idea. Who better to set you up than me?"

He could think of about a million different people. And no doubt each one would set him up with her. All they'd need to do was spend one-point-five seconds with the two of them together to see they created the elusive perfect match. So why couldn't she see it?

"Pretty much—"

His response was cut short by someone knocking on the wood of his screen door. "Anyone home?"

Dierks peered inside, caught sight of them, then let himself in. "Hey, Rach."

"Dierks." She nodded with a smile. He joined them at the counter, and she handed him a cookie.

He bit in. "Okay. These are amazing."

Rach eyed Evan with a devilish glint. "Evan and I were just discussing their amazingness, weren't we?"

Sighing deeply, he turned to Dierks. "What brings you by?"

His friend toggled a glance between the two of them, but wisely said nothing. Instead, he looked at Rach. "Just a little business."

Rachael straightened and grabbed the parsley. "And that's my cue to leave." She headed for the door. "I'm making chicken and rice if you want to stay, Dierks. I'll bring it over in about an hour."

"Wish I could, but I already have dinner plans."

"Next time then," she said as she slipped out the door.

"What's the dinner plans?" Evan settled onto a stool and pushed another one out with his foot.

Dierks joined him. "Mainly they involve eating."

His evasiveness only encouraged prodding. "With someone?"

"Yep." Dierks slapped the files he'd walked in with on the counter, but he didn't immediately address them. "How's PT going?"

"Hard, but necessary." Hated being sore but hated being out of uniform more. "Those the files I was asking about?"

"On Liliana Perez. And STAIRS popped out four others, based on hits from the criteria you sent me. I personally signed them out for you." Dierks had entered the parameters into the Storage and Informational Retrieval System they used that flagged any cases with similar keywords. Just because they shared the keywords didn't promise any connections, but it was a place to start. "I'll admit. I'm intrigued you're asking about this. Cold cases haven't ever snagged your interest." Dierks had tried before to entice him to his one-man department.

"Doesn't mean they can't." He flipped open Liliana's file. He had access to everything here from his computer, but his brain still preferred hard copies. Especially since some details could be missed when scanning information into the system. "I bumped into Hope Perez at the dinner for Searchlight. Rach and I spent some time talking to her, and Rach asked if I'd look into Liliana's disappearance."

"Ah. Now things are making sense." Dierks' fingers drummed against the countertop. "Captain Larry was pretty interested in your new curiosity."

No surprise there. If anything, it was his concern. With Evan's criminology degree and the way he'd lent a hand on a few cases, the powers that be had been trying to get him to move from patrol to CID. But Evan didn't want to work cases after the fact. What good was that? He wanted to stop crime before it ripped lives apart. Protect the innocent. Make a difference. He refused to give in or give up, and this felt like the first step in admitting his shoulder wouldn't heal. That he wouldn't be back in his squad car doing what he was meant to do.

"Tell him not to get any ideas."

"I don't *tell* Captain anything." Dierks straightened, arms crossed. "You can commit that kind of career suicide. No thanks."

"Career suicide would be Cap sticking me with you permanently."

"Would that be such a bad thing?"

"Yep."

"I don't think the families would feel the same." Dierks sighed when Evan remained silent. "It's good work, Evan."

"I'm not saying it isn't important, but for me it's more important to stop the people intent on committing these crimes." He scrubbed a hand through his hair. "A much better way to shrink your pile of case files."

Dierks shook his head. "Rachael nailed it on the head with that crazy nickname she calls you, because you've got a superhero complex." He crossed to the door. "But you're setting yourself up. You can't be everywhere at once, which means my pile of folders isn't going to stop growing anytime soon. I hate that these crimes happened too, Evan. I wish I could have prevented them, but at least I can still see that the people responsible are brought to justice."

With a nod goodbye, he slipped outside, leaving Evan with more than enough thoughts to contemplate, and none were ones he wanted to entertain. He'd look into this case for now, but this was by no means a permanent move. The only option he'd chase was the one he was meant to do. Be a patrol officer. He'd accept nothing less—and his body, along with everyone else, would have to fall in line.

Chapter Ten

"I caught you."

Evan's deep voice from his laundry room doorway startled her. Rachael quickly shoved the T-shirt in her hands behind her back. "Hey there. I thought you were exercising." He'd been in his basement workout room when she returned to fold the laundry she'd started this morning after their shared breakfast.

"That's what I wanted you to think." He inched into the room. "See, these past few weeks things keep showing up around my home."

"Oh?" She aimed for innocence. "What kind of things?"

The look on his face said not only wasn't he buying her cluelessness, but she had no hope of convincing him of it. He leaned against the washer, crossing his good arm over his sling. "Batman paraphernalia. At first it was a magnet on my fridge. But Dierks had visited that day, and he thinks your nickname for me is rather funny."

"It is pretty clever."

He nodded, his lips curling into a smile. "You do seem to think so." His eyes dropped to her hidden hands, then returned to her face. "Next it was a Funko Pop Batman on my bookshelf. But again, Dierks had been by the day before, and I couldn't be a hundred percent sure when it appeared."

"That's some serious slacking for someone normally so detail oriented."

"I blame the pain meds." He straightened. "It was the third piece that pointed my suspicion elsewhere. A Batman nightlight in my bathroom."

"That could come in handy in the middle of the night," she said solemnly.

"Yes. It was very thoughtful." Humor laced his words. "Thing is, with that one, Dierks hadn't been by."

She lifted her shoulders. "That you're aware of. He could have come when you were out. I have no doubt he knows how to pick locks."

"I have cameras in my doorbell. I'd have seen him."

"Could have come in the back door."

"Cameras out there too." Evan straightened and crossed the little distance between them. "There's only one person with all-access to my house." Leaning in, his breath warm against her cheek, he reached around to take the T-shirt from her hands. Though he straightened, he stayed in her space, filling it with a hint of sage and cedar. He shook out the T-shirt. Laughed. "Busted."

She reached for the faded gray shirt with the classic Batman logo in gold and black emblazoned on the front. "I knew I should have waited until you were in the shower." Awareness flared in his irises, and she took a step back. "To put this in your laundry basket. Down here. In the laundry room. Not your bedroom. Not that I don't go in there. Just not when you're showering."

He studied her with complete beguilement, his lips ticking farther up the longer she babbled. Finally, once she quieted, he spoke. "What would have been next?"

"Huh?"

"If I hadn't caught you, what would have been next?"

Batman boxers, but now the thought heated her cheeks. Which was funny seeing as how she'd been folding his laundry for nearly three weeks. "Socks."

His brow arched. "Socks. Really."

Her buzzing phone saved the day. She pulled it out of her pocket to see Jonah's name across the screen. "I should take this."

"Go ahead." He nodded. "I'm going to grab a protein shake from the fridge."

She slid her finger over the screen and answered. "Hey, there. You guys on your way?"

"Unfortunately, no. One of my trucks was in an accident." Jonah ran their family company, All Waste, and had garbage trucks all over Chicago.

"Is everyone okay?"

"Yeah. But I have a bit of a headache to take care of, so it'll be the morning before we're there."

"Not a problem. I'm glad no one's hurt." And that at least they were still coming. She was still processing Gavin's absence.

They covered a few details of the weekend, and then Jonah hung up. Rachael finished taking care of Evan's laundry, then met him in the kitchen. "Thinking about lunch?"

"Yeah, but I thought maybe we could eat out."

"Sounds good to me. Just let me take care of Clooney first."

"Sure." He hopped up. "I'll shower and then meet you over at your house."

Clooney danced at the front door, and Rachael put her into the gated area to run around while she ducked inside for her purse. Nabbing it from the kitchen counter, she noted a small vase with pink carnations, lily of the valley, and yellow crocuses. Seemed she wasn't the only one leaving gifts for people. Evan must have deposited these when she first showed up at his house, and she'd thought he was exercising. Sneaky man.

She picked up the square glass vase and inhaled their fresh scent. A beautiful way to brighten her day. Auna had mentioned that carnations represented a mother's love. As Rachael set the vase on the marble countertop again, her curiosity grew. She pulled out her cell phone to google the meaning of yellow crocuses. *Cheerfulness and joy.* Hmm. Next she entered Lily of the Valley. *Return to happiness.* Okay. This couldn't be a coincidence. Their meanings went together too well.

Tears stung her eyes. Evan was sending her a message through flowers. He knew her heart hurt with Gavin's last-minute change in plans, and he also knew she wasn't ready to talk about it. But instead of ignoring her pain, he addressed it in his own way to make sure she realized he saw it, and he was here should she need him.

It had been a long time since someone had cared for her in such a way.

Her front door opened and closed. "Rach?" Evan's voice called out.

"In here," she responded, dashing at her eyes before her tears could fall. Maybe she should call him Flash because he'd taken that shower in record time.

He entered the kitchen and stopped. His gaze bounced from her to the flowers and back, zeroing in as if trying to ascertain if his eyes were playing tricks on him. "Were you crying?"

Darn him and his timing. "No."

"Because it looks like you were," he said, his words clashing with hers. He took a step towards her. "I'm here if you want to talk."

She so appreciated his offer, but this sadness wouldn't go away if she started playing with it. "Thanks, but you know I'm not a crier."

"I know you don't let people see you cry. There's a difference." He stood strong, but it was his tender scrutiny of her that muscled into her heart. "I wish you'd show me your tears, Rach. I still have one good shoulder for them to land on."

"I appreciate it, but I really don't cry, Evan. Promise."

"Everyone cries."

That answer might truly fit some people, but it was the wrong size for her. She didn't do emotional breakdowns. They helped nothing and focused on loss rather than gain. "What do I have to be sad over?"

"Oh, I don't know, but maybe the fact that your son moved out and you miss him? Or that he reneged on his promise to come home? Perhaps that he told it to you in a text instead of taking the time to call?" Evan's lips swished to the side as his brows arched. "Should I go on?"

"No. That's plenty." She again fought the swell of unnecessary tears. "And I understand how for some people, those things could make them sad, but my situation is different. Gavin's plans might have changed this weekend, but he's still here. He's living a life I wasn't sure he'd even have. I'm thankful for that."

"You're allowed mixed emotions." His deep, rumbly voice offered comfort much like someone handing her a cozy sweater on a cold day.

Wrapped in its warmth, honesty slipped from her lips. "It feels ungrateful. To be upset over something I prayed for."

His entire face softened. "Sometimes grief and thankfulness go hand in hand." He inched closer. "Because you love people deeply, you cherish the moments you have with them. So when those times come to an end, you're thankful you had them, but you can also grieve that they're ending."

Grief was such a wasteful emotion. All it did was take from a person, and she was so tired of its greed. Refusing it entrance felt like the safest route.

She shook her head, the movement the only answer she could muster.

Evan squeezed her hand. "You don't always have to be the strong one, Rach. And you're not alone."

She didn't know how to be anything but that. Staying solitary and strong is what helped her survive.

It protected her.

She straightened and slipped her hand from his, her thoughts clearing. Crying on Evan's shoulder, no matter how good it might feel in the moment, made her vulnerable. Remember Point Four. She wasn't looking for anyone's shoulder. She tapped her stomach. "My stomach is growling. What were you thinking for lunch?"

His full concentration weighed heavy on her, as if her deflection of his comment wasn't acceptable. The longer she knew him, the more he challenged her. Typically it was through humor or a new experience, but this summer he started attempting to breach the locked places of her heart. That was an entirely new ballgame, and she still wasn't sure she wanted to play.

Evan drew in a long breath, then expelled it in a heavy sigh. "Just so happens Hope and Alvaro Perez have a convenience store one town over that supposedly sells pretty amazing tacos. What do you think about eating there, and then I could talk with them too?"

"Sounds like a brilliant idea." A good lunch along with somewhere else for Evan to place his attention? Definitely brilliant. She started for the door. Once on the front porch, she waited for him so she could lock up. "Just tell me where to point Sally."

"Straight to the junkyard," he mumbled as he scooted past her.

"Hey!" She hurried to catch up, donning the perfect amount of fake indignation while actually thankful for his teasing. This Evan challenged her in all the safe ways. But the other Evan who kept showing up, defying everything she thought she knew about their relationship? That Evan she wasn't quite sure what to do with.

"Take a left up there." Evan pointed to the green street sign ahead. The drive to Alvaro's only took twenty minutes, but he'd need every second and then some to wrap his brain around the fact that Rachael thought grieving a portion of her life equated to being ungrateful. Nothing could be farther from the truth.

"How long am I on this road?" Curiosity and a little skepticism dipped her brows as she took in their surroundings. They definitely weren't in downtown Abundance anymore. But though they passed chipped sidewalks and worn-out buildings, it was a safe area or he wouldn't have brought her along.

"About a mile." He looked her way. "Just to prepare you, there will be a few things I need to speak with them about privately."

She puttered along at the thirty-five speed limit. "Such as?"

"Such as things I'd like to keep private for now." Rach wouldn't reveal details to anyone, but he'd learned the fewer distractions while asking questions, the more likely he'd receive answers. Especially when he was asking them to remember a day that occurred fifteen years ago—not that they'd ever forget it.

"Right."

The white building with its blue overhanging roof came into view, and he pointed it out. Picnic tables took up the left side of the parking lot, most of them already filled with the lunch crowd. Rach pulled in, and they stepped out of Sally into the scent of seasoned beef, grilled veggies, and spicy peppers pouring from the propped-open front door. "Word is, these are some of the best tacos this side of the state."

"I'm inclined to believe it based solely on that smell." Rachael rounded the hood and joined him, glancing at the tables as she did. "Let's go order, and then I'll come out and save seats."

He nodded, and they crossed the parking lot. Inside, Alvaro Perez stood behind the counter. Tall and middle-aged, with a wide face and thick, black hair somewhat spiked in the middle, he reminded Evan a little of George Lopez. His big grin added to the effect.

"Hello," he greeted.

"Hi." Evan walked over. "You're Alvaro Perez, right?"

His smile dimmed as caution took its place. "I am."

Evan held out his hand. "I'm Officer Evan Wayne with Abundance Police, though I'm not here in an official capacity at the moment. I met your wife, Hope, at a dinner with Searchlight last week."

"For the mural that's being painted." Alvaro rounded the counter to shake Evan's hand. "She told me about you." He offered his welcome to Rachael next, his accent thick around his words. "And you're Rachael?"

"I am."

"Come. Hope's in the back, making lunch."

"You look a little busy. Is this a bad time?"

"No. Abbi and Ashley can handle the crowd for a bit."

They strolled to where Hope was working over their grill. Her blonde hair was pulled up in a knot with one of those colorful, stretchy fabric things restraining any loose strands. Her pale skin glistened from the heat that also flushed her cheeks to a rosy red. Still, she had a smile for them as they approached. "Officer Wayne. Rachael. It's good to see you again."

"You too," Rachael responded with the warmth of reuniting with a long-lost friend. "It smells amazing in here."

"My mother-in-law's recipes."

"She must be quite the cook." His stomach was already growling. "And please, it's Evan." Two young teens, maybe fourteen or fifteen, stood working the counter. One with black hair like Alvaro's and one with light-brown hair only a shade darker than Hope's. "Are these your daughters?"

"Foster daughters," the chestnut-blonde responded. She passed a loving look in Alvaro and Hope's direction before turning to Evan. "I'm Ashley."

"Abbi." the other lifted her chin in their direction as she bagged an order.

Rachael blinked between them, her forehead crinkled.

Hope wiped her hands on her apron. "Are you here for lunch?"

"Yes, but I also wondered if I could speak with you and Alvaro privately for a moment?" Evan motioned toward what he guessed was a small room down the hall.

They shared a tentative glance, then nodded. "Sure."

"Go, Mamá, we've got this," Abbi assured her.

"I'll order us some tacos and wait outside," Rachael offered.

With a nod, he followed Alvaro and Hope down the hall. They slipped into the small office where Alvaro closed the door. Evan turned to face them. "I wanted you to know that I'm looking into Liliana's disappearance."

Tears formed in Hope's eyes. "Thank you. She didn't run away. I know that."

He tended to agree. "I don't have any answers to give you right now, and you need to prepare yourself for the very real possibility that I won't."

Alvaro took Hope's hand. "We know that, but the fact that you would look into this at all … Thank you."

"Do you mind if I ask you a few questions? They may be ones you've already answered."

"Anything."

Evan spent the next ten minutes revisiting much of what he'd read in the file. Their answers lined up with everything he'd seen. There was one new question that he'd saved for last. "Do either of you remember seeing a blue Ford F150 around the time Liliana disappeared? It would have had a cap over the bed."

Hope straightened. "Yes. I told the police, but they didn't think it was anything." She looked to Alvaro, then to Evan. "I saw it often the week Lily went missing. I'd never seen it in our neighborhood before, but I thought maybe someone was doing work at a neighbor's. The afternoon she went missing, I noticed it drive down the street. I never saw it again."

"Did you give the police a license plate or description of the person driving?"

Her lips thinned. "Like I said, they didn't believe the information worth tracking down."

He'd look up the officer who worked the case fifteen years ago and speak with him to find out why, but he didn't see that going very far. "Do you think you could still describe the driver?"

"It was a man, but he always had a cap on. I couldn't see him well enough, and I never wrote down the license plate." She wiped away a tear. "I thought I was being paranoid, until Lily went missing."

"It's okay," Evan said softly. "You've been incredibly helpful."

Hope nodded and leaned her head against Alvaro's shoulder.

He'd give them a moment. "I'm going to join Rachael outside."

He stepped into the hallway, closed the door, then leaned against it. His nerves thrummed. Two other cases reported a blue truck. And while the connection might prove to be nothing, he didn't believe in coincidences.

With a deep breath, he refocused and headed out to find Rachael. Stepping into the sunlight, he slipped his sunglasses down and scanned the parking lot. She stood near a picnic table, wiping it off with a wad of napkins, and he couldn't take his eyes off of her. A guy must've designed that cut of jeans, because they were meant to be worn by a woman and appreciated by a man. The day baggy came back in style would be a sad one indeed.

As if she felt his stare, she straightened and drew a bead on him. Her right brow arched as she extended her arms and called. "What?"

He had no problem admitting he found her beautiful, if that admission wouldn't shut her down, but he valued his progress too much. So instead he opted to tease her. He strolled her way, waiting until he stood beside her to respond. "Wondering which you'll like better. The cricket tacos or earthworm enchiladas I added to our order."

Rach stumbled. "What?"

Oh, her look was priceless. And a little green. "Relax. I'm only joking."

"I'm not sure I believe you."

"Do you think I'd eat crickets?"

"No." Her hand went to her hip, and she craned her neck to look up at him. "But I think you'd try and make *me* eat them."

"And set myself up for your revenge? No, thank you."

She regarded him with a satisfied smirk. "Yes. The penalty for making me eat crickets would be very severe."

"I have no doubt." He settled on the bench.

She followed suit. "How'd it go in there?"

"As good as could be expected."

"Do you think you'll be able to find Liliana?"

"I'm going to try, but remember, there's a real possibility I won't."

"I know," she said softly.

It wasn't lost on him how important this was to her. She'd formed a fast and strong connection to Hope. The loss of a child no doubt created fertile ground for such associations to grow. "I'm going to do everything in my power to find answers. I promise."

Her eyes lifted to his. "I know that too."

In that moment, she conveyed complete trust in him. How did he convince her to move it from *him* to *them*? To their future together?

"Rach—"

"Your tacos." Hope approached their table, hands full and peacefulness again on her face. "I added some churros with our chocolate dipping sauce for dessert too—on the house." Setting the tray down, she pointed out each type of taco. Street style and size, there were shrimp, fish, and carne asada. "If you need anything else, let me know."

"Will do." Rach returned Hope's wave before picking up the shrimp taco. She motioned for Evan to do the same.

They both bit into it at the same time, and Rach released a tiny groan that encapsulated his own feeling. Definitely one of the best tacos he'd ever tasted. The other two didn't disappoint. He eyed the churros. If he were still able to work out at his normal level, he'd dig in. But he'd already indulged in several cookies this morning, which meant the churros would have to wait. "You go ahead. I'm gonna take a pass on dessert."

Rach picked up one of the cinnamon goodies. "You're the only man I know who counts calories."

"I blame you. You're constantly yammering on about the importance of my abs." Lifting the edge of his shirt, he tapped them. "You could give a guy a complex. Actually, I think you have."

"I think you mean an inflated ego." She reached over the table and grabbed at his shirt. "Put that down."

"Why?" He leaned out of reach. "All these ripples making you hungry for some ice cream next?"

"Ice cream?"

"Fudge ripple. It's one of your favorites." He let go of his T-shirt.

She groaned. "Maybe leave the ab jokes to me."

"Afraid of the competition?"

"I might be if there was some." She dipped the churro into the chocolate sauce. "And I don't yammer on about your abs."

"What would you call it then? Because the subject comes up around you frequently."

"It does not. I've mentioned it maybe three times."

"This past summer alone."

"I also recall talking about other features that would make you attractive to women. Yet you get stuck on the physical. Typical guy."

"Hey. Stereotype-free zone, please." Okay, so his earlier thoughts of her in those jeans completely fell into that category. Thing was, while her beauty might have been what caught his attention, it wasn't what held it captive.

"All right," she said, churro poised by her mouth, "tell me a nonphysical trait that you'd find attractive in a woman."

"I thought we were talking about the ones women like in men. Particularly the ones I contain."

"Except I've already listed those for you. Not my fault if you don't remember them." She finished off her cinnamon treat and reached for another. "Right now you're proving that men don't get stuck on the physical."

"Easy enough." He wiped his mouth, then crumpled his napkin. "Quick wit, caring for others, passable cook—"

"That's generous of you."

"Not looking for Betty Crocker. Just someone to share cooking detail with me." He looked at her. "Now may I continue on the list you requested?"

She motioned outward with her arm.

"Enjoys competition, likes long walks outdoors—"

"Does she like pina coladas and getting caught in the rain too?"

He tossed her a mock glare. "Are you even interested in my answer?"

"Absolutely. How else am I going to help set you up?"

That stopped him midreach for his drink. "I thought we'd agreed that you weren't."

"And I thought you were kidding." She sipped hers. "I promise I'd find you the perfect woman."

He already had, and she was sitting right across from him. "Maybe I already have my eye on someone. Someone who defines the traits I listed."

That set her ramrod straight. "Really? Who?"

For an intelligent woman, she was completely missing the boat on this one. "I'll tell you when I'm ready."

"She probably doesn't exist."

"I promise you, she does."

Her smile dimmed. Drink in hand, she stared him down. "I guess you don't need my help then."

No. But he would take her heart.

Chapter Eleven

Rachael woke to a cold, wet nose against her cheek. She blinked open and Clooney's huge brown eyes blinked back. Her dog's goofy grin offered a split-second warning before she leapt up. Squealing, Rachael dug her hands into Clooney's fur. "You're convinced you're a lap dog, aren't you." Pressing her face into Clooney's, she kissed the top of her head.

"She makes a pretty good alarm clock too." Jonah's voice reached from the doorway.

Rachael peered at him around Clooney. He was here way earlier than she'd expected him. "When you're not the one she's attacking."

"I've experienced that privilege often enough."

"You did buy her for me."

"A decision I've come to regret." A smile lit his icy blue eyes, then strolled into her room. He settled on the edge of her bed. "Since when do you sleep this late?"

That had her checking the clock. She rolled her eyes at him. "It's eight."

"Exactly. The morning's half over."

"Maybe for people who have a one-year-old as their alarm clock instead of a dog." She nudged him with her foot. "What'd you do? Leave at the crack of dawn?"

He shrugged. "Abrielle woke up, so Penelope and I decided to hit the road."

"Where is your better half and my niece anyway?"

"Downstairs." He scrubbed Clooney's fur. "Our little girl is like her aunt. When she's hungry, you better feed her."

"Hey!" Rachael cuffed his arm.

Jonah's deep laughs filled her room. "We brought pastries from Letizia's."

She launched from her bed. "Why didn't you lead with that?"

With Clooney on her heels, Rachael quickly brushed her teeth before meeting Jonah downstairs. Penny sat at the small table in their kitchen, feeding Ellie who sat securely in her high chair. Her niece's hands clapped together when she saw Rachael.

Rachael detoured from the pastries to Abrielle, crouching to give her a kiss.

"How's my favorite niece?" She ruffled the curls that were thickening on Ellie's head. "Can you say Auntie Rachael?"

The giggles in return were more than enough. Rachael turned to Penny. "Sorry, didn't mean to ignore you. Good morning to you too."

Penny waved her hand in the air. "I've been second place to this cutie since I had her."

Jonah delivered a mug of tea, licorice by its spicy scent, to his wife, pressing a kiss to her hair as he did. "You'll always be first place with me."

The love they shared filled the space between them, not only in their looks, but almost tangibly. Like Rachael could reach out and grab a piece of it. She'd already had her share though, and while she keenly felt the hole, she was okay with that space being hollow. The void hurt considerably less than the emptying had.

"Pretty flowers." Penny nodded to the square glass vase. "Where'd they come from?"

"A store." Not a lie. Evan had to purchase them from someplace, but she wasn't about to tell them he'd given them to her. They wouldn't see it for the friendly pick-me-up it was meant to be. Instead, she grabbed a mug of coffee and a cream-cheese Danish from the open box on the counter and joined them at the table. Outside the window, seagulls swerved and dipped through the blue sky and sunlight glinted off the lake. "Looks like we're going to have great weather for the weekend."

"Thankfully." Jonah picked at his muffin. Last year's cool rain forced them all indoors and canceled their annual game of Capture the Flag. They had played every Memorial Day and Labor Day for the past two years, and a win still eluded Jonah's team. He was a man on a mission. "Evan is going down this year."

Penny dropped a handful of Cheerios onto Ellie's tray. "Maybe we choose new team captains this year."

The side-eye Jonah landed on her had both the girls laughing. Ellie joined in too as if she understood the joke. Rachael lifted her mug. "Or choose a different game. You are playing against someone whose job contains SWAT training."

"Ah, but this year he's injured."

As if she needed the reminder. She set down her mug, her appetite waning.

Penny's concerned gaze met hers, and—if Rachael wasn't mistaken—her foot met Jonah's shin under the table. "How's Evan doing?"

"Better. I'm driving him to his PT this morning. Hopefully, he gets his brace off."

"I know he's anxious to be on patrol again," Jonah said.

"He is, but even if the brace comes off, he'll still have quite the wait." Possibly a permanent one.

"I wondered."

Penny held her tea, its steam curling up around her face. "What I want to hear about is this mural you're painting. Do you have any sketches worked out?"

"A few, though I haven't settled on the final compilation. Did you know flowers have meanings?"

"Like yellow roses are for friendship?" Penny asked.

"Yes, but I always thought it was unique to roses. Apparently, flowers have an entire language that people used to use." She blinked to the flowers Evan left her, and an involuntary smile spread across her lips. Penny inhaled, but before she could ask for details, Rachael continued, "I need to do a little more research, but I'm using the idea for part of the mural." She tore off a piece of her Danish. "Before I get too far into that today, I wanted to know if you needed help with anything?"

"Not that I can think of," Penny replied. "I have all the food on order for Ellie's party, along with balloons. We can pick those up Sunday after church."

"And I'll prep all the meat later today for tomorrow's potluck." Jonah and the guys ran the smoker along with a few grills all morning of their annual Saturday potluck. "Other than whatever favorites you told Gavin you'd make, we're set." He stood and wet a napkin to wipe Ellie's face. "By the way, where is he? I thought he was coming in last night."

"He had to cancel."

This had her big brother's eyes on her. "The entire weekend?"

"Yeah. His schedule is too full."

"Things are that busy for him?"

"He's getting used to college. It's an adjustment period." Forcing her into one too. She'd seen it coming. Thought she'd prepared. Which must be why she felt so unprepared for the avalanche of feelings. Blinking away stinking tears again, she stood to clear her dishes and her emotions. "I'm glad he's making friends and finally experiencing some of what he missed in high school."

"He definitely deserves it, but I would have liked to see him," Jonah said. "I'm going to finish unpacking the car." After another kiss to Penny's cheek, he disappeared out the side door.

"You doing okay?" Penny asked as Rachael cleared dishes. "Because I can't imagine Ellie heading off to college."

"You've got a lot of years until that happens." Telling her they happened in a blink was like trying to explain the speed of a roller coaster to someone who'd never ridden one. Until they climbed on and strapped in, they'd have no idea how fast the ride went or what the twists and turns would feel like. "And you'll have me to coach you through it."

"I doubt I'll handle it half as well as you do."

Her compliment strengthened Rachael's resolve. People relied on her to be strong.

"You will." She finished her Danish. "One thing that's helped is the change in scenery. Thanks for letting me move in."

"Stay as long as you like." Penny dished out more Cheerios for Ellie. "I'm sure the company next door plays a role too."

Oh, not her too. "It's definitely good to have a friend around."

Ellie started shoving all her Cheerios to the ground, and Rachael used the distraction to head upstairs before Penny could press the subject further. Quickly showering, she readied herself for the day. By the time she returned downstairs, Penny was putting Ellie down for a morning nap. Rachael nabbed a blueberry yum tart—like a homemade Pop-Tart—from the box and hoofed it over to Evan's. Jonah was chatting with him on the deck.

"I thought you were unloading your car," she noted.

"Evan wanted to give me an update on a few things around the house. Seems someone broke a seal on the window she went through."

Tipping her head, she delivered Evan an exasperated look. "I planned on having that fixed."

He tapped his sling. "Yes, but the guy who usually fixes things is currently out of commission."

"Not by you," she huffed, then handed him his tart. "Here. Thought you'd like some sustenance before your thrice-weekly torture."

"You are too, too kind."

"Yes. Maybe try and emulate my actions instead of tattling on me next time." She settled onto one of his chairs. "I know it'll be difficult, but I believe in you."

"You do provide me with plenty of practice in dealing with difficult," he teased, then shoved a bite into his mouth with a wicked grin.

A quick retort formed on her tongue, until she noticed Jonah watched them with more interest than he followed college football. He didn't need any more of a show. Easy redirect. "You going to bring the TVs out tomorrow for the Michigan-Ohio State game?"

Worked like a charm. Both he and Evan perked up at the mention of the fierce rival. "What do you think?" Jonah asked him.

"I've got plenty of extension cords. Game doesn't start till seven thirty. Great way to polish off leftovers and finish out our night."

The two hashed out details until it was time to bring Evan to PT. They climbed into his jeep and headed that way. "I plan on taking some pictures of the Cummings garden while you're doing therapy, but I'll be back in plenty of time to get you to work."

"You sure?" he asked. "I can always arrange another ride."

"With whom?"

"I do know other people, Rach."

Something prickled inside. She'd prepared herself to set him up with someone, but the idea that *he* had a someone in mind? That his heart was possibly invested elsewhere? Things became a little too real, and she didn't like how it made her feel. Reminded her of the nasty-tasting medicine she used to feed Gavin. He hated it, even if it was good for him. "Like your mystery woman?"

"No. She's busy today."

Relief was not the emotion to feel here. She pulled to a stop in front of the medical building. "Plan on me in an hour."

"All right."

He shut the door, and she drove off. Only took ten minutes to reach the garden. She ducked into the magical place and stood still. Birds swooped from branches, calling to one another as they did. Butterflies danced among tall, pink-capped flowers. Wind tipped with the crispness of fall brushed against her cheeks, and she inhaled the scent of flowers, earth, and pine. Stepping farther in, she walked a few of the paths. Halfway down one, Auna knelt in the grass, digging in the dirt. Not wanting to scare her, Rachael softly called out, "Hey, Auna."

She turned and smiled. "Rachael. Good to see you."

Holding up her camera, she said, "I wanted some pictures to study while I'm painting."

"Take as many as you need. I'm planting some bulbs for spring."

Rachael strolled over to her. Auna had dug several holes along the perimeter of one of the beds and was tossing in bulbs. "What flowers are those?"

"Tulips, crocus, allium, and daffodils." She started pushing dirt over them. "They'll bloom in early spring. Sometimes when snow is still on the ground." She smiled over her shoulder. "They're some of my favorites."

"I know crocuses mean joy and cheerfulness, but what about the others?"

Auna stood and brushed her gloved hands against her jeans. "Tulips are for perfect love. Allium represents strength, and daffodils mean hope."

The allium and daffodils could definitely be used in the mural.

"Thanks." She slung the camera strap around her neck. "I've really fallen in love with this idea of floriography and want to incorporate it into the mural. Do you have any resources you could recommend?"

"Do I!" Auna's eyes brightened. "If you'd like, I can loan you some from my own library."

"That'd be great." She rattled off her phone number. "Text me, and we can set up a time and place to meet." Glancing at her watch, she motioned toward one of the paths. "I should grab a few shots before I need to pick up Evan."

Auna's face softened at his name. "Tell him I said hi."

Her request, accompanied with that look, tossed Rachael off balance. "Will do."

She headed deeper into the garden, her eyes on the flowers but her mind very much on Auna and Evan. She'd seen the easy way they interacted. And just now there was something in her eyes that showed she deeply cared for him. Could she be his mystery woman?

As amazing as Auna was—and Evan deserved an amazing woman—putting a face to his mystery woman and helping set them up was proving to be a tough pill to swallow indeed.

At sixteen, freedom was his driver's license. At eighteen it was the idea he was finally an adult. Moving out at twenty-one beat them both. But nothing, nothing compared to the freedom of this moment.

"So I don't have to wear it anymore?" As far as he was concerned, Becky could keep his sling to use for kindling.

Her eyes sparkled as she laughed. "Well, I think you'll want to wear it still at night. But during the day, unless your shoulder feels fatigued, nope. You don't have to wear it."

She skyrocketed up the list to one of his favorite people. "Does this mean I might be on patrol earlier than expected?"

"I'm not ready to move that date yet."

"But it could?"

"Anything is possible." She handed him his sling. "I can guarantee you, however, that if you push yourself too hard, that date *will* move. Backwards."

He took it from her. "I hear you." Heard her and would listen even if it chafed him. Going backwards would rub worse.

Gathering his things, he stuffed them in his backpack, then headed to the door. Rachael leaned against the Jeep, waiting for him. She practically bounced when she saw him. "She freed you!"

"She did." Her excitement was contagious.

"This calls for a celebratory dinner." She opened the driver's door. "Maybe with Jonah and Penny?"

"Sounds good." He stopped her from hopping inside. "Oh, no. I've been cleared to drive. Those keys are mine."

"Wow. Way to kick a girl to the curb."

"Nope. Just to the passenger side. That's where sidekicks are supposed to ride."

She rounded the hood. "Thought we settled that I'm not a sidekick."

"I know. But it's fun to tease you." He liked how her nose scrunched up when he did.

Shutting the door, she regarded him. "Most people have no clue that Batman has a sense of humor."

"It's the mask."

"Really? I always thought it was the cape. Makes him look like Dracula from the back. And there's nothing funny about draining someone's blood."

"Wow. That took a turn to the macabre."

"Look at you and your fancy words."

"It's all the crossword puzzles I've been doing while recouping. Guess they're paying off."

"Batman does need to be mentally strong as well as physically, seeing as how he doesn't actually have superpowers."

"And we've circled round to my muscles." He tossed her a look. "You are obsessed with them, aren't you."

"I was talking about your brain."

"The sexiest muscle of all."

She guffawed. Real. True. Actual guffawing happening beside him. She spoke between the pops of laughter. "Men do not think the brain is the sexiest muscle of all."

"Untrue. I am incredibly attracted to smart women."

That had her sitting straighter. "So ... your mystery woman, is she intelligent?"

"Incredibly."

"And pretty?"

"Beautiful."

"But her brains are what attracted you?"

"Brains, humor, compassion. And looks. I won't lie." Rachael had it all and then some. He cast another fast glance her way. She was rubbing that thumbnail of hers. He refocused on the road. "Why so curious? I thought we'd already been over this."

"We have, but I'm still trying to figure out if she's real."

"She's very real."

"Then care to tell me who she is?"

The slight edge in her voice surprised him. "Eventually."

"You are so frustrating." She slumped into her seat.

"And funny. Don't forget that."

He caught her eyeroll, and he wasn't even fully looking in her direction. It was enough to distract him from the traffic quickly stopping in front of them. "Hold on!" Their tires squealed as he slammed the breaks, their seatbelts jarring them to a stop. Thank the Lord it was before hitting the vehicle in front of them. Catching his breath, he turned to her. "You okay?"

"Fine." Her blue eyes looked like matching saucers. She pressed into her seat, rubbing her chest. "How's your shoulder?"

"Okay." If he'd been in the passenger seat, the belt would have tightened over his bad shoulder.

The traffic started to inch forward, and he moved with it. Looked like a broke-down car ahead and some rubbernecking knucklehead had caused the backup. Thankfully, he hadn't caused an accident. Flashing lights in his rearview said the stalled car had been called in and the stranded motorist would receive aid, so Evan drove past.

Rachael bent to pick up his backpack and everything that spilled from it. She held up the pictures of other girls. "Are you looking into more than Liliana's case?"

"I am. There's a few possible connections."

She sifted through the pictures, studying each one. "All these girls are missing too?"

"They are." Not as long as Liliana, but long enough that new leads had stopped rolling in.

Rachael's hand stilled on Liliana's photo, and she traced the lines of her face. "Hope said she'd be twenty-seven now."

Her soft heart did something to Evan's. He hadn't been lying about falling for every single thing about her, but her compassion is what captured him most of all.

"Yeah, she would." He flexed his fingers on the steering wheel. "All those years, taken from them. Did she need braces or glasses or did she sail through her teen years? Did her hair grow wavy or did it stay straight?"

"You talk about her like she's still alive."

"Until I know otherwise, I'll pursue this as if she is. She deserves that, and so do her parents." What they truly deserved was for this never to have happened. And if the perpetrator still sucked in air, he'd find him and stop him from ever taking a child again. "No one should have to wonder about the lost future of a loved one."

"I agree." Rachael tucked the photos into the folder and placed it into his backpack.

It hit him again how she was one of those people. She'd lost a future with her husband and little girl. Not through the same type of tragedy, but they'd been stolen from her, nonetheless.

Thankful to be free from his sling, he slipped his hand over to cover hers. "I'm sorry, Rach."

Without missing a beat, she responded, "It's okay. Not that it's what I would have chosen, but life has gone on. And it's turned into a good one."

Good, yes. The mere fact she could utter those words endeared her to him all the more. But the more he got to know her, the more he realized she'd also constructed a controlled and safe life. From the few stories Jonah shared these past few years, she was a much different Rachael than the daring adventurer she'd once been. Understandable, with the losses and hardships she'd endured, but did she ever miss that old side? Or grow tired of always portraying strength? She tried hard to hide it, but he saw her emotional muscles trembling. That she'd practically shown up on his doorstep in her weak moment stoked something deep and protective in him. "You deserve better than good, Rach."

"Says who?"

"Me."

She slipped her hand from his. "What does that look like to you? Better than good."

"Fullness. Freedom from fear." Blunt words might be too much, but he could lay groundwork. "Love."

"I have love." She did, but it wasn't the kind he'd meant. "And fear can be healthy."

"It can also immobilize."

From the corner of his eye, he caught her flinch. "There are times where not moving is the safest course of action."

"Such as?"

"Bear attacks."

"I'm pretty sure they instruct you to move away slowly."

"Unless it's trying to eat you. Then you need to lie flat and still."

"Any other examples besides bears?" he pressed.

"When Gavin was little I'd tell him if he was lost to stand still, and I'd find him."

The precinct came into view, and he slipped into a parking spot. Then he turned to her. "You make a good point with that one."

"Thanks." She climbed out and rounded to his side.

He met her by his door and dropped the keys into her hand. "See you around five?" Last time she'd need to drive him home. Well, technically this time he'd do the driving.

"I'll be here." With a wave, she drove off.

Standing on the corner, he watched her while mulling over her words. She didn't have a clue how they described her, but he did. And they'd forced an internal promise out of him. Rachael Stark was standing still, lost in past pain, and he had every intention of finding her and bringing her heart home to his.

Chapter Twelve

If Evan Wayne thought she was standing still, he was in for a rude awakening. "You know I'm faster than you." His voice deepened as he crouched, ready to dodge around her. After only twenty-two minutes, he'd located their flag and locked eyes on it.

At least he thought he had.

She did her best to hide her grin. Her yellow bandana slipped into her eyes, and she jammed it up on her forehead. "Come on, don't make me look bad to my brother."

"Your brother should have done a better job hiding that flag." He paced to the left, his red bandana wrapped tightly around his corded forearm. "Or a better job of protecting it."

She straightened. "Hey!"

He used the moment to dash past her. She turned on her heel and followed, pushing to her full speed. She still couldn't quite catch him. Didn't matter. He'd drop his guard to grab the flag, thinking he was in the safety zone. That's when she'd make her move.

Sure enough, Evan grabbed the yellow piece of fabric from the tree, raising it overhead with a shout, no clue it was a decoy. She slowed, not wanting to hurt him. If he wasn't nursing an injury, she would have plowed straight into him, taking them both down. Instead, she stopped nearly toe to toe and poked a finger in his chest. "You're caught."

"Nice try. This is the safety zone." He hopped back and forth on his toes. "And I know I can outrun you to my camp, but feel free to try and keep up."

"Might want to take a closer look at that flag."

His forehead crinkled, and he lowered his hands. Yep. There it was. His eyes widened, and she didn't try to hide her laughter as he groaned. "You're a sneak."

"And you're my prisoner." Taking him by his biceps, she walked him to their jail, which already held his sister Hattie and one of his nephews, Jude. "Enjoy." She dropped him off and waved at Belle who was guarding their prisoners. Somewhere out there, Micah, Jonah, and Penny were looking for the red team's flag. Evan's parents and Walter had agreed to watch the littlest kids inside.

Seven-year-old Jude gaped at his uncle. "Seriously? You got caught?" He huffed to the ground. "We're gonna lose."

"Nah. This is all part of my plan," Evan encouraged.

Rachael tossed him a water bottle. "Your plan was to get captured?"

"Keep your friends close, enemies closer, right? Especially when those enemies look as cute in cutoffs as you do." He wiggled his brows, and her knees weakened.

Drat. Her immunity to his flirty charm had worn off completely, and she desperately needed another shot.

A battle cry split through the air behind her. Evan's other nephew, Nick, streaked across the lawn with ... their yellow flag in his hand? Rachael pushed into pursuit, Evan's laughter following her. Her fingers skimmed Nick's shoulder right as he crossed the boundary line and started a dance that looked an awful lot like his uncle's. "It worked! Uncle Evan, it worked! We win!"

Open mouthed—and yeah, a little impressed—Rachael watched Evan strut her way. He high-fived his nephews, then drew himself toe to toe with her, his confident swagger alive and well. "Red team wins. Again."

"I can't believe you tricked me."

"You mean like you *tried* to do to me?" He leaned toward her. "I do reconnaissance for a living. I'm trained to spot the tiniest tripwires. I've led teams into hostage recovery. I'm ready for any move you make."

"Cocky much?" Well, she knew a move he wouldn't be ready for. One that would silence his lips while still putting them to work.

The fleeting idea and resulting image shocked the daylights out of her, and she took a step back. As if he read her unbidden thought, his eyes flared and, oh boy, that look sent fire clear through to her fingertips.

"Don't tell me we lost again." Jonah's voice doused the rising flame.

Sucking in air, she slapped on the world's most awkward smile and turned toward Jonah and Penny approaching across the lawn. Her brother's gaze bounced between the two, and his mouth opened, but Penny slapped a hand against his stomach. "It appears we have," she said.

Nick and Jude were still buzzing with excitement. As Nora, their mom, came from the woods beside Evan's house, they raced to her with the yellow flag in their hand. "We did it, Mom! Uncle Evan's plan worked, and we won!"

Nora braced herself for their impact, hugging them tight. "Great job, you guys. I knew you could do it." Her husband, Tate, arrived from his hiding place and joined the group hug.

Hattie sidled up to her brother and punched him in the arm. "Way to go, our fearless leader. Another year, another win for the Waynes."

Stepping into the fray, Belle and Micah looked to Jonah. "We'll get them next year." Micah slapped Jonah on the back.

A round of commiseration punctuated by smack talk from Evan's family circled the group until Belle piped up. "All right. Pregnant lady who's hungry here. How about those desserts we were promised?"

They'd eaten lunch a few hours ago and put dessert on hold until after the game. As everyone headed to gather their contribution to the table, a car turned up the drive. Rachael glanced over her shoulder, then executed a doubletake. "Gavin?"

Sure enough, her son parked and hopped out of his vehicle. "Hope there's food left for me."

Rachael launched herself at him and wrapped him in a hug. "You came home."

Taller and stronger than she, he was still her little boy. "You're going to snap me in half," he squeezed out on a chuckle.

Clooney dashed across the yard, a blur of fur and barking, until she reached them both. Dancing under their feet, she demanded her own attention from Gavin.

"Oh, sorry." Rachael released him so he could greet Clooney. "Guess I missed you just a little." This had been the longest they'd ever been apart. But it wasn't simply the time, it was the space she felt growing between them. It needed to be there. This transition was right and healthy. Her head knew that, but her heart was taking longer to be okay with the change.

"I missed you too, Mom." He rounded the car to grab his bag from the trunk as Clooney trotted beside him. Most freshmen weren't allowed cars on campus, but because Gavin still had checkups every three months with his doctor in Chicago, he'd been granted a medical exception.

The rest of her family greeted him. Jonah took his bag to drop inside while Evan's mom hauled out leftovers from earlier in the day. Didn't take long for them all to pile their plates and settle into chairs. Rachael spent the next hour catching up with her son before Walter snagged him to round out a foursome for a round of Bottle Bash. Micah needed a partner because Belle was napping.

Rachael swapped seats to sit by Jonah. "I asked Gavin why his plans changed."

"Oh?"

"He said there'll be a dozen more football games he can go to this season, but he realized how much it meant to me that he came home. Especially since he'd told me he'd be here, and a man keeps his word."

Jonah dragged his thumb across the condensation on his glass pop bottle. "You raised a good kid, Rach."

"He is a very good kid, but he's also just a kid." She knew his shortcomings as well as his strengths. "He wouldn't have come up with that on his own."

Bottle in hand, Jonah spread his arms out. "Don't look at me. I didn't say a thing to him, though I definitely wanted to." He relaxed into his chair again and closed his eyes. "Someone beat me to it."

Evan.

Rachael looked across the yard to where he chatted with his sisters. As if he sensed her stare, he glanced her way. His eyebrows dipped like they did when he was reading her thoughts, then he said something to Hattie before walking toward her. Rachael met him halfway, and they strolled to the edge of the lawn behind everyone.

"Need something?" he asked, hands in his pockets. Seeing him out of that sling evoked joy, even if the thing did serve as a constant visual for Point Five— his dangerous job.

"Did you call Gavin and tell him to come home?"

"I called Gavin and encouraged him to keep his word."

"Because a man keeps his word?" she echoed his advice.

Evan shrugged. "Well, yeah. And sometimes at eighteen years old, us guys need a little course correction."

"And you offered that to my son."

Lines creased across his forehead. "I'm sorry. I didn't mean to overstep, Rach, I—"

"Thank you."

His mouth snapped shut, and those big hazel eyes of his held hers. "You're welcome."

Oh, sometimes with this man, her heart wanted more than it could handle.

She smiled up at him, forcing it to behave. "Your mystery woman is going to be one lucky lady, if you ever get around to asking her out."

He rolled back on his heels, then forward again. "I will. I have a plan."

"Going for the long game then?"

"I'm a patient guy."

"Don't be so patient that you lose your chance with her."

"That your honest advice?" he smirked.

"Yeah. Sometimes you just have to go for it."

His smirk deepened and the gold in his irises glistened with that dangerous fire she kept playing with. "That so." He drew the two words out, his voice deliciously low.

Time for some fireproofing before she got burnt.

"Yep, which is why I'm going to help you." She scanned the yard and sure enough, Hattie stood by the dessert table, watching them. "Hattie," she called, "Evan's wondering if you can give him Felicity's number."

"Absolutely!" Hattie set down her plate and headed their way.

Evan's dimple smoothed as his jaw jutted. "Rach—"

She patted his chest as she made her escape. "Thank me later."

Based on his scorching look—this one with an entirely new source flame—*thank you* was the last thing he'd be offering.

Good.

So why did she feel so bad?

By the time he'd extradited himself from his sister's matchmaking prowess, they'd put away the dessert table and most of the group's concentration centered on a nail-biting game of lawn Jenga. Currently Tate had Nick on his shoulders so he could move a block while Jonah conferred with Micah on their next move. Micah's little girl, Anna, bounced beside them begging to be the one to pull the piece. Evan chuckled. The game would be over quickly.

"I sure have liked how our Labor Day celebration has grown," his mom said as she joined him. The top of her curly brown hair reached his shoulder, but she could still grab his ear and drag him to her eye level when making a point. Every once in a while she'd remind him of the fact, in case he'd forgotten. As if he would. His respect for her far outweighed her size.

"Me too."

"They're a really great family."

"They are."

She looked up at him. "Your sister seems rather intent on setting you up with her best friend."

He held in a groan. "I'm aware."

"But from what I can gather, there's another friend you're interested in."

His sisters gave him grief about Rachael. Hattie particularly. Partly because she wanted him with Felicity, partly because she worried Rachael would break his heart. They never discussed any of this around the parents. Yet, as usual, Mom didn't miss a beat when it came to the details of their lives. "Right now that interest is one-sided."

She followed his look to where Rachael sat with Gavin. "I wouldn't be too sure of that."

He could use her optimism. "She wants to set me up with someone else."

"I don't doubt it." Mirth lifted Mom's voice. "I set your father up with my college roommate."

"You what now?" He jerked his gaze to Dad, tossing a baseball with Jude. "You never told us that." Far as he and his siblings knew, Mom and Dad only had eyes for each other from their first date.

"Oh, yes. When I first met your father, I was determined not to fall in love with him."

It was like hearing a familiar word, then learning he'd pronounced it wrong his entire life. "Seriously?"

She laughed. "Quite. I'd recently gotten out of a bad relationship, and in many ways, your dad reminded me of my ex-boyfriend." Across the lawn, Dad raced for Jude's misguided lob. "But he was different in the most important way."

"How?"

Her sigh was the same as his sisters' when they finished off one of those romance books they were always reading on the beach. "His love for me. Patient, unconditional, and all-consuming."

That last adjective she could have left off. And the look on her face bordered what, as a boy, he'd have called mushy. Yet this full-grown man had no problem admitting he wanted Rachael to one day look at him that way.

Mom patted his chest, leaving her palm over his heart. "You're like your father in a lot of ways, Evan. She'll come around. I did."

He stared at her hand on him, then to her warm, hazel eyes. Mom had always been where he'd brought his fears, and she'd calm them. Middle of the night thunderstorms. Baseball tryouts. What happened to Mandie … "What if she doesn't?"

Tenderness tipped up her lips, and a calm assurance steadied her voice. "Then she's not the one for you, and—I know it may sound trite, but—there's someone even better out there who you haven't imagined yet."

If that scenario happened, her words would prove true, because he couldn't imagine anyone other than Rachael.

With one more pat, Mom removed her hand. "I promised your dad I'd beat him at Bottle Bash." She left to join him across the lawn. Evan had always wanted a love story like his parents', he just didn't realize how much like them it would be.

With renewed focus, he headed Rachael's way and the open camp chair beside her and Gavin. "Thanks for siccing my sister on me."

"Did she give you Felicity's number?"

"Programmed it right into my phone." Not that he planned on using it.

"Have you called her yet?"

Evan settled his full focus on Rach. Her fingertips rubbed against her thumbnail. She worked the inside of her bottom lip. And her knee bounced ever so slightly. Her body spoke a whole different language than her mouth. Now if he could get them on the same page.

He lowered into his chair. "Nope."

"Every minute you waste is one less minute without her amazing cookies."

"I'll take that into consideration."

Gavin leaned his elbows on his knees and turned his way. "You're getting set up with someone?"

"That's the plan."

"His sister's best friend."

Their answers toppled over each other's.

Gavin bounced a glance between the two. "Good luck with that," was all he offered, then nodded to Evan's house. "You still have your slackline up?"

Way to divert the conversation. The kid had good senses and knew how to follow them. Smart boy. "I do. Not that I'm using it."

"Mind if I try? The guys strung one up on campus, and I'd love the practice."

"Sure." Evan stood. "But I only have my high line up. We'll need to string one closer to the ground." He'd walked a slackline for years, constantly challenging himself to go higher. His current height was fifteen feet, and he needed a ladder to reach the platform he'd built in the trees. There was something exhilarating about finding balance that far off solid ground, but it wasn't the place to learn the skill.

Rachael followed them. Within twenty minutes they had a line securely strung between two trees and only three feet up. Bright yellow, the taut, webbed polyester was two inches wide and flat. This was the same spot he'd taught himself, and he'd sunk two tall poles into the dirt to grip when climbing onto the line. The trick was letting go. Gavin seemed to already know the basics. While he practiced, Evan focused on Rachael. "You still want to learn?" She'd bugged him about it nearly as long as she had about skateboarding.

Rach nodded. "I've seen you do it. Should be easy." She pointed to the high line. "I bet I'll be up there before the day is over."

"Sure you will," he said as he tapped her arms and hips. "These are your swivel points." He used his feet to knock her knees and ankles next. "You'll use them for balance."

"Like this?" She spread her arms like an eagle.

He jabbed his good arm out and shoved her hard enough to mess with her stability but not hurt her.

"Hey!" She windmilled her arms and swiveled her hips to regain her equilibrium.

"Like that."

Gavin laughed, and Rachael tolerated them both with a narrow glance. "All right. I think I've got it."

That elicited more laughter from them both. Evan nodded to her legs. "Balance on one."

"You gonna come at me again?"

"You wanna learn how to do this?"

She sighed and stood like a flamingo. This time he knocked her from the side and taught her how to use her knees and ankles to hold steady. For the next few minutes he brought her through more movements, and once he deemed them fluid enough, he pointed to the line. "You're next."

Gavin executed his last two steps, reaching the tree at the far end. He'd already made it twice, falling only a handful of times along the way. He hopped to the ground. "All yours, Mom. I'm gonna head over and play with Anna. She wanted me to take her and Sparkles swimming."

Jonah had purchased his niece about a million floats to use in the water, but the glittery unicorn was her favorite. As Gavin returned to the other house, Evan walked with Rachael to the tree. "He's a really great kid. That water is freezing."

"Anna adores him and has him wrapped around her tiny finger. I think she reminds him of Brie."

"They were close?"

"Inseparable. She toddled after him everywhere. I think he misses being a big brother."

"Ever think of making him one again someday?"

Surprise lifted her brow. He'd startled himself too, yet the question didn't feel off base. She leaned against the tree. "Not at all."

"Because you don't want to do diapers again?"

"Because I'm not falling in love again."

"That sounds lonely."

"Not when I have family and friends." Her grin knocked him straight in the chest. "And you."

Except they couldn't sustain this level of relationship for a lifetime. Not when he wanted more. Either things worked out between the two of them, or at some point he'd have to move on. No other woman was going to be okay with their close friendship, and he wouldn't blame her. Whoever he ended up with deserved—and would have—all his heart. If it wasn't Rachael, he'd need some serious excavation to dig her out from where she'd burrowed under his skin.

"Let's see if you still call me friend after trying this out."

"Like I said, easy."

He tapped the line. "All right then, hop on up."

She placed her foot on the line, and it quivered as if made of Jell-O. Backing off, she looked at him. "I thought it was secure."

"As secure as a line strung between two trees can be." He tapped her right foot with his toe. "Use this leg. It's your dominate one."

"And you know this how?"

"From watching you."

Her cheeks lifted above her smile. "You are observant."

"It's my job." And his current fascination. "Now hop up."

She placed her right on the line and rested her weight on it. The line wobbled uncontrollably. Her knuckles turned white as she gripped the pole in attempt to steady herself.

He pressed his hand along her spine. "You can do it. Use your swivel points. It's actually easier once you get both feet off the ground."

She looked at him like he'd tried to convince her she could walk on water, and she braced her left leg under her.

Obstinate. That bullheadedness had gotten her through some very tough times. It also stopped her from experiencing some pretty amazing ones.

Hands lifted, he stepped away and let her fight out her stubbornness against his earned knowledge. She shifted her weight from her left leg to the right, but the moment she leaned into that leg, the line wobbled wildly. She gripped the pole tighter, but no matter her position, with one leg on the ground and one on the slackline, she could not find balance. She peered over at Evan, who remained silent. Arms crossed, he lifted his good shoulder in a nonchalant shrug.

Grunting at him, she returned to trying things her way. After a few more minutes of battling, she looked at him again. Sweat dotted her brow, and frustration puckered her lips. "Can you help me?"

"I did."

That had her facing him like he had a loose screw. "Did I miss it? Because all I've seen is you watching me."

He straightened with a sigh. "I told you, you need to get both feet off the ground. I know it feels like that's less stable, but until you're willing to try, there's nothing else I can do. You'll never walk that line with one foot on the ground."

Hesitation carved tiny lines along the planes of her face. She studied the line with the same intensity he poured over the cold cases. They both searched for answers. Right now, hers were easier to find if she'd just, "Trust me, Rach."

She didn't respond, but she did refocus. Shoulders lifting, she leaned hard into the pole. Then in one fast, fluid movement, she took the leap. Hauling herself upward, she removed her left foot from solid ground. The wobbling immediately lessened.

"Good!" Evan instantly stood at her side, struggling to keep his hands at his side. Her fresh excitement and that look—like she'd conquered gravity itself—made him itch to seal the moment with a congratulatory kiss. "Now stretch your left foot and arm out to the side for balance. Keep your eyes on where the line is anchored in front of you."

She followed his instructions and the wobbling lessened more. But her smile grew, right along with his temptation.

He focused instead on keeping her triumphant moment going. "Now try and bring your left foot in front of your right."

Inching it around, she looked down for placement. The line trembled, and her body swayed.

"Eyes up. On the anchor," Evan coached.

She flicked her gaze to the metal piece then immediately down again as if she couldn't escape the instinct.

"Eyes! Eyes! Eyes!"

Too late. Her hard-fought balance disappeared, she overcorrected, and tipped off the line. Hand still on the pole, she managed to keep herself upright.

Evan wrapped his arm around her shoulder and squeezed. "Not bad."

"Not bad?" She peeked up at him. "I didn't even take a step."

"But you stayed upright longer than I did my first time."

"How awful were you?" She laughed as she turned to try again. Her tenacity didn't surprise him at all.

"Remember, keep your eyes on the anchor."

She hauled herself up and regained her position. "If I do that, I won't know where to place my steps."

"You will. You're going to bring your foot around and feel for the line before placing your weight onto it. But your eyes have to stay on the anchor. The line stretches from it and your next step attaches to it. You maintain your balance by keeping your eyes on what holds the line."

"If you say so." This time only a hint of skepticism lined her words.

Once again she inched her foot toward the line. Her focus shifted down and everything shook.

"Eyes," Evan called.

"Argh!" She fixed again on what was holding her up. "I want to see my next step."

"Trust that the line is there. Reach around, eyes on the anchor, and place your foot. This is about trusting what you can't see. If you try and look down, you'll fall again."

But her eyes possessed a will of their own. Every time she tried to take a step, she glanced down and promptly fell. After about twenty tries, Evan placed his hand on her shoulder. "Let's take a break."

"I can do this."

"I know you can, but you need to keep your focus on the right spot." He hopped up and demonstrated.

She was immediately beside him. "Get down from there. Your shoulder."

"Is fine. I'm only a few feet off the ground. I'm not going to fall"—he paused and took another step— "unlike some people."

"Easy to say when you're hardly shaking."

He laughed. "It wasn't so easy to learn. You'll get there." He turned and walked the other way. "Like everything, this takes practice. You're fighting your natural instincts. Retraining your muscles." He tossed her a grin. "This is really good for the core, you know."

She stood there, watching. "Please, do not use this as another excuse to show me your abs."

"Wouldn't dream of it." He hopped down beside her, enjoying the pink on her cheeks. Did something to him that he had an impact on her. She didn't fight their connection, but she worked awfully hard to deny their attraction. "You'd have a hard time keeping your hands to yourself."

The pink flushed to red. "Yes. The desire to throttle you is often hard to control." She brushed past him, retreating toward Jonah's cottage. "I should check on Gavin."

Huh. Using her teenage son for an excuse as if he were a toddler rather than an adult. With a chuckle, Evan followed her. If she were leaning on such flimsy excuses, he was making headway, and it had to leave her feeling wobbly. Now to convince her to pick both feet up off the ground and chance walking toward a future with him.

Chapter Thirteen

The dawn of a new day was like a tiny miracle Rachael had the privilege to take part in. One that reminded her no matter how dark things seemed, light always prevailed. When she was drowning in grief, she'd wrap herself in one of Chris's sweatshirts, snuggle Brianna's teddy bear, and cuddle up on her front porch. Cracks of sunshine would fracture the black sky, and in that moment she'd hold the hope for the same to happen in her dark world. And while that time had proved to be her darkest hours, she'd survived several long nights. Each of those moments carved out a strength in her she never knew she possessed, and she was thankful for the muscle. Even so, she wasn't looking for another opportunity to grow stronger.

Rachael stifled a yawn as she studied the painting in front of her while enjoying the morning around her. Early signs of fall tinged the air with crispness, but it was warm enough for her favorite cardigan. No one else was up, which meant she'd finished an entire mug of coffee in silence. And there'd been cake left over from Abrielle's birthday party yesterday to accompany her morning cup. Best of all, the empty deck provided privacy for her to work on Brianna's portrait. Jonah and Penny had risen early with Abrielle and joined Belle, Micah, and Anna for breakfast. They'd invited Rachael, but she'd stayed back just for this reason.

Turning, she grasped the buttery yellow that caught the highlights in her daughter's chestnut hair. She squirted some onto her palette as she enjoyed the soundtrack of waves rolling into shore below and seagulls crying for their breakfast. Beside her, Clooney dozed on a lounge. Dabbing her brush into fresh paint, she noted how the soft rays of sunlight dusted the canvas in front of her, highlighting the hills of Brie's cheeks, pulled up in her big grin. Her little girl had been born smiling.

Rachael feathered the bright hue into Brianna's hair. Nearly finished, this yearly project soothed the familiar ache inside. It provided time to spend with her daughter that she'd been robbed of. But these portraits paled in comparison to the vibrancy a lifetime with her would have painted across her heart.

The fine lines of Brie's face blurred, and Rachael wiped moisture from the corner of her eye. Sometimes it felt like she'd used up all her colorful moments, leaving her only with muted tones to fill her days. She could still create beautiful things with those shades, but they lacked the vivaciousness she'd once possessed. A part of her missed living with arms wide open and face to the sky, but that position had left her heart exposed. Each hit tucked her further into herself until she'd curled into a protective ball around her vulnerable places, and she had no intention of unfurling.

Yet, that seemed exactly what Evan was coaxing her to do. His friendship snuck into all those black-and-white places and started coloring them again. But he refused to stay in the lines, and it scared her. All the more reason to set him up with someone.

The sliding door opened and shut behind her. She glanced over her shoulder, ready to turn the canvas around if necessary. Yes, she needed to unveil her mural plans to the families she hoped to involve and also to Evan, but not until the holiday weekend was over. Announcing her direction could easily lead to revealing this painting as well. Hesitancy over that level of vulnerability still plagued her. What if what worked for her heart didn't work for others? Currently, only Gavin knew of her yearly portraits of Brie, but he was her son so it had been like sharing with an extension of herself.

At the sight of him, she exhaled and set down her paints.

"Morning," his deep voice, still gravelly with sleep, greeted her as he settled onto a chair. She might never get used to him sounding like a man. Even though he was starting to look like one too.

Clooney trotted over to nuzzle Gavin as Rachael moved to hug him. "Morning, sweetheart."

He amiably endured her nearly thousandth embrace. "I feel like you're stocking up on hugs this weekend."

"Because I am." She capped her paints and started to clean up, her early morning solitude coming to an end.

"Because I originally canceled this weekend?"

"Maybe."

He sighed. "I'm sorry about that."

Last thing she wanted was to mom-guilt him. "It's okay. Truly. But it has made me realize I better snag my hugs when I have the chance." She pretended to grab for him again.

He leaned out of her reach. "I think we need some ground rules."

"Like I should be able to hug you whenever I want?"

"Nope. Not quite what I meant." He laid a goofy grin on her, and for a second, she saw his dad Kurt. Gavin was the age Kurt had been when he'd ditched her, sixteen and pregnant. Her parents hadn't liked her dating an older guy, but she'd been just rebellious enough to keep up the relationship behind their backs. In those days, she'd been all about leaping without looking, and oh so in need of someone to tell her she was beautiful and loved. For whatever reason, she'd been unable to hear it from the ones who truly did love her. Kurt knew what to say to take exactly what he wanted, and when it was all said and done, she felt emptier than she'd been before him.

But raising Gavin had awoken purpose in her. And through the eyes of a parent, she saw that she always had been loved. That shift in perspective also provided insight to the unconditional, always-faithful, ever-present love of her heavenly Father too. She got her heart right with her family and with God, which opened her to Chris's love—and, oh, they'd fallen madly into it. Such a gift after such pain, and she had no delusions she'd find that again. Even if she did—and lately her heart whispered at the possibility with Evan—she didn't possess the courage to pursue it. Her heart simply didn't have enough muscle left for a third loss.

"Mom?" Gavin nudged her. "You okay?"

She shook out of her stupor. "I am. Sometimes I get hit with old memories."

"About Dad and Brie?"

Gavin knew about Kurt but never called him Dad. He'd never met him. From the time he was four years old, Chris was his dad. "Yeah." She rubbed her thumbnail. "I miss them every day." Always with the same awareness, but no longer with the same intensity.

"Me too," he admitted. "That this year's painting?"

"It is. I'm making good progress too. Should be done early."

"Can't wait to see the finished product."

"You'll be the first one I show."

Gavin's gaze fixed on the stairs at their left. "I'd be okay if I wasn't." Before she could formulate a response, he stood. "I'm going to shower."

She glanced toward the steps. The top of Evan's head crested the stairwell. Was he ... was her son referring to—

"Morning." Evan greeted Gavin, who momentarily blocked him from view. Using the distraction, Rachael quickly turned the painting around. Gavin slipped inside, and Evan leaned against the newel post with his black Teva mug of sludge. He took a long sip as he surveyed the now backwards easel. "At some point you're going to have to share. Especially if you want my help."

He mistakenly thought this was her mural rendering. She'd allow the misunderstanding. "At some point. Not this very second."

"Come on," he coaxed. "I'm a super easy audience. I love everything you do."

The dimple in his chin deepened beneath his lopsided grin. Her stomach flip-flopped, and she jerked her attention to collecting her paints. "Sweet of you, but not yet."

"Consider it an open-ended offer." He sidled up next to her as if he had no clue he disturbed her equilibrium.

She snapped the top of her container closed. "Not that I'm trying to ditch you"—lie— "but I was about to take Clooney for a walk."

"Perfect. I'll join you."

Of course he would. Seemed he intended to invade all her spaces lately.

"Fine. Let me dump all this inside and grab her leash." And recalibrate her defenses toward him.

With each step, she revisited her still very valid four points. *Kissing him would be awkward. It would ruin our friendship. I'm not looking.* Glancing over her shoulder she found him watching her through the glass. His brows lifted in a little wiggle that expanded her final point. Not only did Evan Wayne work a dangerous job, he was danger itself—to her well-being. They could tease. They could encourage. They could share a deep friendship. But they could not, would not, fall in love.

Stacking that last piece firmly in place, she rejoined him, and they descended the opposite staircase leading to the beach. Down here, the breeze intensified, and Rachael buttoned up her cardigan. As they neared the water's edge, she tossed a piece of driftwood. Clooney barreled off after it, barking at the seagulls in her way.

"She sure does love the beach." Evan watched Clooney's antics.

"I think she secretly likes the sand between her toes."

"A dog after my own heart. I knew I liked her." He strolled closer, the sand squeaking under his bare feet. "That was quite the birthday party yesterday."

Most of the large group from Saturday returned to celebrate Abrielle's first birthday, and the theme had been sparkly and pink. "I still have glitter attached to me from putting up the decorations."

"Hey, I offered to join in, but no one took me up on it." He gently rolled his shoulder. "Must be they thought my injury would hinder my abilities."

She bent to pick up the stick Clooney had dropped at her feet. Again. "That would assume you had abilities to start with."

"Hey!"

With a shrug, she flung the stick. Again. "Last time, Clooney," she called after her crazy dog. Wiping sand from her hands, she faced Evan only to find him watching her, one eyebrow cocked, jaw tight, and lips in a thin line. But his eyes betrayed him. They sparked with humor. She tipped her head. "If that's the face you wear when interrogating people, we need to work on it, because it's not nearly threatening enough."

His arched brow rose higher. "First, you insult my decorating skills. Then my work tactics? What's next?"

"Your ability to dodge a bullet? Not very superheroish of you. Though I guess dodging bullets is more Superman than Batman."

His mouth dropped open. "That's it." Demonstrating his reflexes were perfectly capable, he flicked out his good hand faster than she could respond and nailed the soft spot between her neck and collarbone. She squealed and tried to duck away, but he'd anticipated her move, sidestepping to block her escape. His fingers continued their attack. "You don't seem too good at dodging sneak attacks either."

Laughing, she batted his arm away. "Okay! I'm sorry!" she squealed. "Truce!" But Evan intensified his tickling assault. With a loud bark, Clooney barreled into him from behind, knocking him off balance. His full weight slammed into her, and they started to fall.

Evan's shoulder!

She twisted to take the brunt of the landing, his good shoulder ramming into her cheekbone. A small gasp escaped her.

"Rach?" Evan eased off of her, bracing himself on his good hand. "You okay?"

"Yeah." She winced. "I mean, you pancaked me, but I'll live."

He settled into a sitting position, then he brushed her cheek. "Sorry." Clooney nudged in between them, and Evan shoved her away to help Rachael sit up too. "You sure you're okay?"

"I'm more worried about you. How's your shoulder?"

"Just fine."

Except he winced.

"Did you feel anything tear?"

The wince turned to a scowl. "I said I'm fine, Rach. You're the one who's going to have a bruise because you tried to protect my fall. I should have thought about Clooney's reaction." He dragged his hand through his hair, sand slipping from its dark strands. "Headed it off."

"I've had bruises before. Amazing thing is, they always heal." She brushed her palms together. Stood. Offered him assistance to stand. "And who'd've thought Clooney would take you out? I certainly didn't."

That didn't seem to change his countenance. "I know she's protective of you. I knew she was nearby. I had the information and didn't use it." Refusing her help, he pushed to a stand by himself. "It's my fault you got hurt."

Whoa. Okay. Considering his overreaction, he'd landed on more than her.

He'd fallen into old memories. She reached for him. "You didn't hurt me, Evan. Promise."

His brow furrowed. "Tell that to your face."

"My face is fine, and I doubt it'll bruise." She squeezed his upper arm. "I really am okay. Are you?" The man truly did have a superhero complex. A protector who didn't have an ounce of grace for himself when he felt he failed. Thing was, he set impossible standards for himself.

"I already said my shoulder's good." Frustration lurked in the dark shadows of his eyes.

"I'm not referring to your shoulder." She maintained her steady focus. He tried to pull from her grasp, but she held tight. "You are not responsible for everything that happens around you. Nor can you control it."

His attention flickered to the lake where he stared for a long moment as if contemplating her words. Then he blinked at her and shrugged, as if he wanted to believe her but couldn't quite bring himself to. Uncovering that truth for him was like trying to chip through layers of paint covering a priceless work of art to reach the original masterpiece underneath. The process took patience and time.

She offered him both.

"Come on." She wiggled his arm. "I'm hungry, and if we want bacon, we need to get to it before Gavin's done with his shower."

With a puff of air and slight shake of his head, Evan followed her up the stairs.

A few hours later, everyone climbed in their cars to head home. Gavin was the last to leave, and now Evan waited while Rachael said her goodbyes to him. Seeing her face when Gavin's car turned up the drive had been a highlight to his weekend. Seeing her face with the slight bruise he'd given her earlier was a definite lowlight—though she'd tried to convince him she was fine.

Her words on the beach still pinged inside of him. He knew he didn't possess ultimate control, and yet he couldn't seem to stop grasping for it. Being a protector was woven into his very nature, but how did he do that without also being in control?

Gavin lifted his hand in a wave. "It was good to see you, Evan."

"You too." He moved forward to shake Gavin's hand. "You coming in for any of the festival?" Everyone else planned to return in two weeks to visit an apple orchard and celebrate Rachael's start on the mural. The official start of the Fall Flower Fest would begin three weeks after that.

"Yep. I'll be back." After one last hug to Rachael, Gavin climbed in his car and drove away.

Evan peered down at her. "You okay?"

Her eyes remained on the empty driveway for another moment, then she looked up at him. "Yeah. You heard him," she said, then dropped her voice low and attempted an Austrian accent. "He'll be back."

"Is that supposed to be Arnold?"

"Supposed to? I nailed it."

He gave an exaggerated nod. "You did something to it, all right." Her mouth dropped open. Chuckling, he gently nudged her chin up. "Any plans for the rest of your day?"

"I should say a Schwarzenegger marathon so you can see how spot-on my impression was." With a wry look, she pulled from his touch. "But now that the weekend is officially over, I need to work on the mural. Painting starts in two weeks, and I'm still finalizing things."

He tipped his chin toward her house. "I happen to have a free afternoon should you need help." No doubt she'd refuse him like she had this morning, but it never hurt to ask. Again.

Rachael drew her lips to the side and sucked in a deep breath that would no doubt expel in a *no*.

"All right."

He stilled. Wait. That sounded suspiciously like ... "All right?"

"Yeah. I planned on showing you tomorrow, but a few hours won't make a difference." Hands in her pockets, she started for her porch. "Come on."

He followed her inside and upstairs to the third-floor room she used as a studio. She approached her easel, picked it up, and turned it to face him. Her cheeks scrunched as she nibbled her lip. He dropped his attention from them to the canvas below. This was the same girl he'd seen in the portrait in her studio in Chicago, only it wasn't the same painting. A young blonde around the age of twelve with eyes the same color as Rachael's along with a matching, infectious smile.

Stepping closer, he studied the portrait. He'd only caught a glimpse before, but that one look had piqued his curiosity about the familiar subject. He hadn't been able to place her then. He could now, but if what he suspected was true, then Rachael possessed a talent far beyond what he'd realized.

Looking up, he met her eyes. "Is this Brianna?"

Rachael nodded.

He knew she could paint people, but this? This was an entirely different level. This painting didn't only use hyperrealism, but it age-progressed Brianna into the young woman she'd be today. He'd never seen anything like it. "It's …" He stopped. Looked to Rach again. "I honestly have no words."

She rubbed her thumbnail. "In a good way or bad?"

"Good." He nodded. "Very good." His focus returned to the painting. "How did you learn to do this?"

"It sort of came naturally, and then from there a few classes and a lot of practice. Which I had plenty of by aiding the police in Chicago." Surprised didn't come close to describing his reaction. She must have read his wide-eyed look because she offered an explanation before he could form words to ask. "I drew people way before I drew flowers. Chris was an EMT. He worked closely with the police, and we became good friends with a detective there. One thing led to another, and I started doing sketches when they needed it."

A very simple explanation for a huge chunk of her life he'd had no clue existed. "Any other tidbits I don't know about you?"

Her cheeks lifted. "Lots."

He wanted to learn them all. Looked like his lifetime plans definitely included her, because she was a mystery that would take at least that long to unravel. What better way to spend the next sixty years?

"When did you start painting Brianna?"

"The year after I lost her. Her birthday was coming, and I couldn't stop wondering how much she might have changed."

"So you painted her."

Her shoulders lifted slightly. "It's been a way for me to still spend time with her. People may think I'm crazy or handling my grief in an unhealthy way, but losing a child leaves you with so many unanswered questions. This was my way of answering at least one of those."

"I don't think you're crazy, Rach." Far from it. She was one amazing woman. "Grief isn't a one-size-fits-all. God heals our hearts using the language he created to speak to them. For you, that's painting."

His response seemed to allay whatever fears she'd been harboring, which then unlocked that part of her she often kept tucked away. "She'd be twelve this year."

Beautiful, like her mother. "She looks just like you."

Turning the portrait toward her, Rach tipped her head. "I see Chris."

"He's there too, but her smile and eyes are all you."

As if to prove his observation, Rachael smiled. "She had the most amazing laugh. Full-on belly giggles that got us all going." She stilled, eyes closed, as if those peels echoed through her memories. "That sound was all her daddy. Those two were always happy. As if they oozed joy." Opening her eyes, she found his.

"It's been a little hard to find again."

Sometimes raw honesty needed no words in return, but rather a reminder that a person wasn't alone. He reached out for her hand, engulfing her soft skin in his callused palm, and gently squeezed.

She returned the pressure, then let go and crossed her arms, rubbing them as if to warm herself. "You're the first person other than Gavin who I showed this to."

Like her words before, this revelation wasn't taken lightly either. But this time he did sense her need to move the conversation forward. "I'm honored."

"And there's a reason I'm showing it to you now."

Because she was starting to trust him with those hidden places. Though he highly doubted she'd come out and say that. That was okay. He'd take baby steps. He simply nodded for her to continue.

She did. "The mural. I want to age-progress some of the children who are missing and paint them as they'd be today." Once again she was rubbing her thumbnail. "What do you think? Because I know it's not traditionally the type of mural artists enter. I'll still use flowers, but—"

"It's a wonderful idea."

Her eyes met his. "You think?"

"I know." No doubt in his mind. "It's the perfect subject matter for you to paint on the wall. People from all over will see the kids you use. It'll bring exposure to their cases."

"That's what I thought. Hope mentioned people walk right past the pictures on grocery store walls all the time, or they scroll past them on social media. But this mural is something they'll be walking toward." Clooney trotted up the steps, no doubt tired of being alone. She padded to Rach and finagled close for some attention. Without missing a beat, Rachael scratched her ears. "I'm using Liliana for sure, but I also wanted to use the girls whose pictures I saw in your car the other day along with one or two others."

"I can help you find more."

She nodded. "I figured. Also, I'd like to speak with their families before moving forward. First for their permission. But second, so that I can collect family pictures. They help with the age progression."

That made sense. He also understood why she said she needed him. "You want me to approach the families for you?"

"I can come too, but I figured you'd know where to reach them." Bending, she picked up a squeaky toy and tossed it for Clooney. "After all, you are the liaison for the department and this mural."

He'd have said yes either way. "We can start tomorrow, if that works for you?"

"It does." Another toss of Clooney's toy. "I'll work more on the flowers today. I'm using what Auna talked about with the floriography, so each one I add will mean something specific."

"It really is a great idea." And it was sparking his own. "You mentioned doing these sketches for a detective in Chicago?"

"Yes. Sometimes it was faster for me to sketch something he could use rather than send them off to be digitally done." With all the sunshine, it was growing warm up here. She must have felt it too because she crossed to the windows and opened one. "I have a feeling things have come a long way since then."

"Not really." He stepped into the cool breeze. "Unfortunately, there's still more missing kids than there's time to handle all their pictures. We're in line to have these girls' pictures done, but I wondered … Would you be willing to create individual sketches of them that I could put up on our social media sites now?" As her brows drew together, he quickly straightened. "If it's too much on your plate—"

"No. That's not it." She waved him off as a smile took root on her face. "It's the whole *great minds think alike* thing."

"Oh?"

"I already planned on doing individual paintings of each girl to give to their families. I'll make sure you receive a copy."

"Perfect." Distant squeals came through the open window from the people playing on the beach below. He caught Rachael glance from the water to her paints, then outside again. "You know, today is a holiday, and as such should be celebrated rather than wasted on work."

"You think so, huh?"

"I do."

Her head tipped as she contemplated, attention bouncing from her work to him. After a second, she nodded. "I could probably be convinced, if there's an Arnold movie and some cheese somewhere in this celebration." Then she headed for the door.

With a groan, he followed her. "These great minds are no longer thinking alike."

Chapter Fourteen

E xhaustion nipped at Evan's heels as he stretched his feet onto the coffee table in Rachael's living room. In the past week Becky had upped his physical therapy into a realm that left him perpetually sore yet seeing improvements. Made the pain worth it. If he wasn't working with her, he was implementing the exercises at home along with increasing his mileage on the beach. Today he'd pushed hard, and his shoulder protested the extra work enough that he'd been forced to take some of his stronger pain meds. The last hour he'd fought dozing off. Now, Clooney padded over with her favorite toy and nudged his hand. A distraction he'd gladly take.

"I think she's tired of us ignoring her." He set the file he was reading on the coffee table. Others lay open on the couch beside him.

"She can get demanding in the evenings." Rachael's focus remained on the large sketch pad in her hand. She'd cuddled into one of the oversized chairs across from him, her legs tucked under her as she worked. They'd received the go-ahead from all the families, and each evening after dinner she'd work on some aspect of the mural or the individual sketches while he continued to comb through all the case details.

He'd spent a fair amount of tonight, however, studying her. She nibbled her lower lip while scrutinizing her penciled drawing. If she didn't like something, she'd scrunch her nose and tip her head before erasing and fixing it. But when she finally had it to the place she loved, her lips tipped into a satisfied smile and her blue eyes glistened like the lake outside the window. Didn't take him but a second to decide he wanted his kiss to elicit the same response. And if it took a few to get there, he'd happily comply.

Now though, he nabbed Clooney's toy and tossed it at Rachael. The small rubber hedgehog bounced off her forehead and landed with a plunk in her lap. "Hey!"

He tipped his head toward Clooney and lifted his eyebrows. "She's got good aim."

"Right." With light laughter, Rach set aside her drawing and stretched. Her eyes caught on the open files on the table, and she picked up the picture of

Becca Philmont. "Did you know she got this scar from falling out of a tree?" She studied the photo in her hand. "Her parents said she was an adventurous child."

While he'd spoken with the families on the initial ask, Rachael had spent more time interacting with them as they emailed her family photos. "I didn't know that."

"I'm going to put edelweisses by her because they mean courageous and daring."

She'd been pouring over books on floriography—and she wasn't the only one. He'd been intrigued by the language too. "Sounds perfect for her."

Replacing the photo on the stack, she looked his way. "I'm thirsty. Want a drink?"

"Sure." He stood too and walked toward the kitchen. As he passed the small table where she'd set her sketch, he noticed her pencil drawing. His mind shifted gears so quickly he suffered mental whiplash. "What are those?" Among a field of tall grass, she'd layered in different kinds of flowers, but only one captured his attention. Tall thin stalks with poofs on their ends. They jogged a memory.

She switched direction and joined him. "Craspedia. Something's missing in the background, and I'm trying to figure out what. I stumbled across these. They traditionally symbolize good health, but I also read that they refer to a person who lights up your world. I thought maybe I'd layer them into some of the empty spaces." She picked the pad up. "Why? You don't like them?"

"The opposite, actually." The memory pressed in on him. "They were Mandie's favorites. I called them her drumsticks." Hearing their meaning proved they'd suited her. Mandie had definitely lit up his world.

Rachael's shoulder pressed against his. "She played the drums?"

Memories of Mandie didn't always make him smile. This one did. "Yeah. We joined junior high band together. But she was a whole lot better than me."

Returning her sketch pad to the side table, Rachael continued to the kitchen and grabbed two glasses. She headed to the fridge to fill them. "What instrument did you play?"

"Saxophone."

"A real Kenny G." She smiled over her shoulder at him.

"I wasn't quite at Kenny G level. Let's just say the band director suggested I sign up for choir in high school."

"Ah. So that's how your illustrious career as *the* lead actor at Ford High School came to be." She handed him one of the glasses. "Care to sing me a few bars from *Sound of Music*, Captain von Trapp?"

"I still need to pay my sisters back for telling you about that."

"And I still need to convince them to convert the VHS tapes of your performances to digital."

"Those may have mysteriously disappeared."

"You're a cop. You know how to find things."

"I also know how to hide things."

Leaning against the counter, she eyed him. "So, you don't have to answer this, but I've been wondering. Were you and Mandie more than friends?"

If things had gone differently, they might have been one day. "No. We were just friends. Good ones, but nothing more."

"People say it's not possible for guys and girls to be just friends." She set her glass down, then poked him. "But you keep proving them wrong."

He captured her finger with his hand. "I never said neither of us wanted to be more. Only that we weren't."

"She liked you?" Mischief filled her face. "Or was it the other way around?"

"Maybe it was mutual, but neither of us dared say anything." This close, the sweet smell of apples from her hair and soft feel of her skin against his about undid him. Especially with the memory of her advising him to not waste time with his mystery woman. To go for it.

Tenderness lined her face. "You were kids. It's hard to know what to do with all those crazy emotions at that age."

"I don't think it gets any easier when you grow up." He slanted an eyebrow up. "Do you?"

Something shifted between them. Her head tipped ever-so-slightly, and she studied him as if discerning whether his words pertained to his past or their present. Slowly, she shook her head. "No," she whispered. "I don't think it does."

"I think—" he lowered his voice too— "the only difference is you realize that not acknowledging them isn't the same as not having them." Still holding her finger, he tugged her closer. "Feelings, that is."

"True." Her eyes shifted to his hold, then drifted to his lips.

Aw, man, Rachael Stark was one smart, beautiful woman, and he was taking her advice. He released her only long enough to cup the base of her neck, his thumb resting in the well of her collarbone. Slowly, he drifted his fingertips along her soft skin until they tangled in her silky hair.

Cradling her close, he leaned down and pressed a gentle kiss against the tender spot behind her ear, tickling her lobe with his breath. She inhaled sharply, her hand rising to his chest. She created her own trail along the collar of his shirt until she connected with his skin, her movements tentative and slow. He slipped his hold from her hair to return to her neck, his fingertips pressing against her racing pulse. Excited or scared? His uncertainty paused the moment. He'd gladly be the cause of her excitement, but the last thing he ever wanted was to be the source of her fears.

Her phone rang, making the decision for him. The way she bolted from his arms answered loud and clear which emotion fueled her heart rate. A ringing phone wouldn't be an interruption to someone wanting to be kissed. She turned away from him to answer.

"Penny." Her voice broke around the name, and she cleared her throat. "What's up?" Her shoulders tensed. "Nothing's wrong." Pause. "Promise. I'm fine." She peeked over her shoulder, saw him watching, then jerked her gaze out the window.

Not before he caught the pink in her cheeks. Then she raked a hand through her hair. Definitely wasn't the response he'd been hoping for. Giving her some space, he returned to the couch and pretended to work but instead stared blankly at the papers in his hand. She probably hoped he'd leave. Looked like neither of them were getting what they wanted tonight. Pretending they hadn't nearly kissed wasn't an option. It'd only leave things awkward and unresolved. They'd nudged over their friendship line and had to at least address it.

Rach milked her conversation with Penny for all it was worth, keeping her back to him the entire time. But after offering to mail Abrielle's stuffed bunny, did she really need to recount every detail of their shared weekend?

Twenty minutes later she finally hung up, turned, and tried for wide-eyed surprise. "You're still here?"

He gave her a look that let her know he wasn't buying it.

"Right." Her face slacked, and she tapped her phone against her leg. "You're still here." This time a note of dread accompanied the words.

Made him feel super optimistic. "We need to talk."

"No one, in the history of male-female relationships, has ever liked those words."

"Yet talking is a necessity in any relationship." He patted the couch cushion beside him, having settled there while she'd tried dislodging him with her extended phone call.

She nodded but chose the chair opposite him. "Talking, yes. Rehashing moments we both know shouldn't have happened, not so much."

"What if we disagree on which part shouldn't have happened?" He nearly laughed at how wide her eyes grew. Would have too, if they were close to being on the same page. The fact she wasn't sucked all humor from the situation. "For me, it was the phone ringing."

There went her pink cheeks again. "Oh." One word, but it packed sufficient punch. "Yeah, we're not thinking about the same moment."

He wasn't going quietly though, because he still wasn't buying what she was selling. Her tiny gasp when his lips pressed behind her ear and her heated touch against his skin proved her words counterfeit. But to her, they probably sounded like the real deal. "You may want to believe that, but I don't."

"No?"

"No."

She straightened. "It's the truth."

"I disagree." She probably wanted him to walk away, pretend things were the same. He couldn't. Not until they finally talked about the elephant that had been edging into their room since the day they'd met. "Rach, I was serious when I said we'd moved beyond just friends. Whatever's been developing between us, I don't want to ignore it anymore. I want to explore it." He scooted forward and leaned his forearms on his thighs. "Do you?"

Well, she'd completely blown things, hadn't she? But something in his tender caress reached the parts of her that belonged to him. She couldn't deny he'd become more than just a friend, but that "more" didn't have to include kissing—even if her tired, lonely heart said otherwise. She could, however, choose to deny him any more territory. Difficult? Sure, but she'd done difficult before. What she refused to do was fall in love again. Two men had left her. For such different reasons, but she sure didn't feel like finding out if the third time was a charm—or disaster.

Now to extract herself from the situation without damaging their relationship.

"Evan—"

"No, don't." His hand jammed into the air.

"I haven't said anything."

"Your tone said enough, along with your body language."

She glanced down. Oh. At some point she'd crossed her arms. She could try to explain it had been an involuntary protective measure, nothing to do with him, but *it's not you, it's me* sounded as bad as *we need to talk.*

"My tone said I don't want to hurt you." She uncrossed her arms and scooched forward. "I do care for you, Evan, and you are more than just a friend. You're my best friend." Because that trite saying was oh so much better than the others.

"You often kiss your friends?"

"We didn't kiss."

His response came in the form of a look rather than words, and once again, it said plenty.

She sighed. "No, I don't typically kiss my friends. But this has been an emotional few weeks, and I think I needed to be close to somebody."

"Any warm body would do then?" The muscles along his jaw tightened.

"You know me better than that."

"I do." He zeroed in on her. "In fact, I think I know you better than you know yourself right now."

Her insides lit up. "I've always hated that saying. What does it even mean?" She stood. "How can anyone know me better than me?"

"Easy." He stood too, remaining in her space, and his hand went to his chest. "I don't have the same fears inside that you do, so they're not clouding my vision."

"I'm not scared."

"No?" He inched closer.

"No." Except her heart raced as he towered over her. Not because he physically intimidated her. No, he threatened her peace of mind. "And don't you dare say I should kiss you to prove it."

His lips spread in a wide, self-assured smile that made her as wobbly as that slackline next door. "I don't manipulate women into kissing me, Rach. They're willing participants."

She'd seen several sides of Evan through the years, but this steady confidence was a new one. And, oh boy, it only made him more attractive. She reached for a verbal crowbar to pry off his rapidly growing appeal. "This from experience with your mystery woman?"

"I haven't gotten around to kissing her yet."

"But you plan to?"

"Most definitely." He didn't bat an eye. In fact, he steadily held hers.

Heat speared through her, but instead of it being red, it was decidedly green. "Then why were you almost kissing me?"

He tossed his hands into the air. "Because *you're* my mystery woman."

That little revelation sucked all the air from the room. "Me?"

His brow wrinkled, and his face took on this look as if she'd missed the forest for the trees. "Seriously." That one word sounded an awful lot like a frustrated oath. "Yes, Rach. You. I'm not sure how you missed that."

"Because I don't read minds, and you never said anything."

"So my 'I want to explore whatever this is between us' two minutes ago is not saying anything?"

"I'm talking about before tonight."

He gripped the base of his neck, as if trying to rein in budding frustration, and took a slow, measured breath. "You're right. I danced around the subject, but that's because I didn't think you were ready for me to tell you how I felt." Straightening, he rested the full measure of his gaze on her. "Looks like that cat's out of the bag, though, so let me be clear. I'd like to date you, Rachael. I think what we have could become something even better."

Think. Not guarantee. Because life—and love—offered none. What if they tried and it failed and she lost him? What if they tried and it was amazing and she lost him? Holding him at arm's length meant at least she still could hold him. And if the unthinkable did happen, her heart wouldn't be completely decimated because she'd held a part of it back.

Her silence had him straightening. "Looks like I have my answer."

"Evan—" She reached for him.

He ducked her touch, though there wasn't animosity in his movement. "We want different things, and that's okay, Rach. I understand."

She rubbed her thumbnail against her fingers. "Do you?" She inched closer but didn't reach for him again. "I'm not looking for anyone, Evan. Two men have left me, and I know that you wouldn't plan on it, but neither did Chris. And your job is way more dangerous than his ever was." Lifting her shoulders, she slowly shook her head. "I can't do that again."

Sadness creased the corners of his eyes. "I really do understand."

The compassion in his voice nearly undid her. "But will it be weird between us now?" She could hardly stand to voice the question, but it had to be asked.

He studied her for a long painful moment. Then, "Nope. You don't have a thing for me—other than your obsession with my abs—so all's the same on your end. And I don't have to wonder what-if anymore, so I can tuck these feelings away on my end and move forward." His smiled oozed a confidence that didn't quite reach his eyes. "Our friendship will be fine."

She would do everything she could to ensure that too. "Good."

"So, what did Penny need?" His left-field question was like dousing acetone on a misplaced line of paint. Erase it and start again like it never happened. But a remnant of the color always remained under the new layers. She had a feeling their almost-kiss would be the same. Wouldn't that be a special kind of torture. He'd left her undone with a press of his lips against her ear. What would an actual kiss with Evan do to her?

Point Two evaporated under the heat of that thought. Awkward wouldn't even exist in the same realm as kissing him.

"Rach?"

"Oh, sorry." She buckled down her imagination. "They misplaced Abrielle's stuffed bunny and her backup one is here. They need me to mail it." She was pretty sure he could have picked that up from her end of the conversation. Most likely he was as anxious to move them onto a new topic as she was.

"Hopefully, they can get her to sleep tonight without it," he said. Then as if all topics of conversation deserted them, they stared at each other. He cleared his throat. "Okay. Well, I'm beat." He shuffled his paperwork into folders. "I should clear out and head for bed."

She needed things to remain normal between them. "I thought we were going to watch an episode of *Alone* tonight." Turned out the adventure show was one of his favorites. For every Arnold movie he watched with her, she watched two episodes of *Alone* with him.

"Sorry, but I'm exhausted." The way he said it spoke to so much more than his physical state.

She walked him to the door, her heart pounding. "It's okay." Though she wasn't quite convinced it was.

He must have heard the worry in her voice because he stopped at the door. He brushed a few loose strands of hair from her forehead. "It's nothing a good night's sleep won't cure."

"You're sure?" She hated how her voice quaked. Hated that she wanted two such separate things, but most of all hated the thought that she'd damaged their friendship because she couldn't give him what he wanted.

His eyes flickered over her, then his dimple pressed into his chin. "I'm sure." Hand on the door handle, he pushed it open. "Don't stay up too late working on those sketches."

"I won't." She'd stay up too late replaying the last fifteen minutes.

Locking the door behind him, she leaned against it, her mind already on rewind. Okay. So. Evan might be a kissing genius—she strongly suspected that fact now—but he wasn't the man for her. Points One and Two might be gone, but she could hold tightly to Three through Five.

She stared herself down in the mirror to her right. "Point Three: relationships that go from friends to more than friends again never survive—you almost proved it tonight." And she hadn't even kissed him. If romance wound up being what ultimately killed their friendship, she should at least get the joy of kissing him first. "Point Four: you are still not looking! And Point Five: Evan's job is way too dangerous. *Hello!* He's recovering from a gunshot wound." Her reflection did not look convinced. In fact, it seemed to be calling out her logical excuses for being as flimsy as a toothpick bridge.

She'd better find a way to add some reinforcement before Evan blasted through them all, leaving her stranded on the wrong side.

Chapter Fifteen

Evan rapped his knuckles on the doorframe of Dierks's office. "You called?" Dierks looked up from his desk.

"Hey. Yeah." He waved him in. "I have something I thought you'd want to see."

Interest piqued further, Evan strolled in and settled in the worn chair in front of him. "Info on the guy who shot me?"

"No, sorry. Nothing new on that front." Dierks grabbed his computer screen and twisted it toward Evan. "But I do have a video clip that might interest you."

Evan immediately latched onto the rusted blue Ford F150 in the shot. Dierks tapped something and the video rolled. Looked like it was taken from someone's doorbell camera. "Where is this?"

"Cherryville. They got a call from some lady in the neighborhood who said this truck's been trolling a few times a week. Seems to be following the bus schedule."

"Anyone approach the kids?"

"Nope. And when she tried to approach the truck, it took off. So she called the police with her suspicions." Dierks picked up a pen and started clicking it. "They've had a patrol out there this week to increase presence. Seems to be working because the truck hasn't been back. Since we're a neighboring county, we received the heads-up to be watching. One of the guys brought it to me. I went to her, and she provided me with the video feed."

"Tell me you got a license plate." He squinted at the video. The model was old enough and the activity suspicious enough that this could be a real lead.

The clicking of Dierks' pen stopped. "We did, and it's a stolen plate."

Evan scrubbed his face, resting his hand at the nape of his neck. "Of course it is." A break would really be nice. Not that there was any guarantee this was the truck connecting Becca, Morgan, and Liliana's cases, but it was too coincidental for him to ignore. And if this guy was still out there … "Did this woman happen to catch a glimpse of the driver?"

"Not one that'll help. Dark coat. Dark hat pulled low. Nothing we can use."

"Sounds an awful lot like what Hope Perez described. Maybe show her this truck."

"I already called. She's coming this afternoon."

"Let me know?" But even if she claimed it was the same truck, other than putting an APB out for it and alerting the public to keep an eye out, there wasn't much more they could do. And if the guy driving heard increased chatter, chances were slim he'd take it out again. Depended on how desperate he was. Evan straightened. "The timeline is right."

Dierks' brows drew together. "Come again?"

"Liliana went missing fifteen years ago. Becca, ten. And Morgan five." He noted the years in his own file, but they'd all been taken in different months. From different counties. Until now, there'd been no way of knowing if the pattern would continue. "If this is our guy, that fits."

And how did he stop him if he was intent on taking someone else? They could alert other departments, but there weren't enough patrols to watch every school. Every bus drop. Every neighborhood in the state. An overwhelming sense of inadequacy pressed in. "We need to find him."

"We will." Dierks nodded. "We'll spread the word."

"What if he changes vehicles?"

"We'll get people looking, and we'll let the school districts know. They can inform parents to make sure kids stay together walking to and from school. Give them a reminder on safety protocols."

"That'll work for maybe a week or two, then they'll slowly let their guards down."

"But we won't."

It didn't seem enough. He needed to be out there. "I'm going to talk to Cap." Pushing to his feet, he headed to his captain's office.

Captain Larry looked up as Evan knocked. "Evan. Dierks mentioned he called you. What'd you think of the video feed?"

"That I need to be out there." Evan remained standing, feet braced, arms crossed. His shoulder muscles pulled, but the pain was minimal compared to his aggravation at what the wound cost him. "When can I return to active duty?"

Cap looked him up and down, then removed his glasses and reclined in his chair, giving him another once-over. "You pass the physical yet?" The one that would ensure he could perform all the essential functions the department deemed necessary for fitness for duty.

"I can today." Might need an extra dose of Tylenol tonight, but he'd cope.

"Becky give you the all clear?" He spread his hand over his desk. "Because it hasn't made it here yet."

"I'll talk with her."

Cap tapped the end of his glasses against his mouth. "I'm sure you will. It's my understanding, however, that while your recovery is coming along, she still hasn't cleared you for the gun range."

They'd talked about it, and the plan was for her to clear him within the next one to two weeks if his recovery continued the trajectory it was on. "I will be shortly. And I have no doubt my accuracy will remain."

"Until you demonstrate that, and I have a note from Becky saying you're cleared, you won't be in uniform."

Evan didn't break his stance. "You're not hiring anyone into my spot, are you?" The longer he was on light duty, the more he worried it'd become permanent.

"Not yet. The department allots for six months' light duty, and I won't fill your spot one day before that."

He'd already burned through three.

Cap leaned forward, elbows on his desk as he braced one fist in the other palm. "I want you out there, Evan, but I won't put a compromised patrol officer on my streets. Not just for you, but for the people you're supposed to be protecting."

"I expect nothing less, sir. And I wouldn't ask if I didn't feel ready."

"I appreciate your confidence, but I don't go off your feeling. Pass your tests and get Becky to sign off. Then I'll put you on schedule."

Due to the gun range, that meant at minimum another week on the sidelines.

Cap seemed to sense his frustration but read it as worry over his future security. "There'll always be a spot for you here, Evan. You've shown quite the aptitude for these cold cases. Might be a good move for you if we have to go down that route."

"We won't." That had been his biggest concern in telling Rach he'd look into Liliana's case. He didn't want Cap considering the idea of a permanent move.

"All right then." Cap offered a clipped nod. "That all?"

"Yes, sir."

"Then I'll get back to work." Cap picked up a paper from his desk.

Evan turned on his heel and made for the stairs. He itched to head for the gun range, but Becky had been adamant about waiting at least another week. Guess he'd settle for lifting weights. Anything to release the building pressure of the past few days. It had all started with nearly kissing Rachael five nights ago and gone downhill from there. Things had been strained since then, even with his best efforts to return them to normal. He'd yet to make progress on Liliana's case, and this new video acted as a tease that the guy was out there. Which only served as a reminder that his own shooter remained at large. Another assailant running free because he hadn't stopped him.

"I was going to ask if you wanted to grab lunch, but with that scowl, I think I'll pass." Dierks stood near the top of the steps.

"I'm not in the mood." Evan bumped past him.

Despite his words, Dierks followed. "Really? Cause it definitely seems like you're in one."

Evan shot him a glare and kept walking. They hit the exit, and he slapped on his sunglasses to shade the bright afternoon sun. "Thought you were taking a pass on lunch."

"On lunch, yeah. But I have a feeling you need to talk."

He made it to his Jeep before giving in. Leaning against the hood, he faced his friend. "I'm not making headway in any area right now, and I've about had it."

"You know cases don't always move fast. That doesn't mean they're not moving."

"I do know that. But I'm used to a more active role. I feel like I'm at a standstill everywhere." He hooked his foot on his bumper and got to the heart of the matter. "I told Rachael I wanted to date her."

Dierks rolled on his heels. "I'm guessing her response wasn't the one you were hoping for."

He shook his head. "And things have been strained since then."

"Because of you or her?"

Evan thought over the past few days. Rach had shown up each day with a smile he'd half-heartedly tried to meet, despite his promises everything was fine. "More me than her." He scrubbed a hand through his hair. "I'm not sure where to go from here."

"Way I see it, you have two choices. Keep her as a friend or walk away completely."

"Neither?"

Dierks puffed out a laugh. "Not a choice, I'm afraid." He slapped a hand on Evan's good shoulder. "Can you cut her out of your life?"

"No."

"Then I think you have your answer." He let go. "Find a way to make it right."

Evan shifted his gaze to the side, still not wanting to accept that his chance at something more with Rach was over. But it was, and if he continued to sullenly cling to his disappointment, then their friendship would end too. Time to keep his promise to Rachael. His eyes caught on the flowerpot in the storefront a few doors down, and he knew what he'd do.

"You ready to start your mural?" Jonah joined Rachael on the deck of his lake house. He and Penny had arrived last night, and Penny was feeding Abrielle breakfast. They planned on heading to Robinette's Apple Orchard later this morning.

She leaned against the railing, a light breeze tickling the hair loose from her ponytail. Perfect sweater weather today, her favorite. "I think so. At least, I'm as ready as I'm going to be." As of Monday, artists could begin. This past month had flown by.

In this week alone, she'd finished the individual sketches of each girl and delivered them to their families. She'd completed the small rendering to put on display as she painted, and she'd finished creating a grid version to work from. Amazing she'd been able to accomplish any of that with her head and heart focused on her strained relationship with Evan. He'd promised things would remain unchanged, but she'd yet to see evidence of it. Yes, she'd wanted to reintroduce some distance between them, but not an emotional football field's worth. More like a car length. Still near her, but with plenty of room to pump the brakes should they start to get too close again.

One arm resting on the rail, Jonah faced her. "You look worried. Everything okay?"

She could pacify him with her smile and an *everything's fine,* knowing exactly how to deliver it so he'd nod and move on, but maybe he could offer a guy's perspective that would show her the next step. Because she wasn't ready to give up on her relationship with Evan. They'd crossed no lines. They'd remained honest with one another. And it wasn't like theirs was the first friendship between a guy and a girl to experience a flare of attraction. Who wouldn't be attracted to Evan Wayne?

"Rach?" Jonah pressed.

She shook her head, which still clearly was in the wrong place. "Sorry." Down below, someone in a wet suit paddled by on a board. "Evan wants to date me."

Jonah arched a brow. "You're just now figuring this out?" With a sigh, she tipped her head. He held up his hands. "Sorry, but everyone around you two has known for the better part of a year."

"Well, I did not." She ignored his disbelieving look. "Either way, I had to tell him I didn't feel the same. Now things are weird between us." And she hated it. But things were only strained, not broken. "You've been there before with Penny. What do I need to do to get things back to normal? She told you she didn't want to date, but you two stayed friends."

He straightened. "Penelope's and my situation was slightly different."

"You weren't friends as long, true. Still, you were friends."

"We were," he agreed. "All I can say is give him some space if he needs it. He'll come around."

"How can you be so sure?"

Jonah shrugged. "Call it a gut feeling."

She wished hers contained the same one. Right now it was in knots. "Fine. I'll give him space, but I won't like it." At all. "What's the time limit on this space?"

"As long as he needs."

"Gee, thanks. That clears it all up."

Chuckling, Jonah pushed off the railing. "He'll let you know, Rach." He crossed toward the slider. "I'm going to check and see if Penelope and Abrielle are ready to pick some apples."

"Sounds good. I'm ready to go whenever they are."

When they'd planned this on Labor Day, Evan was supposed to go with them. If she was giving him space, did that mean she didn't go knock on his door? Or would her leaving without him only make things more awkward?

"Jonah?" she called as he shut the door.

With a groan, she went to find him. He agreed to go next door for her and see if Evan still planned on joining them. A few minutes later he returned. "He's not there."

Guess that answered things for her.

They packed up and drove to Robinette's, where Micah, Belle, and Anna met them. Parking across the street, they put the kids in jogging strollers, then headed to grab a bag for picking apples. Sunlight from the cloudless azure sky streaked through the rows of trees, bouncing off the deep, ruby-colored apples. Moss and dirt mingled with the sweet smell of the blossoms and fruit, filling the air with the delicious scent of fall. Families wandered through the trees, picking Jonagolds and Red Delicious to add to their wagons. The only thing missing from this quaint scene was Evan. Maybe that was good, because if she missed him on a normal Saturday in September, then her heart had already grown too attached.

Yep. Giving him space would be good for them both. They'd redefine their friendship. A necessity, since Evan would eventually date someone else, and she'd return to Chicago. Space was inevitable, and she was fine with that as long as their friendship remained intact.

"I don't think we need any more apples." Penny's voice reached through her thoughts.

"I concur." Belle stood beside her sister.

Each wagon the guys pulled held a daughter on one side and a few dozen apples on the other. "I hope you're not expecting us to eat all those." Rachael loved apples, but at a rate of one a day, they'd go bad before she could finish her share.

Penny laughed. "Jonah's expecting me to bake all of ours."

"Apple pie. Apple crisp. Apple muffins." Jonah wheeled toward the weigh station, and they all followed. After paying, they found an empty picnic table.

"We'll run in and grab us some donuts and cider," Micah offered.

"Sounds good." Penny let Abrielle out of the stroller, and she toddled around the grass with Anna holding her hand. "So, Rachael, what's up with you and Evan?"

Belle settled onto the bench. "Yeah, spill. Why's he not here?"

No doubt they'd been dying to ask all morning. Since she'd already shared with Jonah, it was only a matter of time until he told Penny. "Evan suggested we start dating."

Belle bounced. "About time."

But Penny shushed her sister with a look. "Except he's not here, so I'm guessing you turned him down."

Rachael nodded. "We're just—" She stopped because she didn't believe it anymore. "He's my best friend. I don't want to jeopardize that."

"Not possible. He's crazy about you." Penny stood and redirected Anna and Abrielle closer to their table.

"And I'm crazy about him. As a friend."

Penny and Belle shared a look. Belle leaned forward on her forearms. "I know it may feel risky to fall in love again, but trust me, it's worth it."

She'd thought the same thing when she'd fallen in love with Chris. But she'd used her second chance and wasn't looking for a third. "I appreciate the advice, but really, we're best off as friends."

Right then, the guys rejoined them. Jonah sidled up beside Penny. "This seat taken?"

That one line was like him telling Penny he loved her in their own secret language. She grinned up at him. "It's permanently yours."

Not going to lie, seeing moments like these made Rachael miss the intimacy couples shared. But she and Evan had that as friends. They often knew what the other was thinking with one look and understood when their tone spoke much louder than words. Hopefully, she hadn't damaged that connection.

After eating their treats, the group tackled the corn maze. Lots of dead ends. Going in circles. Getting lost. Laughter. The entire day was a wonderful one, minus the fact her best friend wasn't there. She felt his absence keenly.

Before leaving, they all bought pumpkins for a carving competition. Jonah eyed them as he opened the trunk at home. "Did you need to pick the largest one, Rach?" He hefted it out.

"I wanted the seeds."

"This one will have enough to last you all season." Arms full, he headed to the door. "Mind grabbing the tiny one we chose?"

"Sure." Nabbing it, she followed everyone up the porch steps. From the corner of her eye, she caught a bundle on the swing. She detoured over only to discover it was flowers. Setting the pumpkin down, she picked them up.

Belle peered over Rachael's shoulder. "Is that mistletoe?"

"Mistletoe?" Jonah stopped halfway through the door. "Who's sending you mistletoe?"

A white tag hung from the white ribbon sealing the brown paper around the flowers. Rachael recognized the handwriting along with the flowers inside. Mistletoe, yes, and zinnias. Smiling, she brushed past her brother toward the books Auna had loaned her.

"With that smile, I'm thinking Evan," Penny remarked as she followed.

Micah and Jonah dropped their pumpkins on the kitchen counter. Belle joined Penny beside Rachael as Anna chased Abrielle around the family room.

"It is from Evan, but he's not sending mistletoe for the traditional reason." Rachael started fanning through the book.

"Let me guess, this is his way of telling you he doesn't need any more space?" Jonah called from the kitchen. "If so, that was fast."

Not fast enough for her.

"I feel like I'm missing something." Micah settled on one of the counter stools.

Standing beside Rachael so she could see the book, Belle peeked up at him. "I'll fill you in later."

Rachael stopped on the mistletoe. *Surmounting all difficulties.* See, she knew it didn't have anything to do with kissing. Although, in this instance, she could see his humor coming through too. The double meaning did help make light of a situation that had weighed heavy on them both all week. Smiling, she flipped to the Zs to looked up Zinnias.

Zinnias. *Everlasting friendship.*

Closing the book, she looked at all of them. "I'll be right back." Then she beelined to Evan's. He answered before she finished knocking. He had on a flannel shirt, worn jeans, and dark hiking boots. His hair was messed up in the best of ways, and he wore the smile she'd been missing all week. The one that made the dimple in his chin stand out.

"You guys already pick apples?" he asked as if they hadn't experienced a blip in their relationship.

"We did. You weren't here."

"Sorry. Dierks called me in."

So he hadn't been trying to avoid her. That soothed her heart. "Everything okay?"

"I don't know." Uncertainty lined his face. "Is it?"

Double-talk that she'd answer directly. "Your flowers seem to say yes."

"And you?"

"I'm inclined to agree with them." Things were always okay when she was around him. "I love them, by the way."

Something shifted in his eyes, gone so briefly she'd nearly missed it. Something that said he wished her words pointed at him rather than his flowers. But his smile never wobbled. "Good." One word. Simple. Soft. "Now, did you save me any apples?"

"Of course. And we're about to have a pumpkin-carving contest."

He leaned into his house, grabbed something from the table beside his door, then straightened. A pumpkin of his very own. "Won't be a contest without some real competition."

She crossed her arms and looked him over. "That's you, I assume?"

"It's definitely not you." He stepped outside. "Why don't you lead the way since it's the only lead you'll take today."

And just like that, they were back.

Chapter Sixteen

"I will happily be your human shield any time, Rach, but to be an effective one, I need a little intel on who I'm hiding you from." Evan peered over his shoulder at her. Ever since yesterday, they'd finally found their rhythm again.

"What makes you think I'm hiding?"

His profile pulled into a grin. "The number of evasive techniques you've executed tonight. I've narrowed it down to two people, but I don't recognize either one so I'm not sure why you'd be hiding from them."

Caught, she slumped. Not that Evan's awareness of the situation or that he'd pegged the right person within his field of suspects came as any surprise. She lifted her chin in the direction of Shona Catto. "Her."

He slowly panned the crowd, acting as if he was taking all the festivities in. The kick-off for the start of the mural painting was taking place in the large lot created for the weekly farmer's market. Hundreds of people milled about in the warm afternoon sun, enjoying live music and food trucks that would be a regular staple for the next several Tuesdays. Dads had toddlers on shoulders, kids darted between strollers, and retirees shuffled through a multitude of vendors selling all things fall. After one large sweep of the area, Evan's gaze drifted round again to Rachael. "The brunette with bangs?"

She nodded.

"Who is she?"

"Shona Catto with *Midwest Art*. She's interviewing all the artists."

He faced her and crossed his arms, something akin to pride on his face. "Isn't that a pretty big publication in your world?"

"Yes." She peeked around him, then met his eyes. "How'd you know what *Midwest Art* is anyway?"

His shrug was way too casual for the knowledge he held. That publication was extremely well known in art circles, but it equated to Timbuktu if you didn't run in them. "I know things. It's what I do."

"Right."

"So why are you avoiding her? I'd think you'd want to speak with someone from MA."

She arched her brow at his use of the slang title, and he lifted his palms with another miniscule shrug as if to play off his familiarity as completely normal. Apparently Evan Wayne was a closet art connoisseur. "The last time that magazine wrote a piece on me it was … less than stellar. I don't have any desire to repeat the experience."

"They obviously know nothing about art. They're a complete sham."

His support of her did nothing to remove these decidedly more-than-friends feelings she'd had toward him lately. "Who plenty of people purchase and read."

"Not me." He peeked down at her. "They've lost a reader for life."

"I think they'll be okay with that," she drolled.

"What could they possibly have had against your work?"

"They didn't agree with the comparisons to Georgia O'Keefe. Said I was a poor imitation who had no right to try and compare myself to her." That review had nearly stopped her from painting. Until Chris lit it on fire and reminded her the only words that mattered were God's. Not that others' verbal jabs didn't sting. "Thing is, I was never the one to draw that parallel. That was another publication."

He gripped her shoulders, leaning down until he was eye to eye with her. "That was an unfair parallel to make."

"I agree."

His dimple came out to play under his full smile. "You're a thousand times better than Georgia O'Keefe."

Laughter and conversation filled the open-air space, along with the scent of apples and cinnamon from the nearby vendors' baked goods. Yet in this split second, all her senses narrowed in on Evan. His tender touch beneath slightly callused fingers. The hint of Downy softness underneath his cedar-and-sage cologne. Those corded muscles along his neck that led to a strong jaw covered in dark bristle that tempted her fingers. Evan was a study in red-blooded masculinity.

Something pulled his attention from her. Correction. Someone. Auna Cummings headed toward them from about ten feet out.

"Hey, Auna." With a final squeeze, he released Rachael. "The flowers look amazing."

"Thanks." Her huge grin said she was pleased with her work as well. "I had fun incorporating the pumpkins, hay, and cornstalks. By week's end I should have all the shops along Rainier outfitted for fall."

"Do you ever sleep?" Rachael asked.

Auna laughed. "Rarely."

Evan rubbed the biceps of his injured arm, a movement quickly becoming a habit for him. "We keep trying to convince her to quit the department and go full time into this flower gig."

Auna leaned toward Rachael, her hand covering her mouth but her words plenty loud. "He's constantly trying to get rid of me. I'm starting to develop a complex about him not liking me."

"And I keep telling her it's because I don't want to see her burn herself out." He eyeballed Auna. "It's called caring."

She warmed under his smile. What woman wouldn't? Evan Wayne possessed the ability to singlehandedly turn women to mush with one look. Another superpower he wielded but wasn't aware of. Auna slid her hands into her pockets. "I cut my hours, but until I know this 'gig' will run in the black, I'm not quitting."

"Stubborn." Evan coughed.

"Learned from the best." Auna turned toward Rachael. "I got your email. I have a few more books you can borrow. I brought them if you want to hook up with me before you leave."

"Sounds great." Evan bounced a look between them, and Rachael responded. "I had some more questions on floriography."

"Ah." He nodded.

Auna chatted for a few more minutes, then headed off to visit with other friends. Evan's eyes trailed her.

"She's a beautiful woman," Rachael commented.

Ever so slowly, he turned Rachael's way. "She is."

"And you two seem to get along. Really well." Pained her to say it. She wasn't feeling super altruistic in this moment, but really, she did want him with someone who could verbally spar with him.

"We do." He rolled onto his heels, then his toes, watching Rachael closely. Like he knew what she was up to.

So she might as well go all in. "You should ask her out."

He crossed his arms as he waited a beat. "Well, see, I would if it weren't for one issue." Leaning in, he brought his face level with hers.

Her breath hitched. Man, she loved his eyes. And that dimple in his chin. Her best friend was one giant distraction. She forced herself to focus. "What's that?"

His lazy smile proclaimed he knew exactly the disturbance he brought to her world, and he was quite proud of it. But because he was a man of his word, and they'd already covered that ground, he straightened. "I don't date women who're already involved with someone."

That snapped her out of her stupor. "She has a boyfriend?"

His grin deepened. "Yep. For two blissfully happy years. Pretty sure they'll be engaged before this year's out."

"Wow. Okay. I really thought there was something between you two." She brushed away a loose hair tickling her cheek. "My sniffer must be way off."

Amusement covered his face. "Not really. Auna and I did date once."

Her fingers stilled against her face. "You two dated?" Their conversation from the dinner with Searchlight careened back. "Is she who you were in love with?"

He nodded. "We were young. Just started college. It didn't last long."

Her stomach jumped. "And you've been friends ever since?"

"Yep."

"Point Three."

"Point what?" Evan's brow crinkled.

Oops. Hadn't meant to say that out loud. "Nothing." Except it was something. Something huge. Because without trying, he'd blasted past another of her barriers. Apparently, friendships could survive breakups.

Her already tenuous reasons for staying away from Evan grew thinner yet.

She spotted Shona Catto behind him in the crowd. Suddenly, speaking with her sounded a whole lot less threatening. "I should"—she nodded in Shona's direction— "get it over with."

He glanced to the left with her. "Need me to come play human shield again? Divert any questions you don't want to answer?"

There were about a million and one questions pinging around in her brain that she didn't want to answer, but he couldn't shield her from them—he was the one creating them.

"No. I got this." She scooted past. "I'll catch up with you later."

Evan watched Rachael scurry away. He fisted his hands, then stretched and shook them. It was all he could do to not follow her. Push her on what he saw in her eyes. How did she look at him like that but tell him she only wanted to be friends? Even worse, try and set him up with another woman? He rubbed his jaw, then slid his hand to massage the sore muscles along his neck and injured shoulder. Nothing was going quite the way he wanted right now, and it threatened to put him in a surly mood.

"I know that look, and it isn't your happy face." His sister sidled up beside him.

"Not now, Hattie."

She immediately stiffened, and he immediately regretted his tone. "Sorry."

She scouted the crowd, her gaze following where his had been, then resting on Rachael. "That tone makes a little more sense now." Before he could respond, she straightened, taking a bead on someone else in the crowd. He spun to see Felicity speaking with Dierks. "Look. Our two best friends in one place. We should join them." She took off before he could say otherwise.

Heaving a sigh at his matchmaking sister, he followed her. Better than her dragging them over his way—which she no doubt would. He nodded at his friend. "Hey, Dierks." Then to Felicity. "Felicity."

She tucked a blonde strand behind her ear and bestowed her huge grin on him. "Hattie said you were out of your sling. Congrats."

"Thanks."

"You should stop by my table for some celebratory cookies, on the house. Chocolate chip's your favorite, right?"

"I'm an equal-opportunity cookie eater."

She laughed. "Okay. Well, I'll see what I have on hand and surprise you."

"You don't have to."

"But I want to."

Dierks piped in, "If he doesn't want them, I'll take 'em."

At this point, anything other than agreeing would be awkward. Plus, Hattie was evil-eyeing him. "All right. I'd love some, thank you."

Dierks groaned. "Thanks, bro. I nearly had a dozen coming my way."

"I'll give you some too," Felicity soothed. "You protect and serve our streets. I protect and serve your taste buds."

Hattie's death-ray glare deepened until Dierks looked her way. She blasted him with it before snapping her gaze to the crowd at their left. Okay. That was strange. Was she worried Dierks was his competition?

He covered his laughter with a rub of his nose. His friend had unknowingly stepped into a whole world of trouble. Hattie was not just anyone to take on. He almost felt sorry for Dierks. Sorry enough, at least, to redirect the conversation. "Hey, Hattie, have you seen Mom and Dad anywhere?"

She blinked up at him. "No, but I did bump into our nephews earlier. Beware. They're angling for one last party at your house for the season."

"Wasn't that what Labor Day was?"

Her hands thrust up and out. "Don't shoot the messenger. If you don't want us all out there, that's fine."

All right then. A simple topic change wasn't touching the mood she'd worked herself into. "I never—"

Dierks spoke over him. "That's not what he said, Hat." Evan jerked his attention toward him at the shortened use of her name, but he continued talking. "You know your brother loves having you all out there. Go with what you know, not what you think you hear."

She pulled in a long breath and looked at Evan. "Sorry."

He regarded her with a hint of confusion she no doubt perceived but ignored. "It's okay." What he really wanted to know was how Dierks defused the situation so well. He was adding up pieces that fit into a picture he wasn't so sure he wanted to see.

Felicity tipped her head toward the vendor section. "I should get moving. Sylvie is guarding my table, and I was supposed to grab us some dinner. Make sure to stop by before you leave." With a wave, she hurried toward the Pink Ladies food truck to order sandwiches for her and her little sister.

Dierks glanced his way. "We still on for the gun range tomorrow?"

Hattie perked up. "Gun range? You can't go to the gun range."

"My PT says differently." Though she'd instituted a ton of rules. Mainly that he shouldn't shoot right-handed yet, which wasn't what he'd expected at all. Demonstrating his ability to manage his firearm meant shooting with his dominant hand. Tomorrow was supposed to check off that box, but Becky was shutting him down. She wasn't in his body though, and his arm felt ready. He felt ready. "Yep. Eight work for you? I'm scheduled with Becky for ten."

"That's like sleeping in. You've gone soft since getting shot."

"Dierks!"

"It was a joke, Hattie. You know I wasn't serious. Think about it." He spoke the words evenly, his focus steady on her.

How had Evan missed this connection between them? Okay, so he had been out of it for several weeks, then preoccupied with his own relationship issues, but this wouldn't have gone unnoticed had he seen them together. Come to think of it, this was the first time he'd seen them in the same place since he'd been in the hospital. Why did he get the feeling it wasn't the first time they'd been together since then?

"I'm going to track down Nora and see when Nick and Jude want to come over." He motioned toward the food trucks. "Want to join me and grab some snacks on the way?"

Hattie shook her head. "I was heading home."

She could handle crowds for only so long.

"Dierks?" He had several pressing questions for his friend.

"Actually, I'm calling it a night too, so I can walk Hattie to her car." Dierks shot him an I-totally-know-I'm-busted look, followed by a silent plea to deal with it tomorrow.

"I'll catch you in the morning then." Evan turned to Hattie. "And I'll let you know what day the boys are coming in case you want to join us."

He took off in the opposite direction, restraining himself from turning around to follow them. Surveillance could answer a whole host of his questions, but he wasn't sure he'd like what he'd see. Thinking about his sister dating was one thing. Having her possibly dating his best friend, another. But watching them kiss—if it had gotten that far—yeah, no, he wasn't there yet. Probably wouldn't ever be.

Didn't take him long to locate Nora and Tate and set up for the boys to come over Thursday after school. Those two had been begging to learn the slackline, and he promised to spend the night teaching them.

After grabbing a Polish sausage with his family, he left to track down Rachael and see how her interview went. As he passed a cheese-on-a-stick vendor, he stopped and grabbed her one. He hopped onto the concrete ledge around the edge of the lot and scanned the crowd but didn't see her. Swiveling around, he peered up Rainier toward the police department. Yep. There she stood, staring at her now white wall. She had a sketchbook in hand and periodically glanced from it to the brick. Must be finishing details before starting tomorrow.

He jumped down and headed her direction. When he was ten feet from her, she turned. It'd be nice to think she was in tune with his presence, but no doubt the scent of cheese grabbed her. Holding out the treat, he made sure his fingers touched hers as she took it. Grade schoolish? Sure. But if it worked to get that blush on her cheeks, the action wasn't beneath him.

"Should I be offended that you look happier to see the cheese than you do me?" he asked.

"I'm equally as happy to see you when you come bearing gifts like this."

He'd purchase all of Wisconsin for her then. Or at least a dairy farm.

She bit in with a groan. "Don't judge, but this is my second tonight, and it's even better than the first."

"I figured it had to be at least your third, so no judging."

"Oh, I had a bowl of cheese curds too." Her grin reached her eyes, and he relaxed with their relationship once again on solid ground. "I like to switch things up. Keep my taste buds guessing."

"Cheese curds? I don't understand how you eat those things. They're like slimy and rubbery—"

"And ooey and gooey." She took another bite. "You don't understand cheese the way I do."

He chuckled while she finished off her snack. The woman was adorable. She'd tossed her hair into a bun since he'd seen her earlier and donned a sweatshirt emblazoned with MIDWEST across the front. It was baggy, but not so baggy that he couldn't still appreciate his favorite jeans on her. She'd jabbed the pencil into her bun and tucked her sketchbook under her arm as he'd approached.

"How'd it go with Shona?"

"Surprisingly well. She loves the idea behind my mural and asked if she could feature it." Rach wrapped her napkin around her now empty stick. "Then she acknowledged the past review and said she didn't agree with the person who wrote it. Seems she's a fan of my work." She paused. "Guess I had no reason to be avoiding her after all."

"Sometimes our past can give us incorrect perceptions about our current situation."

Her eyebrows dipped. "That's an awful lot of big words."

He sighed. "Fine. Let me simplify. Sometimes our past can make us hide from things that aren't scary at all."

Yep. This time she understood what he'd intentionally tried to cloak the first time. Her cheeks pinkened. "I think I preferred your big words." Then she turned and walked away.

Chapter Seventeen

"You sure you're ready for this?" Dierks lobbed the question as they walked into the Silver Bullet.

"More than." He inhaled the familiar mixture of sulfur, metal, and smoke. Three months away from the gun range was too much. And until he could clear it, he wouldn't be on the streets. That stretch of time proved harder than missing this place.

"And Becky really cleared you to come?"

"Sort of." They checked in at the desk and grabbed a few targets before heading to the range.

"That sounds sketchy."

Evan took out a target from his pile, then attached the remaining ones to the magnetic board in his lane. "What really sounds sketchy is you and my sister yesterday."

"You caught that, huh?" Dierks did the same with his targets.

"You're going to pretend I didn't?"

"No. I saw your interest." He set his gun on the counter and leaned against the plexiglass separating their lanes. "I should have told you sooner, but honestly, I wasn't sure where it was going."

"*It* being a relationship with my sister."

"Yeah."

"And you've recently figured out where it's going?" Evan crossed his arms and braced his feet in a tactical stance.

Dierks met his intimidation with an amused sniff. "Yes, *we* have." He stood tall. "Not that either of us owe you details on our relationship—other than we're in one—but you're my friend, so I'll do you the courtesy."

"Kind of you."

His brow arched at Evan's sarcastic tone, but he left it alone. "Your sister is an amazing woman. I always knew it, but we spent a lot of time together after you were shot. One thing led to another—"

"How much of another we talking about?"

That comment had him straightening. "You know me well enough not to ask that, and I'm not answering it out of respect for your sister. Whom you also know well enough." They'd been the only two out here, but now another guy joined them. That meant this conversation was nearly over because it wasn't one to be had shouting loud enough to be heard through ear protection. Dierks picked his up. "Long story short, my intentions are to see how long-term I can make this with your sister."

Surprise licked at him. "It's that serious?"

"Getting to be." Dierks maintained his steady stare. "Is this going to be a problem?"

"No." Though it pinched that his sister and friend were falling in love while he was over here hoping things with Rachael might somehow still be viable. Felt like the perfect morning to be back on the range because he really needed to shoot something.

He slipped on his earmuffs and stapled his target to the board, then tapped the digital screen to send his bullseye out fifteen feet. Starting easy. Well, if he could start with his right hand. As it was, he'd shoot left-handed first.

Picking up his Glock, he took his stance, lifted his arm, and squeezed off a round. He absorbed the recoil with ease. It was just like riding a bike. His muscle memory wasn't even fuzzy. With his confidence building, he shot off a rapid succession of five. All hit paper, but only one landed near the body outline. Sucking in a deep breath, he aimed, and fired. Then grinned. Three landed near the red. Better.

After firing his entire clip, he reloaded and shot off another one before recalling the target to replace it. Dierks angled around the plexiglass. "How goes it?"

"Decent." But he itched to try his right arm. He flexed those muscles, and they didn't quake at all. Dierks nodded and disappeared, then shot a few loud rounds. Evan swapped his targets and sent the new one out the same distance but gripped his gun in his right hand.

Slowly he lifted his weapon. Okay. That pulled, but he should expect to be sore. He'd been lifting one-pound weights, preparing for this, but his loaded gun doubled that. Never would have imagined two pounds could best him, but his arm trembled. With intense concentration, he forced it steady. Then he squeezed.

A little pain. Bad aim. But overall, not bad for his first shot. See? He was ready for this. Aiming again, he sent off five successive shots.

And bit back an oath as his last one left the chamber. Only his training kept his gun in his hand, but man alive, his shoulder burned. His eyes watered, and he clamped down his jaw, trying to smooth his breathing. He set his gun on the counter. Dang it. Something had popped when he'd shot off that last round, and now heat pulsed up and down his arm like electrical currents. Worse yet, every one of his shots had gone wild.

Dierks reappeared, took one look at him, and shook his head. "Was it worth it?"

"Don't know yet," he growled through clenched teeth.

"Shall I call Becky or are you going to?"

Evan glared at him. Shaking his head, Dierks started cleaning up their gear. They walked out to their cars, Evan's shoulder throbbing in time with his kicked-up pulse. Dierks had his phone to his ear, already explaining the situation. He peered in Evan's direction. "Yeah. He was already on schedule, but he needs to come in now." He nodded. "Yep. We'll be there." Hanging up, he stowed both their bags in his trunk. "I'm taking you to Becky."

"I can drive."

That earned him an annoyed look. "Get in the car."

He was in too much pain to respond. Sliding into the passenger seat, he reached across himself to shut the door. "I don't get it. A few rounds with my Glock should not cause this reaction." A rifle, yeah, maybe. But not his Glock.

"Might be nothing. Won't know till you see her." Dierks fired up the engine on his black Mustang and pulled into traffic. "Hattie's going to be on you. You know that, right?"

"Hattie's not going to hear about this."

Dierks drummed his fingers on his steering wheel. "I suppose I could keep my mouth shut." He slid him one of those looks he used when trying to break a suspect. "For the right price."

"You've got to be kidding me."

"Nope." He merged onto the highway.

"Fine. Lay it on me."

Dierks hesitated. "First I need to know where things are with Rachael."

"I took your advice. Smoothed things over with her."

He cast him a glance. "Still only friends?"

Unfortunately. "Yes."

"All right, then this will work. Maybe better than I originally figured." He took a left turn. "Hattie's been trying to set you up with Felicity."

Evan groaned. This was not heading anywhere he wanted to travel. "I'm aware."

"Seems her heart is set on you dating her best friend since she's dating one of yours." His fingers continued their noise making. "My gut says she thinks Felicity is into me. Motivates her to head it off."

"You've never been low on confidence." Evan rubbed his biceps and down his arm, trying to soothe the muscles there. The pain level had lessened some.

Dierks' flashed the grin all the ladies loved. "I have not." Smooth as butter, he slid around two slow cars. "But that's beside the point. What I need is for you to go on a double date with Hattie and me. Put her mind at ease. Bonus points are that I can tell her I set this all up—and I won't be lying."

"You manipulated it. Big difference."

Dierks shrugged. "Seems like a win-win for us both." He waited a beat, then grew serious. "All kidding aside, this is important to your sister, so it's important to me. One date. Which right now might be good for you too. Afterwards, if you don't see it going further than that with Felicity, you don't have to go out with her again. You'll have gotten yourself back out there while also making your sister happy."

Had to go in for the kill, didn't he. "All right. Tell Hattie we can go on a double this Friday. But she better be clear with Felicity that it's just as friends."

"I know you're hung up on Rachael, but she's been pretty clear with you. It's time to move forward, friend, and Felicity is a nice girl. You might surprise yourself." He slowed down as they exited the highway. "I never saw it coming with Hattie."

He had a point. Several, actually.

Didn't mean he liked a one of them.

Dierks parked in front of Lifetime Physical Therapy. "I'll wait out here."

Evan ducked inside, and they ushered him right to Becky. She stood by equipment, finishing rounds with her current patient. After a few words of encouragement to the guy, she turned to Evan, sizing him up. Her lips thinned, and she motioned for him to follow her across the room. She asked him a few questions before investigating his range of motion. She pushed and prodded, not seeming to care when he grunted. If anything, she prodded harder. After several minutes, she stood with her hands on her hips. "You didn't do anything permanent, but you did set yourself back."

He was simultaneously relieved and frustrated with himself.

Becky, however, showed only one of those emotions. "If you're not going to listen to me, then you're wasting both of our time."

Deserved. "You're right."

"I know." Her icy blue eyes frosted.

"And I apologize."

She softened. Slightly. "Apology accepted." Motioning to a small table, she led him over to it. They sat. "Listen, you're not the first officer I've worked with, so I get the stubborn streak. And I know it's hard for you to accept you might not be out there again."

"I will be."

Her mouth snapped shut, and she worked her jaw. All right. He was testing her patience. But he would not accept any other outcome.

"I know that's what you want, but you need to prepare yourself for it not happening. That doesn't make you less than. It makes you human. Your injury was severe, Evan. I'm doing the best I can to give you a fighting chance, but you have to work with me here."

He scrubbed a hand through his hair. "It's taking too long." And every day not out there—no matter what she said—made him *feel* less than.

"It's going to take longer the more you do stupid stuff like this." She stood. "And I will not clear you if I think being out there is a danger to you or anyone else. It's the sucky part of my job, but it'd suck more if I heard you or someone else died because you couldn't perform your duties." Her eyes held compassionate resolve. "No PT today, I'm sending you for a therapeutic massage. We'll repeat it on Wednesday, and you'll rest your shoulder until Friday. Keep up with your stretches, but no exercise."

He didn't have the time for more rest. "You've got to be kidding me."

"Or don't listen. But then don't come back."

"Fine. Rest till Friday."

Then he'd jump back in full force. Those shots had gone wild, but only because he'd pulled the trigger before he'd been ready. He refused to accept that his accuracy was compromised. He'd rest his shoulder. Follow what Becky said even if it grated him.

And next time he stood in front of his target, he'd be prepared.

"You're making good progress."

Rachael turned from the mural toward the familiar voice. "Hey, Belle, what brings you out here?" Setting her brush across her open paint can, she descended her ladder.

"A craving for an almond stick from Kruis Bakery."

A block up the street, they were known for their Dutch treats. "Ah." She wiped her hands on her jeans. "Morning sickness must be getting better then."

"Much." She peered up at the outline Rachael was painting on the wall. "I'm amazed you know where to place the lines."

"Me too." This project was definitely stretching her. "I created a grid to work off of, and I'm praying with every stroke. This is not something I could do on my own." Lots of Jesus, coffee, and cheese.

Belle walked to the framed rendering she'd also set out. Each artist painted a smaller version of their mural, titled it, and wrote a paragraph about the catalyst behind their piece. This year they also added the name and bio of their charity. The town had special frames on stands to store the information so pedestrians could read it as they walked by. Belle studied the info. "Wow. Rachael, this is quite the piece."

"It will be, if my ability can match my imagination."

"I have no doubt it will." She looked up at the outline. "So each of those flowers has a different meaning?"

Rachael nodded.

She walked closer to the wall. "And you're adding the meaning into the flowers." She squinted, then pointed. "I see one! I don't know what the flower is, but the curve along that petal says *hope*."

Her discovery soothed a few of Rachael's ever-present nerves. "You can see it. I worried I'd made the word too small, but I didn't want to make it so large it overpowered the painting." She joined her. "That flower's called hawthorn, by the way."

"It's perfect." Belle's focus remained on the wall. "It's touching"—she glanced at Rachael— "are those carnations? It's kind of hard to tell with only the outline."

"Especially when I haven't finished them yet." This was the section she currently worked on. "But yes, they're carnations."

Excitement lifted Belle's brows. "*Mother's eternal love*, right there on the edge of that carnation where it's touching the hawthorn." She spun to face Rachael, her own eyes misty. "You're going to make me cry, Rach, and you haven't added the children yet."

"Most will be adult faces." Because they'd been missing for so long.

"Now I am crying." Two tears trailed down Belle's face, and she swatted them. "I could blame pregnancy hormones, but I think it's more my mom heart. I can't imagine—" She abruptly stopped. "I'm sorry."

Rach shrugged, unwilling to let her friend's emotions tug out her own. "I know where Brianna is. That's a million times better than always wondering."

Belle looked as if she wanted to say more but Hope Perez and her foster daughters rounded the corner at that moment. "Hey there, we were doing some shopping and wanted to stop by to see the progress."

Rachael made introductions. "Belle, this is Hope Perez, Ashley, and Abbi."

Belle reached out her hand. "Nice to meet you all." She rested her focus on Hope. "Perez. Is Liliana Perez your daughter?" Belle must have made the connection after reading the information on the painting. Rachael had listed each child's name.

"She is." Hope peered up at the wall. "Oh, Rachael, it's going to be more beautiful than I imagined."

"I hope so."

Ashley and Abbi walked over to read the framed information. It was the middle of the school day, so their presence surprised her. Plus, they seemed much more subdued than the last time she'd seen them. "Is everything okay?" Rachael asked.

"They had family visitation this morning."

Ah. That explained their school absence. "They're sisters then?"

"Half." Hope nodded. "Things didn't go quite like they'd hoped, so a little retail therapy was in order."

They were taken from their home for a reason, one Rachael didn't need to know. "They're blessed to have you and Alvaro."

"Oh, no. It's the other way around." Her beaming smile landed on the girls. "We're blessed by them."

With her words, something inside Rachael shifted. Something challenging every one of her internals in ways she didn't want them to. Her life was good exactly the way it was.

They all chatted for a few minutes, then Hope called the girls over. "We've played hooky long enough. Time to get back to school."

Ashley and Abbi groaned, but they followed without argument. Hope waved. "You and Evan come see us for tacos again soon."

"We will."

The clouds covering the sun rolled away, and Belle slipped her sunglasses over her eyes. "I should get going too. I'm bringing Micah lunch."

Even with pregnancy exhausting her, she glowed. "It's good to see you so happy, Belle."

Hand on her slightly rounded belly, Belle smiled tenderly. "It's been a lot of work, but so worth it. A year ago, I never imagined all of this."

None of them would have. With the brokenness in their relationship, and Micah in another state, the idea they'd reconcile hadn't been a blip on anyone's radar. Much like love hadn't been on Jonah's or Penny's when they bumped into one another four years ago. Now they were blissfully happy with a one-year-old. Even Gavin was off discovering his own path. Everyone around her was moving forward. Life didn't stop just because Rachael had stopped living it. But it had been a whole lot easier to disengage when everyone remained in the same place.

Still, she was happy for all of them. "Some things are worth the effort."

"And the risk." Belle hitched her purse farther up her shoulder. "I'll see you around?"

"Yep."

With a smile and a nod, she hustled toward her car. Rachael returned to her work, struggling to focus on the physical wall in front of her. The invisible one she'd placed around herself and the risk required to tear it down had shoved itself to the forefront of her mind. Still, she soldiered on until her arms ached and couldn't go any further. She was definitely developing muscles she didn't know were there.

After packing things up, she headed home. Evan had the gun range this morning followed by PT, so he was sure to be sore himself. They'd talked about going on a hike, but she wasn't sure if he'd be up to it. Either way, she'd have to be because Clooney needed to run.

As if ensuring she was aware of that exact fact, Clooney raced to greet her, barking as she slid across the wood floor. "Hey girl." Rach reached down to pet her. "Give me a second, and then we'll get out of here." She quickly washed the paint from her hands and arms, grabbed Clooney's leash, then headed for Evan's.

Clomping up his steps, she kept an eye on Clooney playing in the grass between their yards. She knocked on Evan's door, then opened it a crack. "You decent?"

"Dressed, yeah. Mood, no." He grumbled from deep inside his house like a wounded animal hiding in its cave. Ha. Cave. Batman. She couldn't stop her giggles, which he clearly did not appreciate. "You and whatever you're laughing about can take a hike."

"Precisely what I was getting ready to do. You still planning on joining me or do you prefer the company of your grumpy attitude tonight?" She peeked around the door. "Personally, I think Clooney and I are the easy choice, but to each their own."

The deepest of sighs expelled his lips, but they also quirked upward. Minimally. "Let me get my hiking boots."

"I'll meet you by Sally."

His not arguing was her first clue. He was definitely sore, or he'd insist on driving.

Five minutes later he was in her Jeep, and they pulled onto the road. "I'm not as familiar with this area as you. Where should we go that Clooney can come too?"

"Oakhollow Park."

She nodded and he navigated them there. Other than his directions, he didn't talk. She understood and allowed him his space. More often than not, quiet didn't need filling with more than a friendly presence. After a short drive, they pulled into a dirt parking lot, and she let Clooney out of the rear seat.

"Since you know the place, you want to pick the trail?" she offered.

"Sure."

More comfortable silence wrapped around them as they strolled toward the trailhead. They ducked into the woods, the trees swallowing them as they walked the pine-needled path. The loamy scent of dirt, sap, and leaves filled the air around them. About a hundred feet in, the area opened to sand dunes leading into a ravine. Across from there stood miles of forest tickled with golds, reds, and oranges. "Gorgeous."

"Yeah."

She didn't look. Didn't have to. She knew what held his focus. Could feel the warmth of his gaze, but couldn't encourage him by meeting it. "I didn't know there were dunes anywhere other than along the lake." Clooney raced across them, getting all the exercise her little heart desired.

"Not many people do."

Now she did look up at him. "Thanks for sharing the spot."

He nodded farther into the forest. "Oh, there's more to see."

By the time they silently followed the trail all the way around its longest circle, she discovered hundreds of trees in horizontal lines, creating rows and rows of nature's perfect paths. They happened across deer and lost count of how many different birds flew past. Plus she discovered a handful of forts people built through the years, and they ducked into a few. Best of all, though, she climbed an old tree whose branches lifted high enough to allow her another gorgeous view.

As they clambered out of the forest, she finally struck up conversation. "Do you come here a lot?"

"Used to. Grew up hiking here with family and friends."

Her curiosity over one of those friends resurfaced. "Did Mandie ever come with you?"

He stiffened. "Yeah, she did." He pointed to another trail. "We'll do that one next time. Leads out to a creek."

In other words, he didn't want to talk about her. One to keep quiet herself, she understood. But, much like he did with her tough subjects, she'd keep bringing them up so he'd know she was there should he want to talk.

"Look out." Evan's arm snaked out to shove a branch away from her face. He grimaced, and it wasn't the first time she'd caught the look tonight. He gingerly tucked his arm to his body. "You almost ate that limb for dinner."

"Thanks," she said. They walked a few more steps. "Your shoulder sore from the range this morning?"

"A little."

"How'd you shoot?"

"I lifted my hand and pulled the trigger."

"And there's your salty Batman voice." She waited for him to look at her. He did, and since she stood on his good side, she nudged him with her shoulder.

He listed to the right but held steady. "Sorry. It didn't go as well as I'd hoped, nor did I expect to feel it this much."

"It was your first time back. You'll get there."

"Not if I keep shortchanging my recovery to work on cold cases."

And now they were nearing the source of his bad mood. "It's important work."

"So everyone says."

"Who's everyone?"

"Dierks." His tone soured. "My captain." He stomped along. "Cap mentioned the work seems to suit me. Like he's forgotten about everything I do on the streets."

"Would it really be that bad to be off the streets?"

"Yes." There wasn't an ounce of give in his answer.

"Why, though?"

"Because I'm an officer, not a detective."

"You seem to have a natural knack for both."

His jaw clenched.

Whoa, 'kay. He really was in a mood.

"I can do the job, Rach, but that doesn't mean I'm meant for it."

"No question?"

"None." Again, the word held no bend.

Which only strengthened her resolve that—while he might be blasting through her points like a pile of TNT—he was not the man for her.

Chapter Eighteen

Somehow tonight had gone from entertaining his nephews to entertaining his entire family. And Dierks. He and Hattie were making their debut as a couple now that they'd outed themselves to Evan. They sat on the love seat component of his patio furniture. Time to throw that piece out.

"I'm thinking lavender and foxglove." Rachael sat in a chair beside Evan as he grilled. One of the floriography books Auna loaned her lay open on her lap, but her focus was on him.

"Huh?"

"It's the flower pairing of choice when you want to encourage a friend to reconsider their decisions."

The woman always knew how to settle him. He chuckled, and as he opened the grill, flames shot up, charring the burgers. Evan shifted the patties around. "My feelings are that obvious?"

"To me." She shut the book. "What I don't get is why? Dierks is a great guy."

He closed the hood. "I'd think you'd be on my side here. He's got a dangerous job."

"So that's your reason?"

"No." He twirled the spatula. "I'm saying I'm surprised it's not yours."

She shrugged. "I personally wouldn't date him—"

"Good."

"But if Hattie's okay with the risk, who am I to stop her?"

He was more stuck on Rach's hang-up. And since she brought it up, "Someone's job shouldn't prevent you from dating them."

"You'd date a stripper then?" He nearly dropped his spatula. She lifted her palms. "I'm just saying, occupations can and do play a role in the dating game."

"That's not close to the same thing."

Her lips thinned, and she gave another shrug, obviously done proving her point.

"Your example is based on a bias, not facts," he prodded.

"Maybe. But you also can't escape the *fact* that police officers have dangerous jobs."

So much for her settling him. "Let's change the topic."

"Fine. What's your reason against them dating?"

"Dierks has been known to be a bit of a lady's man."

"Has been or is?"

"Has." A few more minutes and the meat would be perfect. "He got his act together about two years ago. But he hasn't really dated anyone since then, and I'm not sure I like my sister being the first."

Rach's head bobbed. "Wow. Um, okay. Glad you're not God."

"Come on, that's not fair."

"Holding Dierks's past against him is?"

"You're the one who just questioned me about dating a stripper."

She offered an epic eyeroll. "Stop splitting hairs. My example was given in the present. Yours is in Dierks's past. When we get with God, our past is wiped clean. That's called grace. Extend some to Dierks."

"But we're talking about my sister. I don't want her hurt."

"Hate to break it to you, Evan, but you can't prevent people from getting hurt."

"I can and I have."

"I think I'm going to start calling you Thor instead of Batman. He thought he was a god too."

Evan didn't think he was a god or the God. But he also didn't enjoy her sarcasm. "Pretty sure in mythology, he was."

"Right. Mythology. As in it's a myth. Much like it's a myth if you think you're capable of stopping every bad thing from happening in life."

He popped the hood again and started pulling the meat from the grill. "Burgers are ready. Mind rounding everyone up?"

She stared him down for a lengthy second, then sighed and stood. "Sure."

Everyone but Dierks and Hattie—in a world of their own—were down below in the grass watching Nick and Jude attempt the slackline. He'd given them pointers earlier in the day, and Nick had wobbled across one time before Evan left to fix dinner. Now Rach descended the steps to find them all.

He snagged the last burger, then set a timer for three minutes to let the grease burn off. Shouldn't have shut Rach down like that, but she was dangerously close to some sore nerves. That conversation wasn't going to end anywhere but him owing her an apology, so tanking it was the best strategy. He walked the patties over to the table with all the condiments and side dishes. Down below, Rach called his family to dinner, then footsteps clambered up the stairs.

Rachael appeared last, as if debating staying. He caught her eye and held up a pack of cheese slices. "I added extra to your burger."

That grabbed her smile, dragging it out. "A true friend." She sidled up next to him and started fixing her plate.

Once they'd both piled them high with side dishes—Mom always came prepared to feed an army—he directed her to two chairs in the corner of his deck. The boys hadn't come upstairs yet, and it looked like Nora and Tate were fixing plates to take down to them. He chuckled. They came by their determination naturally.

Rach took a huge bite of her burger, smearing mayonnaise and ketchup in the corners of her mouth while a cheese-laden glob of condiments plopped to her plate. A plate where everything touched. "Um"—he motioned with his hand— "you got a little something …."

She took her napkin and wiped. "Someone had to make the burgers the size of my head."

"Someone covered hers with every condiment known to man."

"The only way to eat a burger."

He held up his with only ketchup and mayo. "That's where you're wrong. Kind of like how you've let your plate become one big mass of food."

She took her fork, speared a bite of mac-n-cheese and dipped it in the baked beans then straight into her mouth. "Mmmm."

He chuckled and took another bite of his burger. After they'd made healthy dents in both their plates, Rach looked over at him. "I shouldn't have said anything about Dierks and Hattie. I know you've been dealing with a lot lately. It wasn't my place—"

"Rach, it's okay." He'd had time to cool some, and he could concede her point on his friend. "You were right about Dierks. He's not who he was, and if he wants to date my sister, then good for the both of them." Though seeing his sisters romantic with anyone took time. Nora and Tate had been married years—had two kids—and he still didn't need to see them kissing.

"Now to get your face to agree with your words."

"Hopefully, I can conquer that gut reaction by tomorrow night."

She popped a blue cheese-stuffed olive in her mouth and talked around it. "Why tomorrow?"

"I'm going on a double date with them."

Her chewing stopped. She swallowed. "With who?"

Huh. It almost looked as if she didn't like this turn of events. Interesting. "Felicity."

Before she could respond, a sharp cry from his yard split the air.

"Mom!" Jude raced up the deck steps. "Mom! Nicholas is hurt."

All the adults were up and moving. Jude led them to Evan's backyard where

Nicholas lay curled on his side holding his arm. Tears rolled down his face.

His dad, Tate, knelt beside him. "Hey, Bud. You hurt your arm?"

Nora scooted to his other side and swiped his hair from his face as Nick nodded at Tate. Evan moved in close, swallowing at the sight of Nick's right arm. It jutted out at an angle that hinted at a bad break.

He looked up at Rachael. "Go inside. Get me one of my small plastic cutting boards, two hand towels, and gauze. You'll find that in the first aid kit in my bathroom."

She nodded and raced off. Nora and Tate remained by Nick, soothing him while Dierks and Hattie talked with Jude to try and figure out what happened. Evan peeked their way.

"He said he wanted to be like Uncle Evan." Tate stared at his shoes.

"So what did he do?" Dierks asked him.

But Evan already knew. Known it the minute they rounded the corner and he saw where Nick lay. He gripped his good hand around his neck and tightened his squeeze. He should have seen this coming. Prevented it. "He tried the high line, didn't he."

Jude looked over and slowly nodded. "We took the ladder from under your deck." Tears slipped down his cheeks. "I'm sorry, Uncle Nick. We shoulda asked."

No. He should have taken that dumb line down before leaving them out here alone. Nick had asked about it several times tonight. Boasted he could walk it with a confidence level that came nowhere near his skill. Leaving it up was like sticking candy in front of a toddler and expecting them not to eat it. The kid was ten. Of course he was going to take the first opportunity to get up there.

Evan looked straight at Jude, willing him to feel his words. "It's okay, Bud. I'm not mad at you."

He was furious at himself.

Rachael rushed back with everything in her hands. Evan went to work securing Nick's arm. Within minutes, he was ready for transport. "I've got his arm stable. He needs to go to the ER."

"On it." Tate jogged inside for his keys while Nora followed Evan, who carried Nick, to her minivan. As they took off for the ER, everyone else returned upstairs. Mom and Dad were packing away all the food.

Evan glared up at the slackline, heat pressing in on him. He stalked to the ladder still leaning against the tree.

"What do you think you're doing?" Rachael's voice reached him from behind.

"Taking that thing down."

"No you're not." She grabbed his good arm. "Last thing we need is for you to fall too."

"Better me than him." A depreciative laugh ripped out. "Guess I'm a little late on that one."

"This is exactly what I was talking about, Evan. Nick getting hurt is not your fault."

He shrugged her off. "Seems we still disagree."

She grabbed him again. "About two things it appears, because if you think I'm letting you climb that ladder, you're wrong."

"Three things then, because if you think you can stop me, you're wrong."

"Stop being a stubborn mule."

"Stop getting in my way."

"You hurt yourself, and you'll be on light duty even longer."

That stopped him. But only for a moment. "So be it."

"Bruce Evan Wayne, you are not responsible for every bad thing that happens around you!"

He kept moving. She didn't know what she was talking about. Didn't carry the burden he did.

"Mandie's death was not your fault."

He'd dodged her words upstairs, but this time he didn't duck fast enough. They hit his sore nerves like an arrow into a bullseye, ripping open a wound she had no clue was there.

He didn't turn. Couldn't. Just kept moving forward like he'd been doing for years. "She called me that night, and I did nothing. She died on my watch. And I'm not letting it ever happen again." He gripped a rung with his good hand and hauled himself up a step.

Rach's fingers slipped over his shoulder in a tender squeeze. "Evan, I'm so, so sorry." Emotion clogged her words, but something else in her tone stalled his anger. He turned, and sure enough, there was empathy rather than pity in her eyes. Because if anyone understood losing someone you loved, it was Rachael. Her lips softly tipped into the barest of a smile that offered companionship he'd never had in this deep well of hurt. "Whatever happened, whatever the full story is—and I'd really like to hear it—that still doesn't make you responsible for the safety of everyone around you."

"It does when I have the ability to stop something and I don't."

She didn't release either of her holds. Her hand still gripped him firmly, and her eyes caught him with a compassionate tether he couldn't break. Especially not when she strengthened its bond with her tender offer. "I'll take down the slackline. Okay?"

He hesitated. It was his responsibility.

"Either that or we're fighting over this ladder, and I don't see that ending well." She quirked her head. "For you."

"Fine." He relented. Stubbornness was a weakness of his, but he could admit she was right on this one. Impulsive action this week had already delayed his healing. Last thing he needed was to fall off the ladder or tweak something else reaching to take down the line. Most important was for it to come down, and Rachael could handle the task.

With his left side, he braced the ladder as she climbed. Within a minute, the slackline fluttered to the ground. The other side could remain attached to its tree. Rach returned to the grass beside him.

"Thanks," he muttered.

"You want to thank me?" she asked. "Tell me the rest about Mandie."

It would have been easier to leave the slackline up.

Rachael wrapped her cardigan closer around her and pushed farther into the corner of her chair. The plastic fabric crackled underneath her, and she debated going for her third cup of crummy coffee from the vending machine. Across from her, Evan held up the wall as he stared out the window into the hospital parking lot. He'd hardly said two words to her since she mentioned how he could thank her. She'd been half kidding. More like a quarter kidding. All right, not kidding at all. She'd unknowingly revived his Batman nickname the moment she'd heard his full name, but the more she'd gotten to know him, the more she understood how perfectly it fit.

Bruce Evan Wayne possessed moments of moodiness, typically brought on by those times he felt he fell short of whatever impossible standard he'd set for himself. He held the biggest superhero complex she'd ever seen along with a deep desire to always be in control. Oh, he masked it behind his humor, but she'd been close enough, long enough, to receive a full picture of who he was. Until recently, however, she'd never understood *why* he was that way. Then tonight, whether he intended to or not, he'd revealed there was more to his story. She wanted all of it.

The chair she sat on shifted as Evan's mom settled beside her. "It was nice of you to come with Evan. He values your friendship."

Rachael turned to Celia Wayne. Evan had her expressive brown eyes, right down to the green and gold lines that darted through their irises. But where Celia's hair was blonde, Evan's was a mahogany brown like his dad's. "I value his as well."

Her lips, always coated in pink lipstick, pulled into a smile. "I'm glad to hear it." She patted Rachael's knee. "He can be incredibly hard on himself. I'm glad he has someone who brings out his light side. That was missing for too long."

"Because of Mandie?"

"He told you about her?" Celia's penciled brows lifted. A lot of women looked fake with all their makeup, but somehow Celia pulled it off with a softness that drew people in.

Rachael shook her head. "Not everything."

Awareness sparkled in her eyes. "Ah. Well, that story is his to tell, and I'll let him."

As if he sensed them talking about him, Evan turned and directed an inquiring gaze their way. Celia stood. "I think I'll go see if Geoff needs any more coffee." She headed toward her husband.

Hands in his pocket, Evan strolled to Rachael. "I'm used to being the one digging for information, not the one being dug into."

"If you'd talk to me, I wouldn't have to dig."

He softly snorted. "Let's take a walk."

"Outside?" She hated hospitals, but she'd come because he needed her.

Not missing a beat, Evan nodded. "There's a good coffee shop around the corner."

"We don't have to go that far. The parking lot would be fine."

"Micah said the surgery could take a couple of hours, and they just brought him back." Micah had been working when they brought Nick in and had been feeding them info. "No sense sitting in the waiting room. You've seen enough of them to last a lifetime."

"If you're sure."

"I am." He motioned toward the door and, after a quick word with his dad, they stepped outside. Bypassing the elevators, they found the steps and silently walked down a floor and exited into the early evening air. The sun was low in the pink-hued sky. She inhaled the crisp air, the temps already dropping from their afternoon high of sixty-six. Up until Nick's accident, it had been a perfect day.

They said nothing as they walked next door to Latte Good, ordered, then settled on one of the tables outdoors. Evan ran his thumb up and down his paper coffee cup. Dark roast. No cream. No sugar. No fun. Normally she teased that his coffee selection was the opposite of his personality. Tonight it suited him.

"I'm glad they were able to fit Nick in for surgery," she said, then sipped her lavender latte.

"Me too. It would have been tough to make him wait through the night with that break." He'd busted through his humerus while also dislocating his shoulder. "As it is, he's going to be in a lot of pain coming out of surgery."

"You would know."

"I would. Which is why I'm such an idiot for leaving that thing up. I knew Nick wanted to walk it. He'd already asked me three times earlier today."

"But you couldn't have known he'd actually try."

"I could have predicted it though."

Settling her cup on the table, she locked gazes with him. "And we're back to Mandie again, aren't we?"

"Yeah," he sighed. "I guess we are." He fiddled with a loose string on one of the buttons of his pine-green shirt. It was one of her favorite colors on him. After a long pause, he directed his gaze into his old memories. "I told you we grew up together. We literally met in kindergarten, and I don't remember a time from that moment on where we weren't joined at the hip." A tender smile curled up his lips, and the edges of his eyes crinkled softly. "She was my best friend."

"And at one time, you'd hoped for more."

"As much as a fourteen-year-old can."

Rachael had only been sixteen when she met Kurt. "First love is a pretty powerful thing."

"Yeah." He dragged his finger along his coffee cup. "It is."

That was the thing with love. It transcended age and relationship labels. It didn't matter what he and Mandie called themselves, his heart had been strongly involved. After all, she and Evan were just friends, and the phone call that he'd been shot had taken her to her knees. What must the news about Mandie have done to Evan when he'd heard it? That thought swung at her more intensely. She took his hand. "I'm so sorry, Evan."

"Me too." He removed his hand from her hold. "I told you she was killed by her stepfather." Those words came out rough, coated in both pain and anger. But how much of it did he direct at himself? "What I didn't tell you was she called me that night. I was the last person she spoke with."

"How can you know that?"

"Because I looked at the report when I became an officer. I know her time of death."

"Oh, Evan." That he'd been touched by such tragedy at such a young age hurt her heart. As did the fact he still carried the effects with him.

"She told me her parents were fighting, and I could hear them in the background." His hand clenched, denting the paper cup he held. "I heard her dad come into her room, angry and yelling at her. And I let her hang up. I let her tell me it would be okay." He lifted tortured eyes to her. "I did nothing but stay silent."

"You were a fourteen-year-old boy in a home with parents who loved you dearly. The idea that a parent could murder their own child wasn't something you'd ever imagine."

"Stepparent," he corrected.

She studied him. He was stuck in one spot. It was time to give him a shove. "All right. Maybe you should have told your parents—"

"Maybe?" he raised his voice.

She kept right on talking. "But you didn't, Evan. You can't change that any more than I can change the choice to paint the night Chris and Brianna died."

She'd pried back the curtain on a hidden part of herself and now waited for the realization of it to reflect in his eyes.

"What do you mean?"

"The night they died, I was supposed to be with them. But I told them to go on without me because I wanted space to paint without anyone underfoot." She peeled the sleeve on her coffee. "I got more space than I ever imagined."

"Rach." It came out softly.

She leaned in toward him. "It's okay, Evan. I've made peace with it." Well, she still struggled with painting, but that was slowly healing too. This mural was encouraging that to happen, something she hadn't expected when she took the project on. "The point is both of us can play out all the *should haves* in the world. They won't change a thing. Mandie is gone, but you know if she were here, she'd never blame you."

He stayed silent although his grip lessened on his cup. She'd love for him to agree. To see the weight lifted from him. One conversation wouldn't remove the hurts he carried, no matter how badly she wanted it to. She could desire freedom for him, but she couldn't force him to seek or accept it. Often silent prayers worked stronger than convincing words. She'd continue to offer both.

"I'm truly sorry for your loss, Evan." She understood it well. "Losing someone we love always leaves a hole. Just be careful what you let fill that spot."

His shoulders sagged, the fight leaving him. "Wise words from someone who's earned that wisdom the hard way."

"And this is one time I'll let you slack off and benefit from my hard work." She tapped her paper cup on the table. "But don't make a habit out of it."

"Deal."

He stood. "Shall we head over?"

His polite way of saying he was finished with the conversation. Understandable. She didn't particularly enjoy talking about her tough past. It was manageable in small doses, and he'd just given her a huge chunk of his.

They strolled toward the hospital, and Evan stopped a foot from the entrance. "You should head home. Things may be awhile here yet, and you have a lot of work to do. Mom and Dad can drive me home."

"All my stuff can wait."

"Not Clooney. She can't feed herself or let herself out. Last thing you need is a bunch of messes to clean up." He nudged his head toward the parking lot. "Go."

He wasn't wrong. Still, she hesitated. "You'll come over when you get home and let me know how Nick is?"

"If it's not too late." He tucked a strand of hair behind her ear, and she squelched a shiver. It wasn't the first time he'd made such a move, but lately even the most familiar touches between them elicited new reactions. Fingers still in her hair, he murmured, "I'll stop by. I promise."

"I won't fall asleep until you do."

Chapter Nineteen

Tired of tossing and turning, Rachael nudged her phone until the screen lit. Five a.m. The sun wouldn't be up for another two hours. Evan no doubt still slept next door, and he needed every minute he could snag. He'd kept his promise and stopped by late last night, looking haggard and tired. Nick had sailed through surgery and would go home later this morning. She'd ordered Evan home with the hope that he'd sleep until he needed to be up for PT today.

Flipping back her covers, she shuffled to the kitchen and made some coffee. She peeked out her windows to find his house still pitch-black. Good. While coffee brewed, she made herself some toast with a few slices of cheddar, then took it all upstairs to her studio. Brianna's painting was nearly finished and the copies of the individual age-progression portraits lay scattered on a nearby table. Evan had already uploaded them to social media sites.

Rachael studied the girls' faces as she ate her breakfast. Creating these along with the mural had birthed a new passion in her, lighting a new direction for her art. She planned to talk it over with her agent, Lanette, but an idea for a gallery showing had firmly taken root in her heart and mind.

First she'd finish her own painting … then one for Evan. She'd snuck his yearbook out of his house to use the pictures of Mandie. His mom also said she'd provide a few from her stash. Without additional family pictures she'd still have some guesswork to do, but she'd drawn enough faces to have an idea how Mandie's would change.

Uncapping her paints, she began the final details of Brianna's portrait. Her daughter's eyes were always the finishing piece. Within their depths, Rach tried to capture the reflection of what Brie might be seeing. Grandparents who had gone before her. Her daddy. Best of all, Jesus. What a party they'd be having in heaven for her little girl's birthday. She had no doubt Brianna was loved beyond measure, both here and up there.

By the time she completed Brianna's brilliant blue eyes, sunlight stretched across the carpet, warming her toes. This year's was her best by far. Brie was losing her little girl look and becoming a young lady. So many conversations they'd have had. Maybe a fight or two. Oh, what she would give to take that bad with the good.

Her hand stilled as the thought split through her current beliefs. Were there good things she was giving up right now because she refused to accept the possibility of the bad? Evan's face drifted into her thoughts.

She sighed and capped her paints. It was too early for facing off with her fears. She'd always taught Gavin not to make a decision when he was tired, hungry, or emotional. Right now she was the first and the last of those things. Rather than working on herself, she'd work on the mural. After a quick shower, she gathered her things and headed to the department. As she set up the ladder to begin, her phone dinged a text from Evan.

YOU'RE ALREADY GONE? THOUGHT WE COULD SNAG BREAKFAST.

While a second breakfast sounded great, her heart still tangled with her early morning question about a future with him. Avoidance of the subject was currently imperative.

SORRY, I ALREADY ATE.

Not a lie, even if her toast and cheese had long since burned off.

LUNCH?

☹ I ALREADY HAVE PLANS.

The frowny face would soften this also loosely true response. Her plans were her own. She intended to grab tacos at Alvaro's, then run by Evan's parents' house to pick up Mandie's photos.

His response dinged. AND I HAVE DINNER PLANS. BREAKFAST AT HOME IN THE MORNING?

She knew he meant nothing by his use of the word home, but it swirled her already churning thoughts, dredging up pictures of what a home with him would look like. Sometimes her ability to take a mere thought and paint it into a scene with vivid clarity worked against her. This was one of those times, because her heart instantly fell in love with the work of art now hanging in her mind.

But she had an entire day to ruminate on what she was going to do about it. Of course, she also had all night to brood about his date.

SURE. I'LL SEE YOU THEN.

By the time her stomach insisted on lunch, she'd outlined the remaining portions of the garden. A few people had stopped by and commented on their excitement over the picture taking shape. She'd chatted with them as she worked, enjoying the sunshine and the company. Now she tapped the lid onto the deep juniper color she used along the edges of the floral stems, then stowed the paint in Sally's tailgate.

Ten minutes later, she pulled into Alvaro's parking lot and made her way inside. Alvaro waved at her. "Rachael. So good to see you."

"You too." She wandered over to him. "I've been craving Hope's tacos."

His face softened. "Then I'm glad you came today. A friendly face will do my wife good."

"Is she having a tough day?"

"Sí."

He offered no further explanation, so Rachael continued to the rear of the store. Hope wiped down the counter, the lunch rush long gone by this time of the day. At the sound of Rachael, she looked up. "Rachael. How are you?"

"Good." She approached the counter. "You?"

"Tired, but good as well." Meat sizzled on the grill behind her. "Did you come for a late lunch?"

"I did."

"Mind if I join you? I haven't had a chance to eat yet."

"I'd love that."

"Wonderful." She straightened. "Let me grab us a few tacos, and I'll meet you outside. Do you have a preference of meat?"

"Not at all. Surprise me."

"I'll be right out."

Rachael headed outside and settled at the same picnic table she and Evan occupied when they'd come. A light breeze balanced the bright sun overhead, creating the perfect fall day. Another few weeks and eating outdoors wouldn't be a regular option. Still, this was her favorite season with its cooler temps and colorful expression. Every tree borrowed from the same palette yet remained unique. Pumpkin everything came out to play. And the holidays were on their way.

Across the lot, Hope emerged from the store and walked her way. Rachael took one of the trays as Hope perched on the opposite bench. "Carne asada and shrimp."

"They smell heavenly." Rachael bit into the steak one first, savoring the seasoned meat topped with grilled onions and guacamole. "You can't keep feeding me for free though."

"I can, and I will. What you've given Alvaro and me is priceless."

As she spoke, a florist truck pulled up. After a moment, the driver hopped out with a bouquet in hand. He disappeared inside only to return a moment later, Alvaro accompanying him their way. He pointed to Hope. "This is my wife."

The delivery guy handed the bouquet of lilies to her, tipped his hat, then went on his way.

"Sweetheart, thank you." Hope stood to hug her husband.

"They aren't from me."

Hope's brow furrowed, and she reached for the card. Tears filled her eyes as she read it. "They're from Abbi and Ashley."

This pulled a warm smile onto Alvaro's face as well. "What does it say?"

"You are an amazing mother, and we know Liliana would think so too." She turned to Rachael. "Today is Liliana's birthday."

Oh, now she wanted to cry. "That's incredibly sweet of your foster daughters."

"They're amazing young girls."

"I'd say you and Alvaro are amazing, opening your home the way you have."

Hope studied her as if her words made no sense. "We have love to give. Those girls desperately needed to receive love. It's a perfect match."

Except it wasn't as simple as she made it out to be. Fostering required they open their hearts but offered no guarantees. Seemed Hope possessed the bravery Rachael desired but had no clue how to grasp.

Evan peeked out his window to see Rachael hauling herself onto the slackline. Strange that she'd come over but not said hi. Before he could prod as to why, his phone rang. It was Dierks with a follow-up on someone he'd interviewed earlier today, thanks to a lead Evan found in one of the cold cases.

"You still there?" Dierks asked.

"Sorry. I was momentarily distracted."

"Aw. Let me guess. Rachael is over."

He released a loud sigh. "Anyway, you were saying?"

"That it paid off, you revisiting attempted abductions." He'd had the idea after the tip on the truck sighting last week. "Kayla Jennings confirms the man who tried to nab her was in a dark-blue Ford F150 with a cap. We pulled the sketch she helped the police draw in 2010. There wasn't much more she could add, but we've already put the picture out there to other departments."

"A guy can change a lot in ten years. Probably won't garner many hits."

"Worth a try. Might jog someone's memory."

Except if people didn't recognize him then, he doubted they would now. "It's sounding more and more like we've got a serial kidnapper out there." Hopefully not a serial killer, but with no bodies, he held out hope these girls remained alive.

"Exactly my thought."

"Hopefully, those age progressions Rachael did for us will generate a lead." They'd been out on social media a few days now with no responses.

"I'm pulling for the mural to do that. It'll get more exposure. Especially this year with the Carltons' involvement."

Because unfortunately, the posts with the age progression photos were often lost in a sea of information on people's social media walls. They were too conditioned to scroll on by. "That's her goal."

"It's a good one." Papers shifted on Dierks's end. "I'll see you at seven?"

"I'll be there." He wasn't hopeful about being set up on a date. Still, he'd go with an open mind since Rachael's was decidedly closed when it came to a future between them.

Shutting off his phone, he jogged outside, stopping at the top of the steps. Rachael's back was to him as she worked to keep herself on the line. Her head tipped down, and she fell. He descended the steps and made it to her side as she dusted off her hands. "I'm going to conquer this thing." Determination furrowed her brow.

"I believe it. But that won't happen until you stop looking down."

She pushed her jaw to the side and regarded him skeptically.

Engaging in the argument wouldn't change her mind. She had to grow tired enough of falling that she was willing to try another way.

Settling his hands on his hips, he leaned against the line. "I was talking to Dierks. He followed up on a possible lead for me since I'm still stuck on light duty."

"And?"

"Didn't pan out quite like I hoped, but it wasn't fruitless either. We're still finding possible connections between Liliana's disappearance and other girls. It's more than what we've had before."

"But not enough to find her."

"Not yet. It's a slow process, Rach."

"That doesn't always lead to answers. I know."

Defeat weighed down her shoulders. Seemed heavier than only Liliana's case, but he didn't have time to ask her about it. He had a date to go on. Joy.

"I need to get ready."

Her face immediately smoothed. "So you are going out?"

Interesting question for someone who didn't want to date him herself. "I am."

"Hattie finally wore you down with Felicity?"

"Dierks, actually."

"Pretty nice foursome. Siblings and their best friends." An unfriendly sarcasm shaded her words, then softened. "Think it'll lead somewhere?"

"I don't know."

"Do you want it to?"

He paused. "I don't know."

She tossed her hands in the air. "Well, what *do* you know?"

Why was she so upset? His first choice had been her. Still was. But she emphatically told him no, so what was he supposed to do? "That I'm single and currently unattached. I was asked out, so I'm going."

"Do you like anything about her other than her cookies?"

"Weren't you the one trying to set me up because of her cookies only a few weeks ago?"

Rather than answer, she clenched her hips, her knuckles turning white. If she tightened that jaw any farther, it'd lock in place.

Her anger proved she felt something more than friendship toward him. He held her eyes, refusing to blink. Unwilling to look away. "If you don't want me to go out with Felicity, just say it. I won't go."

"Why would I care if you went out with her?"

He sniffed. The woman was nothing if not consistent. And he was tired of putting himself out there only to be shut down. "Fine. You wouldn't. I don't know what I was thinking." He turned and walked away.

His foot hit the first step of his stairs before her voice reached him. "Don't go out with her."

Oh, man. Her beseeching tone stopped him. He slowly rounded to face her. "What was that?"

She rubbed her thumbnail, creases deepening around her uncertain stare. But she held his attention. "I said, don't go out with Felicity."

He took a step toward her. "Why?"

"Because"—she sucked in a breath like she was searching for courage—"because she's not right for you."

"Any idea who is?" In her silence, he stepped closer. He could touch her now, and he did, brushing his fingertips along her cheek until he gently held her chin. "You?"

No words. Just a tentative nod.

He smiled. Man, she was beautiful. He brushed his thumb against her soft skin. "Does that mean you're ready to explore things between us?"

She swallowed, an ember of fear flickered in her eyes. "I ... I don't know."

He intended to douse the spark before it fully flamed. "I think you do, or you wouldn't mind me going out with Felicity."

With a step, she disconnected from his touch. "Just because I don't want you out with her, doesn't mean I want to date you."

He waited a beat, doing his best to control his emotions. "You're kidding, right? You literally just said you were the right one for me."

Her hands dug into her hair. "I know, but that doesn't mean you're the right one for me."

Might as well gut him right here. "I cannot believe this." He paced to the steps and back. "Let me see if I have this straight. You don't want to date me, but you don't want me dating anyone else." He tossed her an incredulous look. "That about sum it up?"

"No. I said I don't think you should go out with Felicity."

"Because you're the right girl for me, but I'm not—apparently—the right guy for you." He bit his tongue on what he really wanted to say and searched for words that wouldn't require him to wash his mouth out later. "That's bull crap, Rach."

She flinched. "That's not what I meant."

"But it's what you said. So if you meant something different, then please, clarify." He worked his jaw.

She stood there, mute.

"Fine." He sucked in a deep breath. "I'm going on this date. Not to spite you, but because it's painfully obvious I need to move on. You refuse to take a risk. You're letting fear rule your life." Bending till they were eye level, he said his piece. "Until you decide that living a full life is worth the losses you may incur along the way, there's nothing I can do." He walked away, turned, and stalked back to her. "And let me be clear, you are worth every risk life could throw at me. I'd rather have one second of loving you than a lifetime without."

Her blue irises flared, and her mouth parted. It was all he could do to refrain from kissing her. But he would not erase her fears through giving in to their palpable physical connection. He'd only be writing over them, but they'd still be there and as long as they were, there'd be no future for them. And he wanted her entire future, because she was his choice of a lifetime.

He just wasn't hers.

Chapter Twenty

Well, she'd done a lousy job of avoiding pain, because ever since the moment Evan walked away tonight, her heart smarted. Stupid Point Five posed the primary problem because Point Four dissipated over the past few days as she realized she was, in fact, looking for love. And not with just anyone, but with someone very, very particular: Bruce Evan Wayne. Once she decided to act on her feelings, Point Five dug its heels into the ground. She couldn't seem to circumvent that one inescapable truth: Evan's job was too dangerous.

And she didn't know if she could get past the fear.

Frustrated and antsy, she hopped in Sally and pointed her toward downtown, with only two hours of daylight left. Once upon a time, painting soothed her, and while there were a lot of things she couldn't reclaim in her life, this wouldn't be one of them. She might not be able to risk falling in love with Evan, but she could completely fall in love with the creative process again. Especially with this new project. It felt like a purpose she could claim for herself, and after feeling a little lost lately, that was nice.

Backing over the curb, she parked Sally close to the wall and hopped out. She opened the tailgate, grabbed her paint can, and set to work. The ladder remained on the side of the building, where Captain Larry said to keep it. Seemed he wasn't concerned about someone stealing it since the nearby police station had cameras on every side.

Nearly an hour into her work, she leaned away to gain some perspective and ensure she remained on track. Movement to her right snagged her attention. "Hope?"

"Sorry." Hope waved. "I didn't mean to distract you."

She climbed down her ladder. By tomorrow she'd need the cherry picker to finish the top of the outline. "You're not."

"Liliana loved the path by the river." About a block from town, a wooden boardwalk edged the small river curving through Abundance. "It's one of my traditions, walking it every year on her birthday. After I finished, I found myself pulled here. I didn't think you'd still be working."

"My evening was free, so I figured I'd put it to good use."

Hope shielded her eyes so she could look up at the wall in the evening sun. "You started Liliana's face."

"I did."

"Are those lilies around her?"

"Yes. Not only for her name, but they mean purity."

"I see that. You have it scrolled into the edge of that petal there."

"I do." Rachael looked from the wall to Hope. "Liliana had such a pure, joyful smile. Those flowers felt right."

Hope moved closer to the mural. "And those. Lily of the valley. A return to happiness." She kept studying, reading off other flowers in the garden. "I love how you bordered the entire mural with forget-me-nots."

"It seemed to apply to them all."

"It definitely does."

Even in the midst of Hope's grief, peace shone, a paradox Rachael understood well. But she couldn't understand how to allow her heart to love again.

"Can I ask you a question, Hope?"

"Of course." She turned her full attention to Rachael.

This wasn't where she envisioned having this conversation, yet the street was oddly quiet tonight, providing the needed privacy. "How are you able to love Abbi and Ashley, knowing you most likely will lose them?"

She didn't immediately answer. Then, "Alvaro and I wanted a houseful of children, but I could never get pregnant again after Liliana. It took me some years to grieve that. We started looking into adoption around the time Liliana went missing."

"I'm so sorry, Hope."

"Thank you." She watched a family crossing the street. "Alvaro and I still had a lot of love to give, but we also understood loss. Then we learned about all the children who need someone to love them, but maybe not on a permanent basis. It felt like our hearts had been prepared to open up to more children than I could ever birth."

Rachael heard what she was saying but couldn't quite grasp it. "You've fostered more than Abbi and Ashley?"

"They're our twenty-sixth and twenty-seventh."

She couldn't stop her widening eyes. "That's an awful lot." To love and give up. To live through what had to remind her daily of losing Liliana. "How do you do it?" Her throat closed around the question, but she desperately wanted to know.

"What was our other option? To shut down our hearts and close our door? What kind of life would that be?"

A safe one.

Yet Hope willingly placed herself in the situation to love and lose over and over again.

"Doesn't it hurt every time you have to let them go?"

Hope looked at her a long moment. "Hold your arm out for me." Rachael complied. "Good, now keep it there." About a minute later, her arm began to shake. "Keep holding it."

She made it another minute before her arm dropped to her side. She shook it out.

Hope's eyes remained trained on her. "Does your arm hurt?"

"Yeah?"

"Now tell me," she said, nudging her chin toward the mural she'd begun, "does your arm also hurt after a full day of working on that?"

"Yeah." This time she drew out the word.

Hope nodded. "So you experience pain either way, the only difference is, with that"—another nudge toward the mural— "you're creating something beautiful that will last long after the pain is gone."

Oh.

"Life has pain. You can't escape that fact. But why would you willingly shut out the beautiful parts too, in a futile attempt to avoid experiencing hurt?" A large group headed their way, but Hope added one last piece. "Shutting out love is shutting out the best parts of life. You're not getting rid of pain. You're just allowing it to win."

The group of teens passed by, laughing and chatting. Hope stood to the side, allowing them room. After they were gone, she met Rachael's eyes. "I should go. Alvaro and the girls will wonder where I am."

Rachael merely nodded. She couldn't find her voice, not when emotions clogged her throat. Over what Hope said, yes, but …

She turned and faced the wall, blinking. She'd been a fool. She wasn't trying to avoid falling in love with Evan. She was *already* in love with him and—even with Hope's words ringing in her ears—the realization still terrified her. Yet those words bolstered her sagging courage. Provoked her to push through the fear.

She packed up Sally and headed for home. Evan was still on his date. The one she'd told him to go on. But she'd be there to greet him. Make sure he never wanted to go on another date with anyone else—if she wasn't too late.

She didn't think she was.

Pacing by the windows, watching the clock. An hour slowly ticked by. Then another. Had they hit it off? Did he take Felicity out alone afterwards? Great. She loved the guy, and she'd sent him off with another woman. A sweet woman who baked amazing cookies and wasn't scared to fall in love with him.

What was wrong with her? She'd deluded herself into thinking she could stand to see Evan loving someone else. Building a life with another woman. Making a home with her. But that future was hers. That home, theirs to share. Like a mental image she needed to sketch before it dissipated, her chance at creating this perfect picture could evaporate because of her hesitance.

She continued pacing, the tips of her fingers rubbing against her thumbnail. Worrying. Wondering. Another half hour, and headlights lit up her downstairs. Sneaking to a window, she peered outside. Evan parked and hopped out. He was home. The dim moonlight provided only enough glow to outline him as he stared at her house. His broad shoulders lifted in a weary sigh, one she felt in her own bones, and she launched out the door before she felt her hand on the knob.

Her eyes trained on him. She didn't slow. Took the stairs with one purpose in mind, to get to him. She couldn't see his face, but she heard the surprise in his voice. "Rach?"

She let her actions answer. Not breaking speed until she reached him, she slipped her hands into his thick hair and tugged his mouth to hers. His sharp inhale and slight pause proved she'd caught him completely off guard, but the man was trained in quick response. His hands gripped her waist, and he pulled her tightly against him before turning his head to take full control of what was happening with their lips.

He dove in deep, and she swam into the depths with him. Exploring. Tasting. Touching. His abs were rock-hard beneath the soft cotton of his T-shirt. He chuckled against her lips as she slid her hand along his stomach, then he spun her so she rested against his Jeep. Lowering his mouth to her neck, he tickled her with soft brushes of air as he nudged her jaw for better access. Oh, man, she'd been right. Evan Wayne was a kissing genius. She'd taken much too long to prove the fact, but she'd be more than happy to make up for lost time. Hands returning to his hair, she lifted his mouth to hers again.

If he wasn't careful, he'd lose control of the situation. He was almost there already. The way she'd come out of her house, trained on him like a woman on a mission. He'd had no clue of her intent, but the second he realized he was the target of her operation, he decided to take over command.

She tasted sweeter than he'd imagined. He broke away from her mouth once more and slid to her neck, inhaling the soft scent of apples and … He smiled. Paint. She'd been painting tonight. A dried swath of it roughened the softness of her collarbone. His hands tightened on her waist as hers slid across his back. Her breath hitched as he rose to that tender place by her ear. She pressed in closer to him.

Yeah, all right. Time to close things down.

He slowly navigated to her lips for one last touch. He lingered, ensuring their first kiss would always be the one they'd try and live up to. Softly nipping her lower lip, he also promised there was so much more to come one day.

But not tonight.

Still holding her waist, he added a little room between them. Heart racing, he dropped a kiss to the top of her head. "That was quite the welcome home."

She buried her face in his chest, her soft puffs of laughter warming his T-shirt. "Sorry."

"That kind of welcome never needs an apology. It needs a repeat." He waited but she kept her face hidden. "In fact, you can make that your official greeting for me."

She shook her head, then finally peered up at him. Right. They needed to find a couple of chairs. Outside.

Taking her hand, he led her up to her porch. She settled on the swing, leaving room for him. Instead he draped a blanket around her and grabbed the chair a few feet away. He dragged it over to sit facing her.

Hand on top of the blanket, she rubbed her thumbnail. "How was your date?"

The question and tone were both tentative. How on earth she could feel that way after their kiss he couldn't fathom. But he had no intention of letting it continue. "Felicity is a sweet girl, but you were one hundred percent right when you said she's not the one for me. Tonight confirmed it long before I got home." He chased those last words with a grin that had her dipping her chin. His guess? She was also blushing.

"Then why were you out so long?" she asked.

Ah, she'd been waiting for him. Which meant her movements were premeditated and not on a whim. Had his blood warming again. "The date was over hours ago. Then my parents needed help with something, and after that I drove to the state park and watched the sunset."

"By yourself?"

Okay, sounded strange, a guy sitting alone watching the sunset. He hadn't really gone for the view though. "I had some things to think about."

"Like me?"

"Like us." He'd come to the conclusion that trying to maintain a friendship with Rachael while also moving on had reached the impossible stage. He'd worried over his next move. Now he looked forward to it. Immensely.

Taking hold of her hand, he brushed his thumb against her skin. "You cleared them up, though. And I kind of like the way you chose to do it."

"That why you're sitting over there instead of next to me?"

"That's exactly why."

"I thought Batman was stronger."

"Every superhero has his weakness."

She smiled. "And you're much too heroic to give in to it?"

"Rach." Voice low, it held a subtle warning.

"Sorry. I did enjoy our kiss, but I suppose I like your hero side even better."

"Good, because he's the side that's about to say good night." He stood and gripped the back of the porch swing, one hand on either side of her. "Let's finish this conversation in the daylight after we're both rested." Because there was too much temptation tonight. He leaned down and pressed a kiss against her lips. "Good night, Rach."

Her fingers skimmed his cheek. "Good night, Batman."

He straightened before he could second-guess the move, turned, and headed for his house. His head buzzing, there was no way he'd be sleeping anytime soon. Instead, he picked up the notes he'd made on the missing girls. Flipping through, he stopped on the picture of Kyla Jennings's attempted abductor. Something about him niggled the edges of his brain. Had he bumped into him on another case? Somewhere on the streets?

Not knowing drove him crazy. Especially if it meant putting someone behind bars who was hurting others.

He scanned all the papers, though by now he knew them by heart. Then he opened his laptop and scrolled through comments on the age-progressed photos. Lots of heartfelt wishes to find the girls, but no one mentioned recognizing them. They'd been shared hundreds of times. How did people disappear into thin air?

His phone buzzed on the table, and Hattie's face appeared. He picked it up. "Everything okay?"

"It is."

He waited, but she didn't say anything else. "Did you need something, Hat?"

"I wanted to know if you had a good time tonight."

"I did. Felicity's a nice woman. Just not the woman for me."

Silence.

"She's also not the woman for Dierks."

"I know." Hattie's voice raised.

"I hope so, because it's clear to me that no other woman is going to turn his head but you." And tonight showed him they were good for one another. "So you don't need to set me up with Felicity."

"I wasn't setting you up with her to keep her away from Dierks."

"Piece of advice, Hattie?"

"What."

"If you're going to date a detective, then you need to be prepared for him to deduce your motivations in every situation." He could imagine her frown. "You're not going to pull anything past him."

"He said that's why I set you and Felicity up?"

"Mm-hmm. He also said you have nothing to worry about."

She was silent a moment. "I really like him, Evan. I'm not used to feeling like this, and I think it's made me a little crazy."

That was the most vulnerable he'd ever heard his sister. Let alone her mentioning anything about feelings. He held in the chuckle that wanted to escape. "Love can do that. Feeling a bit crazy is perfectly normal." He should know. It'd practically been his permanent state since Rach showed up.

Hattie sighed. "I'm not sure I'm cut out for this."

"You are. Hang in there and trust that Dierks is feeling as unbalanced as you are."

"You think?"

"I do."

"You're an amazing little brother. Just in case I never told you that."

"I recall pesky, bratty, bothersome—"

Now she laughed, a sound becoming more regular the more time she spent with Dierks. He was definitely good for her. "Well, those too."

"Goodnight, Hat."

"Night."

Evan hung up, then tucked away the papers he'd been looking through. Time to put in a few exercises for his shoulder before calling it a night. He shuffled to the weights in the corner of his living room. Clooney's muted barks slipped through his closed windows, pulling him the opposite direction and to his slider door. Rach slipped down her deck stairs to the beach below. Bright moonlight reflecting off the water colored the night like an old black-and-white movie. He headed outside and leaned against the railing, watching her. Making sure she was safe.

She tossed a stick a few times for Clooney, then watched the waves as Clooney dug in the sand. After about fifteen minutes, she turned to ascend her steps. The soft glow of the Edison bulbs Jonah had strung on his deck and stairs warmed her features as she stepped into their haze. Halfway up, she caught sight of him. "Playing guardian?"

"Maybe."

Forget the moon. Her smile could light his night. "Can't shut it off, can you?"

"Nope." It was who he was, no off switch. Only the burden to carry when he messed up. A heavy load, but he'd grown used to the weight. Someone had to protect others, and that job fell to him.

"Breakfast in the morning?" she suggested as she reached her slider.

"I'll be there."

She waved and ducked inside. He waited to hear her lock slide into place before heading inside to tear through his exercises with renewed vigor. Tonight reminded him that anything was possible—and he planned to prove it yet again. He would regain his strength, and he would be back in uniform.

And he'd be doing it with Rachael at his side.

Chapter Twenty-One

They'd fallen into a routine over the past two weeks. Breakfast together, exercise or PT, then Evan would try and chase new leads while Rach completed her mural. In between, they found plenty of time to explore her new greeting for him. He might have commandeered it to use a few other places during the day as well. Was thinking of it now.

"What time is everyone coming?" With her head in his lap, he played with her hair. They'd settled on the couch after breakfast, and he'd stretched his legs to the coffee table while she curled up to use him as a pillow. Clooney lay on the ground beside them.

In a few hours, her family would arrive for the kickoff of the Fall Flower Fest, and they planned to stay through the weekend. As of last night, all the murals were completed. Today marked the start of the two-week voting period. The Carltons would be in town to visit each artist's entry, which meant news crews would arrive too. More so than typical for their little town's festival. Already Rachael's mural had sparked interest from several places, and she was on schedule for a few interviews this afternoon.

Rachael rolled so she could see him, providing clear access for another morning greeting. "Gavin's coming tonight. Jonah and Penny will be here in a few hours. He had a meeting he couldn't reschedule."

Evan couldn't ignore the perfect opportunity her position presented. Leaning down, he brushed his lips against hers. "Good. I kind of like having you to myself." He pressed in for another kiss.

Her tiny hum against his mouth said she was as much a fan of the situation as he. Might have taken her awhile to jump off the cliff, but now that she had, there wasn't a hint of shyness in her affections. Luckily, they both drew their lines in the same place. That did not, however, make holding that line any easier.

He pulled away. Pressed his shoulders against the couch. "Probably a good thing they're coming though."

"Yeah," she sighed. "Probably."

"How many we-knew-its do you think we're going to hear?" The news of their status change had spread like wildfire through their friends and family ranks. His family was on board—even Hattie was coming around, thanks to Dierks. Gavin had called and given him his blessing, which still made Evan smile. Belle and Penny had inundated Rachael with phone calls, while Jonah and Micah had been suspiciously quiet. Had a feeling he was in for some serious ribbing since he'd dished it out to both of them over the years.

Rachael laughed. "Too many." Reaching out, she ruffled Clooney's fur. "We should make it a game. Every time someone says it, we kiss."

"That'll only encourage them more."

Her flirtatious grin could entice a man to forget he even had a line. "I know."

"All right." He gently removed himself as her pillow. "Time to get our day moving."

She pressed up, those blue eyes bright and assessing. "In a different direction, huh?"

He pointed a finger at her. "You are not helping matters."

Her tiny shrug said she wasn't repentant at all. She stood and pressed a kiss against his cheek. "Not my fault you're so irresistible." With a pat on his chest, she turned and strolled to the kitchen, giving him some much-needed—albeit not-wanted—space. Only downside to dating your best friend was the getting-to-know you stage had passed. Made other phases move faster. If things kept their current pace, there'd need to be some rapid changes in their relationship status.

He followed her to the kitchen where she'd poured another mug of coffee and stood staring out the window. "Nervous for today?" He'd come to discover that, while she handled it well, the spotlight wasn't her favorite place to be.

"A little." She turned, mug captured in both hands. "I don't really look forward to chatting about myself or having pictures taken, but I'm really happy with how the mural turned out. Felt good to paint again." Her fingernail clicked repeatedly against the ceramic. "Felt even better to find a new reason for painting."

"Planning on moving into murals permanently?" He said it half-jokingly, but he honestly wondered if that was her thought. "You'd be great at it."

"No." She shook her head as indecision rolled across her face. It didn't last there long. She set her mug on the counter. "I'll be right back." Then she disappeared.

Her footsteps clipped up the stairs. Probably headed for her studio. Within minutes, she returned to the kitchen, a thick sheet of paper about eleven by fourteen in hand. "Painting Brianna every year really helped my heart, and it sparked the idea for the mural. Then I did individual portraits for each family, and they all told me how much those meant to them. It made me start to think about the direction I want my work to take after this contest." Her voice wobbled slightly as if she could see a new path but wasn't sure she should take it. Without another word, she handed him the paper.

Curious, he took it and turned it over. A myriad of emotions slammed into him, making his eyes water. He blinked away the moisture. "Mandie?"

Rachael nibbled her lip and nodded.

She'd captured the mischievous look in his friend's eyes as she lay looking up from a field of flowers like in the yearbook photo. Her red hair fanned out all around her with yellow buds of Craspedia decorating her soft curls. But this was Mandie as he'd imagine her today. Seeing her this age … her peaceful smile with life still in her eyes …

He set the paper down and pinched the bridge of his nose.

Rach's hand grasped his bicep. "Evan?"

He pulled away. Turned. Couldn't speak past the lump in his throat.

Now her hand touched his back. "I'm sorry. I didn't mean—"

He held up his own hand. Shook his head to cut off her words. Cleared his throat to try and find his voice, because she'd done nothing wrong.

Turning, he sniffed. "It's perfect."

Rach's brows practically connected beneath her wrinkled forehead. "You're not mad?"

"Not at you." He sniffed. All he could see when he looked at that picture was his own failures. Mandie should be here in the flesh, not in a picture that showed him what could have been.

Rachael had gone silent. This wasn't how he meant the morning to go. He hauled in a long breath, slowed his racing heart, and picked up Mandie's portrait, trying to reassure Rachael. "You're really gifted, Rach."

She shrugged. He'd hurt her, and that twisted inside him. There'd been a reason she'd retrieved this picture, and he thought to the start of the conversation. She'd been talking about the direction she wanted to take her painting—and he'd shut her down.

"Rach?"

Arms hugging herself, she stared at a spot on the floor behind him. "Yeah?"

"Thank you for this."

"You don't have to keep it."

She reached for the paper, but he held it away from her grasp. "I want to. We all may handle grief differently, but that doesn't change the beauty of what you're doing. If painting lost loved ones is the direction you're taking your career, you're going to touch so many lives. In such an amazing way." He paused, waiting for her to lift her eyes to his. When she finally did, he added his next words. "You already have."

It took her a long moment, but then she attempted a smile. "As long as I only do commissioned work rather than surprise a person?"

"I could have handled my reaction better."

"Like you said, we all grieve differently." Clooney chose that moment to pad into the kitchen and nudge Rachael's hand, seeking attention. Rach obliged her with a scratch between the ears. "I can understand that."

"I know."

They absorbed the silence for a moment before she motioned toward the staircase. "I should get ready. I'll see you downtown?"

He had PT this morning, and she had her interviews. They planned to meet up for lunch. "I'll be there."

She turned to go, paused, then spun his direction. With two steps she stood in his space and pressed a quick kiss to his lips. "See you there."

He watched her leave, then let himself out, Mandie's picture in hand. He hadn't lied when he told Rachael her paintings were a gift. This one served as a physical reminder of why he couldn't let up the fight to be back on patrol.

"Can I get a picture of everyone together?" Shona Catto motioned for Rachael to move closer to Blake and Harlow Carlton.

Rachael had finished all her local news interviews before meeting again with Shona from Midwest Art. Blake and Harlow chose the same moment to check out her entry, which actually calmed her nerves because she didn't have enough time to process the fact she was standing with Hollywood royalty. By the time Shona finished the bulk of her interview, Rachael discovered Blake and Harlow were sweet, kind, and perfectly normal, and nerves wouldn't be necessary.

From across the street, random people snapped pictures as Harlow scooted in close to Rachael. Shoving her red hair behind her shoulders, she smiled. "Your mural is amazing."

"Over here," Shona directed. They looked her way long enough for her to capture the moment. "Blake, I'd love to grab a few quotes from you about the contest."

"Sure." He joined her a few steps away.

Harlow peered up at the wall to take another look. "I love how you used the flowers too. This is such an incredible piece."

Flowers in all shapes and sizes swirled around the faces of five young women, all of them a missing child of a family member from Searchlight. Three stemmed from the cases Evan believed were connected. "Thank you. I hope the publicity not only shines a spotlight on this charity but also sparks leads for these families."

"We'll do all we can to get the word out." The intensity of Harlow's words matched that on her face, promising she meant what she said.

Finished with his interview, Blake joined them, wrapping an arm across his wife's shoulders. The top of her head reached only to his chest, yet they made an impressive couple. Didn't hurt that they looked at each other like their love remained a fresh discovery they couldn't explore enough.

Blake held out his hand. "It's nice to meet you ..."

"Rachael." Harlow pressed her palm to her husband's chest.

"Rachael," Blake repeated as he shook her hand.

His smile could win awards. The man was movie-star handsome and standing this close only enhanced the fact. Whatever cologne he wore was pretty amazing too. But he had nothing on her personal superhero.

As if Rachael's thoughts conjured him, Evan strolled up the street. "Hey, Rach," he said as he joined them and nodded to the Carltons. "Blake. Harlow."

"Good to see you again." Blake returned the nod.

Surprised, Rachael turned to Evan. "You know him?"

"We've bumped into each other." Evan shrugged as if this were a minor detail he'd merely neglected to mention.

"Abundance Police helps us out every now and then. For the most part, everyone here respects our privacy, but once in a while someone thinks the gate around our house is merely a suggestion," Blake supplied. "Evan's come out on a few of those calls."

He'd never said a thing.

Harlow's gratitude showed on her face. "We appreciate it very much."

"Just doing my job." He scanned the growing crowd. "If you don't mind me making a suggestion, I think it'd be wise for you two to head home for the day now that you've seen everything. Word seems to have spread that you're out and about, and there's a lot of tourists in town with the festival starting today."

Harlow frowned. "So much for shopping."

"Darn." Blake attempted to match the forlorn look but didn't quite pull it off.

"You could at least try and sound disappointed."

He took his wife's hand, his award-winning smile turning devilish. "Having to choose between a day shopping or spending it alone with you, holed up at home? I couldn't fake that disappointment even if I wanted to try."

Her cheeks reddened beneath eyes that said she was anything but embarrassed.

Evan cleared his throat. "Come on, I'll walk you to your car."

"We're good." Blake waved him off. "Only a block up."

Rachael caught the hesitation on Evan's face and gripped his hand to hold him in place. "It was nice to meet you both."

They returned the sentiment, then started up the street. At the corner, a group of teens stopped them. Evan tugged against Rachael's hand to head that way. She held firm. "They're fine, Evan. I'm sure this is their normal. If they needed help, they'd ask for it."

Sure enough, they signed a few pieces of paper, posed for a few selfies, then disappeared around the corner. Still, he hedged like he should follow them, so she did the one thing she knew would distract him. She kissed him.

And, oh yeah, it worked.

"And I thought Blake and Harlow Carlton were the most surprising thing we'd see today." The humor in Jonah's voice broke them apart.

Still in Evan's arms, Rachael turned. "Oh, hey there."

Her brother arched one brow. "Am I going to need to move into the lake house for a few weeks?"

Standing beside him and their stroller, Penny slapped his stomach. "Be nice."

Rachael disengaged from Evan and greeted Belle, Micah, and Anna who'd also arrived. Mischief lit Micah's eyes and his lips parted, but Belle shut him down too with a nudge. He gave her a look. "Oh, come on. The man has earned a little razzing."

"Rachael, however, has not."

The guys clearly didn't like their wives' approach but were wise enough to listen, though Evan was no doubt in for it later.

Penny, pushing Abrielle's stroller, walked over to the framed information about the mural while Jonah pulled Rachael into a hug. "You did good, sis. This is amazing."

She settled into his embrace. "Thanks."

"I may tease, but Evan's a great guy," he whispered in her ear. "It's good to see you two finally together."

Pulling away, she met his blue eyes. "We're just exploring things."

"Yeah, I saw."

"You know what I mean."

Chuckling, he let her go and joined his wife. A few feet away, Micah had Anna on his shoulders, and she stretched out her hands to touch the painted flowers. Belle stood beside them. "How did you come up with this idea?" she asked.

"A long, winding story that I can fill you all in on later."

Penny joined them. "I'd love to hear."

"Me too." Jonah snagged a fussy Abrielle from the stroller and bounced her in his arms. Seemed she didn't want to sit. "How about we grab a big table at The Landing, and we can all have lunch while you tell us about it?"

"Sounds good." The crowds along the street were thickening, and Rachael needed to chat with people as they stopped by. Still, she needed to eat too. But there was sure to be a wait. Luckily, The Landing had a large fenced-in grassy area where Abrielle and Anna could run free. "You'll text once you have a table?"

"Yep."

As they turned to leave, Dierks strolled around the corner. He waved and headed their way. "Heard you guys were coming into town."

"Couldn't miss the start of the festival," Jonah said as he nodded a greeting.

Dierks stopped as he reached the group. "Your sister's going to win this thing."

Racheal's cheeks heated as everyone agreed. "You all are biased."

"Yeah, but they know a good thing when they see it." Evan pressed a kiss against her temple. "Just like me."

Dierks looked from them to the others. "I'd just like to say, I knew these two would wind up together."

"So did I."

"Me too."

"No-brainer."

"Had to be blind not to see it."

All their voices eclipsed each other.

Rach craned her neck to peek up at Evan who wiggled his brows her way. "By my count, that's five."

"I concur."

He dipped to her lips.

"Eww, they're kissing!" Anna's little voice split through the air.

Evan's lips curved into a smile against hers. "Can I bank the rest?"

"Only if they accumulate interest."

He chuckled.

Jonah groaned. "All right, you two. This brother can only handle so much."

Evan turned, his whiskers brushing against her cheek. "Better get used to it."

"Remember you said that," Dierks warned good-naturedly.

Hattie walked toward them.

Evan straightened. "Oh, no."

"Oh, yes." His partner met her and tugged her in for a greeting that had Evan averting his eyes.

Jonah laughed and clapped Dierks on the shoulder as he came up for air. "Thanks for that."

"Anytime." He entwined his fingers with Hattie's. "Need me to reinforce the point?"

"No," Evan answered for him.

Hattie's eyes bounced between Dierks and her brother. "Am I missing something?"

"Not at all," Dierks pressed a kiss against her hair.

"You two heading for lunch?" Micah asked.

"Yep."

"Want to join us?"

Dierks looked at Evan, who nodded. "Sure," Dierks responded. "Good with you, Hat?"

"Definitely."

Jonah wiggled a quickly-growing-fussier Abrielle. "We'll text once we're seated."

They started down the street, and Evan turned to her, taking advantage of the momentarily quiet street. "Now about that interest."

Chapter Twenty-Two

Fall had definitely taken root. Trees bursting with colors begged Rachael to pull out her watercolors in attempt to replicate them. The desire to capture nature's beauty on paper swelled inside like a wave she was prepared to dive into rather than dodge. It was still a little strange to smile again when she thought of painting. Familiar in some ways. New in others. Kind of like what was happening between her and Evan.

With all these changes bubbling inside, Rachael had ducked away from Evan and their friends to stand alone in his backyard. Next door everyone was enjoying a final cookout before Jonah and Penny returned to Chicago and Gavin to school. But this slackline beckoned her.

She'd come so far lately. Today she would conquer this.

Hopping up, she steadied herself using the pole beside the line and the stabilizing techniques Evan had taught her. She focused, sucking in a determined breath. "Eyes on the anchor," she coached herself.

A little wobbly, she fought her natural instinct to look down. She could do this. Take a blind step. She brought her left foot around, felt for placement, leaned into it. One step! Okay. She had this. Eyes up, she released the pole, lifted her right foot, and began to move. But even with correct focus, the line still swayed. Unprepared, her focus jerked down, seeking assurance. And she promptly fell.

This time she landed on her rump. She stood and dusted herself off.

"You okay?" Evan's voice came from behind.

She turned. "Frustrated, but otherwise fine." Strolling toward him, she brushed her hand along the slackline. "I thought I wasn't supposed to be so unsteady if I was looking at the anchor."

His forehead crinkled. "You'll still feel movement, but you'll maintain your balance."

"Well, that's not very encouraging." She blew a loose strand of hair from her face. "I don't know if I'll ever overpower my instincts while that thing doesn't feel solid."

"It's a trust issue. You have to believe it is solid even when what you feel says it's not." His words made sense in theory, but not in application. At least as far as she'd experienced. "You're not there yet, but you will be."

"I'm beginning to doubt it."

The dimple in his chin deepened, and he switched his focus to the trees lining the perimeter of his yard. Without a word, he hiked over to an oak tree and grabbed a low limb. Bending it toward him, he snapped off a small branch, then walked it over to her. The leaves were a deep umber, and a spray of acorns remained attached.

Rachael took his offering. "Thanks?"

"Oak symbolizes bravery." He shrugged. "You're rediscovering yours. Celebrate the small steps you've made. I have no doubt you'll make it across that entire slackline eventually."

This man might very well melt her heart. That shaky step on the slackline mimicked the ones she'd taken recently in her life, and here he was, celebrating her tiniest of achievements. Oak branch in hand, she leaned in to express gratitude.

"I should give you foliage more often," he said against her lips before diving in for more.

Kissing him was quickly becoming her favorite pastime. She wrapped both arms around his neck and pushed up on her tiptoes so she could slide her mouth across his bristled jaw. He retaliated by tickling her with his soft breath behind her ear before nipping at her lobe.

"Aw, man. I cannot unsee this."

Rachael startled at her son's voice and pulled away from Evan as if she were the teenager caught by him, the parent. "Gavin. Hey."

Evan maintained his hold on her, most likely because Gavin wore a huge smile and his words had been heavily doused in a teasing tone. "Need something?" he asked.

"Uncle Jonah sent me to tell you food's ready." Gavin inched away. "But I can tell him you're busy."

"Thanks."

"Gavin!" She eclipsed Evan's response as she simultaneously slapped his chest.

Gavin laughed but kept moving.

She pushed off an also-laughing Evan and hurried to catch her son. "Hold up. We're coming."

Evan followed on their heels. They crossed the yards and joined everyone on Jonah's deck. A spread of food filled one table, and after a quick prayer, they all piled their plates. Rachael filed through the line with Evan, but as they turned to find seats, she spotted Gavin in the corner. They hadn't really had any time alone all weekend. "I need to speak with Gav."

With a nod and kiss to her cheek, Evan went to join Dierks and Hattie. Rach settled into an Adirondack rocking chair beside her son. His chestnut hair had come in thick after chemo and radiation, and he'd recently grown it long enough to do that messy spike in the front. He wore a Michigan State sweatshirt and worn jeans, his body conveying a strength she remained thankful for every day. He'd inherited the same clear blue eyes she and Jonah had and Kurt's square chin. Every time she saw him now, he looked a little older. More like a man than a boy. His outward appearance had finally caught up with his inward maturity, which had developed too early thanks to the hardships they'd faced.

"Having a good weekend?" she asked.

"I am. Not quite as much as you, though." Grinning, he bit into his hotdog.

This was yet another angle to their mother-son relationship she'd need to get used to. His being old enough to talk frankly about her love life. The fact it had been just the two of them for a decade now accounted for part of the openness. That and all the things they'd gone through. They'd learned to have conversations most parents and children never did.

Still, she was Mom and he was her boy. She'd worked hard to maintain that delineation even as they leaned on one another. "Are you okay with me dating Evan?"

Poised to take another bite, he set his hot dog down. He looked at her for a long moment. For as much as they did talk, she'd felt for a while now that there were some things unsaid between them. She'd wondered if it was simply adapting to this season of change, but his face said otherwise.

"I'm not only okay with it, Mom. I'm incredibly happy for you." He peered out over the lake, then to her as he cleared his throat. "My decision to go to school was one of the hardest I've ever had to make, but I knew I needed to. For both of us."

Caught off guard, she straightened.

Gavin continued. "You've put me first for too many years, and if I'd stayed, that wouldn't change."

"Gav, I'm a mom. I will always put you before myself." There was an internal switch that had automatically flipped on the moment two pink lines showed up on the pregnancy test. "It's what we do."

His smile carried echoes of Brianna in it. "I know that's what all parents say, and until I am one, I probably won't understand it. But somewhere in the last couple of years, it stopped feeling like you were putting me first because you were Mom, but because it was a way for you to hide from jumping back into life." He worked his mouth as if searching for his next words. Or worried over saying them.

"Go ahead, Gav. You can tell me anything. That's always been our deal."

He still hesitated a moment. Then, "It's just … It was like I started needing you less and less, but you started needing me more and more."

Now his eyes came up, a hint of worry in them as if he'd upset her. She understood why. The truth hurt, and he'd delivered it.

But she'd needed to hear it.

Rachael reached for her son's hand, giving it a quick squeeze. "You're one smart kid, you know it?" He quirked one eyebrow like his uncle. "Sorry," she laughed. "*Young man.*" When that arch in his brow lifted farther, she shrugged. "That's as far as I'm prepared to go. Give me a few years before I strike out the word young." Thinking of him as a man was one thing. Saying it made it all too real. A mama's heart could only handle so much at one time.

Her smile drifted away as she tackled the more serious topic he'd bridged. "You're absolutely right, by the way. It wasn't something I consciously did, but for so long you needed me. Focusing on your needs was easier than dealing with my … everything, I guess." Because her emotions included every nameable one and then some. "You leaving for school kind of forced me to."

"It's good to see you really smile again, Mom."

She tipped her head. "I always smile around you."

He nodded. "But not like you used to before Dad and Brie and my cancer. I've missed that."

"Oh, Gav." She'd thought she was shielding him from so much, but he'd always been perceptive.

He straightened like a deer in headlights. "Please don't start crying."

She rapidly blinked. "Wouldn't think of it."

"Good." His shoulders relaxed slightly. "Anyway, I'm happy you're painting again, but I'm even happier you and Evan are giving it a go. I like him."

The two had hit it off well over the past few years.

"I'm glad you approve."

He popped a chip in his mouth and munched on it. "Yep. So if you decided to make it something permanent—"

She held up her hand. "One step at a time." Not that she wasn't thoroughly enjoying the one she'd just taken. She shifted a glance toward Evan, and her lips tingled while her stomach fought knots. If only she could see what a future with him held, she'd feel a whole lot safer walking towards it.

They'd cleaned up from lunch, and while Penny put Abrielle down for a nap, everyone sat around outside talking. Evan settled into one of the Adirondack chairs beside Rachael, content to let the conversation happen around him. The momentary break from the craziness of the festival was welcomed. Yesterday, Rachael spent a good chunk of her time near her mural, speaking with tourists passing through. Already her popularity was reawakening. Her old agent, Lanette, had called about a gallery interested in a possible showing of her past work mixed with her new pieces. It no doubt helped that the festival had blipped across national news, thanks to an interview with Blake and Harlow, who happened to use Rachael's mural as their background.

While this small pause was nice, he wasn't worried about her busyness becoming a problem. Not when he fully intended to be in uniform again sooner rather than later. With all the leads on Liliana's case meeting dead ends, he filled his extra free time with exercise, and it seemed to be providing results. He'd done considerably better at the gun range yesterday. No bullseye, but his shoulder handled the shots with minimal pain. Now he needed to stop the mild tremor and regain his accuracy.

The slider door opened and Penny stepped outside. "She's asleep."

Jonah hopped up. "Time for me to redeem myself then."

Within minutes they split into teams of five for an impromptu game of Capture the Flag. Evan's team consisted of Micah, Hattie, Penny, and—being that he never lost—he took Anna too. Jonah's team included Dierks, Gavin, Rachael, and Belle. Seemed like a fair split, so no one could say he'd stacked the teams when he won again.

Twenty minutes in, he peered around a tree, laying eyes on Rachael who stealthily snuck toward his team's flag. He'd watched her closely during lunch while she talked with Gavin. It seemed like an intense conversation, but whatever they'd covered apparently brought them closer together. He'd probably hear the details tonight once everyone went home. For now, he had a game to win.

That meant stopping Rachael. And he had a good idea how.

Darting silently through the trees, he navigated to a spot behind her, then waited to make his move. She peeked to the left and right, but never checked over her shoulder. Rookie mistake, and one he'd happily use to his advantage. As she snuck toward a large bush, he raced forward and caught her in his arms, enjoying her shriek as he dipped his mouth near her ear.

"Gotcha."

She twisted her face to try and see him. "For a kiss will you forget you saw me?"

He loosened his grip enough so she could turn while remaining in his hold.

"Tempting."

"Yeah?" She leaned in and connected with him in a way that erased all ability to forget her but dangerously close to making him ignore where they were.

"Rach." He pulled away enough to speak her name.

She followed with another kiss.

"Rach," he tried again, this time with slightly less oomph. Especially when her hands started wandering up his chest. He reciprocated with one of his digging into her hair while the other slid along her neck till his fingers pressed against her pulse. This pastime was much better than any game.

Except kissing her wasn't a game, and he needed to stop playing like it was before he lost himself. With a strength born out of convictions he'd carried too long to desert now, he added space between them. The way she looked at him—hungry eyes and swollen lips, like she wanted to dive right back into his kiss—had him taking another step. He had no doubt he looked the same because he definitely felt it. The closer they grew, the blurrier his lines became, and he was well aware of his frailties.

This wasn't only about physical, which honestly only made things more difficult. He'd fallen for every part of her. That left him wanting more than a kiss. Which meant he needed to ask for more than just dating. If only he could be sure she was ready.

The last thing he wanted was to fail her in any way, shape, or form.

Her fingers drifted across her lips. "Am I free to go?" Behind her hand, her lips tipped up.

He loved flirting with her almost as much as kissing her. "You do know I'm trained to withstand persuasion tactics of all kinds."

She lowered her hand. "So that's a no then?"

Eyes never leaving hers, he crossed his arms and slowly nodded.

"Guess I better run." She faked left and dodged right, running past him.

With a chuckling sigh, he turned and took off after her. "I already captured you," he called.

Full-on laughter was her response. She didn't break speed. They dashed toward the front yard, and he noted Dierks jogging his way. Evan changed course to meet him. "What's up?"

"Just got a call. Someone thinks they recognized one of the girls on Rach's mural."

"Think it's legit?" With the buzz around her entry, they planned to weed through tips that would take them nowhere. The fact Dierks would leave their get-together said something about this one warranted a second look.

Dierks tipped his head for Evan to follow him to his car. "Guy pegged Becca

Philmont. Said she looks like one of his neighbors. They live pretty far out in the country, but he has seen her when he's on his tractor. Seems his land butts up against hers. She'd never meet his eyes. Scurried back inside the few times he caught her out, and he found it strange."

"But never said anything."

"She'd been outside. He figured if she was in a bad situation, she had the freedom to leave."

That wasn't always the case.

"Get this though." Dierks pulled his keys out and stopped by his car door. He met Evan's eyes. "Cops did a drive-by, and guess what they spotted along the back of the property."

Evan sucked in a deep breath. "Blue Ford?"

With a clipped nod, Dierks opened his door. "I'll keep you posted." He climbed in and took off down the drive.

Not going about killed Evan, but he hadn't been cleared for active duty, which meant he stayed put.

Rach had stopped to watch them. Now she joined him. "Everything okay?"

How much should he tell her? She'd been in this from the beginning, and her work had allowed this lead to crop up. Hands on his hips, he regarded her. "Someone thinks they recognized Becca's picture."

Her eyes widened. "Did they find her?"

"Dierks is heading to check it out now." It would start with a knock on the door and a few questions. Dierks would be able to assess a lot with one look. "There's more. With the info we've received, there's a slim possibility this could be tied to Morgan and Liliana too."

Rach grabbed his hand. "How long until we hear anything?"

"Could be a while." He led her toward the backyard. "Let's call the game and see if people want dessert instead." Sweets didn't seem any more enticing of a distraction to her with the way she glanced over her shoulder. Looked like she wanted to climb in her car and follow Dierks. Oh, boy, did he share that feeling. "Come on." He tugged her along.

The next three hours passed slower than any he remembered wading through. After everyone had packed and left, he, Rach, and Clooney curled up on his couch. He'd even put in a Schwarzenegger movie. On second thought, that choice might have made the evening drag all the more.

Right in the middle of an over-the-top action scene riddled with bad puns swathed in Arnold's thick Austrian accent, his phone finally rang. His heart thudded when he noticed Cap's number, not Dierks's. He stood as he slid his finger over the screen. "Cap?"

"Evan. You need to come to the hospital. Now."

"Why?" He was already moving to the door. Rach followed, her own face a mask of concern as she tried to discern what was happening.

"Dierks has been shot. It's not good."

"I'm on my way."

Rach slipped through the door with him. "Evan?"

"Dierks was shot. I don't know any more than that." His voice shook.

"Should we call Hattie?"

"Not yet."

They climbed in and Evan disregarded the speed limit as he headed toward the hospital. Rach pulled out her own cell phone. "I'm calling Micah. He's working an overnighter."

Evan listened to her side of the conversation. A bunch of nonverbals, but he picked up plenty from them. Seemed Cap hadn't been overstating things. When she hung up, Evan looked at her. She blinked rapidly. "He was shot in the head, Evan."

He pressed the gas pedal harder. This could not be happening. Had to be a bad dream. Then Rach's hand grasped his, her freezing touch proving it wasn't. His fingers shook in hers, and she tightened her hold.

They arrived at the ER, and he slammed to a stop out of the way of where any ambulances might need to land but far from a parking spot. A nurse waited at the entrance for them.

Eyes full of concern, she greeted them. "Are you Evan?"

He nodded. She motioned for them to follow. "I'm Dawn. I'll take you to where everyone is."

Using her badge, she led them into a restricted area and down a long hall to a waiting room filled with other officers. Captain Larry stood outside the door, deep lines creasing his face. Tonight he looked every moment of his sixty years.

"How is he?" Evan asked.

Cap shook his head.

Dawn turned to leave. "If you need anything, I'll be at the nurses' station."

Cap placed a staying hand on Evan's shoulder. "Before you go in, there's something I need to tell you, because it's going to hit the news if it hasn't already."

Dread pooled in his gut. "What?"

"Dierks went to check out a tip with a few of our guys."

"I know. I was with him when he received the call."

"It proved to be a good one. Becca Philmont and Morgan Childress were both there."

"Liliana Perez?" Rachael quietly asked.

"No sign of her yet, though we have reason to believe she was held there too." Cap looked at Evan. "I'll keep you abreast of all those details, but what you need to know is, along with the blue Ford we found, there was also a maroon minivan there."

That info landed like a blow. "Same guy who shot me?"

Cap nodded. "Suspect and car match what we had on your dashcam. He's the same height and build. Dents are in the same corner."

Heat rolled inside him. "Where is Dierks?"

"Surgery."

"He got off a shot?"

Cap nodded again.

Evan clenched his neck and walked a few paces down the hall. "I had this guy. Pulled him over. If it weren't for me—" His throat closed around the words. If he'd done his job, Dierks wouldn't be lying in surgery, fighting for his life.

Rach reached for him as the door at the far end of the hall opened. A surgeon walked out, his eyes met Cap's, and Evan knew before he said anything.

Once again he'd failed, and someone he cared about had paid with his life.

Chapter Twenty-Three

Rachael hadn't cried this much in a long time. She could stave off her own pain, but when it came to the pain of those she loved, her tears ran freely. Evan was deeply steeped in grief right now, but beyond that, guilt had dug its ugly claws deeper into him. No matter what she said, she couldn't pry its talons out. Best she could do was stand by his side.

Today was Dierks' funeral. Evan dressed in his uniform and stood guard over the casket. He'd acted as Dierks's family liaison as well, but he'd also insisted on taking part in at least one watch beside his friend as he lay in rest. Along with the family, he'd followed Dierks from the church while his fellow officers served as pallbearers.

A long line of police cars made their way to the cemetery where Abundance officers, along with others from several surrounding cities—Holland, Grand Rapids, and Hidden Lake—stood at attention, hats on, black bands over their badges, while the twenty-one-bell ceremony rang through the silence of the afternoon. Gray clouds covered the sun and a soft cool breeze brushed against them as if the day itself participated in their mourning. As the echo of the bells faded, the final radio call for Dierks sounded. Rachael looked toward Evan as Dierks's badge number was read one final time, and he was placed out of service by the dispatcher. Tears welled in her eyes as Evan rapidly blinked. Strains of "Amazing Grace" played through bagpipes as the Honor Guard retired the colors and presented Dierks's mother with the flag and their gratitude for his service. It seemed so little when he'd given so much.

Rachael waited as the crowd dispersed. Evan remained by Dierks's family. Across the carpet of grass marked by headstones, Hattie stood, watching. She wiped her pale, tear-streaked cheeks. Rachael and Evan had sat in silence with her much of this week. Now Rachael walked her way.

"Do you need anything, Hattie?"

She shook her head. Rachael understood her silence, borne of a grief deeper than words could touch. Hattie might not have been married to Dierks, but she loved him. Plus, his death had to stir memories of her brother being shot. They'd definitely darkened the edges of Rachael's mind this week, and she'd done her best to hold them at bay. But today had infused them with power beyond what she had the strength to endure. Every time she looked at Dierks's casket, she saw Evan lying there.

She tried once more to focus on Hattie, but her standard practice of helping others to avoid her own chaos wasn't working like usual. "Are you ready to leave? I can give you a ride."

Hattie shook her head.

Rachael remained beside her, willing her usefulness to work for them both. Hattie's family eventually joined them and gave her hugs while Rachael slipped away to find Evan. He stood by as Dierks's family pulled from the cemetery to return to the church for a luncheon. As their car exited the lot, she joined Evan and placed a hand on his back. "You doing okay?"

He shook his head.

"Do you want to attend the luncheon?"

"I should, but you can go home."

He'd been pushing her away all week, and she'd been ignoring the nudges. She might not know what the future held, but she knew in this moment Evan needed her. "I'll come with you."

He stared at her a long moment, then slowly nodded, turned, and walked to his car. She followed. At the church, she joined the women bringing out food while Evan mingled with his fellow officers who were sharing stories about Dierks. He participated, but she caught the look of self-reproach in his eyes. He'd convinced himself that Dierks's death was his fault.

After several hours, she helped tidy up as the church cleared and then rejoined him.

"You're still here?" he asked. No condemnation. Just simple, tired surprise. "You didn't have to wait for me."

"No, but I wanted to. Plus, you're my ride home." She hoped the light comment would breathe a little levity into the moment, but it flopped.

He picked up his hat from the table he'd settled at with a large group who'd since departed. "Let's go, then."

She reached for his hand, and he allowed her to take it but didn't return the hold. He fired up his Jeep and turned toward home in the waning daylight. One thing about fall was how early night seemed to arrive.

Evan didn't say one word the entire drive. They hopped out, and she went to follow him to his house. He stopped. "It's been a long day, Rach."

"I know, but I wanted to finish that load of wash I put in this morning."

"I don't need you doing my laundry anymore." He still wouldn't look at her. "I can handle it."

Probably, but, "You're still injured."

This whipped his attention to her. "You'd like that, wouldn't you."

Was his misplaced guilt eating away his common sense? "Are you kidding me? I hate that you were shot."

"But you don't hate that it's keeping me off the streets." He roughed a hand through his hair, a scowl darkening his handsome features, his voice terse. "Do you."

Oh. Okay. So he might have approached it the wrong way, but he was right in his assumption. And it brought them both to the heart of what had hovered over her since the moment they heard of Dierks's death. "I've never lied to you about not wanting you out there. You nearly died." It still twisted her insides. "And Dierks ..."

She couldn't say the words. Speaking them made it all too real. And it was that very reality she'd tried to fool herself into believing couldn't happen again in her life.

"Dierks's death is my fault."

Even with her fear screaming at her, she loved him too much to let him believe that lie. "You are not responsible for his death, Evan."

He didn't speak for a long moment. Then, "Ezra Mabbitt." He turned and looked her way. "I missed him twice. Once when I pulled him over, and he got me instead of the other way around. Then again when I looked at the sketch Kayla Jennings did and didn't recognize him. If I'd done my job, Dierks would be here."

"That's not true. The guy ambushed Dierks like he did you." The truth nearly paralyzed her vocal cords. Reminded her that on any call, in any split second, Evan could be ripped from her life. Her heart buckled against the thought, but she remained focused on him. "That picture was ten years old. You said yourself people change too much for it to be recognizable."

"It's my job to catch things others miss."

"So what? Let's say you'd made the connection. No one found that van until after Dierks was shot. It wouldn't have changed anything."

"Might have made him more cautious."

"Why? If he didn't know the connection?"

"Because!" Evan shouted the word, then seemed to catch himself. He stilled. Calmed his breathing. Looked at her. "You're right. Recognizing Ezra in that picture might not have changed anything. But me pulling him off the streets four months ago would have. You can't argue that."

"Ev—"

He held up his hand. "I'm tired, Rach."

And suddenly, so was she. So tired of trying to pretend this could work between them. Her footing would never be solid in this relationship because he couldn't guarantee her the one thing she needed. "This is it, then. Isn't it."

He didn't pretend to not understand what she was saying. That told her enough.

"Do you want it to be?" Thick and rough, his voice scratched out the words.

"Are you determined to return to patrol?"

"Yes."

Tears threatened, and she swallowed. "Can you promise me you won't end up like Dierks?"

"You know I can't." Sadness creased his eyes with the finality of his words.

She never should have given in. Never should have kissed him. She'd known all along where this would end.

"Good night then, Evan." She backed away. Good night was so much easier to say than goodbye.

He didn't try to stop her. Didn't offer false promises. Just silently let her go. In that moment, she knew. She hadn't needed five points to keep her distance from him. She'd only needed one. Evan Wayne would shatter her heart if she gave it to him.

Unfortunately, she'd missed that point until it was too late.

Evan didn't bother to head upstairs. He wasn't sleeping tonight. Guilt over Dierks weighed heavily on his shoulders. He shook his head at that thought. At least his busted-up shoulder could carry something.

With the living room as dark as his mood, he crossed to his window and peered toward Rachael's. She'd let Clooney out for a brief bathroom break but hadn't taken her for a walk. No doubt she worried he'd keep watch over them, and she didn't want to see him. Couldn't blame her. He needed his distance as well.

Sighing, he headed for the fridge, wishing he had something stronger to drink than water while also glad he didn't. He'd been drunk once in his life, and all it had left him with was a nasty hangover. He had enough to regret come morning. He didn't need a pounding headache too.

After snagging a water bottle, he settled onto his couch. He'd seen this coming all week, and the more time passed, the more he became convinced that letting Rachael walk away was the right thing to do. These past few days reminded him of all the ways he'd failed the people around him. It wasn't only Dierks. He could barely bring himself to look at Hattie, knowing he was the cause of her heartache. And he'd never forget the sound of Dierks's mother sobbing as they handed her his flag.

As much as he wanted Rach in his life, he'd just mess it up and hurt her. And she'd been hurt enough. Which was why, when she'd turned away from him, he'd held steady. It had taken every ounce of strength he possessed.

Needing to talk to someone, he reached for his phone to call Dierks, and reality slammed his reflex to a nasty halt. Cursing, he hurled his phone across the room. A soft knock sounded at the door.

He ignored it. Cowardly? Sure. But if Rach had come over to say she'd made a mistake, he'd be in for a world of trouble. He wasn't dumb enough or proud enough to think he had the ability to walk away from her, which was why he'd let her do the walking. Just because he knew it was the right thing to do didn't mean he wanted to repeatedly do it. Once had been enough.

Another soft knock preceded his mother walking through the front door. "I know you're awake because I heard a crash."

He held in a groan. "What are you doing here, Mom?"

"I just left Hattie's. I got her to sleep, but I knew she wasn't the only one of my kids hurting tonight." She shuffled over to him and took a seat on the other side of the couch. Leaning her arm across the back, she faced him. "What was that crash?"

"Nothing." He refused to admit he'd lost his cool. "And I'm fine. You can go home."

She sat silently for a moment. "I thought maybe I'd find Rachael over here too."

Might as well rip this Band-Aid off in the cover of night. "Rachael and I aren't together anymore."

"Oh?" She straightened. "That's a fairly recent development because you were together a few hours ago."

"We decided when we got home, and I really don't want to talk about it."

"Did she break it off with you?"

"It was mutual." He took the cap off his water bottle. "And like I said, I don't want to talk about it."

She stood and wandered across his room until she found his phone. Picking it up, she studied it. "Well, that was one expensive outburst." Then she returned it to him. "Want to talk about this?"

"Nope."

Placing her hands on her hips, she looked down at him with a mixture of motherly concern and determination. "I never should have let your siblings talk me into naming you Bruce Evan Wayne."

This had him sitting up. "What?" He'd never heard this origin of his name.

"Your sisters and older brother played superheroes every day. Superman, Wonder Woman, and Supergirl. And when they found out I was pregnant with you, they called you their Batman from day one. We didn't know if you were a boy or girl, but they were convinced." She smiled. "Around everyone else they called you Bruce to protect your identity as Batman."

"You always told me you and Dad picked the name."

"Because by the time you were old enough to realize the connection, Nora and James were too embarrassed to admit they'd once been that into playing superheroes. And then you struggled with it enough to start going by Evan, and we didn't want you upset with your siblings." She settled beside him. "My point is not about all that though, it's about how you've tried to live up to the name. But, my dear sweet boy, it isn't your job to keep everyone safe." Placing her hand over his heart, she looked at him. Enough moonlight slipped through the windows that he could see the love in her eyes. "The weight of the world doesn't rest on you, Evan. So please, let it go."

He shifted beneath her touch. It was too late, and he was too exhausted to let her words sink deep. They sounded good, but just because something sounded good didn't make it truth. If nothing else, Mom had calmed his brewing storm enough for him to find a little rest. He'd unpack what she said tomorrow.

"Thanks, Mom."

With a sigh, she stood. "Want me to make you some hot cocoa before I go?"

When he was little, her hot cocoa had been his favorite solution to life's problems. At least the ones he'd let her see. He had a feeling she'd been more aware of what ailed him than she often let on. "No. It's getting late, and you need to get home." He walked her to the door. "Will you call me to let me know you're safe?"

"I would, but I'm not sure it'll do much good."

Oh, right. His phone. "Then email me. I'll have my computer on."

"Deal." She pressed a kiss to his cheek, then slipped out the door.

He picked up his phone and headed to bed, her words still lingering in his mind. They rang with a freedom he longed for. But if it wasn't his job to protect the people around him, then why did he burn with a desire to do so? It felt like a part of who he was. A part he continued to fail miserably at yet couldn't seem to release.

Falling into his bed, he tried to sleep. The darkness seemed the best place for him right now.

Chapter Twenty-Four

Tonight should have been the gala to close out the Fall Flower Fest and announce the winner of this year's mural. The committee canceled the event in honor of Dierks, but there'd still be an announcement. Blake and Harlow would post a live video to their Facebook page. First they'd called to personally let Rachael know she'd won.

Her initial instinct had been to share the victory with Evan. It would take time to retrain that knee-jerk reaction. They'd been best friends for several years now. She'd give herself at least that long to erase the habit of him. His absence provided that painful process with a solid start as she hadn't seen him, other than from a distance, since the night of Dierks's funeral. She'd spent the week beside her mural, answering questions and providing interviews since the rescue of Becca and Morgan had made national news.

By today, things had died down, and she'd made her way to Alvaro and Hope's home. Yes, to tell them the mural won. But she also wanted to pay her respects to the woman who'd started all of this and become a friend along the way. They'd found answers for Hope. If only they'd been the ones everyone prayed for.

Liliana's remains had been found on Ezra Mabbitt's grounds. She'd been his first victim, and he held her captive until she passed away during childbirth. After a failed abduction attempt on Kayla, he snatched Becca and five years later grabbed Morgan. The day he shot Evan he'd been stalking his next victim.

Becca and Morgan had given him children as well as raising Liliana's daughter, Evangeline, who now was ten years old. She'd recently been united with her grandparents. Rachael wasn't sure what she'd find when she knocked on their door. She did take notice of a few cars parked along the street. Seemed the story remained newsworthy.

Strolling up the sidewalk, she tapped on their front door. It opened a crack, and Hope peeked out, smiled, and invited her in. "Rachael, it's so good to see you."

"You, too." She returned Hope's hug. "How are you?"

Hope led her into their family room. Pictures lined the walls of so many children, and right in the center was Liliana. Their love hadn't shut off because of pain, it had multiplied.

Sitting across from her, Hope clasped her hands together. "We're doing okay." She paused a moment. "It wasn't the news we wanted, but at least we know. At least we can lay Liliana to rest."

"When will that be?"

"As soon as we can have her body." She cleared her throat and grabbed a tissue to dab her eyes. Then she reached for a photo on the table beside her and handed it to Rachael. "This is Evangeline. She's upstairs with Abbi and Ashley, but she's not ready to meet others yet."

"I completely understand." Rachael took the picture. "She looks so much like Liliana."

"She does, doesn't she?" Another sniff. "Our prayer is for her healing now. She doesn't fully understand everything that's going on. Becca and Morgan shielded her from so much. But I know she'll hear the stories as she grows older. We want to prepare her for that."

"I've been praying for all of you. I can't imagine trying to navigate any of this."

"One day at a time." She took the picture as Rachael returned it.

Rachael rubbed her hands together. "I wanted to let you know our mural won. They're announcing it tonight."

Hope's eyes widened. "That's wonderful news. Though I'm not surprised in the least."

Neither was she. Not because of anything she'd done, but because of the life, loss, and love all the families had allowed her to share. "Thank you for letting me get to know Liliana."

Reaching over the small table separating them, Hope took Rachael's hands. "Thank you for listening to that little nudge to do so. You crafted something beautiful from your own pain, and you used what you discovered to reach others. Always remember, there's a purpose found in what we walk through."

Words she'd said to others so many times because they were the right ones to say, but hearing them spoken over her broke something inside. Through those cracks, truth pressed its way in and erupted in cleansing tears. Hope pulled her into a hug borne from shared pain, deep grief, and a healing only God could bring.

After their tears dried, they both straightened. Rachael stood. "I should go, but I'll come visit again, maybe next week?"

"We'd like that." Hope walked her to the door, and Rachael slipped outside. She climbed in her car and made her way home.

As she pulled up the drive, she spotted a familiar car. Gavin sat on the front porch but stood to meet her as she parked. "Hey, Bud." She gave him a hug, tears threatening again. So much for not being a crier. "What are you doing here?"

"I wanted to congratulate the winner of the Fall Flower Fest in person." His smile was contagious. "Congrats, Mom. I am so proud of you."

"Thanks." They walked together to the door. "You hungry?"

"I need to come home more often if you've already forgotten my answer to that question."

She laughed. "Let me whip us up some dinner."

"Is Evan coming over too?"

"No." She didn't elaborate, and as if he sensed her sadness, he didn't press.

They ate dinner together, and he filled in all the spaces with stories about his job, new friends, and college classes. "Did you finish Brie's portrait?" he asked.

She stood. "Let me grab it."

Instead, he followed her up the stairs. She opened the door, and Gavin crossed the floor to his little sister's picture on the easel. "Wow, Mom. It turned out great." He leaned close and studied the reflection in her eyes. That was always his favorite part. After a moment, he turned. "I think you're going to blow up the art world by offering these."

"You do, huh?"

"Yep." He pawed through other paintings she'd begun as part of the series for a gallery showing. She once again incorporated floriography to tell stories of children who were missing. Each piece portrayed a bouquet, single flower, or a small garden paired with the face of a missing child. The media attention surrounding her mural and how it led to Becca and Morgan's release only increased the desire for her paintings. Lanette already had received calls from several art museums, asking if they could show the exhibit once she finished it. And individual collectors were placing orders for her to paint loved ones no longer with them.

She hadn't sought this success. Hadn't thought much of her gifts or how they intersected with her past, but they did. Viewing her life's work of art, the full process of creation became evident, and it reminded her of how she painted. For so long, all she saw was the bare outline of her life. Huge blank spaces that left her feeling empty, and while they defined certain areas, she couldn't grasp the full picture. And just like she'd never have left the mural as a black-and-white outline, God hadn't left her that way either. He began filling her spaces with color.

Light and dark combined to give depth and meaning. The tones worked together, both needed to create structure and beauty. She could not craft a painting without using colors from the entire spectrum—much like her moments of joy and pain swirled together to make her who she was today. Someone with a unique ability to reach into another's life and help them heal.

This heartache with Evan would add another brush stroke. It felt dark right now, but even dark tones were needed to paint a masterpiece. That's what her life was, a beautiful masterpiece. She could stand back and see that now. And like any work of art, she'd use it to reach others.

Even if it wasn't with Evan by her side.

"Evan?"

He looked up to find Captain Larry standing in the doorway to what had been Dierks's office. Still not cleared for active duty, Evan was filling in for his friend no longer here. It was the least he could do. "Yes, sir?"

"There's someone I'd like you to meet."

Evan straightened as Cap moved to allow an older gentleman access. "This is Gerald Philmont, Becca's father."

Standing, he offered the man his hand. "Nice to meet you, sir."

"The pleasure is mine." Gerald removed his black cap, showing off dark-brown hair edged with silver. Not tall, he stood with perfect posture like he'd once been in the military. If Evan remembered from the files, Gerald was twenty years his senior.

"Please, have a seat." Evan motioned as Cap turned and left, closing the door behind him. Gerald perched on the chair across from Evan's desk, while he returned to his spot behind it. "How can I help you?" Most likely he had questions about Ezra Mabbitt, but Cap would have been better at answering those. So why'd he bring him in here?

"Your captain seems to think it's me who can help you. But first I wanted to say thank you for bringing my daughter back to me."

Evan cleared his throat. "That wasn't me. That was Detective Dierks Holden."

"Yes." Gerald's voice held sorrow. "If I could thank him too, I would."

Because of Evan, he couldn't. He fisted his hand, squeezing to stop its shaking.

Gerald continued. "But it's because of the work you did, you and that artist Rachael Stark, that my Becca was found. It took all of you, and that's not something I'll forget."

He didn't deserve those words and wouldn't sit here accepting them. "Actually, sir, if I'm being honest, I ran into Mabbitt months ago on another violation, and I let him slip through my hands. In light of that, I'm sure you'll agree it isn't your thanks you should be offering me."

Rather than condemnation filling Gerald's features, compassion softened the creases around his eyes. "I'm aware of your run-in with him and that he shot you. Your captain filled me in when he also shared about the role you played in finding Becca. One doesn't cancel out the other."

"Maybe we'll have to disagree on that."

Gerald studied him long and hard. "Think I'm starting to see why your captain prodded me to come in here and share what I'd told him with you." He turned the cap in his hands. "Did you know that Ezra Mabbitt gave each of those girls a different name when he took them?"

He'd read that in the reports. "I did." Ezra gave them each Biblical names connected to wives and mothers. He'd thought of himself as some sort of father of faith, and they were creating his lineage.

"Called her Leah. For the past ten years, my Becca has answered to that. He tried to strip her of her identity, right along with her worth. And over time, she started responding like his lies were her truth."

There were no words he could offer to ease the atrocities Becca endured.

Gerald's hands stilled, and he looked Evan in the eye. "None of that changed the truth of what I called my daughter though. Every day I prayed for my girl, and I called her by the name I'd given her. I knew who she was even when she'd forgotten. And now, I'm going to help her remember." He stood. "I don't know you or what you're carrying, but I get the sense you're listening to some lies too, thinking they're the real deal. Maybe it's time for you to do some remembering as well." He slipped his ball cap on his head, tipped it toward Evan, then walked out the door.

His words lingered, slamming into Evan harder than the bullet that tore through his shoulder. Gerald may have fired them off, but Cap had aimed them with an accuracy that struck dead center into Evan's guilt. Was it true? Was he believing lies?

The silence of Dierks's office screamed over any answers. He couldn't process here. Not when every inch of space reminded him of an all-too-familiar failure. One he desperately wanted to shed for the freedom he sensed in Gerald's challenge.

Standing, he grabbed his jacket and headed out. Wasn't sure where he was going until he pulled up at the cemetery. The sun hung low in the sky, casting golden light on the trees bordering the edge of this place. They were cloaked in a myriad of colors, cementing autumn's firm hold on these shortened days. With the leaves crunching underfoot, he strolled to the last row, turned left, then stopped at the third headstone.

Amanda Nicole Johnson.

"Hey, Mandie." He brushed away dust from her name, then pulled a few weeds. Once he'd cleared her stone, he wasn't quite sure what to do next. Why he'd come. Except ... he had to bury the past. Dragging it with him all these years hadn't brought Mandie back or saved Dierks.

But it was suffocating him. Killing his future. And neither of his friends would want that.

Evan touched the cool granite. Letting go started with allowing room for the honesty he'd dodged for years. "I'm sorry, Mandie. Sorry I didn't say anything that night." He coughed past the sudden lump in his throat. "But I was just a kid. I didn't think anything like that would happen."

He'd suspected her stepfather wasn't a nice guy. He'd prodded her for info, but she played it off. Even that night she told him she'd be okay. And he believed her, because his mind couldn't comprehend the ugly possibility that a man who should have protected her would kill her.

Sniffing, he squatted and traced her name. "I failed you, but you wouldn't have blamed me." He could still see her smile. The one Rachael had captured in her portrait of Mandie. "So why have I spent so long blaming myself?"

Because all he could hear were all the voices asking him why he hadn't done something. People at the funeral home. Her grandparents at the school assembly. His older brother even. Felt like every time he turned around someone, in some form, reminded him he should have acted. So he'd made the decision to never be in that position again.

Such impossible standards. No wonder he always fell short. Had it been anyone else, he'd never have placed those expectations on them. His fourteen-year-old self couldn't see that, but the man he'd become finally could. It was time to let that boy off the hook so this man could move forward.

That meant also accepting he couldn't have saved Dierks. Facing his grief head-on, and not shutting down. For all the times he'd accused Rach of being afraid to fully live, he should have recognized he was doing the same.

Standing, he gazed at Mandie's name one last time. "I'm so sorry, Mandie. And I'm even more sorry I clung to your death more than I did your life. That stops now."

He was done listening to the lies of his past. Done allowing them to shape who he was. And done letting them keep him from the woman he loved.

Chapter Twenty-Five

"Need anything else from the house?" Gavin asked as he loaded her bags into the car.

"No. I packed light."

"I'd say." He shut the tailgate, then held out his arms. "Want to get your last hug in until Thanksgiving?"

She smiled. "Absolutely." Then she tugged him to her and held on tight.

"You can let go now." His chin bounced on top of her head as he spoke.

"No way. This has to last a month."

Gavin endured another minute before stepping away. "You going to be okay, Mom?"

"I will."

"Promise?"

She nodded. "Now get on the road. I'm going to take Clooney for a walk so hopefully she'll sleep the whole way home."

"Call me when you get there?"

"That's my line."

His smile still held memories of her little boy. With a wave, he climbed into his car and drove off. Each time it became a little easier to say goodbye. Yes, he'd always be her baby, but she loved the man he was becoming. It happened way too fast, but she was settling into this new season. Because that's what time did, it passed in seasons. Some were barren while others burst with new life and color. Then there were moments like now when those colorful moments led to letting go so new things could grow. She was finding her rhythm again.

Patting her leg, she called Clooney and they strolled to the beach. After nearly an hour of tossing driftwood for her, Rachael started up the steps. Unbidden, her eyes strayed to the slackline in Evan's backyard.

She stopped. He wasn't home. This was her chance, because it might be next summer before she returned to the lake house—if she returned. Determination settled her decision, and she changed course.

Reaching the line, she rested her hand on the taut yellow webbing, but she didn't let that feeling fool her. The moment she applied her weight to it, the thing would sway. Difference was, she understood what she needed to compensate for the movement, and she finally felt ready to conquer old habits and create new ones.

Grabbing the wooden pole for steadying purposes, she hauled herself up. She used her swivel points to gain balance, then—eyes on the anchor—she brought her left foot around and settled it onto the slackline. As she applied her weight to it, the line wobbled, but she maintained her grip and threw out her left arm to calm the movement. The next step required her to release the pole. Maintaining her focus, she let go and brought her right foot around.

Oh, she wanted to look and see if her step lined up, but she forced her eyes to remain on the anchor and trusted the process. Her legs shook, the line swayed, and she adjusted her body to remain upright. Leaning her weight onto her foot, she completed the next step. And then another. And another. While each one grew slightly steadier, the slackline continued its movement beneath her. But she'd come to expect the trembling and had learned how to remain steady and take a step in the midst of it all.

As her hands latched onto the rough bark of the tree at the other side, pure joy welled up inside of her. She thrust one hand into the air. "I did it!" Silence greeted her celebration.

Hopping down, she dusted her hands together and peeked at Evan's house. Conquering the line wasn't the only victory she wanted today. Facing down her fears in other areas topped that list. This time, she'd put herself out there first. Yes, Evan let her walk away. Agreed they couldn't work. But he'd been hurting too. For years he'd pursued her with patience. Now it was time for her to do the same with him. She had to at least try. Evan Wayne was worth every effort and more.

Slapping her leg, she called Clooney. "Come on, girl. Looks like we're not leaving quite yet." Not before Evan came home.

They walked to her house and climbed the porch steps. As she reached the door, she caught sight of a small bundle sitting on the little table by her porch swing. She walked over to it, and her eyes widened. A huge bouquet sat beside a gorgeous black book with flowers across the front and a delicate font scrolling the title: *Floriography*.

She looked around, but no one stood in either yard. Still, there could only be one person responsible for this gift. Picking up the book, she reached for the card attached to the bouquet. No signature, but rather the names of each flower. With a smile, she settled onto the swing and cracked open the book's pages. Her artist's heart leapt at the beautiful illustrations of flowers inside. Each had a description opposite it along with its meaning and a tiny story about how the meaning came to be. She flipped to the first flower listed.

Asphodel: to indicate regret that will follow you to the grave

Columbine: foolishness

Hyacinth: please forgive me

Oh, the man was speaking her language. She peeked up to find their yards still empty, then back down to the remaining list of flowers.

Buttercup: you are radiant with charm

Dogwood: our love will overcome adversity

Chrysanthemum: I love you

Dahlia: eternal love; commitment

"Those last two are my favorite, but it's the hyacinth that I hope you'll respond positively to."

She jerked her gaze up. "Where? How? I just looked, and you weren't there."

His grin curled a familiar warmth through her. "I do serve on SWAT. We're trained to be covert."

But it was the uncertainty chasing his confidence away that had her reaching for him. "I thought maybe it was because you're Batman."

"That too." He climbed up the steps and slowly approached. "I definitely nailed his dark side recently."

"I did a rather good rendition myself." She scooched over so he could sit beside her. "I'm sorry."

"You're forgiven." He settled onto the swing, his thigh pressing against hers.

"You are too." She picked up the bouquet, holding it between them. "And your apology's much prettier than mine." Leaning down, she inhaled their fragrance. "They're gorgeous."

"You like them then?"

Nose still in their petals, she peeked up and nodded. "Very much."

"Good." He took the bouquet, then leaned in to place it on the table beside her. Man, he smelled even better than the flowers. He lingered in her space. "But Rach, you deserve the apology from my own mouth, not just in flowers."

She could think of another use for his mouth that she'd much prefer.

His pupils dilatated as he caught her look, but he didn't move closer. "I'm sorry."

"Still forgiven." Her fingers trailed along his arm. "If you're planning on apologizing a third time, I have suggestions."

"You do, huh?" That dimple in his chin deepened.

This time, she finally gave in to her impulse. Reaching up, she placed her finger in the dent, relishing the warmth of his skin and the scratch of his whiskers. "Just like I thought. Perfect fit." She flickered her eyes to his.

He captured her hand and caught her lips with his own. With ease, he spoke a message far sweeter than any bouquet he'd ever give her. Clooney's barks were the only thing that brought them up for air.

Evan tucked Rachael under his arm and rested his chin on top of her head. Their hands remained joined together. "I saw you on the slack line. You finally made it across."

She curled closer to him. "I did."

"Even though it wobbled."

"You were right. When I kept my eyes focused on the anchor, I was able to keep walking through those wobbles."

"Wait a sec. Can you repeat the part where you said I was right?" His chin nudged her head as he spoke.

She laughed. "No. It was hard enough to say the first time."

Now he laughed. With his foot, he pushed them into a gentle sway. "I know your car is packed, but what do you think about staying?"

"For how long?" she asked.

His voice, rich, warm, and full of loving hope, reached down. "A lifetime?"

She twisted in his arms so she could see him. His camouflage eyes weren't hiding a thing from her. She saw her future there, and it was one she couldn't wait to grab hold of, for however much time they had together. And she didn't want to waste one more minute.

Reaching over, she slipped a flower from the bouquet and held it out to him. He smiled when he saw it. "Eternal love?"

"Forever and always." Then she leaned in to seal their promise with a kiss.

Epilogue

Memorial Day on Lake Michigan was not traditionally this beautiful. But today boasted a clear cerulean sky, temps touching eighty, and spring flowers in full bloom. Last fall, as a part of their first official date, Evan had shown up with tulip bulbs to plant. They represented deep love and, when they bloomed, new beginnings. Together they'd planted them around his home. Now they sat on his porch as their families hung out in their combined front yards. They'd shared a potluck lunch and were waiting to start their game of Capture the Flag.

Rachael leaned against him on the swing, using his lap as the most comfortable pillow. He ran his hands through her hair. "I think we should add more bulbs this fall."

"You do, huh?" She smiled up at him, accepting his tender kiss as he bent down.

"I do."

Sunlight caught on the diamond solitaire and matching band on her finger. He'd proposed on Thanksgiving, and they'd married on New Year's Day. Seemed fitting to start their new chapter in the freshness of a new year. Five months in and things definitely remained fresh. As he kissed her again, she had a feeling they always would. The man could curl her toes and light her insides on fire in the most delicious of ways.

"Aw, c'mon." Gavin's amused voice broke them apart. "I'm happy you guys are happy, but maybe stow that level of bliss until I'm back at school."

Rachael sat up and grinned at her son, who jogged up the porch steps. "I make no promises."

Gavin had decided to stay in Lansing and work through the summer while taking a few classes. He was thriving in both. Even better? The same foundation that had paid for Micah's schooling had contacted Gavin and offered him a scholarship—as long as he maintained his grades and continued working in a hospital setting. She had the sneaky suspicion that Micah played a huge role in that surprise, but he and Belle remained mum on the subject.

Gavin nudged his head toward the yards. "We're ready to start."

Rachael hopped up and grinned at her husband. "You know you're going down this time, right?"

He stood, a devilish smirk on his face. "It's so sweet that you think you can beat me. I love your optimism in the face of impossible odds."

"Pride goeth before a fall, Batman."

"Not pride. Confidence in my team's track record. I believe we've never lost."

"First time for everything." They joined the group in the middle of the grass. Penny and Belle came from Jonah's house. "Nap time successful?"

"Abrielle is passed out, thanks to Gavin chasing her all morning."

"My pleasure." He smiled at Penny.

Belle slipped under Micah's arm, her hand resting on his chest. "And little Eli is out too." At only two months old, their baby boy already had the chubbiest of cheeks and the sweetest smile.

Jonah passed out the bandanas to everyone. "I feel like it's finally yellow team's turn to win."

"Sorry," Evan said as he held out his arm for Rachael to tie his bandana around. "I'm not one to take turns when it comes to winning and losing." Rachael smacked his shoulder. "Hey!" He grabbed it. "That hurt."

"Sure it did." She studied his trying-to-be-indignant face. Would work better if his lips weren't fighting a smile. "You're perfectly fine, other than your overconfidence. Now tie my bandana on."

She offered him her arm and stood patiently as both his hands went to work. He'd fully healed, though it took much longer than he'd hoped. In the months of hard work, when he wasn't sure if it would pay off, he found emotional healing right along with the physical. And in March, he finally donned his uniform again. In fact, he had a shift starting in a few hours. She still fought a tremor every time he walked out their door, but she could not deny that he was doing what he was made to do. And not because guilt drove him, but because protecting people truly was in his DNA.

So while he worked, she painted. Within the past several months, she'd created a series and her agent secured a showing for it in Chicago. That would happen over the summer. And several orders waited for Rachael to paint portraits of lost loved ones. She too had found her footing again.

Evan patted her bicep where he'd tied her yellow bandana. "All set." He addressed both their families. His mom was inside in case the babies woke up, while his dad, sister, and nephews donned their bandanas. His brother-in-law held their team flag. Even Hattie had joined them. It had been a long winter for her, but like everything else around them, she was slowly returning to life again. "Ten minutes to hide our flags, and then the game begins."

As they started to scatter, Evan pointed a finger Rachael's way. "You're a Wayne now. You could join the winning team."

"I'm already on it."

He laughed. "Don't say I didn't offer." Then he raced the opposite direction.

Half an hour in, Rachael tiptoed around a bush, her eyes on her husband, who'd locked his own eyes on their yellow flag. She didn't stop him. In fact, he was playing directly into her hands. Sure enough, he scoped out the area. Satisfied his reconnaissance was complete, he snuck toward the yellow team's flag. Rachael waited until his hands were on it to show herself. "Going somewhere?" she asked as she ducked out of her hiding place.

He didn't startle. Turning, he graced her with that cocky, confident look of his. "I knew you were there."

"I figured." Her husband didn't miss a thing, especially when it came to her. Well, not most things.

She suppressed a smile. "But you still thought you'd go for it."

"Wasn't too concerned you could stop me."

"No?"

He tucked their flag into his back pocket. "I love you, sweetheart, but you can't outrun me."

"I wasn't planning on it." She crossed her arms over her chest.

"That's not like you, to give up so easily."

"Who says I am?"

He edged toward the right, no doubt readying himself to make a break for it. "Trying to lull me into complacency then? Let me warn you, your kissing tactic won't work again." Scanning her from head to toe, he wiggled his brows. "Though I'll happily let you try."

She was half tempted, but there'd be plenty of time for that later. "Maybe I have another tactic."

"Such as?"

She lifted a shoulder in a shrug.

His eyes caught on something over her shoulder. "Ah, you're trying to stall me. Thing is, I'm closer to the finish line and faster than your brother."

She turned. Jonah had found the red flag and was racing up from the beach. He had stairs to tackle. Evan had an open yard.

And he was making his move.

That was okay. She had no doubt hers would stop him cold. "Evan?" she called.

He spared her a glance as he dodged past. "Not stopping."

She gave him two more steps before lifting her voice. "I'm pregnant."

And her husband, trained to maintain his cool in every situation imaginable, tripped over his own two feet. To his credit, he landed in a roll and bounced back up in one fluid movement. He turned. Eyes wide. "What?"

She smiled. "I'm pregnant."

For the space of a breath, he stood perfectly still. Then he was charging her. He scooped her up and spun her around, his laughter and kisses drenching her.

Jonah's victory cry reached her as he crossed the finish line, and she lifted Evan's face from hers. "We won."

"Yeah." His voice broke with emotion. "We did." His forehead rested against hers, eyes filled with love and wonder, before pressing a gentle kiss against her lips. Then, with that dimple-inducing grin, he lifted his face and yelled, "We're pregnant."

Everyone stopped, and then chaos broke out. The wonderful, amazing kind of pandemonium borne from joy and love. Gavin reached them first, his face filled with pure happiness as he hugged them both. Then the rest of their families descended on them.

Engulfed in their embraces, Rachael met Evan's adoring eyes. There was a vulnerability to loving someone the way she loved him. It was big and scary ... and amazing and lovely, and oh, such a gift. One she'd treasure for as long as she had it, and even longer. Because loss wasn't more powerful than love. There were no boundaries to love, no endings. Only beginnings and its unending ability to multiply.

As she placed her hand on her belly and looked around at her family, she felt the blessing of both those things. And when Evan reached for her, engulfing her in his arms and placing the sweetest of kisses to her lips, she had no doubt their love would continue to grow. Sweeping vibrant colors across their lives.

Creating a beautiful masterpiece.

The End